HE KNOWS THIS WOMAN INSIDE OUT, KNOWS ALL HIS WOMEN.

They are all the same, when their veneer of culture has been stripped away. With some, it takes more work than others, but the hunter has his ways. They all reveal themselves in time, with proper coaxing.

He is never disappointed in the end.

He takes the latest video cassette and rises from his desk, moving toward the Sony, past the coffee table with its pair of matching skulls. A photograph between them, in a simple frame. Twin sisters smiling over birthday cake.

He slips the video cassette into his Sanyo VCR, picks up the remote, and keys the tape to a familiar street scene. Erin Gerber locks the front door of her house behind her, coming down the concrete steps, across the scruffy lawn. She wears a hot-pink jogging suit and Nike pumps, hair tied back in a ponytail.

The camera tracks her for a block, until she turns the corner. Cut to a deserted children's playground. Approaching from the west, oblivious to her surroundings, Erin paces off the sidewalk with her measured, loping strides. The jogging suit is molded to her breasts and thighs.

The hunter rolls it back to watch again. . . .

Cat and MousE

MICHAEL NEWTON

POCKET BOOKS

New York   London   Toronto   Sydney   Tokyo   Singapore

An *Original* Publication of POCKET BOOKS

POCKET BOOKS, a division of Simon & Schuster Inc.
1230 Avenue of the Americas, New York, NY 10020

ISBN: 0-671-89738-1

First Pocket Books printing June 1995

10 9 8 7 6 5 4 3 2 1

POCKET and colophon are registered trademarks of Simon & Schuster Inc.

Cover art by Tristan Elwell

Printed in the U.S.A.

For Sam and Laura

Acknowledgments

The author owes a special debt of gratitude to several individuals for helping make this book a viable reality. They include: the two Eds, for living a part of the story; Judy, for the seed of an idea; my agent, Nancy Yost, at Barbara Lowenstein Associates; Dana Isaacson, at Pocket Books; Steve Fisher and the gang at Laurel Entertainment.

Sometimes accidents happen in life from which we need a little madness to extricate ourselves successfully.

—La Rochefoucald, Maxims

Prologue

———•———

The basement trophy room was sixteen feet by thirty-two. On all four walls and overhead there was cedar paneling, well oiled and fragrant. Underfoot, the deep-pile carpeting was beige, its heavy pad providing insulation from the concrete floor below. The furnishings were sparse but comfortable: a heavy sofa done in leather; a matching easy chair; an oaken desk and coffee table; twenty-six-inch Sony console television with a VCR attached. The room was windowless and virtually soundproof, but there was a small light set above the door that winked in crimson flashes when the doorbell rang upstairs.

It was a man's room, custom tailored for its one and only occupant. The solitary tenant was responsible for its remodeling and decoration. No one else had set foot in the room for seven years, since he acquired the house.

It was a sanctuary from the world outside, where dreams unfold and sometimes come to life. A place to plan and reminisce.

The hunter's trophy room was unconventional in its display of artifacts. There were no mounted heads or varnished fish, no hanging pelts or severed legs converted to umbrella stands. The weapons neatly racked in two glass-fronted cases were not those a sportsman would select for stalking normal game.

But "normal" was a fluid concept, after all. To each his own.

The hunter's trophies were divided into three broad categories: physical mementos of the hunt, selected photographs, and items borrowed from the media. He was meticulous in the arrangement of his souvenirs, but their diversity required imagination. Jewelry was a simple item to display, but scalps and bits of tattooed skin required more maintenance. His scrapbooks ran to thirteen volumes bound in imitation leather: snapshots, dated clippings from the local papers, here and there a MISSING flier, credit cards, a driver's license.

Nothing went to waste.

The video cassettes were dated, chronologically arranged, one shelf below the scrapbooks. Roughly one-third of the information they contained was gleaned from television news reports, including two brief spots on CNN, the rest of it surveillance footage of the hunter's chosen prey.

He always did his homework, nothing left to chance.

This autumn evening, he was finalizing plans for yet another hunt. The prey had been selected, scrutinized at home, at work, and at play. His cameras had recorded any minor detail that the hunter may have missed in his surveillance: little things, minutiae that could make all the difference in the world.

The chosen one was Erin Gerber. Blond, petite, late twenties. Single. Childless. Spotting a potential mark was easy, but the rest of it took effort, patient research, and time invested in a job well done. He followed the intended target home, confirmed addresses, checked against the fat reverse directory. It cost him fifty dollars yearly to obtain the book, but it was worth its weight in gold.

He understood that secrets, in the modern world, are few and far between. It only took persistence to discover anything and everything about a total stranger. Push the necessary buttons. Phrase your questions in the proper way.

Ask, and you shall receive.

The hunter understood these things and cherished his privacy all the more because he recognized its fragility. His secret was secure right now—this minute—due to his capacity for taking great pains with details. Every move he made was planned out in advance, rehearsed, evaluated for potential risk. He was not caged because no one suspected him. He had given them no cause.

His mother did not raise a fool.

The snapshots, first.

As a beginner, he was satisfied with Polaroids. That was before he learned they would fade with time. These days, he favored a Minolta, took it with him everywhere, did all of the developing himself. No half-wit flunky in a drugstore or the local Photomat to point a finger at him from the witness stand.

Security.

His women shared a certain photogenic quality, a kind of radiance. Erin Gerber was no exception. The candid shots were basic, nothing artsy-fartsy, but they captured her vitality and confidence. A sense that she had found the secret of success and put her life on track, that nothing could derail her plans.

It would be interesting to study her reaction when she found out she was wrong.

First shot, five minutes after the initial sighting, give or take. She had her back turned to the camera, loading groceries in the backseat of her Cutlass, short skirt riding high on those golden thighs. He could not see her face, but all good things come to those who wait.

Next shot was a profile. She, still unaware of the camera, flicked back her shoulder-length hair in a gesture the hunter now recognized as habitual. Not smiling, quite, but neither was she somber. Waiting for the next act in her life to start, on cue.

He brushed past a photo of her car, the license plate recorded for posterity. Next up, the duplex where she lived alone. No pets, unless she kept them shut up in the house.

The other shots spanned nineteen days of hit-and-miss surveillance. He could not afford to watch her all the time and make himself conspicuous. It taxed his imagination, using different cars, disguises, checking in at varied times of day and night. He knew her hours at the flower shop, had purchased roses from her, made small talk, and the knowledge of her daily schedule made it easier to chart her movements. He had followed her on three dates, never with the same man twice. None of them had been privileged to stay the night.

A woman of discriminating tastes.

It was a sham, of course. He knew this woman inside out, knew all his women. They were all the same when their veneer of culture had been stripped away. With some, it took more work than others, but the hunter had his ways. They all revealed themselves in time, with proper coaxing.

He was never disappointed in the end.

Two maps were open on his desk, beneath the fan of photographs. He turned his full attention to them now, the snapshots pushed aside. The first was standard issue, readily available at any service station in the county. Streets and parks and public buildings drawn to scale and mass-produced for travelers. The other was a personal creation, Erin Gerber's neighborhood reduced to eight-by-twelve, individual houses sketched in by the hunter, with notations of potential danger points. A barking dog. An alley lined with trash cans. An insomniac, three houses down, whose lights burned all night long.

The duplex was a problem. Adequate construction, at a glance, but long experience had taught him how sound carries through connecting walls. It might be possible for him to penetrate the house, subdue his prey and cart her off without a struggle, but he did not like the odds.

Besides, a measure of resistance makes the game worthwhile.

The flower shop was out, too many witnesses. Giving her a lift from work, in midtown traffic, was preposterous. He would be seen, identified, run down, and caged.

Impossible.

A challenge, then. He needed a better plan.

He took the latest video cassette and rose from his desk, moving toward the Sony, past the coffee table with its pair of matching skulls. A photograph between them, in a simple frame. Twin sisters smiling over birthday cake.

A masterpiece of composition . . . or *de*composition, as the case may be.

The wordplay made him smile, but only for a heartbeat.

4

He focused on the task at hand, a pretty problem for a master at his craft. For every riddle, there was a solution. All he had to do was find it, work the details out, prepare his strategy.

He turned the Sony on, the all-news channel. Comedy and drama held no interest for him, life reduced to tidy scripts wherein the players knew their lines by heart and every move was mechanical. Tawdry puppet shows where justice triumphs and the good guy always got the girl.

In real life, as the hunter knew, it seldom worked that way.

He liked his entertainment true-to-life, chaotic, reeking of the charnel house. An earthquake in the Middle East. A plane crash in Detroit or Boston. Gang-related shootings in Los Angeles. A teenage mother putting her baby in the microwave. Pit bulls attacking a Girl Scout selling cookies door-to-door. A Catholic priest confessing to molesting adolescent boys. In Little Rock, a plumber cleaning drains in an apartment complex flushed out the remains of a dismembered six-year-old.

The stuff that dreams were made of.

Television's talking heads called each new segment of the passion play a tragedy, but they could not deceive the hunter. Pain and suffering were part of life, an educational experience for those who managed to survive. The losers hardly matter. They were simply pawns in an elaborate game, too ignorant and self-involved to understand the rules. Like sheep, their function was to keep the higher class of predators amused and fed.

He slipped the video cassette into his Sanyo VCR and stepped back to the stout recliner. He picked up the remote and keyed the tape. A train wreck in the Rockies winked out, replaced by a familiar street scene. Erin Gerber locked the front door of her house behind her, came down the concrete steps, across the scruffy lawn. She wore a hot-pink jogging suit and Nike pumps, her hair tied back in a ponytail.

The camera tracked her for a block, until she turned the corner, out of sight. A cut from curbside to a children's playground, at a park six blocks from Erin's home. The slides and swing set were deserted, darkness closing in. Approaching from the west, oblivious to her surroundings, Erin paced off the sidewalk with her measured, loping strides. The jogging suit was molded to her breasts and thighs.

The hunter rolled it back to watch again.

Except on weekends, or in rainy weather, Erin Gerber did her jogging after work. The hour varied with her schedule, but she did not fear the darkness. There were streetlights here and there along the way, a two-mile course that brought her home in something under half an hour. He had mapped the route, examined every foot of ground along the way. The park had possibilities, but there was little in the way of cover near the street, where he would have to make his move. A better ambush site lay on the final quarter mile of Erin's course, beneath an ivy-covered railroad overpass.

He tapped Fast Forward, losing track of Erin for the moment. Rolling footage of the course, the camera mounted on his dashboard. Coming to the overpass . . . right . . . now.

Freeze-frame.

Deep shadows there, beneath the stony archway. Nothing in the way of streetlights. Lifting off the button, he was through the minitunnel in a heartbeat, rolling free and clear along a gentle curve that took him back to Erin's street, her doorstep. Sanctuary.

She did not avoid the overpass in darkness. He had followed her on two occasions, in a different car each time, once passing her within a few yards of the tunnel's maw. She did not flinch away from vehicles or break her stride.

Determination.

He would not be driving when he met his chosen quarry in the shadows. Fifty yards beyond the overpass there was a gravel turnout, oil drums painted blue to serve as garbage cans, a narrow foot track leading down through waist-high weeds to meet the bank of a canal.

He thought ahead to Wednesday, maybe Thursday evening. He'd use a pair of cold plates on the car and park it in the turnout, waiting. Lead his prey by several minutes, time enough to jog back from the car and reach the tunnel just ahead of her. No loitering, in case another vehicle should happen by.

The rest was easy. Drop her with the stun gun. Lift her in the fireman's carry for the short run to his car. Handcuffs and duct tape waiting in the trunk. His tools beside her in a leather bag.

No sweat.

The rest of it would be private time, a little one-on-one to get him through the night. Exploring horizons of pleasure and pain. Melding diametric opposites into one long scream before death's sweet release.

He viewed the brief segment of tape three more times, forward and backward, before he was satisfied. A trial run tomorrow, in daylight, to scope out the ground, and then would come the waiting. If the pickup was delayed, so be it. Patience was a part of hunting, part of the challenge.

Delayed gratification.

Any fool with one eye and a trigger finger could cruise down the street, dropping sheep in their tracks. The act of killing, in and of itself, required no intellect, no great imagination. Most destructive energy was wasted in the heat of passion, spent on friends and family. Such killers were beneath contempt.

It took an artist to enjoy his work, refine techniques from one hunt to the next, avoiding capture, learning from mistakes. The greatest minds had always dwelt on homicide, at least in passing. Even then, most lacked the courage to proceed beyond the theoretical.

He switched off the VCR, the all-news channel coming back. The Sony's twenty-six-inch screen showed a familiar face. The hunter felt his heart stop, skip a beat, resume its task with just a bit more effort.

Bender.

Thumbing up the volume, the announcer was halfway through her spiel.

". . . continues to reject all efforts to delay his execution, scheduled for the early morning hours of December fifth. Authorities say Bender may have killed as many as . . ."

The same old story. Names and dates extracted from police reports. A glimpse of Bender in the courtroom, stone-faced as his sentence was pronounced. Truncated interviews with civil libertarians who hoped to save his life in spite of Bender's stolid opposition.

The hunter knew a soul mate when he saw one.

Granted, Bender had experienced a kind of mental lapse

in custody. He should be fighting for his life, defying his unworthy captors. Still, he had pursued his suicidal course with quiet dignity, a wily predator who knew that he would never be released to hunt again.

Why live, without the hunt?

What else provided the same rejuvenation and release?

He switched off the television, rose from his chair. A pause before his desk, surveying snapshots, maps, a notepad marked in shorthand; pieces of a puzzle he had already completed in his mind.

The hunter's thoughts were elsewhere now. They wheeled and circled over Bender's prison like a flock of vultures, following the heady smell of carrion. He willed himself inside the tiny cell with Bender, tried to replicate the anguish of a bold, free spirit caged.

No, thank you.

It had been clumsy, getting caught like that. He blamed it on the alcohol, a weakness any veteran of the hunt should recognize. Still, few men had the hunter's strength of will. It was unfortunate that Bender let himself be taken—there was no real competition on the street these days—but judging him would not undo the past.

The hunter felt a sudden need, surrendering for once. He left the trophy room and locked the door behind him, taking extra time with the alarm. He was alone, as always, in the house, but you could never be too cautious. Burglaries were rare in this part of town, but no one was immune.

Shit happens.

Upstairs, in his den, he whipped a plastic cover from the IBM Selectric, settled in his chair. The trophy room was just below him. He could feel it, pulsing like the black heart of a world he had created for himself.

Inside the top drawer of his desk was a box of rubber gloves, packed like tissues for the surgeon's convenience. One size fits all. The hunter knew that he was going overboard on the security precautions for a simple letter, but he liked to keep in practice. Never let your guard down for a moment, even in your sleep.

Preparedness made all the difference in the world between himself and Bender, sitting in a box and waiting to die.

He took a sheet of plain white paper from the tray immediately on his left and rolled it underneath the platen, lining up his margins. He typed the date and salutation, paused.

What to say?

How do you say good-bye to someone you have never even met?

He had it now. One soul mate to another, an appeal to reason. It was not the same as talking, face-to-face, but he would never have that chance.

The words flowed easily, once he began. He was wholly focused on the paper, blotting out all else. No further thought of Erin Gerber, for the moment.

She was dead.

The dumb bitch simply didn't know it yet.

CHAPTER
1

The snow had tapered off since midnight, but a biting wind remained to keep the temperature in single digits, buffeting the rental car as Adam Reed approached his destination. Carson City's neon lit the sky behind him, but ahead lay darkness more befitting his mission. The radio featured a heavy metal hour, and he turned it off to concentrate on driving over pavement slick with ice.

He understood the institutional psychology involved in scheduling an execution to be carried out at 2 A.M. Although committed to proceed, the state was secretly ashamed of its behavior, and the dirty work would be conducted under cover, while decent folk were fast asleep. Nine months of headlines climaxed by a furtive scuttling in the dark.

Reed saw the prison now, a stark, medieval fortress looming in the night. Its only modern features were the floodlights and the loops of razor wire surmounting chain-link fences. It had been grim the day before, in sunlight. Now, in darkness, it reminded him of something from the Inquisition.

Demonstrators, numbering perhaps two dozen, had begun their vigil on the outskirts of the prison parking lot, restrained by guards from moving any closer to the fence.

The arctic wind had thinned their ranks and forced the hearty remnant to rely on flashlights, rather than the mourning candles they preferred. Their placards were illegible at thirty yards, but Reed had seen them all before. He could have quoted them from memory.

A deputy examined his credentials at the entrance to the lot and waved him on. The rental's heater could not match the cold outside, and by the time he rolled the window up, Reed's teeth were chattering. He parked beside a state police car, shut the engine off, stepped out before he had an opportunity to change his mind.

A television crew was setting up outside the gates, technicians grappling with lights and camera while the talking heads stayed snug and warm inside the van. They missed Reed going in, and he was thankful for the accident of timing as he stepped inside the gate house, proffering the necessary paperwork.

His invitation to the party was a simple business card, black-bordered, with his name typed in below the printed date. Three guards took turns examining his driver's license, tucking it away beneath the counter with his wallet and the other contents of his pockets. In exchange, they let him have a plastic clip-on badge that named him VISITOR and passed him through a metal detector, into the waiting arms of his escort.

Cold, again, as Reed fell in beside his baby-sitter for the short walk to the main administration block. The waiting room reminded Reed of every small-town courthouse he had ever seen. Plain wooden chairs and benches, with a humming water cooler. Plaques and glossy photographs of politicians on the walls.

The only exit from the waiting room was through an air lock, manned by uniforms inside a cage of armored glass and stainless steel. A high sign from his escort got Reed through the checkpoint. He was directed to his left, along a sterile corridor, to reach the meeting room where journalists and scheduled witnesses had been arriving since half-past twelve.

It was the same room where, some thirty hours earlier, Reed had conducted one last interview with Thomas Edward Bender. Short of time, so many questions still unanswered, he had tried to share the dying man's perspective, understand the private demons that had driven Bender through his wasted life, destroying others in the process. Reed had done his best to solve the riddle, and he found no consolation in the thought that no one else would have a chance to try.

He counted thirteen faces, recognizing three. The DA from Las Vegas, Cochran, had arrived to witness justice in the raw, resplendent in his Stetson, bolo tie, and snakeskin boots. The court-appointed lawyer, Goldstein, having tried in vain to change his client's mind about appeals, looked painfully uncomfortable, reflecting peevishly on failure. Finally, McGill, the Reno newsman who had hounded Reed, in vain, for interviews. Their eyes met, briefly, and McGill dismissed him with a vague expression of disdain.

The strangers were divided into chosen witnesses and stringers for the media, the latter readily identified by harried looks and spiral notepads. Of the witnesses, aside from Cochran and the lawyer, Reed pegged three as law enforcement officers, the rest as civil servants drafted to fulfill the mandatory quota. Two, a pair of bleached-blond secretary types, were whispering to one another, but the rest were silent, almost painfully self-conscious. Children in a new school, on the first day of class.

The conference table he recalled from Wednesday afternoon had been replaced by several rows of folding chairs, a podium in front. The chairs outnumbered witnesses by nearly two-to-one. Reed found an empty one on the sidelines, sat and waited for another quarter hour while a handful of reporters filtered in and helped themselves to coffee from a stainless steel urn.

At last, the warden entered. Flanked by uniforms, he moved directly to the podium. He was a beefy man, with chins that overflowed his collar. Twenty years of prison life had leeched the color from his face; the artificial sunlamp tan did little to restore a first impression of vitality. He wore a hairpiece that did not appear to fit his lifestyle or his scalp.

"If we could come to order, please . . ."

The warden's voice was thin, high-pitched, belonging to a man one-third his size. Reed shut his mind off to the speech. When it was time, the uniforms would lead him to his destination, tell him where to stand and when to leave. The rest of it was window dressing, and he did not need a course on execution etiquette.

Instead of listening, he asked himself what Bender must be feeling at that moment. Reed had learned the drill beforehand: Valium with dinner, and again at one o'clock. He did not know the dosage, but he knew enough of Thomas Bender, and if Reed was any judge of men, the killer's mind would still be functional. Was Bender looking forward to the moment of his death with awe? Anticipation? Inside the cold machine, was there a trace of fear?

The warden fielded several questions from the press and then retreated, leaving officers behind to shepherd the assembled witnesses to their destination. Reed fell in step behind the secretary types and followed as they made their exit through a side door, one guard leading, with another bringing up the rear. The cold was waiting for them, numbing flesh on contact, turning breath to plumes of smoke.

Beyond the fence, a bank of television lights blazed on, illuminating cameramen in miniature. The demonstrators had begun to sing, but they were few and far away, their voices tattered by the wind. Like extras in a dream, they had no substance.

Three abreast, the small procession passed beneath the silent, darkened windows of a cell block, tracked by cameras and the nearest tower guard. Another corner, and they lost the klieg lights, entering a courtyard bounded on three sides by brick and stone, reminding Reed of New York tenements that he had visited while working on an article some years ago.

Their escort paused beside a narrow metal staircase, bolted to the cell block's outer wall much like a fire escape. The landing, twenty feet above their heads, was dominated by a metal door that had been painted olive drab.

"I'll ask you all to watch your step and use the handrail," said their escort. "Single file, until you're safe inside."

Reed took his time, uncomfortable with heights in any weather, doubly so on steps made treacherous by freezing rain. Behind him, someone slipped and went down, cursing, on one knee. Reed thought it sounded like McGill, and he could not suppress a smile.

The newsman had been after him since Thomas Bender signed the contract naming Reed as his biographer, a firm exclusive clinched in black and white. His mercenary attitude and whining voice had grated on Reed's nerves from the beginning. After half a dozen calls, Reed let McGill do all his talking to an answering machine.

Reed's legs were trembling as he stepped across the threshold, whether from the chill or nerves he could not say. When all the stragglers were accounted for, the door locked tight behind them, they were herded through a dimly lit corridor. The walls were blank on either side until a few yards from their destination, when they met adjacent doors. One granted access to the deathwatch cell, where Bender had been housed, under suicide watch, for the past twenty-four hours. The other—small and oval, with its central wheel, like something from a submarine—would open on the execution chamber.

Reed was fifth in line to reach the observation room. He bellied up against a whitewashed rail, the others crowding in behind him, adding their aromas of cologne, tobacco, perspiration, to the air, until he felt a surge of claustrophobia. Suppressing it, Reed concentrated on the plate-glass window, close enough to touch, and the peculiar, tiny room beyond.

In fact, he saw the execution chamber was a dome, its floor recessed, with outer walls slapped on to bolster the illusion of a normal room. Inside, beyond the glass, a padded table was the central feature, fitted out with leather belts and fleece-lined cuffs. An EKG machine was mounted on a stand between the table and the observation window. Yards of rubber tubing hung suspended from the ceiling, one end disappearing through a vent, on Adam's left.

Nevada's mode of execution had been cyanide before the legislature voted for a switch to chemical injection. Their decision was pragmatic, firmly based on economics and expedience. When killer Jesse Bishop was gassed in 1979, after a twelve-year hiatus in executions, it was discovered that the chamber leaked. Observers had to be evacuated;

ditto for the occupants of homes within a half-mile of the prison. Architects of death determined it would cost the state some thirty thousand dollars to repair the leaks—or they could spend a paltry grand to drill some extra holes, rip out the belted chairs, and string some hose. By that time, the injection method had already proven itself a dozen times in Texas. It was deemed humane *and* inexpensive: perfect.

Reed had done his homework. While the state played coy, refusing to discuss the details of the execution, he had made some phone calls, boning up on basic chemistry. He knew that Bender would receive a lethal mixture: sodium thiopental, to induce near-instant unconsciousness, followed by Pavulon and potassium chlorate, to shut down heart and lungs, respectively. The killer cocktail had not failed so far, though there had been one ugly scene in Texas, when technicians failed to tap a proper vein.

Distracted by his thoughts, Reed nearly missed the submarine door's opening. One moment, he was staring at an empty room; the next, and Bender stood before him, dressed in jeans and denim work shirt, manacled with cuffs connected to a chain around his waist. His sleeves had been rolled up above the elbow, showing off tattoos and hairy forearms. Shackles stopped him at the elevated threshold, and his burly escorts lifted him across, hands tucked beneath his armpits.

Bender scanned the audience, found Reed, and cracked a small, lopsided smile. He offered no resistance as the uniforms removed his chains, one of them falling back to drop the hardware in the corridor. When he was situated on the table, Bender lay inert and let them fasten belts around his chest, his waist and thighs, with padded cuffs securing wrists and ankles. It startled Reed to find he wore no shoes.

When they were midway through the buckle-up-for-safety operation, Bender caught Reed's eye. His lips moved silently behind the glass.

"It's cool."

Reed groped for a response, remembered Bender could not hear him anyway, and let it go. One of the uniforms stepped back, a long arm reaching out of frame to find a hidden cord and pull the sliding curtains shut. The next phase would be carried out in privacy, as if the witnesses selected to observe a death would be offended by insertion of a needle in the subject's arm. Reed waited, watching shadows on the blinds, attempting contact with the mind of Thomas Edward Bender.

What must it be like, anticipating death, when he had always been the one to mete it out? Would any of the victims come to mind or were his thoughts consumed entirely with himself? Was there remorse behind the twisted smile or mere chagrin at getting caught?

The curtains opened and the uniforms retreated, closing off the airtight hatch behind them. Bender lay with catheters inserted in both arms, the EKG machine hooked up to monitor his heartbeat, while it lasted. His narrow eyes were focused on the ceiling, tuning out the strangers who had come to watch him die.

Offstage, the warden passed a signal to the executioner, and taps were opened to release the flow of chemicals. It took a moment for the subject to react, but then Reed saw his eyelids flicker, drooping as the sodium thiopental kicked in. The hands that had extinguished thirteen lives relaxed, unclenching.

Sixty seconds, and the other drugs came through in tandem, etching ragged peaks and valleys on the EKG. Bender convulsed, heaving against his restraints, and his fists clenched again, knuckles whitening. His feet turned inward, pigeon-toed.

A second spasm, weaker than the first, as if the dying man was coughing in his sleep. Reed forced himself to watch, remembering that Bender couldn't feel a thing. Or could he?

Concentrate!

The Dallas women, strangled, raped before and after death. Two more in Vegas, left in Dumpsters with the other garbage. Five in Southern California, one of them Bender's own wife. More bodies in Wyoming, Oklahoma, Utah.

This was justice. Bender had been moving toward this moment since he started strangling puppies at the age of seven. Pity was misplaced in application to a human monster.

Flat line.

Reed ticked off another ninety seconds in his mind before the uniforms appeared and drew the curtains shut. The show was over. Numb inside, he waited for the escorts to return and lead them out again. Reverse track, through the sterile corridor, immediately followed by the shock of frigid air. The stairs seemed doubly treacherous as Reed descended, with the weight of other bodies piling up behind him, threatening to bowl him over. Klieg lights, bright and painful on the short walk back to the administration block.

Inside, the witnesses lined up to sign a ledger, like the guest book at a wedding party, verifying that they had observed the death of Thomas Edward Bender, carried out on such-and-such a date. As if there would be any doubt, five minutes or a year from now. Some doubled back to the reception area, to share their words of wisdom with the press, but Reed was outward bound when he ran into Father Frank.

The prison chaplain seemed to function well enough without a surname. He was simply Father Frank to the administration and the inmates, personal denominations notwithstanding. In his time, the priest had ministered to Catholics, Protestants, Mohammedans, and Jews. He played no favorites and in fourteen years of service had been more or less immune to the assaults and injuries incurred by other members of the prison staff.

Reed had been hoping to avoid the priest, pass on the platitudes, but Father Frank waited for him in the lobby, staking out the only exit. All in standard black, with hair to match and olive skin betraying Latin roots. At the sight of Reed he tried a smile on for size, thought better of it, let it go.

"I missed you at the send-off, Father."

"I was there." The priest remained unruffled. "Had to keep the warden company."

"Of course. How is he bearing up?"

"He'll live, I think." The priest held out a fat manila envelope. "Tom wanted you to have these."

Tom.

The boyish name rang hollow. Reed experienced a sudden rush of mixed emotions—anger, jealousy, confusion—as he pondered Father Frank's relationship with Bender.

Opening the envelope, he found a Bible, ten or fifteen letters, and an audio cassette.

"He didn't answer any of the mail," said Father Frank. "It's up to you."

"The Bible?"

"Tom requested it. We spent a fair amount of time together in the past few days. I like to think it helped."

"You never know."

He shook the padre's hand and joined a uniform for the return trip to the gate house. Silence from the officers on duty as he swapped his plastic badge for wallet, keys, and pocket change. They would not meet his eyes, as if the fleeting contact might infect them. Mark them with the stain of death.

The television crowd waited for him as he cleared the gate house, brandishing their microphones like magic wands. He faced them squarely, fed the Minicams some noncommittal pap about a sobering experience, and managed to escape without suggesting that they buy his book to get the details. Time enough for self-promotion down the line, when he was stumping talk shows with a finished book in hand.

The demonstrators sang "Amazing Grace" as Reed approached his car. He drowned them out with heavy metal, rattling the windows as he drove the rental back to town. Across the bridge, with ice below. Past the capitol, with floodlights canted toward the dome. Casinos losing money in the frigid dark, and staying open anyway.

A side street brought him to the mortuary, where fluorescent lights shone through the frosted basement windows. Parked outside, a vintage Cadillac, a sleek Mercedes, and a compact Ford from Hertz, the latter rented by a Stanford grad assistant sent to pick up Bender's brain. The university had plans to check for lesions, evidence of trauma or pathology contributing to Bender's homicides.

Reed wished them luck.

No scientist, he would have bet his life that it was all a waste of time. Their microscopes and tissue samples would not solve the riddle, for solutions lay outside of flesh and blood. If there were scars on Thomas Bender, they were soul-scars. Clinical technicians had no means of quantifying pain.

There seemed to be no point in waiting for the hearse. A man was dead, and now the task remained of resurrecting him on paper, offering a glimpse inside a twisted world where sex and death walked hand in hand.

Reed turned the screaming music up another notch to drown out his thoughts, and started back toward his motel.

CHAPTER

2

———•———

The Pair-o'-Dice Motel did not appear in any Triple-A brochures, but it was cheap and reasonably clean. The neon dice out front flashed lucky seven all night long, but Adam Reed was scarcely conscious of them as he pulled into the parking lot.

The lot was almost empty when he parked outside his room. Reed palmed his key, was on the sidewalk when he remembered the manila envelope and had to double back, his fingers clumsy from the cold as he unlocked the driver's side. He retrieved the meager cache of Bender's last effects. A Bible—wonders never cease.

The door was open. She was waiting for him. Warmth and light, and Dana bundled in her robe. She closed the door behind him, threw the latch, and stepped into his arms without a word. Reed held her tightly, cherishing the fragrances of shampoo and bath soap. She wore nothing beneath the robe, but at the moment, all he wanted was her presence and silent understanding. Moments passed before they stepped apart, her green eyes searching Adam's face for signs of life.

"How are you?"

"Fine."

21

"The truth?"

"I think so. Yes."

"I'll take your coat."

He let her slip the parka off his shoulders, juggling the parcel as he shed each sleeve in turn.

"What's that?"

"The last effects. A tape. Some fan mail."

And a Bible. Jesus.

"Want to play the tape?"

"Not now." He sat down on the queen-size bed, bone-weary. "I could use some coffee."

"Coming up."

The in-room coffeemakers were a "special extra" at the Pair-o'-Dice. Reed had a fifth of Seagram's on the nightstand, and he spiked the steaming mug that Dana handed him before he brought it to his lips.

"Okay?"

"You saved my life."

"We aim to please."

She sat beside him, slid a weightless arm around his shoulders, pressing close. Her robe gapped open, offering the soft curve of her breast, but Adam could not bring himself to touch her.

"You were on the tube," she said. "They broke in on 'The Love Boat' for a special update."

"That's the big time for you."

"Was it terrible?"

"I can't explain it. He was there, and then he wasn't. I expected worse." He took another sip of coffee, waiting for the chill to break. "I can't get warm."

She slipped her other arm around his waist and snuggled closer. "I can help with that, I think."

"Just let me catch a shower, first." He felt unclean, refused to share the taint with Dana.

"Sure." He caught a note of disappointment in her voice. "I'm sorry, Adam."

"Mmm? What for?"

"I should have seen it through."

"It's better, this way." He was not prepared to tread that ground again. "I mean it."

"Well . . ."

"It's separate, not a part of us."

He rose and slipped his jacket off, undid his tie and dropped it on the bed. Kicked off his shoes and crossed the room in stocking feet.

"Ten minutes."

"Right."

He closed the bathroom door behind him, both for warmth and privacy. There was a hook behind the door, and Adam hung his slacks up by a belt loop. Never mind the shirt and underwear; his perspiration had soaked through them, in defiance of the cold, and now he left them wadded on the floor, his socks on top. He stood before the glass, with goose bumps starting on his back and arms, examining the mirror image of his face.

Okay, for thirty-five, he thought. His eyes were clear, the shadows underneath them easily attributed to stress and time of day. The sandy hair was thick, betraying no signs of erosion. If he forced a smile, the teeth were white and even. Not a face that strangers recognized, despite the jacket photos on his last two books. But soon, with Thomas Bender's help, perhaps . . .

Reed turned on the shower and waited for the steam before he stepped inside. It stung at first, but he adapted quickly, relishing the heat that baked his flesh and opened up his pores. He bowed his head beneath the spray, as if in prayer, and waited for the drumming on his skull to clear his mind of conscious thought.

No go.

He could not shake the mental image of the execution chamber. Bender lying on the padded table, buckled down as if he were preparing for a space shot. Lethal hands relaxing as the chemicals took hold. The rising steam left Adam short of breath, intensifying his reaction to the flashback. Did the anesthetic do its job? How did it feel to strangle in your sleep, before your heart stopped beating?

Suddenly light-headed, Adam pressed both hands against the sweating tile to keep himself from falling. Opening his eyes to keep the dizziness at bay, he watched the water streaming off his body, swirling down the drain.

Snap out of it!

He had the soap in hand when Dana slid the plastic shower curtain back, stepped in beside him, pulled it shut again behind her.

"Here," she said, and took the soap away from him. "Let me."

Her auburn hair was plastered to her skull before she finished soaping Adam's back and flanks, the washcloth pleasantly abrasive on his skin. Upon command, he turned to face her, let the shower rinse him clean while Dana started on his chest. When she had lathered him from neck to waist, she reached around him, groping for the washcloth, close enough that he could feel her nipples on his soapy chest. She had to rinse the washcloth twice before her work was done.

"You missed a spot."

"Be patient."

Lathering her hands, she caught him by surprise, a moment's energetic scrubbing giving way to longer, more demanding strokes. In spite of everything, he felt himself responding, stiffening in Dana's grasp, while she pretended not to notice.

There were soapsuds on her breasts from leaning into Adam, and he took advantage of them, kneading pliant flesh with greedy hands. She caught her breath and closed her eyes, allowing him to tease her while she finished with the washcloth. Adam slipped a soapy hand between her legs, to match the magic action of her fingers with his own. When both of them were close, she pushed his hands away.

"I haven't finished." Breathless. Bright eyes shining.

Dana knelt before him, soaping first one leg and then the other, languid motions interspersed by teasing feather-kisses on his glans. Her tongue delighted and infuriated him, first here, then gone, now flicking back again to sear his flesh. At last, she finished with his legs, warm fingers cupping Adam's testicles as Dana took him in her mouth. He let the velvet fire consume him, one arm braced against the wall to keep himself from falling.

In their eighteen months together, they had practiced pleasing one another, making it a loving game. She knew what worked for Adam, and she used her knowledge now to maximum effect. He gave himself to the sensation. Drifting. Free.

When he was trembling on the edge, Reed broke the spell and pulled her to her feet, strong hands beneath her armpits, lifting. Dana wrapped her legs around his waist, heels prodding Adam's buttocks as she welcomed him inside. He pinned her back against the tile, short lightning thrusts, the moment too intense to last. They came together, melting into sweet release, warm water beating upon them like tropic rain.

Outside, the shower off, they dried each other, taking turns. He felt wrung-out, but Dana's touch revived him, made him new again. When he had dried her back, she stepped against him, sleek and naked, while he reached around in front of her to finish. Taking longer than he needed with the towel.

"Again?" she asked.

The misty mirror offered him another view. Perfection multiplied. His body was reacting, prodding Dana from behind.

"Again."

"In bed, this time." She led him from the bathroom, pulling back the sheet and blanket, sliding in ahead of him.

"The lights?"

"I like the view," he said.

Reed took his time and worked at pleasing her, in no hurry as he found her secret places with his mouth and hands. She cried out softly, twice, before he entered her, and then she clung to him with something close to desperation, missing several beats before she found his rhythm, matched it with her own.

Reed understood the psycho-babble explanation for his sudden ardor. Any shrink would tell him that he was reacting to a brush with death, the image of his own mortality, by reaffirming life in its most primal form. He knew the rap and didn't give a damn. Right now, his world consisted of this room, this bed. This melding of the flesh. Whatever lay outside could wait until tomorrow.

Dana got there first this time. She bit his shoulder as the rocking spasms hit her, fingernails like talons digging into Adam's back. He wasn't ready, couldn't stop. Beneath him,

Dana shuddered, rolled her head from side to side. Somewhere in the distance, Adam heard her voice, entreating him to join her, calling him by name.

It was enough. He stiffened, instant rigor setting in as Dana peaked again, her supple body arching off the mattress. Soaring. When they came back down to earth and separated, Reed could barely find the strength to fetch the blankets up around them.

"Love you," Dana said, all dreamy now.

"I'm counting on it."

Stretching like a cat, she rolled away and killed the light, then scooted back to mold herself against him, settling in her favorite sleeping posture. Reed fit well against her, loins against her satin flanks, his knees tucked in against the back of Dana's thighs. His left hand slid around in front of her, to cup the fullness of her breast and monitor the rhythm of her breathing as she slept.

His body was exhausted, but his mind was wide-awake, refusing to unwind. He made a point of timing Dana's heartbeat, firm and strong against his hand, but in his brain the bright, electric pulse of an EKG was spiking, losing any semblance of a normal rhythm. He could see it, when he closed his eyes, speeding up, then faltering, then receding into silence as the line went flat and still. As cold and still as death.

His eyes snapped open in the darkness, sudden panic chilling him, defeating drowsiness. Beside him, Dana shifted, grumbling in her sleep, disturbed by his convulsive movement. She was breathing. Still alive.

Reed held her close and did not close his eyes until the first pale light of dawn crept in to drive the shadows back. Aware that he was drifting then, he gingerly released his grip on consciousness, praying he would not dream.

CHAPTER

3

———•———

By Monday morning, he had learned to cordially despise the telephone. The calls, since Friday's early coverage of the execution, had been evenly divided up between the media and sundry flakes. Reed spoke to neither. Most of the reporters had moved on to other things by Monday, but the cranks would need more time. He was considering the luxury of an unlisted number when the phone began to ring once more. He left it to the answering machine.

"I hate these damned things, Adam. Am I talking to myself?" It was the voice of Roland Nash, his agent and a friend.

"How are you, Roland?"

"Beautiful is how I am. You holding up okay?"

"I'm fine."

"That's good to hear. You're up to working, then?"

"I'd say." A tingle of excitement at the prospect of a deal. "What have you got?"

"A cauliflower ear is what I've got. I've spent the whole damned morning on the phone, but it's encouraging. The weekend coverage on your buddy helped, of course, but still—"

"What *is* it, Roland?"

"Simon and Schuster is interested. We've got an offer."

"How much?"

When Roland told him, Reed suppressed a sudden urge to drop the telephone and clap his hands. It wasn't milk and honey, but it equaled the advance on Adam's last two books combined.

"Okay."

"Okay, he says. I wanted more, but what the hell, we'll make it up in royalties. Did I mention Pocket Books is interested in paperback rights?"

"You damn well know you didn't."

"Well, they are." He pictured Roland grinning, in New York. Self-satisfied. "It's not for sure, but I've got friends there, so keep your fingers crossed. On second thought, make that your toes. I want your fingers free for typing."

"How long on the paperwork?"

"A couple weeks. Have you got everything you need to nail it down?"

Reed glanced around his office, at the files stacked on his desk, the floor around him.

"I've got everything that's coming. It's enough."

"All right already. I've got confirmation calls to make, so I'll stop taking up your time. Expect the bluebacks on your desk in three weeks, tops."

"Thanks, Roland."

"You can thank me with my ten percent. Get busy, guy!"

He cradled the receiver, reaching out to hit a switch that cleared the answering machine. He felt like kicking up his heels and shouting, but it would have been ridiculous, a grown man capering around the empty house. He thought of calling Dana, but he didn't know where she was shooting, and she didn't need the interruption. It would wait till she got home.

And, in the meantime, he had work to do.

The files were sorted, chronologically and geographically, but there was still the matter of coordinating and condensing, fleshing out the basic outline while eliminating useless trivia. Reed had enough material on hand to rival *War and Peace* for length, but he would have to pare it down to something like a hundred thousand words. Maintaining focus, all the way.

Between their interviews and periodic phone calls, Thomas Bender had inscribed the story of his life in longhand, filling up nine legal pads, the last installment mailed a week before his death. More information came from confidential sources—school and psychiatric records, files from law enforcement agencies and penal institutions—grudgingly released as Bender fired off notarized petitions from death row. The rest derived from legwork, interviews and correspondence with survivors, pit stops on an odyssey of death. The autobiographical material was in itself, book-length, and while Reed planned to utilize his subject's words throughout the final manuscript, they needed polish. Not to mention factual corroboration.

Start at the beginning, then, with childhood. There the seeds of evil put down roots and flourished, fertilized with alternating violence and neglect. Born to alcoholic parents in the spring of 1950, Thomas Bender had endured vicious beatings from the time he was old enough to walk. In later years, he would recount the details with a crooked smile, unable—or unwilling—to recall the pain with any clarity. It would be Adam's task to make his readers share that pain, experience the outrage of repeated, unprovoked assaults. Long, hungry weekends, spent inside a closet, with the door locked. Small hands clenched above an open flame.

A travesty of childhood, with predictable results. At age eleven, Bender was arrested in a stolen car, too drunk to recognize the uniforms that towered over him. Probation for a first offense, but nothing in the way of leniency at home. More beatings, more arrests. Shoplifting. Vandalism. Curfew violations. Graduating into burglary.

At school, the counselors threw up their hands. The Bender boy again, more trouble than he's worth. Reports of petty theft and truancy. Repeated confrontations with his so-called peers, the violence escalating over time. Suspensions, with a week in juvey for possession of a knife. More fighting, no holds barred. Applying lessons learned at home. Relief came, when Bender dropped out of high school in his junior year to prowl the streets full-time.

In 1968 he joined the army, hoping for a crack at Vietnam. *Real* action. Guns and shit. Twelve weeks in uniform, and he was chafing at the discipline, unable to control his drinking. That Christmas Eve, his sergeant was in his face about some chickenshit assignment, giving Bender grief about his attitude. The hate came boiling out, in search of physical expression, and it took four men to pull him from the sergeant's prostrate body. Brig time, with a discharge designating him unfit for military service.

Bender started drifting, working long enough on this or that to keep himself in liquor. It was warm in Dallas, more or less hospitable to nomads. Killing time in seedy bars, he met a regular named Randi Sue. The randy part was right on target, and he found that she could match him drink for drink. True love. The courtship lasted fourteen days, and they were married in a civil ceremony, settling in a cheap, three-room apartment. If you blinked, you missed the honeymoon.

So much for romance. Randi Sue put on her wedding band in the belief that no ring ever plugged a hole. When she was drunk—and that was pretty much all the time—she felt like balling. If her old man wasn't home or couldn't get it up, there was a whole wide world of men from which to choose. In time, the sloppy sex was interspersed with screaming free-for-alls. Police were summoned. Bender's face became familiar at the county lockup. Finally, convinced that Randi Sue was servicing all their neighbors in his absence, Bender bought himself a can of high-test, lugged it back to the apartment house and set the place on fire. The charge was arson, and he offered no defense. Served twenty-seven months on five years maximum. He felt nothing, when he heard that Randi had been flattened by a hit-and-run in Houston.

Drifting.

Bender had a weakness for the Southern California climate. San Diego struck him as a laid-back town, the close proximity of Mexico a sweet fringe benefit. The Broadway neighborhood was perfect. Tattoo parlors and massage joints, porno houses, hookers offering their wares to sailors and civilians, any time one cared to take a stroll. It was a smorgasbord of sex, sensation, sleaze. Bender knew that he was home.

He tried the hookers on for size. Worked two-bit, dead-end jobs to keep himself in spending money. Rolled a drunk or two when times were hard. The sex was fair, but there was something missing. Violence. The excitement of a shouting, screaming punch-out that resolved itself in frenzied, sweating pleasure-pain.

He started to experiment with prostitutes. Some roughhouse, escalating rapidly as Bender realized that working girls did not complain to the authorities. A razor-flashing confrontation with an angry pimp left him trembling with excitement. Blood as aphrodisiac: a psychic breakthrough.

Bender had become a predator. No longer satisfied to pay for sex, he took it as it came. In parking lots and residential neighborhoods. At knife point. Needing booze and blood to make it happen. Stopping short of homicide, but edging closer every time he hit the street.

At Easter, two years into his parole, he went for broke. The lady was a topless dancer, not averse to entertaining after-hours, though not with Bender. She recognized a hard case when she saw one. Checking out Bender's eyes, she sampled a taste of hell on earth. He lost it when she started screaming, slashing her in an alley fifteen times. He surely would have killed her if a beat patrolman had not wandered into earshot, creeping up on Bender's blind side with a nightstick. Ninety days of psychiatric observation, with the catch-all diagnosis of an "antisocial personality disorder." Charges of attempted murder were bargained down to aggravated battery. At twenty-four, he had attained the danger age, when random killers typically emerge from their cocoons, but no one picked up on the signs. He served the minimum with time for good behavior, and emerged a wiser man.

Within the next eight months, he killed three San Diego women. Targets of opportunity, selected in bars, lured away by Bender's charm, his promises of liquor, love—whatever. In his car, he kept a ball peen hammer and a hunting knife. The rest was simple. Satisfying.

Boozy introductions long forgotten, Bender did not give a damn about their names. Reed managed to identify two victims by reviewing news reports. Maria Alvarez, a part-time prostitute, had been the first to die, in June 1975. Louise Frechette, "masseuse," was Bender's bloody Valentine, discovered on the ides of February. Another victim, sandwiched in between those two, had failed to make the papers. Later queries from Reed to police were useless. San Diego's finest never laid a glove on Bender, and they still refused to credit his confessions, writing off his murders as a string of unrelated incidents involving violent pimps.

Imagining himself in peril, feeling heat where none existed, Bender fled the state. He settled in Las Vegas, passed a quiet fourteen months before he felt the itch again. No problem. Escort services are all the rage in Vegas. Bender dialed a number, placed an order for his dream girl, waited in the dark outside a cheap motel for Sherry Ransom to arrive. She never knew what hit her. Bludgeoned, strangled with her own brassiere, eleven stab wounds in her chest and abdomen. He raped her after death, then moved on in search of other prey.

Thermopolis, Wyoming, in the heat of August. Catherine Littlefeather made it number five, assaulted in her own apartment. The investigating officer—assistant chief, these days—agreed to talk with Reed, then clammed up tight when told Bender stubbornly denied removing hidden cash from underneath his victim's mattress. Seven hundred dollars missing, with a live-in boyfriend crying foul. It was intriguing, but Reed knew the legal staff at Simon and Schuster would never touch it.

In Oklahoma City, Bender celebrated New Year's with a classic binge, waking to find an unknown woman in his bed. Part of one, at any rate. More of her was in the bathtub and further remnants were in the kitchen sink. He had no memory of picking up his latest victim, did not check her handbag for ID before he started shoveling the pieces into garbage bags. A quick run to the dump, where trash was burned on Thursdays. City homicide detectives later shrugged at Bender's confession, unable to proceed without substantial evidence. Reed believed the story. Bender knew the neighborhood by heart, described it to a tee.

Eight months elapsed before he played his game again, this time in Beaver, Utah. Misty Price, a Mormon housewife, disappeared while loading groceries in her car outside a supermarket. Hikers found her skeletal remains in mid-November, her identity confirmed by dental charts. No clues as to her murderer, until a Texas lifer started talking six years later.

Back in San Diego, Bender played it cautious, then began to unwind when he discovered he was not wanted by police. He met another lush, Drucilla Spencer, and they tied the knot on Halloween. An instant replay of the galling images from childhood. Randi Sue revisited.. A week before Thanksgiving, waitress Julie Farthing paid the tab in blood, component parts retrieved from several Dumpsters in the neighborhood of Broadway.

Drucilla survived through spring, when Bender felt the tender pangs of wanderlust. He strangled her with loving care and wrapped her body in a blanket, tucked inside a closet of their rented duplex. The authorities regarded her death as suicide, but Bender had no way of knowing. He was on the road again.

Another Vegas pit stop, long enough to meet Melinda Ross, a former show girl five years past' her prime. He dumped her lacerated body fifty feet from where police discovered Sherry Ransom two years earlier. Times change. Nevada voters have restored capital punishment since Bender's last visit. It makes all the difference in the world.

In Dallas, Bender came full circle, looking for familiar faces but finding only strangers. Targets. In the space of eighteen days, he killed three women, but the fever made him reckless. Patrons in a bar recalled his face—or did they? Homicide investigators pulled him in, along with several dozen others.

We want to talk about the woman, a cop says to him.

Bender smiles and asks, Which one?

Jaws drop. Case closed.

He drew three concurrent terms of life imprisonment, with parole a possibility inside eleven years. From out of nowhere, in the spring of 1984, he sought an audience with prosecutors from Las Vegas. He copped to Sherry Ransom and Melinda Ross. Waived extradition. Filed a guilty plea and asked for death, resisting all appeals on his behalf.

When Reed attempted to define Bender's motives, the killer hedged, expressing no remorse or guilt. It was convenient to dismiss his choice as suicide, the final action of a coward who had always preyed on victims weaker than

33

himself, afraid to take his own life in the crunch. Reed understood the rationale and somehow didn't buy it. Bender took his secret to the grave.

Perhaps, before he finished off the manuscript . . .

Reed broke at noon, to fix himself a sandwich, and returned to eat it at his desk. The time had come for him to deal with Bender's last effects. He had allowed himself the weekend, gaining distance, objectivity, but he could see no point in stalling any longer. He wiped his fingers on a paper napkin, opened the manila envelope, and spread its contents on the desk.

The Bible, first. Why had Bender requested it? It would not be the first time that a death row con was "born again," but Bender had revealed no trace of sudden piety in interviews or correspondence. Reed thumbed through the Bible, seeking tell-tale marks or dog-eared pages, finding none. He gave it up and set the book aside.

The audio cassette was next. He held it in his hand and stared at it awhile, as if the message could be picked up by osmosis. Finally, reluctantly, he slipped it in the Sony compact, keyed the Play command, and fiddled with the volume. Braced himself as static whispered from the speaker, giving way to a familiar voice.

"Hey, Adam. How's it hanging?"

Short hairs stirring on his nape. They really *do* stand up.

"We haven't got a lot of time to chat," the dead man told him. "Anyway, I think we've covered everything. I'm trusting Father Frank to pass some things along. The letters are a hoot. I think you'll find a couple of them interesting. And now . . . some music, maestro, please!"

A clumsy cut-away to Springsteen, singing "Downbound Train." Reed heard it through and listened to the trailing static for a moment, making sure that there was nothing else, before he punched Eject. The sound of Bender's voice was trapped inside his head.

There were thirteen envelopes. A lucky number. Sorted out by size, the smaller ones on top, held together with a rubber band.

Anticipating hate mail, Reed found nothing of the kind. No threats, obscenities, or serves-you-right-type letters. Prison censors must have thinned the crop . . . or, maybe no one cared enough to put their hate on paper. Saving it for other candidates who were not caged and waiting for the ax to fall.

The bulk of Bender's mail—six out of thirteen letters—brought religious tracts of the Repent-and-Be-Ye-Saved variety. Hellfire and brimstone. Personal redemption in the blood. Four correspondents, women in their early thirties, had included snapshots with their chatty notes. Reed studied them, one nude and three self-conscious portraits, wondering what moved a stranger to expose herself that way. Approaching Thomas Bender in the final moments of his life, with hopeless bids for an emotion Bender did not recognize.

I think you'll find a couple of them interesting.

Reed noted a resemblance among the women. Timid smiles, except the nude who boldly licked her lips. Dark hair, worn shoulder-length. They might have passed for sisters or for any one of Bender's victims. Carbon copies.

That left three white envelopes with Bender's name and prison address typed, unlike the others that were written out by hand. For the return address on each, a small adhesive sticker of the sort traditionally hawked by mail. According to the stickers and the postmarks, Michael Sturgess, with a P.O. box in Santa Rosa, California, had been moved to write three times inside a week. Reed checked the dates and took the envelopes in order of arrival.

The first contained a single sheet of yellow legal paper, folded twice, the message typed in single-space, without regard to printed lines. It had been written on November twenty-eighth and mailed the twenty-ninth. Reed scanned the message.

Mr. Bender—

I have followed your experience through television and the press. I recognize your courage in the face of overwhelming odds, but it disturbs me when I hear that you are giving up without a fight.

I hope you will consider new appeals, before it is too late. We both know that the failure is society's, not yours. Your life has value. Let us learn from your example, if we can.

No signature. The author's name typed out, as if he feared to leave his mark upon the page. A second reading yielded no more clues about his personality, beyond the bid to get on Bender's good side with a show of understanding.

Number two from Sturgess had been written on December second, posted the same day. Typewritten, once again on legal paper, letting Bender read between the lines.

Dear Mr. Bender—

I hope this finds you well. It must be terrible for one of your vitality to be confined, unable to exert yourself. Society exacts its price from individuals.

I hope you have been giving thought to my suggestion of a new appeal. It seems a shame to throw away your knowledge and experience when there is so much still to be accomplished.

With that in mind, I hope you will consent to answer several questions. First, what visions fill your mind in the commission of The Act? Is there a conscious pattern in selection of your subjects? What events produced the interruption of your work? (Police are lucky, sometimes, but they aren't too bright.)

Please, *please* consider fighting for your life! The feminizers and betrayers will not triumph!

Reed frowned as he returned the letter to its envelope. Four days, and Sturgess had progressed from vague expressions of concern to open admiration. Chalk up one more application for the Thomas Bender Fan Club. Questions rooted in the standard morbid curiosity.

The final letter had been written on December second, posted on the third. Reed pictured Michael Sturgess, man without a face, returning from the mailbox, sitting down to write again. Compulsive. Driven.

Thomas—

I got home just in time to see your picture on the TV news. It is the first time I have seen your picture and the similarity between us was amazing. Not that we resemble one another physically, but there was something in

36

your eyes—a recognition of the best (and worst) life holds in store.

I would have known you anywhere.

Believe me when I say I understand what you have been through. Pain and victory make up our common bond. I wish that we could meet and talk, but realize it is impossible in present circumstances.

Once again, I urge you to resist your enemies! Don't let them steal your life, when there is so much you could offer to society. Your death would be a tragic waste!

That said, you have my blessing in whatever you decide.

The work goes on.

Reed set the sheet of yellow paper on his desk, imagined Bender watching with his twisted smile.

The letters are a hoot. I think you'll find—

The work goes on.

That Sturgess was a flake, no doubt about it. Morbid hero worship, like the women with their photographs. Poor bastard.

Reed double-checked the author's address: Santa Rosa. Something on the news. His background research. Reed had been collecting clips on other serial murder cases for comparison, perhaps a thoughtful prologue. There was something he should know.

It clicked.

He crossed the room, retrieved a folder from the filing cabinet, and shuffled through a stack of dated clippings. Pulling out several, he sorted them by date before he read them through.

The articles spanned seven months, providing sketchy details of the fruitless manhunt for a killer known in headlines as the Santa Rosa Slasher, credited with murdering and mutilating twenty-three young women in the past three years. Another seven were missing and presumed dead, with police no closer to a breakthrough than they had been on day one. A madman stalking human prey in peaceful Santa Rosa. Crazy Michael Sturgess firing letters off to Thomas Bender from the psycho's happy hunting ground.

Reed knew it was insane. Some killers write to the police or to the press, like Son of Sam and Jack the Ripper, but they don't write back and forth to one another. *Do* they? Wasn't Hinckley stung for sending notes to Bundy on death row? And they were *both* inside. God only knew what sort of freaks were sending mail to Lucas or Berkowitz.

The sound of Dana's Fiat in the driveway brought him back. He met her on the threshold, with a kiss, and he could smell the ocean in her hair.

"You're early."

"Mmm. Chick got the shots he wanted."

"Good old Chick."

"He's working on a cover for me. *L.A. Style.*"

"He wants you *under* covers."

"What he wants and what he gets are different things."

"Does he know that?"

She teased him with a smile. "You're jealous."

"Not a bit."

Her pout was so delicious that he had to slip his hands around her waist and pull her close.

"Well, maybe . . ."

One more kiss, a quick one, and she wriggled free. "I'm starving. Early dinner?"

"Fine."

They worked together in the spacious kitchen, Adam tossing salad and preparing garlic bread while Dana fixed spaghetti. She described the shoot for Adam, knowing he enjoyed the details of her work as a model and that he valued her for who she was.

"I got some news today," he said, when she was finished. Briefing her about his talk with Roland Nash, their deal with Simon and Schuster, the possibilities with Pocket Books.

"That's wonderful. Congratulations."

And another kiss, no quickie this time. They were interrupted by the pasta boiling over on the stove.

He saved the Sturgess letters for dessert, while they were cleaning up. "There's something else," he told her, and she listened while he ran it down, complete with his suspicions. Skepticism showed on her face.

"It seems unlikely, hon. I mean, these people don't just correspond like pen pals."

"There was Hinckley," he reminded her, "and Manson still gets crazy letters."

"Right, but everybody knows about them. Wouldn't the police have checked this Sturgess out by now?"

"If someone sent them copies of the letters, I suppose."

"Well, there you are. The warden would have passed them on if they meant anything."

"I guess."

She heard the echo of his doubt. "But what?"

"Suppose they only check the mail for drugs, escape plans, things like that? For all I know, they've never heard of Santa Rosa or the Slasher."

Dana frowned. "If you're concerned, I think you ought to tell someone."

It was his turn to frown.

"I'll think about it."

When they were finished with the dishes, Adam dialed directory assistance in Santa Rosa, and an operator gave him the police department's address. He made copies of the Sturgess letters on his Canon PC-25—no hope of fingerprints on the originals by now—and typed a cover letter, laying out the basic facts and his suspicions. He weighed the parcel on his postal scale and filled the right-hand corner up with stamps. He found Dana working out, with Christie Brinkley on the VCR.

"I'll just be gone a minute."

"Right." She flashed a perfect smile, not missing a beat.

He loved their quiet Pasadena neighborhood, convenient to the L.A. action, yet removed—or, so he told himself—from all the major lunacy. It was a short half-block through gentle darkness to the corner mailbox. At the final moment, with the envelope in hand, Reed nearly changed his mind. He felt foolish playing Sherlock Holmes.

To hell with it. The stamps were wasted already.

The mail slot swallowed up his offering, and he reversed his steps without a backward glance. Already feeling better, he turned toward home.

CHAPTER

4

───●───

Nine days later. The nuisance calls had tapered off by
Sunday night, cranks moving on to pester new celebrities
and try to grab their fifteen seconds in the spotlight. Adam
Reed was thankful for the respite as he tried to put his
thoughts in order and words on paper. He started with the
kitchen sink and all, vowing to edit with a vengeance in the
second draft.

The wall beside his desk was decorated with at least two
dozen glossy eight-by-tens of Thomas Bender and his wom-
en. There was Bender as a child in grade school, smirking
for the camera. A copy of his wedding photograph with
Randi Sue, all smiles. A service photo, Bender dressed in
olive drab fatigues. Assorted mug shots, the expression
ranging from bemused to bored.

The women, most of them, were captured in before-and-
after shots. "Before" meant candid photos for the most part,
some of them procured from family albums. The obligatory
smiles ranged from hesitant to manic, now frozen for
eternity on film.

There were no smiles depicted in the "after" shots,
though one of them—Louise Frechette—had faked a grin of
sorts, her pale cheeks slashed from ear to ear. A couple of
the bodies lay facedown; all ghastly to behold.

40

Reed used the photographs to keep focus, glancing up from time to time or stopping in the middle of a sentence, swiveling his chair around to simply sit and stare. He knew the women only from obituaries or interviews with relatives when there were any to be found, but there was something in the eyes, a kind of vacancy, that bound them all together. Reed had never met them, had never known a one of them in life, but he felt confident in his belief that each of them was *searching* when she died—for love or its facsimile. Companionship. A friendly face.

Instead, they found Thomas Edward Bender.

Reed was winding down on Chapter One, a summary of Bender's Texas murder trial that paved the way for flashbacks to his childhood, when the telephone shrilled its demand for his attention. He had set the answering machine to screen his calls, and now waited through the greeting message, tapping keys to save up three new paragraphs.

The voice was male, a solid baritone, unfamiliar.

"Mr. Reed, I'm Sergeant Roy McKeon with the Santa Rosa Homicide Division, answering your letter of December—"

Adam lifted the receiver, killed the answering machine. "Hello?"

The startled caller echoed him. "Hello?"

"Yes, Sergeant. You were saying . . .?"

"Mr. Reed?"

"I just walked in."

It was a pointless fabrication, but it did the trick. The caller cleared his throat and started over, as if reading from a script.

"I'm Sergeant Roy McKeon, Santa Rosa Homicide. I'm looking at the note you sent us on December ninth, with the enclosures."

"Yes?"

"We'd like to clarify the circumstances under which you got these letters, Mr. Reed. You're a reporter?"

"Free-lance author. I write books."

"And you were corresponding with this Bender fellow up in Carson City?"

"On death row, that's right."

"And he received these letters, I'm assuming it was several days before his execution?"

"Right again."

"And you obtained them, how?"

"The prison chaplain passed them on to me with Bender's last effects."

"As part of your research?"

"That's right."

He would not test McKeon's understanding on the strange rapport he had developed with a killer, Bender locked in a cage, he free to come and go. It was irrelevant in any case, and trying to explain would only make the sergeant think he was another bleeding heart.

"Well, Mr. Reed, it may be nothing . . . but we're interested."

"I see."

It was the only thing that he could think of, questions churning in his mind, too fast and furious for him to put them into words.

"We've tried to check this Michael Sturgess out the past few days," McKeon said, "but there appears to be no record of him in the area."

"Appears to be no record?"

"What I mean to say, he's not in the directories for Santa Rosa or Sonoma County. Altogether, we've checked twenty-seven towns. He's got no telephone, no driver's license, and we can't find any record of him paying taxes to the state or IRS. According to the FBI, he hasn't been arrested since their records were computerized in 1969. We drew a blank on military records, and he never signed up for the draft. He's got the postbox, but the home address he listed is a janitorial supply store and they never heard of Michael Sturgess. So . . . we're interested."

"I see."

Reed sensed a story shaping up, or maybe it was just a footnote with potential, but it had The Feel. If Sturgess *was* the Slasher, it could be a whole new ball game. Thomas Bender had become a piece of history the moment that he closed his eyes in death. He wasn't going anywhere.

The Santa Rosa Slasher, on the other hand, was *news,* a

breaking story. Headlines yet to be written. If Reed played his cards right, some of them might carry Adam's name.

"You had an interview with Bender, I believe, a day or so before he . . ."

"Died. That's right."

So, they had checked him out with Carson City. Fair enough. Reed would have done the same.

"There was no mention of the letters at that time?" McKeon asked.

"They came as a complete surprise."

"And these were all the letters Bender got?"

"From Sturgess, right."

"Assuming 'Sturgess' is an alias, I thought he might have tried to reach your guy some other way."

"The other letters mostly came from women, plus a few religious types. I kept them all, if you want copies."

"Would you mind? It's probably a washout, but you never know."

"You think it's worth pursuing, then."

He did not phrase it as a question, waiting for McKeon to deny the obvious if he was so inclined.

The sergeant thought about it for a moment, cleared his throat before he spoke. "You've obviously done some reading on our problem here," he said.

"I have. That's why I sent the letters."

"What we've got right now is twenty-three dead women and another seven missing. One or two of those could still be runaways, but we assume the worst."

"So, call it thirty dead."

"That kind of killing doesn't sit well in Sonoma County, Mr. Reed. It's not your everyday occurrence, if you follow me."

"I do."

"Which means we've got no end of pressure on us, here, to find the man responsible."

"I understand."

"Smart money says your Michael Sturgess is an ordinary flake, okay? For all I know, he keeps a postbox in another name so he can order girlie magazines and hide them from his wife."

43

"You may be right."

"It comes back to the letters, though," McKeon said. "The general tone, for one thing, and this part about 'The work goes on.'"

"I caught that, too."

"You know, a deal like this, it could go either way. Some kind of harmless psycho groupie, or . . ."

"I guess you never know," Reed said.

"You never know," McKeon echoed. "It'll be three years next month since all this started. We've had false confessions, women turning in their husbands, landlords fingering their tenants. We have to check 'em all, of course. Three years, and I could name a dozen suspects who were hot enough to make the finals. Every one of them washed out on background checks and all we've got to show for it is twenty-three dead women."

"You could use a suspect."

"We could use a miracle," the sergeant told him, frankly.

"Maybe, if you watched the postbox, you could get a look at Sturgess, run his license plate or something."

"That assumes he picks up every day," McKeon answered. By his tone, Reed knew the simple plan had been considered, possibly attempted, but without success. "We're running short on men and money, as it is."

"I understand, of course. If there was some way I could help . . ."

"I don't suppose there's any chance you'd ever hear from him again?" the sergeant asked.

Reed felt his pulse rate quicken. Just a little, but enough to register.

"I never heard from him at all," he said. "The letters went to Thomas Bender."

"Right. That's right. And Bender's dead."

He recognized the bait. It was so obvious, a blind man could have seen it. Still, the smallest nibble wouldn't hurt.

He drummed his fingers on the desktop, then took the plunge.

"Suppose I answered him?"

"I couldn't recommend that, sir."

"Let's make it 'Adam,' shall we?"

"Adam, we've got stringent regulations when it comes to

44

the involvement of civilians in an active case. If anything went wrong—"

"It would be my responsibility," Reed interrupted him.

The guy was probably a harmless crank. At best, his offer to McKeon would produce some morbid correspondence from a psycho groupie. They were rarely violent. It might make a quirky epilogue for Adam's book on Thomas Bender once he changed the names around to satisfy the libel lawyers.

And, at worst?

Sturgess would have Reed's address from his letterhead. A postbox would have spared him that, but it had never seemed worthwhile. And, anyway, he was in the telephone directory.

"Officially," McKeon's baritone cut through his reverie, "I can't request that you take any action on this matter."

"Understood." The word caught in his throat at first, but Adam got it out. "I'll send you a release, if necessary."

"No, no, that's all right." McKeon chuckled at the thought. "We'll let it go with a suggestion that you take no steps to put yourself at risk."

"Received and noted, Sergeant."

"Well, in that case—"

"There's a fifty-fifty chance he may not answer me."

"But if he does . . ."

"I'll be in touch, of course."

"You know, he's probably some couch potato with a stupid sense of humor. Even so . . ."

"I always take precautions," Adam said.

"You do this kind of thing a lot?" McKeon asked.

"Hang out with lunatics, you mean?"

The laugh again. "It *is* a little strange, you know?"

"It sells books," Reed told him, knowing there was more to it than that. "Besides, I've always had a thing for monsters. Finding out what makes them tick."

"You figure that one out, I wish you'd let me know."

"I'm working on it."

"How'd you get along with Bender?"

"He was . . . different."

"I guess. They filled me in a little when I called . . ." McKeon caught himself and hesitated.

45

"When you called to check me out in Carson City," Adam finished for him.

"Nothing personal."

"You must get mail from crazies all the time."

"It happens now and then. The ones you really have to watch just walk in off the street."

"Protect and serve, remember?"

"Off the record, half the people I run into on a given day could use a keeper. Not that most of them are dangerous to anybody else, though I sometimes wonder how they look out for themselves."

"Sometimes they don't."

"That's right. They don't."

He felt McKeon looking for a way to disengage, get back to the mechanics of his job.

"Well, Sergeant, I should have a letter off to Sturgess in another day or so. I'll let you know if he responds, ASAP."

"Appreciate it, Adam."

"Maybe you'll get lucky in the meantime."

"That would be a change of pace. 'Bye now, and thanks again."

Reed cradled the receiver, switched the answering machine back on, and sat for a moment, staring into space. It was a simple thing, one letter. Ten or fifteen minutes, tops. No rush about it either. Santa Rosa wasn't paying him, and he had other business on his plate. In fact, if he forgot about it for a day or two—

Reed caught himself reviewing lame excuses, frowned, uneasy with the qualms he felt surrounding such a simple task. Write Sturgess back, explain in fifty words or less how he had gotten Bender's mail, and let it go at that. An open invitation to respond, no pressure. Nothing that would make your basic psycho groupie cut and run.

He tried to calculate the odds against a "lucky" hit, and did not have the first idea of how or where to start. His atlas, two years out of date, showed some 300,000 people in Sonoma County, more than one in four from Santa Rosa proper. Eighty thousand plus, not counting transients, and the odds against any one of them being the Slasher were . . . what?

Never mind.

He had promised McKeon. Backing out now would be childish. Worse, it would make him a coward, ducking and hiding from shadows. Running away from a story. Away from himself.

It would not cost him anything to try, and if he caught a lucky break, it could put him over the top. If Sturgess answered him, if anything developed from their correspondence, he could hold McKeon up for an exclusive. Sell the TV movie rights to Hollywood, six figures after Roland's ten percent.

Slow down.

He had to write the letter first, mail it, then wait around to see if Sturgess answered him. And in the meantime, there was Thomas Bender's story, on an eight-month deadline for delivery at Simon and Schuster.

Reed double-checked himself to verify the chapter had been saved, before he started up a new file. Standard business letter format. Typing out the date and inside address.

> Michael Sturgess
> P.O. Box 1165
> Santa Rosa, CA 95402

And where to start?
At the beginning. Take it nice and slow.
Dear Mr. Sturgess . . .

Adam broke the news to Dana over dinner, halfway through a Caesar salad. She had finished telling him about her day, a shoot with bogus furs for *L.A. Style.* The next two days were open. She was looking forward to the break.

"I got a call this afternoon from Santa Rosa."

"Who's in Santa Rosa?"

"The police." He reminded her of the Sturgess letters.

"Oh?"

"They tried to check him out, but he's a blank. No telephone, no street address. They're interested."

"Which means . . .?"

"I'm writing back to him, see what he has to say."

"Oh, Adam, I don't know."

47

"What's wrong?"

She hesitated, poking at her salad with a fork. "If the police can't find him, how are you supposed to?"

Adam shrugged. "I'm not. I write back to his P.O. box and introduce myself. He either answers or he doesn't."

"Why don't the police do that? They must have someone who can write a letter."

"He was interested in Bender."

"So? The cops could fake it. They could tell him whatever he wants to hear, set up a meeting, then grab him when he keeps the date."

"It's not that easy, Dana."

"Why?"

"In the first place, it's not against the law to mail a letter. All the task force wants right now is background information, to find out who this joker is and why he doesn't leave a paper trail."

"You volunteered for this," she said. There was a hint of accusation in her voice.

"The cops can't draft civilians." Adam smiled.

"Because it's *dangerous,*" she finished for him, having none of it. "You're not a homicide detective, Adam. You're not qualified."

"To write a letter? Jesus, Dana."

"It's a story, right?" She made it sound like something wicked, a forbidden vice. "Another maniac."

"It all comes back to Bender."

"Bender's dead, remember? He was locked up when you started working on the story. This is something else."

"Listen, Dana, if the cops thought there was any danger, don't you think they'd say so? This guy's probably a harmless Walter Mitty type. He probably won't even answer me."

"I wish you wouldn't do this, Adam."

"Well . . ."

"You wrote to him already, didn't you?"

"This afternoon."

"And mailed it?"

"Right."

"Terrific."

"Dana . . ."

"Never mind. It's your decision."

"If I'd known that it was going to upset you—"

"You'd have kept it to yourself."

"It's business, Dana."

"I just hope it doesn't blow up in your face."

"It won't."

But even as he spoke, McKeon's words came back to him. *If anything went wrong . . .*

Chances were, the crazy bastard wouldn't even write him back. And if he did . . . well, Reed would think about that when it happened. In the meantime, he had work cut out for him at home. A book to write. Bruised feelings to assuage.

He hadn't done a damned thing wrong, but there it was. The guy who wrote *Love Story,* Reed decided, had been full of crap. Love meant *always* having to say you were sorry, even when it made no sense.

Still, she was definitely worth it.

Dana would forget about the letter soon, and if he were ever to hear from Sturgess—damned unlikely, Reed decided, if the guy was guilty—he would keep it to himself.

He let her see his most engaging smile and said, "How's good old Chick these days?"

CHAPTER

5

——•——

At half-past ten on Friday morning, Howard Michael Starr prepared to fetch his mail. This occasional journey was no simple task. In the interest of security, he shunned any predetermined schedule. He knew his enemies would love to catch him at it, claiming he was up to something nasty, using any old excuse to punish him for someone else's sins.

No problem.

They would have to get up *extremely* fucking early in the morning if they wanted to stay ahead of Howard Michael Starr. He had them figured out from way back, knew exactly how their little minds worked, spinning webs to snare him. All in vain, with their pathetic meddling, sniffing after something they would never truly understand.

He felt like being blond today. The wig was custom-tailored for his shiny, hairless skull. A special weave, no stinting on the cost. He used theatrical adhesive to prevent unsightly accidents. You had to get up close and personal to tell that he was wearing it.

And no one got that close to Howard Michael Starr.

It was a quirk of Starr's that he invariably thought about himself in the third person, an observer of his own unfolding life. And when he thought about himself—an exercise that filled his waking hours—he invariably saw himself as Howard Michael Starr.

Not simply "Howard Starr," nor even "Michael" for a change of pace. Absolutely never "Mike" or "Howie."

Starr detested nicknames. They diminished one's identity, subtracting from the whole, which was dangerous. The world was rife with peril, even for a man who kept himself intact and knew exactly who he was. Surrendering a portion of himself, however trivial it might seem, was tantamount to suicide.

Besides, his name had power. He could feel it burning in his veins each time he closed his eyes and turned the three words over in his mind. A proud gift from the father who had died when Starr was barely eight months old.

Starr heard his mother's voice, inevitably slurred by alcohol. *Your father left us money and his name. That's all you need to get along these days.*

She had been wrong of course, as mistaken in her philosophy as in her choice of men. Starr had forgiven her for lying to him, as well as for all her other foibles. By the time he was old enough to understand her words, he had also recognized the error of her ways. He took steps to save himself before it was too late.

The eyebrows were more difficult than the wig. It took real craftsmanship to weave and trim a lifelike pair. He used a touch of spirit gum, taking extra care in setting them precisely.

There.

A pragmatist by nature, he had come to view the alopecia as a gift, instead of the affliction it had once appeared to be. He was reborn each day, as sleek and naked as when he came into the world. Starr knew that he was born at night, and in the middle of a raging thunderstorm, because his mother had incorporated all the details in her litany of grievances against the son who had tied her down. Too young to be a widow with a child in tow, she did her best to compensate with liquor, chemicals, and mindless sex. Still, she could always spare a moment to complain.

Long ago, he had decided that the weather on his birthnight was an omen, proof that his arrival on the planet was significant enough to rate a show of fireworks.

He decided to forget about the mustache, having worn a beard the last time out. He would avoid any subtle pattern based on facial hair. He toyed with the idea of trying on a scar, then dismissed it as more trouble than it was worth.

Blue-tinted contact lenses next, to camouflage the slate gray of his eyes. Blue added warmth, so he had been told. No matter how he searched his mirror image, warmth eluded him. If he had ever known the feeling, it was long since dead and gone.

The finished man stared back at him and tried a smile for size, rehearsing for a minor walk-on part. He had no lines in this performance, but he was prepared to ad-lib if the script was altered by his enemies.

A walking masterpiece, was Howard Michael Starr.

He left his dressing room, moved through the silent house, no sound to violate the perfect stillness as he passed from room to room. He picked up his car keys from the dresser, then stopped to finish off a quart of orange juice in the kitchen, storing energy. He rinsed the empty carton out and crushed it, dropped it in the trash.

There were two cars in the garage. They represented half his present rolling stock; two more were stashed in rented quarters under different names. The Porsche was registered to Howard Michael Starr, the Volvo to a corporation he had organized in 1985 to cover his investments and the remnant of his father's legacy.

He chose the Porsche because it seemed to match the face he had selected for his outing. Youth and style, supported by a bank account and stock portfolio that left him ample leisure time. The Volvo went with brown hair, maybe gray, and pin-striped business suits.

Before he climbed into the Porsche, Starr checked on the black widow spider he had noticed for the first time six days earlier. Her tangled web was underneath his work bench, out of sight unless you made a point of searching for it. Starr would never have discovered it had he not dropped a cartridge case last Saturday while using his reloader. He spied the widow when he stooped to fetch his brass.

It would have been easy to kill the spider, but he chose to let her live. Starr felt a grudging kinship for the tiny, jet-black killer, hanging motionless and waiting for her prey to make a house call.

And the widow was expecting young ones any time now. Two fat egg sacs were tucked up in a corner of the web like little cotton balls. In a few more days, he could kill a thousand spiders for the price of one.

He spent another moment watching the widow eat a fat bluebottle fly, then left her to it. Sliding in behind the Porsche's steering wheel, Starr triggered the garage door opener and waited as a narrow slash of daylight widened to reveal the yard and sloping asphalt drive.

Starr liked the atmosphere of this serene, old-money neighborhood in Santa Rosa. He was six or seven years below the average age of residents in Willow Run, a subdivision notable for stately homes and manicured lawns maintained by Mexicans who knew their place. Aside from Fletcher Boles, a widower at sixty-one, three houses down, Starr was the only bachelor on the block.

The neighbors did not trouble Howard Michael Starr. His house sat well back from the street, with weeping willows out in front for privacy. Geography and some strategic landscaping prevented anyone from spying on him in his own backyard. He came and went by car, odd hours of the day and night. Some of the neighbors recognized his vehicles, might nod or lift a hand if they should pass him on the street, but it was generally known that he was not the social type. He would certainly not be insulted if his name was automatically deleted from prospective guest lists, parties and the like. Starr did not mingle well.

Starr had his own diversions. An audience of one was ample for his needs, and he preferred to choose the players on his own.

He drove the Porsche with skill but did not test its power. Racing up and down the streets of Santa Rosa would have been a fool's game, drawing undesired attention. It was enough to have the sports car noticed and admired, its driver likewise, while remaining perfectly anonymous.

The driver's license in his wallet and the pink slip in the Porsche's glove compartment bore his true name and address. At home, inside a basement floor safe, Starr had half a dozen sets of personal ID in different names. None of them matched the postbox he was visiting today, but that was not a problem. Starr had always paid his fees on time, in cash, and none of the distracted postal clerks had ever given him a second glance.

He used the P.O. box for recreation, corresponding with an ever-changing list of strangers under several different names. On any given day, he might have letters waiting from Miami, Dallas, New York City, Montreal. He answered personals at random, scanning several major dailies, singles magazines, what have you. Starr had trained himself to read between the lines.

On rare occasions, once in every eighteen months or so, he sought out a pen pal. No warning of his visit. Some detective work beforehand, running down the home address. Reconnaissance, to spare himself from any rude surprises. In and out like magic.

There was always someone ripe to take the fall.

Downtown, he managed to ignore the Christmas decorations that the city put up every year. The carpenter from Nazareth held no appeal for Howard Michael Starr, although it occurred to him that the two of them enjoyed one common trait: No one who laid a hand on either of them came away unscathed.

He found a parking space, locked up the Porsche and set the car alarm before he made his way inside. Starr held the door for three departing customers, the last in line a young blonde with a rugrat on her hip and one more in the oven.

"Thanks." The bare suggestion of a smile.

He pictured gutting her, the warm blade crimson-slick and gliding on the upstroke. Watching as the fetus slithered out and dangled at the end of the umbilicus. The youngest bungee jumper in recorded history. A footnote in the *Guinness Book of Records*.

It was crowded in the drab post office lobby, patrons lined up almost to the door while three clerks took their time processing packages, accepting cash and making change. Clerks and customers alike looked bored. If any one of them was thrilled about the coming holidays, it didn't show.

The crowd was good and bad for Howard Michael Starr. It provided him with an extra bit of anonymity as he proceeded to retrieve his mail from Box 1165. Still, he realized that it was also easier for enemies to hide in a crowd. They could have spies on duty, waiting for him, looking for a chance to trip him up.

He dawdled past a wall display of stamps depicting dead musicians. Elvis in his twenties. Buddy Holly singing "Peggy Sue."

The young die good.

More stamps, with scenes from World War II. Starr leaned in closer, checking out the beach at Tarawa, but he was disappointed. No blood on the sand.

He turned away from the display case, saw his opening, and moved before a fat old woman with her granddaughter in tow could block the way. He had the key in hand and ready when he reached his box. Glancing left and right without appearing to, he satisfied himself that no one was observing him.

There might be hidden cameras, of course, but there was little he could do about technology. Starr trusted his disguise to throw the snoopers off, if they were watching him. And if they somehow traced the car . . . well, he would think about that when the time came.

In the box was a flyer from his congressman. A plea for him to send a starving child in Asia thirteen cents a day, as if the little bastard could survive on that. Three letters from pathetic women in Chicago, Denver, San Francisco. One more with a man's name and return address he did not recognize.

He stashed the letters in a pocket of his navy peacoat, dropped the junk mail in a forty-gallon trash can that would soon be overflowing. He held the door for two more patrons coming in, then slipped outside. The chill was bliss compared to the oppressive, sweaty atmosphere he'd left behind.

Long strides across the parking lot, not hurrying, but moving with a purpose. Several strangers straggled out behind him, none appearing to give Howard Michael Starr a second glance. They had their own lives, filled with whining children, jobs that made them wish their days away, the various pedestrian concerns of money, health, and fleeting time.

He was not followed to the Porsche, although he could not

absolutely rule out spotters watching from a distance. Anxious as he was to read his mail, Starr left the letters in his pocket, gunned the Porsche's engine for a heartbeat, then released the parking brake. He kept watch in the rearview mirror as he left the parking lot behind him and merged with traffic.

This would be the time for any followers to make their move.

As far as Howard Michael Starr could tell, with senses finally honed from long years of preparedness, he did not have a tail this afternoon. Even so, he took no chances. To err was human, and he practiced every day to purge himself of that humanity. Defensive driving was a habit, evasive movements second nature. Starr would no more drive a straight path back and forth from home than he would masturbate in public.

Make the bastards work.

Assume the worst.

Be ready.

He spent close to twenty minutes on a drive that should have taken ten, twice doubling back to shake off motorists who showed a trifle too much interest in the Porsche. Starr did not feel the least bit foolish taking strict security precautions in his daily life. He was alive and walking free today because he never gave his enemies an edge. He took nothing at face value.

Question everyone and everything.

It would be death, in no uncertain terms, to let his guard down.

Starr opened the garage door from a half block out, stopped several yards beyond his driveway. Shifted to reverse and backed the Porsche in. Got it right the first time, everytime.

It was a routine Starr never varied. Always park the cars with an escape in mind. There would be little or no warning when his enemies came knocking. Every second he could shave from his emergency departure time improved his chances of survival and escape.

He shut the door, relaxing somewhat once the pleasant residential street was cut off from view. Starr left the Porsche and took his keys, no spare time now for the widow in her web as he retreated to his living quarters. In the dining room, he sat at the broad oak table where he took his meals alone and spread the letters out in front of him, like playing cards.

The women were a mixed bag, physically and psychologically. Chicago was a dancer. Slim, athletic, blond. She called herself Lucille, no last name yet, but it would come in time. It always did. Lucille could certainly have found herself a man with little difficulty, hanging out at bars, but she had done that scene, with uniformly bad results. These days, she craved a little distance. Space. A vague, no-strings relationship with someone who was not about to turn up on her doorstep. It was distance that permitted her to tell him things, explore dark fantasies, and pose for photographs that showed a side of her that her friends and family would not recognize.

Starr answered each and every letter he received. He was adept at tapping into other minds and rummaging around for nuggets long forgotten or suppressed. When asked about himself, he fabricated details from a life he might have led if he were someone else. The photographs he sent to women on request were clipped from ancient magazines and fashion catalogues, rephotographed and printed in his basement darkroom.

No loose ends.

His pen pal out of Denver was a red-haired, thirtyish divorcee with a three-year-old who kept her off the dating circuit, more or less. Starr recognized excuses when he saw them, knew the woman—Christie Stanwick—was afraid of taking chances in her life. Once burned, twice shy. Her ex had been abusive, prone to use his fists when he was drunk or pissed, which had been nearly all the time. He had abused their daughter, too, in ways that Christie hinted at but never specified. The woman needed risk-free reassurance now, that she was still desirable, intelligent, and capable, a valued person.

Howard Michael Starr enjoyed the sideshow that was human nature. So much agonizing over trivia, the trappings of a "normal" life, and what it all came down to was the bottom line of Me, Me, Me.

His little friend from San Francisco offered superficial

deviation from the norm. Marissa was a sadomasochist who cultivated naughty friends around the country. It amused Starr to allow her brief, distorted glimpses of his private life, assessing her reactions, feeding her erotic fantasies. One day, he thought it would be pleasant to surprise her with a visit, test Marissa's limits for himself. Starr knew that he would have to alter his technique, with Frisco being dangerously close to home, but he was nothing if not versatile.

The final letter was a riddle. Starr examined it for several moments, studying the envelope, the stamp and postmark, the return address. He did not know an Adam Reed, had never written to the Pasadena address. There was no particular aroma when he held the letter underneath his nose and sniffed it. No suspicious lumps or thickness when he smoothed the envelope beneath his fingertips.

One sheet of paper, he decided, folded into thirds.

He slit the envelope along its top crease, placed the sleek bone-handled switchblade on the table, at his elbow. Took the letter out. Pale stationery, somewhere on the color scale between off-white and ivory. The author's name and mailing address centered at the top. A date—December eighteenth, two days previous—typed beneath the city, state, and zip code.

Starr read through the letter twice, before he put it down.

Michael Sturgess
P.O. Box 1165
Santa Rosa, CA 95402

Dear Mr. Sturgess:

I am—or was—a friend of Thomas Bender. We became acquainted last July and grew to know each other through interviews and correspondence, working on a book about his life which has been scheduled for delivery to Simon and Schuster in June. I was among the witnesses who viewed his execution on December sixth.

Because he had no living relatives, Tom designated me as the recipient of his effects. Among the items given to me by authorities in Carson City were your letters, written in the week before Tom's death. He wasn't big on writing, but he left a note suggesting that it might be worth my time to get in touch with you.

Now, having read your letters, I agree.

I would be very interested in learning more of your opinions on the problems Tom was faced with in his life and the unique approach he chose in coping with those problems. Any insights you may offer would be much appreciated, and they would be credited in print . . . or not, as you prefer.

Thanks for your time. I look forward to hearing from you soon.

Sincerely,
Adam Reed

Starr placed the letter on the tabletop and smoothed it with his hands, slow gliding strokes. He picked up nothing from the paper, no vibrations that would help him see beyond the words and into the author's mind.

He supposed a book on Thomas Edward Bender's life was inevitable, but he had thought some more prestigious scribe would get the job. The name Adam Reed stirred nothing in his memory, but that was no surprise. Some fledgling hack perhaps, who had cajoled and wheedled Bender's story out of him for chump change and the siren song of immortality in print.

Or could it be a trap?

Starr frowned, considering the possibilities.

His notes to Bender had been mailed on impulse, something in the stranger's face, his television interviews that spoke to Starr on a subconscious level, telling him they were soul mates. Even so, Starr recognized the danger when he sat down and began to type. He had conceived a new identity specifically for Bender, taking care with fingerprints until he had the letters safely tucked inside their envelopes. A decent lab could take saliva samples from the stamps, but Starr's blood type was A: the only common thing about him, shared with forty-two percent of human beings on the planet. As for DNA, the lab would need a subject for comparison, which meant that they would have to track him down.

It would never happen.

It concerned Starr, for a moment, that a man he had

trusted would pass his letters on to someone else, a total stranger, but he let it go. With only hours left to live, he understood the urge that Bender must have felt to leave a record of his work behind. Beyond the tabloid articles that garbled facts and fabricated motives, all painting Thomas Edward Bender as a hopeless madman.

Starr had seen through that distorted portrait, recognizing Bender at a glance for what he truly was: an artist.

True, he had been clumsy toward the end, consumed with passion for his work. He made mistakes and wound up in a cage, condemned to die. Starr wrote it off to simple over-zealousness, forgiving Bender for his momentary lapse. Recalling the achievements that preceded Bender's fall.

Starr brought his mind back to the here and now, considering the note from Adam Reed. He tried to form a mental picture of the man, came up with rumpled hair and wire-rimmed glasses, tweed and corduroy. A bookish type by inclination and profession. Soft and pale from working at a desk indoors.

No danger there.

Still, it could be a trap. Starr understood that mail was monitored in prison. Several dozen people might have read his letters, passing them around and psychoanalyzing him before they reached death row. In fact, he had no way of knowing whether Thomas Bender ever saw his correspondence. It would be a simple thing, routine, to intercept his mail and weed out any notes the warden or his staff deemed inappropriate.

And what would happen, then? Delivery to the state police, perhaps? A consultation with the FBI at Quantico, Virginia? Starr knew all about the federal shrinks who took such pride in drawing "psychiatric profiles" from the slimmest evidence. They called it science, palming off their guesswork on police departments where the average homicide detective barely finished high school. Keeping labels vague enough so that almost any evidence would fit a given profile if you closed one eye and squinted through the other.

They were fools and charlatans, no threat to Howard Michael Starr. The men they captured were invariably careless, some of them apparently intent on leaving clues to their identity.

Oh well, it took all kinds.

It never crossed Starr's mind that he would place himself at risk by writing back to Adam Reed. There were precautions he would have to take, of course, but they were trifles, automatically incorporated in his daily life.

He only questioned whether it was worth his time.

It might be interesting, a change from the pathetic women who depended on his letters for some meaning in their wasted lives. Another man might understand him, given time and guidance. Literary types sometimes possessed surprising insight. If they could establish trust, he might—

Starr caught himself and drew back from the brink of fantasy.

If he wrote back to Adam Reed, it would be one more game devised for personal amusement. There was nothing he could learn from lesser men, but he might teach the scribbler something. Give him just the smallest glimpse inside a world so stark and terrifying it would change his life.

And if the letter *was* designed to bait him, Starr could deal with that as well. A bit more vigilance from now on when picking up his mail could only do him good. Another exercise to keep him on his toes.

And he could always find a way to punish treachery.

It was decided. He would respond cautiously. Starr did not want to frighten Adam Reed away by showing too much at once. It would diminish the experience for both of them, and that would be a mistake. Anticipation was the prime ingredient in any satisfactory experience. A buildup to the main event, with a flawless execution as the ultimate reward.

His mother's voice: *You always were a nasty, stupid little boy.*

Starr silenced her, recovering his composure in a heartbeat. Smiling. It was easy when you had the knack.

He read the letter's final sentence one more time.

Be careful what you wish for, Adam.

Howard Michael Starr was smiling as he rose and took the letter with him, moving toward his den.

CHAPTER

6

Beginning was the hardest part. Staring at a blank computer screen and waiting for the words to come, searching for that certain turn of phrase that would grab the reader on page one. The research, preparation, outlines, all came down to nothing if you couldn't find that hook.

Day seventeen since Bender's death. Adam Reed had finished the preliminary work on Saturday. His notes were organized, cross-referenced, sorted by chapters. Everything done, in fact, except the work of writing.

Simple.

He had signed the contract Friday morning, shipping it back to Roland Nash by Federal Express. The clock was running, but he still had seven months and change before his deadline. No real pressure yet, until he thought about the missing hook and began to get paranoid. Once into it, Reed knew from past experience, the narrative would flow, but getting there was still a problem. On his first book, it had taken him a month to get the first page right, and just six weeks to finish off the next three hundred.

Adam backed up and deleted his initial thirteen words. The Apple screen was blank and silent, waiting. It could wait forever, unlike certain editors.

At least he had the title. That was something. It had come to Reed while he was listening to one of Bender's interviews on tape. An observation on the link between his crimes and alcohol. "Deathwork is thirsty business," Bender said. "It helps to have a couple six packs going in." And there you had it: *Deathwork*.

All he needed was another hundred thousand words or so, and he was done.

It hit him then, or maybe he had known it all along. If Bender could provide the title, he could also bait the hook. What better way to draw the reader in than letting Thomas Bender introduce himself?

Reed pushed back from his desk and retrieved the Sony tape recorder and a shoe box filled with audiocassettes. The tapes were labeled, names and dates, approximately one-third of them interviews with Bender, mostly on the telephone, collect from Carson City in the weeks before his death. A printed index told him which tape he was seeking. Adam plugged it in and hit Fast Forward, watched the counter, stopping just before the segment he desired. He hit Play and let it run.

"You ask me what it feels like, killing people. Women. I suppose I'd have to say it's different every time. My first kill, I was really nervous, thinking of a hundred different things that could go wrong. I almost lost my nerve, but what the hell. Once I was into it, the nerves were nothing. There's a rush, you know? Like nothing else you've ever felt before. A kind of power. After that, it just got easier. Same rush, without the worries."

From the killer's firsthand statement, Reed could move directly to a murder scene, catch Bender in the act. Red-handed, as it were. The reader gets a glimpse of hell up close and personal, no holds barred. He'd use Dallas, follow through on the arrest and trial before flashing back to Bender's childhood to unearth the roots of evil.

He was getting there. Bender would break the ice and help him past the first-page block that had him stymied. Reed could carry on from there.

He started over, wound the tape back, making sure he got it right. Sometimes it felt like magic, watching letters march across the blank screen of his monitor, form words and sentences before his very eyes.

He lost the next full hour, slipping into Thomas Bender's world. It was an easy place to find once you acquired the mind-set, but it always left him feeling soiled. Despair and degradation had a way of rubbing off. Cops had it worse than writers, but he had to watch himself.

What was it Nietzsche wrote in *Thus Spake Zarathustra?* "When you look into an abyss, the abyss also looks into you."

He was a fair way down the rabbit hole when something called him back. A sound, from the direction of the living room. He shifted gears, ran down the short list of familiar noises. It was almost noon; the postman.

He saved up on the Apple, rose and stretched to work the kinks out of his back and shoulders. Reed was grateful for the interruption. Now that he had found his way inside the story, he could pace himself. A break would do him good.

The postman had already disappeared when Adam reached the porch. He glanced inside the box from force of habit, then retrieved his mail, an average Tuesday haul. Two bills. Junk mail addressed to Dana and her roommate Occupant. Three Christmas cards. A long slim envelope.

He blinked at the return address and froze. It took a heartbeat for him to recover.

Michael Sturgess. Santa Rosa.

Reed checked both ways along the quiet street, as if expecting some ungodly character to appear on the sidewalk, breathing like Darth Vader through a hockey mask. Feeling ridiculous, he went back inside and dropped the other mail on the breakfast counter. He took the Sturgess letter to his office. Reed set it on the desk in front of him and stared at it for several moments.

Fingerprints came instantly to mind. The smart thing, Reed decided, was for him to send the plain white envelope unopened to the Santa Rosa task force. Type a cover note and let McKeon do the rest.

He had volunteered to get in touch with Sturgess, draw him out through correspondence. And he couldn't correspond with someone if he never read their letters, could he?

McKeon expected him to read the letter—or, at any rate, he should have.

Reed caught himself, realizing he was making up a lame excuse to have a look inside the envelope, to find out if he were dealing with a monster or a common flake. Curiosity gnawed at him like a rodent nibbling cheese.

He picked the letter up and turned it over in his hands, as if he might learn something by osmosis. Stalling. Wondering if he was qualified to judge this total stranger on the basis of a simple note. False modesty aside, he had become an "expert" on the case of Thomas Bender, but that expertise was nontransferable to maniacs in general. He was not a shrink or criminologist, could not remember squat from the semester he had spent in Psych 1A, his freshman year in college.

Reed made up his mind. He would read the letter, shoot a copy on the Canon, taking reasonable care with fingerprints. Send the original to Santa Rosa for analysis and let the experts carry it from there.

He slit the envelope and shook a single piece of folded paper out. Felt awkward trying to unfold it without smearing fingerprints or adding dozens of his own. A pencil and a plastic ruler pinned the letter down. He read the neat, typewritten lines.

Dear Mr. Reed,

I was surprised to hear from you, as you may well imagine. It would be presumptuous of me to say that I regarded Thomas Bender as a friend since we were never privileged to meet, but I believe you will agree with me that he was "an original." It pleases me to know that he will be immortalized in print.

It takes a special kind of man to stand alone against the world.

The correspondence you suggest might be instructive, though I fail to see what insight I can offer into Mr. Bender's life or personality beyond your own exhaustive research. Possibly, if you could pose specific questions and approach the subject philosophically, we both might profit from the exercise. I have some limited experience in that regard.

65

Best wishes on your work, until I hear from you
again.

Sincerely,
Michael Sturgess

Adam read the letter twice more, trying to imagine
Sturgess at his typewriter. He pictured someone dumpy,
nondescript. Joe Average. The syntax spoke of education,
almost certainly beyond the high school level. Not a dimwit,
although tidy sentence structure did not make a genius.

*It takes a special kind of man to stand alone against the
world.*

I have some limited experience in that regard.

Like what? Reed wondered. Was it ego talking? Had he
flattered Sturgess by responding to the death row letters and
expressing interest? Was the guy a self-styled expert, tapping
into true crime paperbacks and back issues of *Psychology
Today?*

Not quite. He had contrived a false identity, for starters,
and a false address to back it up. The Santa Rosa task force
couldn't track him down, though Adam had no way of
knowing how hard they had tried.

One suspect out of—what? how many?—in the past three
years. They must have gone through dozens, maybe hun-
dreds, in their manhunt for the Slasher. Better leads than
this, without a doubt. It was ridiculous of Reed to think that
he could wander in from nowhere, crack the case, and take it
to the bank.

Dana would be pissed if he pursued the matter, that was
understood. He saw two possible ways to play it. He could
keep it to himself, the wiser course, or give a nod to honesty
and try to minimize the risk involved.

What risk?

He had the Santa Rosa task force standing by to land on
Sturgess like a ton of bricks, assuming they could ever find
him. Call it ninety-nine to one that he was just a harmless
crank, perhaps a psycho wannabe who studied human
monsters in the press the way some followed rock stars. If he
came off sounding like an expert in his letters, chances were
that it was all hot air.

Reed found McKeon's number in his address book and hesitated with the telephone receiver in his hand. He tapped out the eleven digits, waited. He was startled when a female voice came on the line.

"Detective Janus, homicide."

"Detective Sergeant Roy McKeon, please."

"He isn't in right now. Is there a message?"

Adam left his name and number, feeling disappointment as he cradled the receiver. It was silly—they had more important things to do, of course—but he had counted on a swift response, some kind of action.

Get back to work, he thought. You're wasting time.

He read a portion of the Bender text again, but it felt awkward now. He was preoccupied with Sturgess, sidetracked from the main event. A rumbling in his stomach gave Reed the excuse he needed to desert his office and make himself a sandwich, pass on beer in favor of a decaf Coke. Too early for a drink, despite the dictum that it must be four o'clock at some point on the planet.

He was nearly finished when the phone rang, feeling stupid when the shrill sound made him jump. He took it in the kitchen.

"Good morning. Mr. Reed?"

It's afternoon, he almost said, before he recognized the voice.

"Sergeant McKeon."

"Right. I got your message. What's the word?"

"I heard from Sturgess," Reed informed him. "Can you hold on while I take this in my office?"

"Sure."

A moment later, he was seated at his desk, the telephone receiver wedged between his shoulder and his ear, hands restless in his lap.

"Okay, the letter came this morning, just before I called. I opened it before I got my brain in gear, but I was careful with the fingerprints."

A partial truth, at least.

"Uh-huh." No disappointment evident in the detective's tone.

"It's short," said Adam, "if you'd care to hear it."

67

"Please."

He read the letter through and waited for a moment, while McKeon mulled it over.

"Well, that's something," the detective said at last. "Offhand, I don't know what to make of it."

"It may be nothing," Adam said, belaboring the obvious.

"That's true. I'd like to have it anyway, if you don't mind."

"Sure thing."

"If there's a way for you to get it back inside the envelope without a lot of excess handling, that would be ideal. I don't expect much in the way of prints, but you never know."

"I'll see what I can do."

"You probably have gloves around the house?"

"Of course."

"I'll have our people take a look and see what they can see."

"About responding . . ." Reed began.

"I'd wait a bit on that," McKeon said. "No reason to suppose our buddy's going anywhere. I'd like to have some people read the note and give me their impressions, before we make another move."

The brass, thought Reed. More probably a shrink. A good lab could identify the make of typewriter. Forensics might come up with fingerprints, perhaps a blood type from saliva on the stamp or gummed flap of the envelope.

"I understand."

"It won't take long. I know you've got a book to write."

"That's true."

"I don't want to monopolize your time on this," McKeon said. "I'll touch base after we've reviewed the letter."

"Right."

"And, Mr. Reed, we do appreciate your help."

"It's Adam."

"Adam, right. I'll be in touch."

He hung up, walked back to the kitchen, cleared the other telephone. A pair of baggy rubber gloves lay folded in a drawer beside the sink. Reed slipped them on and flexed his fingers, feeling like the crazy doctor in a piss-poor movie from the Late, Late Show. He rinsed the gloves off, dried them on a dish towel, to eliminate potential grease or cleanser traces.

Adam walked back to his office, switched the Canon on, and waited for the blinking light to stabilize. He picked the Sturgess letter up between a thumb and forefinger, the upper left-hand corner, and aligned it on the window of the copier by nudging at the edges. Shot two copies of it, just in case he managed to misplace one.

The gloves felt clumsy, folding up the letter, but he took his time. The envelope resisted him until he ditched one glove—the outside prints were useless, anyway—and got it open wide enough to slip the folded letter back inside. A six-by-ten manila envelope would do the trick.

He scrawled a cover note by hand, typed out the label, weighed the envelope and stamped it. Sitting on the corner of his desk, it looked innocuous. Like nothing.

Which, he thought, was probably the truth.

There was no rush to mail it. It was Christmas Eve tomorrow and the post office would be swamped. It would be New Year's, maybe later, by the time McKeon got the envelope. Still, Adam felt a sense of urgency that he could neither ignore nor explain. A need to get the damned thing out and on its way. Find out what happened next.

McKeon had an interest in the letter, but he wasn't jumping up and down with great excitement either. If you took out one or two suggestive lines, the note was bland, innocuous. A total stranger writing out of simple curiosity or loneliness.

Reed wasn't signing on as anybody's pen pal for the fun of it. There were suggestions in the note—"It takes a special kind of man . . ." "I have some limited experience . . ." —that suggested a world of possibilities. It could be total bullshit, but it shouldn't take Reed long to check it out.

McKeon told him to wait. The task force had priorities, and capturing a homicidal maniac was clearly more important than the writing of a story. On the flip side, he did not regard the two pursuits as mutually exclusive. Sometimes you could have your cake and eat it, too.

He started on a mental checklist. Tap the papers—Santa Rosa, Frisco, Oakland, any smaller locals—and collect their coverage on the murders going back three years. Compile a list of victims, witnesses, detectives. Interviews and research. Background information, ranging from geography and local history to private lives. It didn't matter if the Sturgess angle came to nothing. Whatever happened, he would have the Slasher's story down in black and white.

Reed stopped himself, came back to first things first. He had a book to write before veering off on a tangent in pursuit of something else. The Santa Rosa business was nothing more than a sideshow and he would not allow it to distract him from the work at hand.

He stared at the envelope addressed to Roy McKeon, knowing he would have to mail it if he wanted any piece of mind. Unload the problem for a while and concentrate on Thomas Bender. Do the job that he was being paid for. It would only take a minute to walk down to the mailbox and back.

Adam slipped his shoes on, grabbed the envelope, and stepped into sunshine filtered through the normal layer of smog. Another lazy, hazy day in Southern California. It was cool outside, but any physical resemblance to the Christmas season was a matter of coincidence.

Reed did not know his neighbors well, but he imagined their reactions if they saw him strolling down the sidewalk in the middle of the day. The questions that would come to mind regarding source of income, for example, when he never wore a suit and tie or punched a clock.

On second thought, he had no reason to believe that anyone noticed him at all. Reed did not have a dangerous look about him, and he wasn't "anybody" in the L.A. scheme of things.

Not yet. But soon, perhaps.

The corner mailbox took his offering. Whatever happened next would be decided by the Santa Rosa task force. It was out of Adam's hands.

Retreating toward the house, Reed changed his mind about that beer.

It didn't seem so early after all.

CHAPTER

7

———•———

Sometimes it was difficult for Howard Michael Starr to tell if he was dreaming or awake. The hunt had certain dream-like qualities, but he was always in command, the master of his craft. And when he dreamed of hunting—three, four times a week at least—the outcome never failed to satisfy.

Control was everything. If Starr had chosen a religion for himself, its one commandment would have been: *Control thyself and thy surroundings.* Self-indulgence and denial would have been the only sacraments, contradictory at a glance, but symbiotic in practice. Yin and yang. Two sides of a coin.

The dream-hunts left him feeling satisfied and lazy, like a well-fed predator, but there were *other* dreams, tapped into wells of memory, that Starr found painful and unsettling.

He was not afraid of pain, per se. A little agony was educational from time to time. A source of energy. Almost erotic. Starr was not a masochist in the accepted sense, but he had taught himself by slow degrees to live with pain, to draw strength from suffering and use it for his own devices.

Howard Michael Starr was not insane by any modern definition of the term. He understood the law, knew right from wrong and recognized the consequences of his actions.

He never once suspected that his neighbors might be aliens from Jupiter. He *did* hear voices now and then—one voice—but that was memory, and not to be confused with a psychotic episode.

Still, there were times when he would gladly have forsaken memory and dreams.

He sipped a glass of orange juice, storing energy, and thought of Erin Gerber. She had tricked him, just a minor thing, but still a deviation in his plan. For three days running, she had not appeared for work, no sign of her around the house or on the jogging route. Belatedly, Starr understood that she had left town for the holidays. The Friday after Christmas, he had dressed up in his postman's uniform to check her mailbox and reassure himself that nothing had been transferred to a forwarding address. A bill from J.C. Penney cinched it for him, and he let himself relax.

She would be back and he would be there, waiting for her.

Even so, the glitch was irritating. Starr believed in psychic bonds between a hunter and his prey. He should have known that Erin would be gone for Christmas, should have made allowances, anticipating her. His irritation was a natural result of being caught off guard.

The dreams were something else.

In essence, they were history. Mind-movies sketching out the life of Howard Michael Starr. The early days would normally be lost, but Starr could thank his mother for the hours she devoted to his education, drumming details into his impressionable mind. The stormy night when he was born, plus all that went before and all that followed.

Lucy Kendrick was a twenty-year-old waitress working in a San Francisco supper club when she met Aaron Howard Starr. His family was old money, publishing and petro-chemicals, and Aaron was the only child. Divorced for seven years at forty-six, he had begun to face the prospect of a lonely middle age, no heir to carry on the family name. It was a fluke that pretty Lucy Kendrick crossed his path, a novelty when Aaron asked her out, a family embarrassment when they were married four months later.

Whatever impact marriage had on Lucy Kendrick Starr, it did not compensate for immaturity or any private quirks she brought to the relationship. No virgin on her wedding night, she understood that she was giving up the party life for marriage to a wealthy older man, but there were times when she would still resent the swap of freedom for security.

Aside from business, Aaron Starr was chiefly interested in fathering an heir. His sperm count wasn't anything to brag about, but after three years trying, drugs and perseverance finally did the trick. It was all downhill from there, as far as Lucy was concerned. The morning sickness, swollen ankles, feeling fat before she even started showing. Barely twenty-three and she was finished. Nine months carrying her husband's brat, and then eighteen years of playing second fiddle to him down the line.

It didn't work out that way, of course. She had her own agenda, Lucy did. Back on the pill, as soon as Howard Michael Starr was born. No risk of a repeat performance, thank you very much. If Aaron ever thought about it, he was too preoccupied to care. He had his precious son—the living, breathing, diaper-shitting proof of his virility—but he was not concerned with the details of parenting. The family business needed his attention. There were egos to be stroked and grown-up games to play.

His favorite toy, in those days, was the *Juvenal,* a custom yacht that sometimes carried Aaron south as far as Ensenada, northward to Vancouver Island if he felt the urge. He said the ocean helped him think. If his young, spoiled wife suspected leaving her behind was part of the attraction, she would not have been far wrong.

In over twenty years of sailing, Aaron Starr had never run afoul of weather or technology. On April Fools' Day 1958, his luck ran out. A Coast Guard cutter found the *Juvenal* adrift, unmanned, a mile off Point Arena. There was nothing to suggest the skipper's fate, investigators filling in the gaps with educated guesswork. It was easy to suggest an accident. Man overboard, the forty-footer gliding swiftly out of reach. Fatigue and hypothermia. Perhaps a hungry shark.

Starr's will left Lucy and their son secure for life, with a provision that forbade her meddling in the family business. That was fine with Lucy as long as the checks kept rolling in. Her interest in the earning side of things had long since been exhausted. She was into spending, and making up for time lost in her husband's shadow. Men were everywhere, and Lucy Starr was young enough to interest most of them.

She left the chores of motherhood to her employees. One of them, a governess named Bridget Eisley, took a special interest in the boy. She dressed him in the morning, bathed him daily, tucked him into bed at night and read him fairy tales until he fell asleep. If Bridget's take on Mother Goose was somewhat different, skewed toward punishment of parents who neglected children, heavy on the pleasures of rebellion, no one seemed to notice. Likewise, when she carried little Howard to her room so they could share a steamy bubble bath.

He remembered Bridget well enough, with no assistance on his mother's part. Lucy Starr had never known about their secret times together. Would she have cared? It was a moot point now, and Howard Michael Starr was never one to play "What If?"

He had been conscious of his mother's men for years before The Incident. Not knowing why they came and sometimes spent the night. He saw no link between his mother's visitors and the sensations he experienced with Bridget, squirming while she stroked and kissed him.

One night, when he was nearly six years old, a nightmare woke him. Muffled voices, moaning, inarticulate. At first, he thought the creatures of his dream had followed him across the line to consciousness, but then he realized the sounds were coming from his mother's room next door. He scrambled out of bed, still groggy and confused, remembering that he was Bridget's little man and the defender of the house.

He listened at the tall, locked door between their rooms, confirmed that he was not imagining the noise, and made his way into the hall. His feet were cold, and gooseflesh rippled underneath his flannel PJs. Moving toward his mother's door, he walked on tiptoe, careful not to make a sound. Pale light beneath the bedroom door.

He used both hands to turn the knob. No squeaky hinges in his mother's house. He pushed the door back silently and stepped into the light.

At first, he did not recognize the figures tangled on the bed. The only other naked person he had ever seen was

Bridget when they bathed together. This configuration—
thrashing arms and legs, a mound of hairy buttocks pumping in between the woman's thighs—was new and frightening. The sounds these strangers made spoke volumes of their
suffering, but they were trapped somehow, unable to escape.

What were they doing in his mother's bed?

Reluctantly, he circled to the left, a different point of
view, and that was when he glimpsed his mother's face. At
that, Starr almost failed to recognize her with her hair down,
eyes closed, lips drawn back in something like a snarl. He
felt a sudden impulse to protect her, but he had to satisfy
himself that there was no mistake.

He called to her, a whisper. Wasted. Found more volume
when he tried a second time. Her eyes snapped open, swept
the room in sudden panic. Found him.

"You!"

The man between her legs lost rhythm, cursing, turned to
glare at Howard Michael Starr across one shoulder.

"What the fuck?"

Starr's mother pushed him off and scrambled out of bed, a
grimace from the stranger as they separated, rolling over on
his side with no attempt to hide the fleshy pole that pointed
toward the ceiling. Starr had never seen his mother move so
quickly, wobbling breasts reminding him of Bridget in the
bathtub. Reaching for her nipples as she came to him. No
danger, after all. A game that he knew how to play.

His touch changed Lucy Starr's expression from a look of
shock to outrage. Lashing at him with an open hand that
knocked him sprawling.

"Dirty! *Filthy* little brat!"

Talons closed around his arm and jerked him upright,
held him while the other hand slashed back and forth across
his face. Cheeks livid, throbbing, Starr was dazed as Lucy
dragged him back along the hallway to his room. Across the
threshold, toward the bed. Another jolting slap, before she
dumped him on the mattress.

"Nasty boy! Don't leave this room again until I come for
you!"

He lay awake all night, but it was Bridget who retrieved
him in the morning, making sympathetic noises as she
stroked his poor, bruised cheeks. He wept against her bosom

and she managed to console him. Stroking. Squeezing. Bringing raisin toast and cocoa afterward.

It took a few more days for Lucy Starr to plot the game out in her mind. It was years before her son decided for himself what must have happened in the bedroom after his surprise visit. The naked stranger more excited and demanding than before, ignoring Lucy's protest that she wasn't in the mood. A reaming she would not forget.

It took another week or so before she finished working out the details of the game. The next time she had a visitor, his mother unlocked the connecting door between their rooms and left it open just a crack. He couldn't miss the sounds that way, and when he moved on trembling legs to watch, Starr found *her* watching *him*.

If Lucy Starr had been an actress, that night would have cinched her Oscar nomination. She was everywhere, did everything, denied the stranger nothing. She made moves her son would not begin to understand for years, accompanied by moaning, gasping sounds of real or simulated ecstasy. She sweated through the sheets and left them crumpled on the floor, pretending concentration on the thing that pierced and pumped between her legs.

Eyes wide open.

Staring at her son.

For Howard Michael Starr, the tingling in his loins and burning in his cheeks were hopelessly confused. Excitement, shame, and fear competed for the upper hand, none of them the clear-cut winner. He could watch because he sensed that Mother wanted him to see her that way, but he also read the malice in her eyes.

Much later, when the nameless man had gone and Starr was back in bed, his mother came to him through the connecting door, a naked fury, one hand clenched around a stylish alligator belt. Cheeks flushed and nipples rigid as she threw the covers back and began to whip his legs and buttocks.

"Filthy boy! I *saw* you watching me. You *like* to watch me, don't you? Does it make your little pecker hard, you *filthy* boy?"

Starr didn't know a pecker from a penguin, but he answered yes to everything because he sensed that negative responses would infuriate his mother even more. The message loud and clear, despite her cursing, flailing with the belt.

She wanted him to see her, wanted to make his little pecker hard. For all the whipping, Lucy never got around to telling him he *shouldn't* watch—and why would she unlock the door between their bedrooms otherwise? Why leave it open far enough for him to hear and see if there were secrets in the other room?

A lesson took shape, unconsciously at first, but filed away for future reference. The first link was forged between desire and pain; a valuable pointer toward the future.

Bridget helped to forge the second link as she consoled him in his suffering. He had never recognized her overtures as sexual—did not, in fact, have any grasp of what sex was at that age—but he understood the next time Bridget used her mouth and hands to make him squirm. He learned a bit about the way those men felt in his mother's bed. No whipping afterward, so he could concentrate on pleasure for a change. When Bridget showed him what to do to make her feel good in return, the boy was happy to reciprocate.

The game assumed a schedule of its own. The strangers came to see his mother once a week, on average, a different man each time. She may have had her regulars, for all he knew, but there were never any duplications in the game. In time, Starr understood that repetition of the scene, a young boy spying on his mother, might have prompted questions, maybe gossip in the clubs where Lucy found her playmates.

It was curious, Starr thought, that he was only beaten as an adjunct to the game. It seemed to be the only time his mother really noticed him, except for carping lectures over meals, when she was in her cups, regaling him with all the many failings of his late and unlamented father.

Lucy hated Aaron for the fact that he had tied her down, used up the best years of her life to propagate an heir, then summoned the audacity to die and saddle her with the responsibilities of motherhood. She hated Aaron's parents and attorneys for adhering to the stipulations of his will, denying her free access to the corporate accounts. Above all else, she hated Howard Michael Starr for the offense of drawing breath, a flesh and blood reminder of her servitude.

In Mother's eyes, he was a stupid little boy, no matter that his grades in school would average well above the norm. If Mother found him reading, he was lazy, a pathetic bookworm. If he went to play outside, he was a ruffian, uncouth and filthy.

Always filthy.

Even so, she never punished him at home, except for joining in the game. When he began to play with fire and vent his spite on animals, she never seemed to notice. Bridget cleaned up after him whenever possible and endeavored to distract him with her body.

Sex and violence.

Fire and blood and pleasure-pain.

Inevitably, the sensations ran together, mingling into one.

He came to realize that punishment was the objective of his mother's game. She might enjoy the rutting with her playmates, but she lived to catch her filthy man-child watching, whip him for his indiscretion, always stopping short of an injunction to desist.

When they had played the game for several months, he learned to make it better. He slipped off his PJs when he heard the moaning start next door. Appearing naked in the doorway, tugging on his little pecker, he was pleased to see the flush suffuse his mother's cheeks. He received an extra special whipping that first time, carried out in total silence, as if Mother did not trust herself to speak.

Refinements. Learning to manipulate the game and satisfy himself.

He understood the rule of silence, knew that it would ruin everything if relatives or teachers learned about the games he played with Bridget and his mother. Punishment would have to fall on someone, and a child was always first in line. The worst he could imagine was an interruption of the lifestyle he had come to view as normal and pleasurable. Friends were not a problem, since he made none. He lived for the private times.

The alopecia came in seventh grade when he was twelve years old. While other boys were sprouting hair in brand-new places, Howard Michael Starr was losing his. Within six months he was completely bald, no eyebrows, lashes. Nothing. When he lost the hair inside his nostrils Dr. Buller warned that he would always be at risk for allergies, infections, this and that. Defiantly, Starr clung to health. He took vitamins in wintertime and antihistamines in spring.

Starr's thirteenth birthday present, from his mother, was a custom-tailored wig. Of course, the other kids at school all *knew* it was a wig and they delighted in humiliating him. The taunts and insults were routine, monotonous, the childish repertoire exhausted in a few short weeks. Starr rode it out, developed a facility for laughing at himself. He practiced in the mirror, rolling back the mental tape of jibes and smiling till his jaw ached. Making sure he got it right.

The manufactured sense of humor served him well, except for Ronnie Dunstan. Held back in the eighth grade for his academic failure and a general shitty attitude, the Dunstan boy was older than his classmates, larger, dumb, and mean.

Too dumb, in fact, to recognize a kindred soul in Howard Michael Starr.

Ron Dunstan never realized they both had certain interests in common. Naked women. Furtive masturbation. Taking pleasure in the mortal pain of lesser species. Looking down on Howard Michael Starr, the bully saw a target, soft and bald and vulnerable.

Two days short of Christmas break, the students were released from class for an assembly. Choral music in the junior high's gymnasium, with bodies massed on folding bleachers, ancient perspiration in the air. Starr joined his classmates, had no choice. It was a minor test of will for him to sit between two boys he had despised since second grade. Not bullies, but simply morons.

The choir was halfway through its presentation when a hand came out of nowhere, fastened on his wig, and whipped it off. The spirit gum was no match for teenage muscles. Ronnie Dunstan jumped on his feet, arm cocked to make the pitch.

"Watch out!" he shouted in the momentary silence. "It's *alive!*"

He tossed the wig some thirty feet toward the center of the floor. It landed just behind the choir director, almost at his feet, resembling a deflated cat. The choir director turned at Ronnie's shout, just in time to see the wig come arching toward him. He took a quick step backward—flying squirrel alert—losing his footing on the polished wooden floor. He went down on his ass.

The crowd exploded into gales of laughter, Ronnie Dunstan bowing to his audience before old Mr. Kroker reached him, leading him away. Starr rose among his fellows, bitter tears of anger streaming down his cheeks, and went to fetch his hairpiece. Past the gaping choir and out of there, with laughter ringing in his ears.

It was the last time he cried.

The upshot was a conference with the principal, a lame apology, and two days off for Dunstan. An extended Christmas holiday. Starr's mother smiled and nodded at the principal. Of course, she understood. Boys being boys. She ragged her son the whole way home.

"I can't *believe* you would embarrass me this way! What are you *thinking* of, you stupid, nasty boy?"

That night, he let his fingers do the walking. Nineteen Dunstans in the telephone directory. He called them each in turn, hit paydirt on the second from the last. Is Ronnie home? Hang up before the slimy bastard gets there, jotting down the address. He checked a street map.

The best part of neglect was being able to escape unnoticed from the house. He bundled up against the cold and took along a can of gasoline the wetback gardeners had left in the garage. Twelve blocks through misty darkness, dodging headlights like a pro.

The Dunstan house was smaller than his own, one-story, stucco painted beige. Starr didn't know how it would burn, but he was determined to find out. Two gallons wasn't much to start with, but he found a way to make it stretch. Broke into the attached garage and poured the gas around in there, on cardboard boxes, on a plywood workbench. On the family station wagon, making sure to take the gas cap off.

He struck a match and watched it happen.

Merry Christmas, asshole!

Two days later in the *Chronicle,* he found a tiny article about the fire and clipped it for a scrapbook he had yet to buy. No injuries, but arson was suspected. An explosion. Major damage to the house. The family was staying with relatives till further notice. They wound up moving. Starr had seen the last of Ronnie Dunstan, even though he never got to watch the bastard fry.

It was the best fire ever, when he thought about it. Not his best *night* ever—that was still to come—but Howard Michael Starr had learned a thing or two since junior high.

The rest was history—or would be, years from now, if someone ever wrote the story of his life. It would require a special kind of scribe to do him justice, look beyond the sequence of events for motivations, grasp his genius and portray it for the world at large.

Perhaps, when he had time, he should write the story out himself.

But not just yet. He still had work to do, no time for resting on his laurels. Fame would have to wait. Just now, he was devoted to the game.

CHAPTER

8

The telephone was ringing as he walked in from a shopping expedition, a case of typing paper heavy underneath one arm. Reed left it to the answering machine, three rings before his prerecorded voice cut in to ask the caller for a message, name, and number.

"Mr. Reed, Detective Sergeant Roy McKeon calling. I was hoping—"

Adam lifted the receiver, switched the PhoneMate off.

"Good morning, Sergeant."

Flustered, the detective missed a beat. "That's twice you got me."

"Nothing personal."

"I'm glad I caught you. Have you got a minute?"

"Give or take."

"I have the letter from our pen pal, here. Still nothing I can hang a charge on, but it's definitely interesting."

"I thought so, too."

"It's odd, the way he seems to sympathize with Bender. Almost like some kind of hero worship. Do you see a lot of that?"

"Celebrity offenders often pick up groupies," Adam said, "but this feels different. Sturgess has identified with Bender, somehow. He seems to believe they share some common background or experience."

"I had the same impression reading over it," McKeon said. "I showed the letter to a friend of mine. He helps us out from time to time with profiles, this and that."

"Forensic psych."

"That's it. I'd like to have him join us, if you don't mind."

"Join us?"

"On the line."

"No problem." Adam feeling stupid, even as he said it.

There was nothing in the way of clicks or static to announce a new participant in the discussion. He was suddenly there, another voice in Adam's ear, and Reed suspected he had been on the extension all along.

"Good morning, Mr. Reed. I'm Jacob Nesbitt."

"*Doctor* Nesbitt," said McKeon. "Out of Stanford's criminology department."

Reed sketched a mental picture of an academic, tweed and horn-rimmed glasses, maybe favoring a pipe, with graying hair that tended to defy a comb. He would be wearing wing tips, scuffed around the toes, with mismatched socks.

McKeon's voice cut through his reverie. "We talked about the letters, as I said. It's early, but we have a few preliminary notions. Dr. Nesbitt?"

"Yes, indeed. It's definitely premature to brand this individual a killer on the basis of his correspondence, but his pattern of behavior—pseudonym, the false address, and so forth—clearly indicates a furtive personality. He covers up. It may be simple paranoia, or there may be something that he feels compelled to hide."

"Like thirty murders?" Adam asked.

"I wouldn't risk a guess on that, right now," said Nesbitt. "I can tell you that his various precautions and apparent skill at wiping out his paper trail suggest a personality that may—I emphasize that qualifier—*may* fit the Slasher's profile. Definitely organized. Are you familiar with the FBI's taxonomy of random killers?"

"Vaguely."

As a point of fact, Reed had devoured all the standard

texts by Ressler, Douglas, and the other federal brains as part of his research on Thomas Bender. He was interested in hearing Nesbitt's take.

"In essence," the psychologist went on, "the Bureau has divided killers into three broad categories. Organized offenders plan their crimes in advance, prepare meticulously, target strangers for the most part, and take pains to cover up their tracks. The flip side, a *dis*organized offender, acts on impulse, may kill relatives or friends as readily as strangers, and he seldom gives coherent thought to an escape. It stands to reason that disorganized offenders spend more time in jail."

"That still leaves one," said Reed.

"Excuse me?"

"One more category."

"Ah. That would be the so-called 'mixed' offender, sharing traits of both disorganized *and* organized. It's fudging, I'm afraid, but life is like that. Nothing's ever quite as neat and clean outside the laboratory."

"No."

Like Bender, Adam thought. He often killed impulsively, while drunk, then sobered up and took advantage of his high IQ to ditch the evidence.

"We're basically agreed," McKeon interjected, "that the Slasher's highly organized."

"Without a doubt." The doctor's voice was ageless, playing games with Adam's mental portrait. "Organized offenders typically display superior intelligence. A high birth-order status seems to be the rule: an elder son or only child. He may present a fair degree of social competence, but loners aren't uncommon, either. If he socializes, it's a safe bet no one *really* knows him. Far too dangerous for anyone to get a look inside."

"We're basing most of this on the forensic evidence," McKeon said.

"I understand."

"The organized offender presents a trademark pattern of behavior," Nesbitt said. "Private rituals and pleasures vary, as I'm sure you realize, but there are common traits. Mobility, for one. Disorganized offenders hang around the old home neighborhood until they get a sudden urge to kill.

The Slasher trolls and transports victims in a vehicle which, following the law of averages, is fairly new and well maintained. He brings the necessary tools and weapons with him, binds his victims to insure submission, and typically commits aggressive acts like rape before the coup de grace. Fantasy and ritual dominate his mind. He may eroticize the killing, as with torture, and victims are frequently personalized—through one-on-one conversation before the murder or with some elaborate postmortem display."

"All common factors from the Slasher crimes," McKeon said.

"But it's impossible to say, from what we have, if Sturgess is connected to the homicides."

"So far, that's right. He seems to have an interest in the case, and he's adept at hiding his identity. Beyond that, zip."

"You've looked at birth certificates, I gather?"

"Starting to," McKeon said, "but that means fifty states, and we don't even have a year of birth to start from."

"Yes, I see your problem."

"Guys like this," McKeon said to Reed, "can pick up new identities the same way you and I go shopping for a change of clothes. Check out obituaries for a given year, to match their birth date more or less, and find a kid who died in infancy. The obit names his parents, probably a hospital. From there, you can request a copy of the birth certificate, say the original was lost or burned up in a fire, whatever. Six or seven bucks, it's yours. With the certificate, you can get anything you want: new driver's license, passport, bank accounts and Social Security—name it."

"Yes, I see."

"We have an estimate on age," McKeon said. "Mid-thirties, based on evident maturity and self-control, but that's only an educated guess. He could be ten or fifteen years beyond that."

"Or he could have made the name up on his own," said Reed.

"Or that."

"I'd say you've got a problem, Sergeant."

"I was thinking—that is, we were thinking—there's a way we still might pull it off and find out who this guy is."

"I'm listening," said Reed.

"Last week, you indicated willingness to follow up with Sturgess."

Adam's smile felt like a nervous twitch around the corners of his mouth. "That's right, I did."

"If nothing's changed . . ."

"I'm interested," said Adam, "but I frankly don't know what to ask him next. I can't just blunder in and ask for a confession."

"Goodness, no," said Nesbitt. "This requires a bit of subtlety."

"Suggestions, Doctor?"

"First, we have to try and understand the man's psychology. The Slasher clearly views himself as brighter, more courageous than the average man. Superior to the police and those who try to analyze his crimes. He basks in that sensation of superiority, presumably without an audience."

"Presumably?"

"There have been cases where a *team* of random killers worked together. L.A.'s Hillside Strangler case is one example, but we've seen no evidence of multiple offenders here in Santa Rosa."

"None at all," McKeon echoed.

"Michael Sturgess may not be the Slasher," Nesbitt said, "but he presents a similar attitude. What was it that he wrote? Ah, yes: 'It takes a special kind of man to stand alone against the world.' And further on: 'I have some limited experience in that regard.'"

"False modesty?" asked Reed.

"Perhaps. In any case, the attitude is similar enough to warrant scrutiny."

It came to Adam, then, how serious the shrink and the detective were. Within a few short moments, casual interest in a stranger's letter had become much more. Reed felt the pulse beat in his temples, the excitement flavored with a dash of apprehension. Instinct told him he was being used—or would be, if he gave the Santa Rosa team a chance. And that would be fine as long as he went into it with eyes wide open, using them along the way.

"You have to find him first," he said to no one in particular.

"That's right," McKeon answered. "And we're thinking there's a chance to draw him out, assuming you still want to volunteer."

"I'll hang up on you if it gets too scary," Adam said.

"You understand that I am not empowered to request—"

Reed interrupted him. "We've been through that. I know my rights. Let's hear the plan."

"The key to drawing out an organized offender of this sort is through vanity," said Nesbitt. "The Slasher lives primarily within his own imagination, nurturing his fantasy. It's obvious to him, if no one else, that he is the most fascinating creature on the planet. All men would admire him—or, at least regard him with a sense of awe—if they could only grasp his master plan."

"He's conceited," Adam said.

"It goes beyond that, but the symptoms are similar. Response to flattery. Reaction to a challenge."

They were getting somewhere. "You don't want me to challenge him, I take it."

"No. I haven't seen the letter that you sent to Sturgess, but you obviously struck a chord. Some small appeal to vanity, perhaps."

"I did my best."

"And he's responding. Cautiously, I grant you, but his latest comments indicate a willingness to share. He craves a sympathetic audience."

"For what?" asked Reed. "I've told him I'm a writer. Do you really think he's likely to confess?"

"The fact that you're a journalist may be our hole card," Nesbitt said. "Most organized offenders have a tendency to track their cases in the media. They read and clip newspaper stories, tape the radio and TV broadcasts. Some are moved to write or call and brag about their crimes, correct perceived inaccuracies in the coverage."

"Like Son of Sam."

"There was another case in Wichita some years ago. Unsolved. The killer was unhappy that he didn't get his fair share of the nightly news. 'How many do I have to kill,' he wrote, 'before I get some national publicity?' "

"So, what should I tell Sturgess?"

"You're the writer, Mr. Reed. I won't presume to dictate,

but the general tone should draw him out. He knows you're interested in Bender, but the man we're after craves the spotlight. Center stage. He needs to think you find him every bit as fascinating as he finds himself. Not all at once, you understand. No gushing. Nothing that would seem contrived or hasty. Somewhere down the line, though, you should strive for a facade of empathy."

"And then what? Try to set a meeting?"

Even saying it, Reed felt a chill.

"Ideally we can pick him up before it goes that far," said McKeon. "We'll have the postbox covered from the time you send your letter till he picks it up. I'm working out the details as we speak. With any luck at all, he'll lead us home, and we can mount surveillance. Find some probable cause and reel him in for questioning."

It sounded like a piece of cake.

"Okay. I'll have a letter in the mail first thing tomorrow and a copy for your files. Let's find out what he's made of."

"We appreciate your help on this," McKeon said.

"It's premature. I may be wasting everybody's time."

"We'll see."

I guess we will, thought Reed.

"I wish you'd let it go, that's all."

"It's just a letter, Dana."

"No, it's not," she told him, in that frosty tone Reed recognized from their infrequent arguments. "You're working for the cops now."

"That's ridiculous."

"Oh, really?"

They were westbound on the Colorado Freeway, near the Rose Bowl, coming up on Glendale. Keeping up with traffic on a New Year's Eve. The party thrown by Dana's agent was a semiformal bash in Coldwater Canyon, 90210. The dress that Dana wore was tight, low-cut, electric blue. She looked exotic and desirable, but Adam's mind was elsewhere.

"Was I working with the cops on Bender?"

"No comparison," she answered. "He was doing time before you ever heard of him. It's not the same at all."

"What is it then?" Compelled to drag it out of her.

"They're using you, okay?" An echo of his own thoughts. "How many years, without a suspect?"

"Three."

"Three years and now you hand them one. But they can't *find* him. Jesus, Adam."

"How's that using me?" he asked. As if he didn't know.

"Don't act naive. You're fronting for the cops on this. They're using you as bait. It isn't even *legal*, Adam."

"Answering a letter is illegal?"

"Now you're being flip. I don't think we should talk about this any longer."

"Dana . . ."

Getting off the freeway on Ventura Boulevard, he drove past Universal City, picking up Mulholland Drive. The slower traffic gave him time to think.

"I wouldn't be involved in this if there was any risk," he said. Not strictly true, of course, but he was angling for a truce.

"You don't even know what the risks are, Adam. What if they arrest this person and he's *not* the killer. Say he gets pissed off and sues you for entrapment."

"Never happen." Reed was smiling now, but cautiously. "He'd have to sue the cops. I'm not arresting anyone."

"And if he *is* the killer?"

"Then, they've got him. What's the problem?"

"I can see you've got it all worked out."

"Please, Dana . . ."

"I don't want to talk about it anymore."

"Okay."

"You've got your blood up, that's the problem. You can smell a story and it just takes over."

"Are we going to discuss it?"

"No."

"All right."

"You need to watch yourself, that's all I'm saying."

"Right."

"Because your friends in Santa Rosa haven't done much good so far. Three years and nothing. They'll be absolutely useless if you get in trouble."

"I know what I'm doing, Dana."

"Sure. You want to be a hero."

"Wrong."

"What is it, then?"

"A *story*, Dana. I'm a *writer*. Get it?"

"I don't want to talk about it anymore."

"You said that."

"Just remember what I told you."

"How could I forget?"

"It's up here on the left."

"I know Chick's house."

A blaze of lights announced the party. BMWs, Jaguars, Benzes stacked up in the driveway. Signals of conspicuous consumption. Adam's Chevrolet was definitely out of place. He left the keys with a valet who looked like Salman Rushdie's younger brother, trailing Dana toward the house.

"Remember it's a party," she instructed him. "No murder talk."

"To hear is to obey."

Reed hoped there would be something stronger than champagne on tap. It had the makings of a long, cold night.

CHAPTER
9

———•———

Howard Michael Starr felt gray on that Saturday, the third of January. It was not a function of his mood, which seldom varied, but a whim that struck him as he planned the day's disguise. Outside a bank of storm clouds massed and muttered, threatened rain. No silver linings visible.

He chose a wig and matching eyebrows that would add at least a decade to his age. Still active, virile, somewhere in the neighborhood of forty-five or fifty. Skip the contacts for a change. The nylon windbreaker was charcoal, two or three shades darker than his slacks. The shirt he chose was deep maroon, so he would not present the aspect of a walking corpse. Black running shoes, selected on a whim.

It had to be the Volvo on a day like this. Conservative and sturdy. Brown. The very opposite of bright, eye-catching, and adventurous. He would present the image of a trim, successful businessman, not quite relaxing on the year's first weekend, though he left his suit and tie at home. Perhaps a golf game scheduled, if the rain held off, or catching up on light work while he had the office to himself.

It came to Howard Michael Starr while he was drinking half a quart of orange juice from the carton that he ought to change the Volvo's license plates. An impulse, nothing more. He had no reason to believe that he was being followed, had detected no signs of surveillance in the past few days, but there it was. A sudden urge for extra anonymity.

Howard Michael Starr collected license plates the way some people gathered matchbooks. Some nights, when the restless mood was on him, he would drive for hours, stopping here and there to make an acquisition. Shopping malls and supermarkets, theaters and restaurants, motels and residential neighborhoods. He carried tools and worked in darkness, there and gone, a shadow in the night. Took front plates only, so the owners of the target vehicles were less inclined to notice, minimizing any risk they would be stopped by traffic officers and so report the theft. He washed the plates at home, to clean off splattered bugs—a tip from "Adam-12" on television, thank you very much—and validated half of them with registration stickers shaved from *other* plates with an Exacto knife. The other half he used as front plates, so his vehicle of choice would show a different license number rolling toward a witness or away.

The end result, three dozen plates at last count, filled a drawer of Starr's workbench in the garage. He never lifted license tags from out of state, believing that a "foreign" plate drew more attention. Santa Rosa had its share of tourists passing through, but it was not the cosmopolitan community you found in San Francisco or Los Angeles. A change of California plates would do just fine, and Starr did not expect a traffic stop in any case.

If that should come to pass, against all odds, he had the Smith & Wesson semiautomatic pistol, with its load of sixteen Teflon-coated rounds for piercing body armor. Purchased like his other firearms, at an urban gun show, off the record. Screw the Brady Bill.

He took an extra moment to make sure the connecting door to the garage was locked behind him as he left the house. Unscrewed the front and rear plates of the Volvo, left them on the bench, and chose a mismatched set of alternates at random. Paused to wish the fat black widow spider a good morning.

No response. Ungrateful bitch.

Five minutes saw him finished with the plates, and

Howard Michael Starr was ready to retrieve his mail. While it was a simple errand, he did not feel the least bit foolish over his elaborate security precautions. Better safe than sorry, as his sainted mother used to say.

He opened the garage door by remote control, pulled out and waited for the door to close again behind him. Willow Run was braced for rain, cars tucked inside garages, sidewalks empty, curtains drawn against the threatened storm.

"Bring out your dead," he muttered, cruising past the silent houses. Feeling fine, without a problem in the world. He might call Erin Gerber later on, see if she was back at home.

Geography dictated limitations on the choice of routes he used to reach his destination. It was physically impossible for him to choose a new path every day, but he had worked out seven, alternating them without a conscious pattern, making sure he never used the same route twice within a five-day period.

Christmas decorations would be coming down on Monday, but for now they still remained at downtown intersections and in the windows of department stores. The effigies of Santa Claus looked weary and bedraggled, ready for another year in mothballs. Strings of tinsel drooped as if the weight of so much cheer had borne them down. The flocking in store windows suddenly reminded Howard Michael Starr of soap, applied by vandals.

Happy New Year.

With 355 shopping days left until Christmas, the post office parking lot had plenty of spaces to spare. He nosed the Volvo in beside an Oldsmobile and checked his rearview mirror as a matter of routine. No watchers he could readily identify.

The gray man locked his car and went inside to claim his mail.

A pair of dark eyes followed him, as they had followed every other adult male who stepped inside the post office that morning. The observer was a stocky six-foot-one, around two hundred pounds, most of it muscle on a solid frame. His dark hair, lightly salted with a touch of gray and thinning at the top, was overdue for trimming by department standards. When he frowned—and that was often—it carved furrows in his weathered cheeks.

Before the Slasher came along, Detective Sergeant Roy McKeon had been cutting back on weekend shifts. You never had an iron-clad guarantee, of course, but the advance in rank was something, and the rate of major crime in Santa Rosa never rivaled San Francisco, much less Oakland. It was not unheard-of for a month to pass without a homicide, and most of them were quickly solved. Domestic altercations spilling blood. A lethal grudge between two neighbors. Children playing with a gun.

The usual.

But there was nothing usual about the Slasher. Twenty-three dead women. Seven others gone without a trace and almost surely dead. Autopsy protocols and crime scene photographs that documented torture, sexual assault, and mutilation. Ghastly souvenirs.

McKeon knew from personal experience that random killers were the worst, almost impossible to catch unless they made a critical mistake. The Son of Sam might still be killing in New York, if he had not received a parking ticket near the final murder scene. Another headcase in Los Angeles had dropped his driver's license in a victim's driveway.

The Slasher was another story, though. In three years' time, the bastard hadn't dropped a stitch. With thirty victims on the list so far, McKeon did not have a single tire track, fingerprint, or useful sighting by a witness. Nothing in the way of hairs or fibers. Semen traces had been found on half a dozen of the bodies, so they knew the killer's blood type—A—which hardly narrowed the field. For any kind of match on DNA, they would require a subject for comparison, and that meant laying hands on Mr. Right.

No clues to speak of, but they had *too many* suspects. As of Halloween, the task force had 357 names on file, most of them average citizens who had been fingered by a neighbor, landlord, ex-wife, or employer. Eighty-odd percent of them were cleared by a preliminary background check, corroborating alibis for two or more known murders in the Slasher series. Half a dozen had been weird enough to rate a trip downtown, complete with polygraph and blood test.

One of those had been arrested twice on child-molesting charges, pulled a two-year jolt for lewd behavior at Tehachapi, but he had never been attracted to a female over ten years old, no homicidal indicators on his psychiatric sheet. Another had two rape convictions, but his blood type didn't match the Slasher's. Two had gone away for homicide, both bargained down to manslaughter. The crimes were drug-related, though, and they had skated on their polygraph exams. A fifth potential suspect actually bragged about the crimes, but he was short on details, pulling thirty days for mental observation on the county's dime. The sixth collected books on homicidal maniacs, his small apartment decorated with the garish covers of detective magazines. He also kept a scrapbook of the Slasher's clippings, but investigation showed that he had spent the first year of the murder series in Atascadero, working out some mental kinks.

Which left McKeon with a big fat zero for his efforts.

Since he pulled the task force duty, his routine had gone to hell. It hardly mattered on the home front—he had been divorced six years ago, no children from the marriage—but McKeon didn't like to feel that he was wasting time. It pissed him off and made him wish that he could meet the Slasher one-on-one. Five minutes in an alley somewhere. Settle this and put the whole damned thing behind him.

As it was, instead of a dramatic showdown, he was playing watchdog. Parked a block west of the post office where "Michael Sturgess" rented Box 1165. No driver, cutting back on hours where he could, but there were still three other men assigned to lookout duty on the box.

Down range and facing in the opposite direction, Joey Hollander was on his own, assigned to follow any westbound subject, so McKeon didn't have to give himself away with an illegal U-turn in the middle of the street. Doug Washburn had the parking lot, relaxing with a copy of *Sports Illustrated*'s swimsuit issue in a Plymouth borrowed from the impound lot. His partner, Eddie Dudeck, was inside pretending to complete an application for the U.S. Postal Service when he wasn't reading junk mail—anything to let him keep an eye on Box 1165.

McKeon checked his watch and grimaced. It was coming up on ten o'clock, two hours wasted, no one going near the suspect's box. He listened to the cross-talk on his two-way radio, wishing he had somewhere else to go.

Two hours left before they had to fall back on Plan B.

Officially, the post office shut down at noon on Saturdays, but access to the rented boxes was available throughout the day. A cleaning crew came on at 8:00 P.M. and locked the doors behind them when they left, say half-past nine or ten o'clock. Between the time the postal clerks went home and janitors arrived, surveillance would be dicey, anyone who lingered in the station longer than it took to fetch his mail would automatically become suspicious. They could risk it, leave a spotter on the job and yank the Plymouth out of sight, but there was still a chance their subject might get hinky, give the box a pass or come back later for another try.

If anybody showed up twice, McKeon was prepared to run the plates and risk a tail, divide his forces if he had to, but he recognized the built-in danger. Say their suspect made a pass at one o'clock, got spooked by Eddie Dudeck, and returned an hour later for another try. If Eddie showed his face the second time around, their game was blown, with no clear grounds for an arrest. Conversely, if McKeon started changing spotters every time a patron wandered in to get his mail, it would degenerate into a Chinese fire drill. Any casual observer could stand back and watch the Keystone Kops at play.

The solitary option—pulling everybody out at noon and simply watching from the street—was no improvement from McKeon's point of view. In that scenario, they had no way of knowing whether anyone tapped Box 1165. The best that he could do was run the plates of every patron who arrived and hope for . . . what?

They knew that "Michael Sturgess" had no driver's license. He had never registered a vehicle or signed up for the draft, paid a tax or cast a ballot in the state of California. He *existed* without a visual ID for the postbox he had rented. Roy McKeon might as well select a name at random from the telephone directory.

He watched a Volvo enter the parking lot and park near the entrance. Force of habit made him scrutinize the driver. Six-foot-one or -two, around 190 pounds. Gray hair worn long enough to overlap his collar. Stylish clothes matched the vehicle. A businessman perhaps, though you could never really tell. For all McKeon knew, the stranger could be maxed out on his credit cards and eating TV dinners in a two-room flat.

The first fat drops of rain were speckling McKeon's windshield as the new arrival disappeared inside.

The post office provided several waist-high counters for its patrons, spacious areas designed for juggling parcels, sorting mail, or paging through the massive book of zip codes that was shackled to the wall. As Howard Michael Starr pushed through the swinging door, he registered a young man on his left, hunched shoulders and unruly hair, a pencil scratching at the boxes on a printed application form.

Good luck.

Starr didn't need an hour in the young man's company to recognize that he was short on writing skills, a fair sign of intelligence below the mean. His flannel shirt was not tucked in and it was anybody's guess when he had last washed his jeans and denim jacket. Reeboks on his feet that could have used new laces and a cleaning. A bemused expression on his bland, unshaven face.

On second thought, he should do well in a bureaucracy of bottom-feeders. Lugging sacks of mail around for twenty years, going haywire down the line and shooting ten or fifteen drones exactly like himself.

Good riddance.

There were several other patrons in the office as he entered, three lined up with packages or questions at the service counter, and a shapeless woman in her forties pulling junk mail from a postbox on his right. Starr noticed each of them in turn, without appearing to. Dismissed them as potential enemies.

The key was in his hand as he approached his box. No hesitation as he opened it and reached inside. Two letters waiting for him: one from Pasadena, one from Jacksonville. He blinked at Adam Reed's return address and shut the postbox. Locked it, turning toward the door.

The denim drone was watching him.

More accurately, he was trying *not* to watch as Starr picked up his mail. A sidelong flicker of the eyes, before he found his place again and scribbled something on the application form.

A dullard's idle curiosity, perhaps? Some people had to gawk and stare because their lives were empty, wasted. Meaningless. They sought diversion scrutinizing others at the most mundane of tasks. They went on aimless drives on Sunday. Sat around in shopping malls and watched life pass them by.

The first alarm sounded in his brain as Howard Michael Starr retreated to the parking lot. He unlocked the Volvo. Slid behind the wheel and dropped his letters on the empty seat beside him. Two full minutes passed as he sat waiting for the young man to emerge.

He could be wrong, of course. Starr recognized that he was sometimes cautious to a fault, suspecting enemies where none existed. It was part of who he was, the reason he was still at liberty instead of sitting in a cage somewhere with shrinks and lawyers lined up at his door.

Another thirty seconds, and the drone did not appear. Starr turned his key in the ignition, backed the Volvo out, and left the parking lot, eastbound. His home was in the opposite direction, but he did not feel like taking chances.

No one rushed into the parking lot, but there was movement at the curb, perhaps a block beyond the post office. A nondescript sedan had pulled out from the curb, no rush about it. Falling in behind him, keeping pace.

He felt the warm, familiar tingle of excitement that he normally experienced at the beginning of the hunt. It did not matter, seemingly, if he was predator or prey. The hunt was all that mattered. Playing out the game.

The rain picked up, preventing Starr from checking out the drab sedan in any detail. One man in the car, as far as he could tell. It was too far away for him to see if it was an official vehicle. Police were often careless, branding "unmarked" cars with whip antennas and official plates. The institutional mentality at work.

Starr took no chances. It was probably nothing, but he wanted to be sure. Disposing of the tail would be good practice either way.

The light turned red in front of him, and Howard Michael Starr made up his mind. He stood on the accelerator, blasted through it, grinning fiercely at the angry sound of bleating horns and squealing brakes.

McKeon was about to light a cigarette when Eddie Dudeck whispered to him from the walkie-talkie.

"Comin' atcha, guys. Gray hair, dark jacket. Box 1165."

McKeon watched the Volvo's driver exit, walk back to his car. Unlock the door—a cautious man—and slide behind the wheel. He didn't pull away, though. He sat there killing time.

McKeon shot a glance at Washburn through the rain-streaked windshield, half afraid to take his eyes from Mr. X. Doug had a fix on Kathy Ireland, never looking up, but he had shifted in his seat, prepared to jam if necessary. Waiting.

The Volvo's backup lights were on. The snappy dresser had it in reverse. McKeon raised the walkie-talkie to his lips and thumbed the button down.

"Heads up. He's moving out."

Too far away for him to read the license plate, McKeon wishing he had time to reach in back for the binoculars. They could roll up on him when they worked out which way he was going. He had come in from the west, behind McKeon, but you couldn't go by that.

In fact, the Volvo left the parking lot and headed east, past Joey Hollander. The young detective kept his head down, no big double take to make the pigeon fly. He would allow McKeon and their boy to grab a lead, perhaps a block, before he swung around and got in line. By that time, Eddie would have joined Doug Washburn in the confiscated Plymouth, linking up with the parade.

McKeon switched on his wipers and left the radio alone as he accelerated, shortening the Volvo's lead. No reason to believe the subject had him spotted, but he didn't want to show the walkie-talkie just in case.

He had the plate, now. California, PBA1035. Committing it to memory. They had no cause to stop the Volvo, but McKeon meant to follow it all day if necessary. Find out where the subject lived and who the hell he was.

"You're mine, asshole."

Third block. McKeon saw the light change up ahead, brief

amber shifting into red. He would be on the Volvo's bumper in another moment, close enough to see the driver's eyes reflected in his rearview mirror. Take a guess at what he's made of.

Suddenly, the Volvo took off like a rocket, charging through the intersection, traffic on the cross-street screeching to a halt. McKeon had to make a choice, then. It was fly or die.

"You fuck!"

He mashed the pedal down and lurched off in pursuit. In front of him, the shaken motorists were starting to recover when McKeon came through, leaning on his horn to give them one more shock. He cleared the intersection, saw the Volvo running arrow-straight in front of him, and plucked his walkie-talkie from the shotgun seat.

"He's running! East on Roosevelt. I'm on him."

At the next intersection, the Volvo cornered smoothly, barely slowing down despite the rain. A wink of brake lights, there and gone. McKeon clutched the steering wheel in both hands, hanging on. He fought the drift and brought his own vehicle back in line, but Sturgess had increased his lead.

McKeon risked a quick grab for the glove compartment, brought the red light out and slapped it on his dashboard. He could pull the bastard in for reckless driving now, but they had to catch him first.

Behind McKeon, Joey Hollander was catching up. No sign of Washburn yet, but maybe he was attempting an interception, cut the tricky bastard off and box him in.

Keep dreaming.

Up ahead, the Volvo made another turn and started running east again. McKeon fought the steering wheel and almost clipped a taxi, making it just inches short of impact. He was mad enough to use his pistol, but he needed both hands on the wheel. Besides, there were civilians on the street. There were strict rules against the discharge of a firearm from a moving vehicle.

The Volvo swung into a smaller side street, northbound. If it lost speed on the turn, McKeon couldn't tell the difference. Christ, this prick could drive!

An alley came up and brake lights flashed as the Volvo

swung in that direction. Then the driver changed his mind and kept on going.

What the hell—?

A garbage truck came out of nowhere, huge and gray, a barricade across both lanes. McKeon cursed and threw his full weight on the brake, fishtailing. Rubber smoking as he saved it by a foot or less. Behind him, Joey Hollander swung broadside, rocking to a halt.

McKeon rode the horn and shouted curses at the gray behemoth. Peering down at him through sheets of rain, the driver had a pained expression on his face. He grappled with the stick, gears gnashing, finally got it in reverse and started backing up. Put two wheels on the curb and smacked a mailbox, stopping short. He had to try again, from scratch, McKeon screaming at him, pounding both fists on the steering wheel.

The street was empty when McKeon got his first glimpse past the garbage truck. He raced down to the intersection, looked both ways. Another block, repeat the process.

Zip.

He double-parked and found the microphone beneath the dashboard. "Lincoln twenty-six to base," he snapped. Rain drumming on the roof.

A sexy female voice came back. "We copy, Lincoln twenty-six."

"I need a make on California license Peter Bacon Adam one-oh-three-five. Copy?"

"Working."

Fifteen seconds felt like half an hour, Joey pulling in behind him, blocking other cars against the curb. Tough shit, if anybody had to leave this minute.

"Lincoln twenty-six."

"I hear you."

"California license Peter Bacon Adam one-oh-three-five fits a Honda Civic, 1989. No wants or warrants. Registered to Ralph James Collier, D.O.B. 9/16/33."

"Well, shit."

Gray hair or not, their rabbit hadn't been *that* old, and no one could mistake a Volvo for a Honda Civic. Stolen plates, for Christ's sake, and the prick was gone.

101

McKeon put a terse description of the Volvo and its driver on the air. They might get lucky, but he wasn't betting on it. Sturgess had eluded them and now knew the box was being watched. Their only lead had just gone up in smoke.

"What's up, Sarge?" Joey standing in the street and looking tense, hair plastered to his skull.

"We're screwed," McKeon told him. "That's what's up."

CHAPTER

10

———•———

The chase, while brief, had been exhilarating. Starr had been *that close* to capture, handcuffs, listening to high-school dropouts read his legal options from a dog-eared index card. The fucking pigs had been *right on his ass*.

And he had beaten them.

He stood before a full-length mirror in the bedroom, naked, admiring himself. The hairless body, once repugnant to its owner and the butt of lewd, disgusting jokes from others, pleased him now. He worked out regularly, used a sunlamp in the wintertime to hold an even tan. The alopecia gave him clean, sleek lines, a look most bodybuilders struggled to maintain with razors and depilatories.

Howard Michael Starr decided he was perfect.

For a heartbeat, as the chase was starting, Starr believed he was afraid, but then he recognized it as the hot rush of adrenaline that always gave him extra strength and cunning, special clarity of mind. He did not have to think about the streets he chose, or how the Volvo would perform. The pigs were strictly second-rate, unworthy of respect.

Although they had tracked him to the box.

He half-turned to survey his profile. Rounded buttocks. Smooth pectorals. His erection standing proud. Starr gave himself a stroke and smiled.

Not yet.

He had to solve the riddle, first. Ejaculation would be his reward.

Starr had been using Box 1165 for sixteen months. He would have automatically exchanged it for another one in sixty days or so, but the police had forced his hand.

He kept a roster of his pen pals on a floppy disk, downstairs, but Starr did not require a list to know that he had corresponded with a minimum of fifty strangers, using Box 1165 as his return address. They knew him by at least a dozen names, and while the content of his letters ranged from mild flirtation to the rankest filth, he could not picture any one of them complaining to authorities. If they had done so, U.S. Postal officers would be assigned to the investigation.

Nothing federal, then.

Three times he had visited correspondents in the flesh, but they were past telling on him now. He had carefully expunged all traces of himself: old letters, diaries, scribbled entries in address books. It was always possible that one of them had spoken to a friend or relative and dropped his name in passing—but his *address*?

He left the bedroom, walked back to the living room, still naked. On the coffee table were two slim envelopes, the last he would receive until he found himself another postbox. Skipping Jacksonville, he reached for Pasadena.

Adam Reed.

The man had written to him twice, and police were waiting on the very day his second letter arrived.

He held the unopened envelope in his hands and played connect-the-dots. His notes to Thomas Bender, passed to Reed by someone on the prison staff at Bender's death. Reed's follow-up, as research for his book . . . or something else? Starr's own response to Reed had been a calculated risk. Reed didn't know his name, could not have traced his whereabouts.

Except through Box 1165.

Reed was a reporter, more or less. His work in progress was the story of a man who stood outside society and preyed on weaker specimens. It was entirely possible that he had researched other cases for comparison. Starr's game playing in Santa Rosa had been headlined up and down the state, a spot in *Newsweek,* half a page in *USA Today.*

Starr thought about the letters to Thomas Bender. He could not recall his own words verbatim, but he had been excited when he wrote them. Almost feverish. Convinced that he could forge a mental link with Bender, or at least provide some solace while a kindred soul was waiting for his date with death. A rash endeavor, possibly, but he would do the same again.

Acknowledgment of error was impossible for Howard Michael Starr. If Reed, a total stranger, chose to meddle in his game and side with the police, so be it. Reed would find he had made a ruthless enemy.

Starr wanted to be positive before he made another move. He had already stripped the bogus license plates and stashed them in his trophy room. Outside disposal meant unnecessary risk. The police could be stopping any Volvo they could find. Conceivably, they could obtain a master list from Sacramento, question every owner in the state. Track Starr through corporate records, with a bit of effort. Turn up on his doorstep with their bland, shit-eating grins.

But they would never get downstairs without a warrant. If it came to that . . .

He tore into the envelope, unfolded the familiar stationery. It was dated New Year's Eve.

Dear Mr. Sturgess,
    Thank you so much for your prompt response. I know how busy you must be, and I appreciate your taking time to write. You are correct in saying Thomas was a special man who played by no one else's rules. One of a handful, I suspect, who know exactly what they want from life and go for it, at any cost.
    I would be *very* interested in hearing more from you about your own experience and personal philosophy in that regard. True individuals are hard to find.
    Until I hear from you again . . .

Starr smiled and read the note a second time. *I know how busy you must be.* In fact, Reed knew precisely nothing, but he would soon find out.

Before dwelling on betrayal and the fitting punishment, however, Starr would satisfy himself that there was no mistake.

The first step was simplicity itself. Risk-free.

Starr took the letter with him as he padded toward the telephone.

"The last thing I remember in Thermopolis is sitting on the couch with what's-her-name, the redskin."

"Catherine Littlefeather."

"Right. We're drinking through the afternoon and evening. Three, four different bars, and wind up back at her place. She starts taking off her clothes, and that was it. What can I say? Shit happens."

Adam stopped the tape and closed his eyes. The sound of Thomas Bender's voice was trapped inside his head.

Shit happens.

Meaning people die for no good reason. If they drink a bit too much, start feeling frisky with a stranger. It was no one's fault, exactly. Calculated losses. Everybody was expendable. Some deaths were worse than others, but nobody got out of life alive.

It was a rotten Monday morning, gray and drab outside. He wished it would snow, just once. Dump tons of crystal white across Los Angeles and offer the facade of cleanliness, if only for a little while. The way it worked in L.A., though, whatever snow you found was made for snorting, and it didn't have a thing to do with holidays.

The shrilling telephone made Adam jump. A quick glance at the answering machine told Reed that he had failed to turn it on that morning.

"Shit."

He had a simple choice: pick up or miss the call.

"Hello?"

"Good morning, Mr. Reed?" Male voice, no recognition.

"Speaking."

"This is Michael Sturgess."

Adam's mind went blank for half a second, then it hit him. Groping for a suitable response, he managed: "Mr. Sturgess, this is a surprise."

106

"I got your letter."

"Yes?" Of course, he *had* the frigging letter. Why else would he call? Why *had* he called?

"I thought you might not mind a small intrusion," Sturgess said. "It seemed more *personal* somehow."

"Of course."

Reed thought of getting it on tape, but that meant he would have to switch the PhoneMate on, then punch the button to record. There would be distinctive clicking noises on the line.

"I'm glad to hear from you," he said. A lie. Glad didn't cover anything that he was feeling at the moment. There was nervous, apprehensive, jittery, and weird. *Glad* wasn't on the list.

"How is your work progressing?"

"Work?"

"On Thomas."

Get your act together, stupid!

"Fairly well, I think. First drafts are difficult to judge."

"You're modest."

"No, not really. Mr. Sturgess—"

"Michael, please."

"Okay. Are you at home now, Michael?"

"Home?"

Be careful. "I could call you back, reverse the charge. You'd save some money."

"Money's not a problem."

"What I'd really like is a substantial interview."

"With me?"

"That's right, but at the moment—"

"Why the interest, Adam?"

"Pardon me?" A stall. Reed knew he was skating on thin ice.

"It's flattering, of course, but to be frank, I'm still not sure how I can help you with your project."

"Well—"

"Unless, of course, you're interested in something else."

Reed hesitated. "Something else?"

"A layman's point of view on Bender. Grass-roots observation, as it were."

"In fact—"

"But then, I have to ask myself: Why me? You must have experts at your beck and call."

"Not quite."

"Or we could talk about my work in Santa Rosa."

"That's intriguing. When you wrote to Bender—"

"Sadly, I don't have the time this morning," Sturgess said. "Just touching base. I'll have to call you back."

"My dime, next round. If you could let me have your number . . ."

"Never fear. I'll be in touch. 'Bye now."

And that was all. Reed sat there for another moment, the receiver in his hand, as if persistence would retrieve the contact. Finally, distracted by the dial tone buzzing in his ear, he gave it up. His hand went out on reflex, switched the PhoneMate on.

What now?

He started typing furiously, screw the punctuation, trying to record the fleeting dialogue verbatim. It was touch and go, the details garbled by distraction and surprise. Reed thought about the standard exercise they ran on students at the FBI Academy. The middle of a boring class, a wildman rushes in, shouts something, turns around and splits. Three dozen junior G-men are required to write detailed descriptions of the stranger: hair and clothing, his demeanor, what he had to say. From what he understood, no two of them came out the same in any given class.

To hell with it. His notes were close enough. If Sturgess wanted to contest his transcript somewhere down the line, he could produce his own tape of the conversation. Fuck him.

He would have to let McKeon know as soon as possible. The game was heating up. He paused with one hand on the telephone and asked himself: Am I afraid? Not yet.

But he was getting there.

Six days a week, Detective Sergeant Roy McKeon sat behind his desk and faced the Victim Wall. Arranged in three long rows were photographs of thirty women, twenty-three before and after, seven left with space for crime scene photographs if they were ever found. These women watched

108

McKeon shuffling papers, making phone calls, getting nowhere. Some accused him with their eyes, while others
seemed indifferent to the grim fate that had overtaken them.

It took all kinds.

He could recite the thirty names from memory, fill in the
details of their lives without a reference to the task force
files. Sometimes, McKeon thought he knew these women
better than he knew his own ex-wife, though he had never
met any of them alive. A few were prostitutes or runaways,
but there was no clear pattern in the choice of victims. Santa
Rosa's monster was as likely to select a third-grade teacher
as a topless dancer, killing anyone who crossed his path with
fine impartiality.

Most random killers focused on a certain type of victim
—hookers, nurses, red-haired eight-year-olds with freckles
—but the Slasher was eclectic. Staring at the photographs,
McKeon saw no striking similarity between the victims,
overall. A few could pass for sisters, but he thought that
anyone who murdered thirty women from the same community was bound to pick up half a dozen lookalikes by
sheer coincidence.

Aside from that, the victims were Caucasian. Ages ranged
from seventeen to thirty-three. Physique was variable, five-
foot-one to five-eleven, weighing anywhere from ninety-
seven to one hundred thirty pounds. Hair color varied, with
at least one dye job and a punk style that defied description.
Seven of the twenty-three known dead wore glasses. Eighteen were employed, but if the Slasher was obsessed with
any given occupation, he concealed it well. He butchered
students, waitresses, exotic dancers, housewives, hookers, a
librarian, a nurse, a student teacher. When the crimes were
plotted on a map, they yielded nothing in the way of
geographic patterns.

After nearly three years on the case, McKeon had jack
shit.

Except for "Michael Sturgess."

Even that was slim, of course. An empty postbox rented
with a phony name and address. Stolen license plates that
led back to a sixty-year-old former railroad engineer. The
Volvo might be stolen too, for all McKeon knew. He
wouldn't put it past the crafty bastard.

Still, for all of his suspicion and the indicators of a furtive life style, there was still no proof that "Sturgess" was their man. Three hundred *thousand* cars were stolen in the state of California every year, God only knew how many license plates. If every car thief was a killer, there would be a nonstop massacre from Redding down to Baja. Zero population growth, and then some.

Still, the first thing he had learned working homicide was to suspect coincidence. If they had been in San Francisco or L.A., some headcase writing to a death-row con would be routine. McKeon knew that Santa Rosa had its share of flakes as well, but circumstance and timing set alarm bells ringing in his head.

McKeon started ticking off the high points. "Michael Sturgess" wrote three times to Thomas Bender—not just any con, a lady-killer—in the week before Nevada punched his ticket. Sturgess used a phony name and address when he hired a box to catch his mail. He drove a car with stolen plates. Wrote cryptic letters making reference to his "work" in Santa Rosa—meaning what?

The stolen plate and fancy driving were enough to bust him on, albeit small potatoes. Make it grand theft if the Volvo came up hot . . . but they would have to find him first. And that, McKeon realized, would be no easy task.

The telephone was ringing, and he scooped it up. "McKeon."

"Sergeant, this is Adam Reed. In Pasadena?" Making it a question, like he wasn't sure.

"What can I do you for?" Distracted by the faces on the Victim Wall.

"I got a call just now from Michael Sturgess."

"Say again?"

"He called me here at home."

McKeon's mind was racing. "Is your number on your stationery, Adam?"

"No. I'm in the book, though. He could get it from directory assistance."

"Right." The scary part. "Was it long distance? Could you tell?"

Reed thought for a moment. "Probably," he said at last. "I think so, yes. It had that sound, you know?"

"Uh-huh."

"I asked where he was calling from and tried to get his number, but he wouldn't play. He said he'd call me back."

"That's it?"

"He wonders why I'm interested in him," said Reed. "It didn't seem to put him off, though. He suggested we could talk about his work in Santa Rosa. That's a quote."

"I don't suppose you had a chance to tape him?"

"Sorry."

"Never mind. We need to make arrangements for a trace in the event he does call back."

"He got my letter. Did you spot him at the postbox?"

"Ah, we had a little problem there."

"I see."

McKeon didn't feel like going into detail and making himself look stupid, so he let it go. "We'll need coordination with your local agency. That's Pasadena P.D.?"

"Right."

"You wouldn't know their number?"

"Not offhand."

"I'll look it up, no sweat."

"What else should I be doing?"

"For the moment, not a thing. I'll be in touch before the day's out."

"Sure. Okay."

Impulsively, McKeon asked, "You wouldn't have a gun around the house, by any chance?"

"A gun? No, why?"

McKeon thought about the California two-week waiting period for handgun purchases, considered telling Reed to buy himself a riot shotgun now, today.

"Forget it. False alarm."

"Okay." The writer's voice was strained with apprehension now.

"I'll be in touch," McKeon promised.

"Right."

McKeon cradled the receiver, thinking through the next call he would have to make. A touchy one, invading someone else's jurisdiction, but he couldn't help it. And he couldn't put it off.

111

He turned his back on thirty lifeless women, felt them staring at him as he called out to the room at large.

"Yo, people! Listen up! Has anybody got a number for the Pasadena P.D. filed away somewhere?"

Detective Steven Driscoll had been working Pasadena homicide for nineteen months. It was a change from vice, where he had spent two years before that, and a definite improvement on patrol, where you got stuck with everything from vandalism to domestic beefs and drive-by shootings. He was out of uniform and young enough, at thirty-one, to still believe he might be chief someday. Beyond that . . . well, his only limits were ambition and imagination, both of which Steve Driscoll reckoned as his strong points.

Pulling homicide in Pasadena wasn't bad, all things considered. They had three or four a month, on average, versus five or six *a day* in L.A. proper. Gangs were moving in, of course, but most of Driscoll's cases were impulsive crimes, committed by a friend or relative of the deceased. For the most part, he didn't have to wade through convoluted psychiatric texts to find a motive. Sex, love, jealousy, and greed were still the basic causal factors, even in the nineties.

Take the latest case on Driscoll's desk, for instance. Sophie Gellen, forty-two, three kids. Assaulted on Sunday night in her driveway with a baseball bat. Skull fractured, DOA at Pasadena General. The husband was distraught, from all appearances. He was also dating someone younger on the side and keeping up a life insurance policy on Sophie that would put a million dollars in his pocket if she died by accident—a legal euphemism that included murder, when the beneficiary was not involved.

Steve Driscoll had a few more questions for the grieving hubby. He was listing them on paper, making sure that nothing was forgotten when the telephone demanded his attention.

"Driscoll, homicide."

"Detective Driscoll, is it?"

"Yeah. Who's this?"

"Detective Sergeant Roy McKeon, Santa Rosa P.D. homicide."

"What's up?"

"Long story short, we've had a guy up here the past three years, he's killing women. Maybe you're familiar with the case?"

"It rings a bell." But faintly. Jesus, random killers were a dime a dozen in the Southland.

"Anyway, I'm on the task force."

"Yeah?"

"We've got a lead that crosses over into your backyard," McKeon told him. "I was hoping we could get cooperation on the follow-through."

"Why don't you fill me in?"

McKeon ran it down in simple terms. A local writer, working on a book about some piece of shit they executed in Nevada. Letters to the prison from a guy in Santa Rosa who was using fake ID and stolen license plates. He didn't spell it out, but Driscoll had a hunch the flake had burned McKeon's squad somewhere along the way. Now, the psycho was calling Pasadena, talking to the writer at his house.

"It's interesting," said Driscoll, as McKeon finished. "Thin, but interesting. What are you looking for?"

"A trace, if possible," McKeon answered. "Reed's cooperating. Find out where this joker's calling from with any luck."

A sudden thought made Driscoll frown. "You don't have any reason to believe he's down this way?"

"Not yet."

He didn't like the sound of that. "Potentially?"

"I couldn't rule it out," McKeon said, "but it's a long shot."

Driscoll felt him holding back, but that was standard when you had an interface between departments. Christ, LAPD was so antagonistic toward the county sheriff's office that the FBI was forced to operate two squads on bank heists, one each for municipal and county jurisdiction, to avoid offending anyone. It all came down to petty bullshit as a daily fact of life.

"I doubt my captain would involve himself without a local hook," said Driscoll.

113

"Understood. I'm mainly calling out of courtesy. We'll trap Reed's line at home, go through the operator if we have to."

"Are you coming down yourself?"

"Tomorrow or the next day probably."

"Okay. Why don't you call me when you set it up. We'll do lunch, like they say in Hollyweird, and see what's what."

"Appreciate it, Driscoll. Have you got a private number, there?"

"Extension two-three-nine."

"Okay. I'll be in touch."

"Look forward to it."

That was not exactly true, but it would be a small diversion anyway. You heard about these cases all the time, but Driscoll was a virgin when it came to psycho-stalkers. Maybe he could learn a thing or two, cash in on the reflected glory if a lead from Pasadena helped to bag their man.

Three years, though. Driscoll shook his head. It sounded like a wild-goose chase, but you could never tell. The Hillside Strangler had moved to frigging Washington before they nailed him on an unrelated beef. It could be educational.

But in the meantime, he still had work to do. Another little chat with Russell Arthur Gellen, all about insurance and his passion for a twenty-two-year-old from Hollywood.

And that was the appeal of homicide, thought Driscoll.

It would always let you see a charming slice of life.

CHAPTER

11

———•———

The phone call told him everything he had to know. Instead of Erin's answering machine, he got the bitch herself after three rings.

"Hello?"

Good-bye.

Starr never spoke to any of his women in advance. It was against the rules he made up as he went along. There was no wooing or seduction. He did not attempt to gain their confidence or impress them with his charm. His pen pals didn't count, the courting ritual of lies exchanged on paper. Once he had begun to stalk a target in the flesh, they would not speak until the bitch was absolutely at his mercy.

Soon.

He drove past Erin's duplex in the Chevrolet Caprice. Cold plates, a matching set this time. The vehicle was registered to Howard Stone of Fulton, north of Santa Rosa. In fact, there was no Howard Stone. The address on his pink slip was a bowling alley Starr had randomly picked from the yellow pages.

It was getting dark when Starr pulled over, half a block from Erin's house, and took a street map from the glove compartment. Spread it open on the steering wheel. His rearview mirror framed the duplex, keeping it constantly in his sight, though any passerby would see a helpless motorist attempting to discover where he was and how his navigation had gone wrong.

His heartbeat quickened at the flash of color in his rearview. Erin's jogging suit *de jour* was a fluorescent green that shimmered in the twilight. Watching her approach, Starr felt the first warm surge of an erection.

No. Not yet.

She passed him on the sidewalk, not even glancing in Starr's direction. If she sensed the presence of her judge and executioner, the feeling was beyond her conscious grasp.

Starr let her reach the intersection, turn the corner, disappear from sight. No hurry as he folded up the map, replaced it in the glove compartment, reached for the ignition key. There was an instant—echoes of an old frustration dream—when he expected the Caprice to fail him, leave him stranded, but the engine caught at once, and he rolled out on Erin's trail.

He took it nice and slow, caught up with her a block before she reached the park, and kept on going. Not a glance to warn her, as he passed. He saw her in the rearview mirror, shifting toward the middle of the street as she approached the park, and Starr was glad he had not planned to take her there.

The rest of it was timing, dawdling at the stop signs so he didn't get too far ahead. The longer he was parked to wait for Erin at the chosen ambush site, the greater risk he ran of being spotted by another motorist. He would not seem suspicious, at the time. No one would stop to offer help or ask his business. Only later, when the word of Erin's fate was circulated by the media, would any casual observers stop and rack their brains.

Starr had it covered—car, cold plates, disguise. Still, he preferred to make the lift without a witness. A perfect crime, rather than *almost* perfect. Any glitch could snowball if you let it get away.

He estimated he had five minutes, give or take, as he drove underneath the railroad arch and pulled into the gravel turnout fifty feet beyond. He doused the headlights, took his keys, and stepped out of the car. Despite the chill, a rancid odor wafted to his nostrils from the bright blue garbage cans nearby.

Starr's wig was black, with matching eyebrows and mustache. He wore a plain gray sweatshirt underneath a lightweight jacket, faded denim jeans, Adidas running shoes. The stun gun pulled his jacket down a little on the right. He didn't mind.

Starr took a moment with the cap, adjusting it. He wore it low on his forehead for a bit of extra camouflage. It was a minor point, but he had spent three hours shopping for the cap one Saturday. Its emblem was a grinning skull above the words LIVE FAST, DIE YOUNG.

It was nearly dark by half-past five, when Erin Gerber locked the door behind her, dropped the key into a pocket of her jogging suit, beside the can of pepper spray, and angled off across the lawn, running westbound at an easy pace. Despite the warm-up exercises, stiffness lingered in her calves and thighs, a painful side effect of dropping ten days from her normal schedule.

Family. The holidays.

She wore a rueful smile and concentrated on her breathing as the first block fell away behind her. Getting into it. The duplex with her Cutlass in the driveway shrinking by the moment.

Twenty-eight years old, and she was hanging in there with a regimen of daily exercise. Resisting time and gravity as much as possible. She didn't hear the ticking clock so many women talked about—most days, at least—and she got off on feeling young.

But family didn't help.

Her parents lived in Bakersfield, and since they never traveled farther than the nearest shopping mall, a flock of relatives converged on them for Christmas, many hanging on through New Year's.

Fish and visitors, thought Erin. There was something in the old saw, after all.

In truth, her parents weren't that bad. They didn't fit a Norman Rockwell portrait, but they weren't the Simpsons either. Erin loved them dearly, but they *worried* so damned much. To Jack and Edna Gerber, life was fraught with danger, each new day delivering another threat. And when the Gerbers worried, mother Edna felt an overwhelming urge to share.

Her weekly mailings were the worst, chock-full of horror stories from the papers that she clipped with pinking shears. A panoply of urban nightmares. Radon gas. Satanic cults. Carcinogens in health food. Air pollution. Gang rape. Acid rain. Drunk drivers on the freeway. Kids with guns. Asbestos in the walls and air ducts. AIDS.

The Slasher.

Erin no longer read the clippings. She skimmed her mother's chatty letters, threw the rest away, and wasted no more time than absolutely necessary pondering the decay of society. She had enough to think about just living day to day without a cloud of paranoia darkening her skies.

At Christmastime, with Erin and her siblings safely home, the Gerbers let themselves relax a bit. Of course, they never really gave it up—there was cholesterol and heart disease to think about, with those heavy meals; and the countless risks of traveling—but for the most part they were cool. As luck would have it, most of Erin's aunts and uncles also lived within an easy drive of Bakersfield, and their arrival turned the holiday week into one long organ recital: prostates and kidneys, livers and spleens, gall bladders and bunions. It was a morbid contest of who was sicker. Which pathetic soul had suffered more in the preceding year? Can you top *this?* I'll see that and raise you a dysfunctioning bladder.

By suppertime on Christmas, Erin felt the yuletide spirit wearing thin. By New Year's Day, it was a challenge to be civil, feigning interest in the aches and pains of people who ignored her all year long, birthdays included, counting on a sympathetic ear as if the Constitution guaranteed each hypochondriac a captive audience.

She felt the old resentment and swallowed it like bitter medicine. The season was behind her for another year, and Erin could look forward to the months ahead. She never wasted time on New Year's resolutions, but she did have prospects. Saving up to start her own shop with the cash, hands-on experience, and knowledge she had gained from Mr. Rosenblum the past four years. A shot at making something of herself.

And Todd.

Their second date had been on Saturday, and he had called her every day she was down in Bakersfield. Her sister Cathy made a joke of it, the little snot, but Erin wasn't laughing. After all this time, no real relationship since college, she had trouble laughing at the ups and downs of modern romance.

Granted, Todd would not have been her first choice as a knight in shining armor. He was no Mel Gibson, but at least he tried to keep himself in shape and earned a decent salary. Computers. He was thirty-one and single, didn't smoke, was not addicted to the tedious pursuit of TV sports. They hadn't gone to bed as yet, but he was straight, presumably without disease. If things went well the next few dates—

Whoa, girl.

She caught herself skywriting and returned to solid ground. Two dates and ten or fifteen phone calls did not make a lasting love affair. When Erin's mother asked about the new man in her life, she tried to play it down, reduce the typical embarrassment of having to explain how things went wrong if this one blew up in her face.

It wouldn't be the first time, but at least she tried to learn from her mistakes.

Again, she heard her mother's parting words. *Be careful, Erin, please. Your father and I worry so.*

I worry, too, she almost said, but kept it to herself.

These days, reluctantly, she thought about impending middle age. It didn't roll around at fifty, fifty-five. How many people lived to be a hundred, anyway? The average life expectancy for middle-class white women in America was pushing eighty, if they didn't smoke or drink or fool around. Twelve years to go, and Erin would have crossed the halfway mark.

Terrific.

So, she hit the health club at least once a week and went out jogging every day despite the weather. Carrying her can of pepper spray.

If anybody asked, she would have smiled and told them that the spray was meant for dogs, but no one had to ask. The Slasher didn't surface much these days, in conversation on the job or at the beauty shop, but every Santa Rosa female over ten years old knew he was out there hunting. Looking for another human sacrifice.

Or, maybe not.

It had been four months, give or take, since number thirty disappeared. The name eluded Erin, and it made her sad. The cops were cagey when they talked about the missing victims, throwing out the possibility that some of them had vanished voluntarily. It didn't wash, but Erin understood their need to minimize the problem. They were spokesmen for the city, with an image to protect.

And it was only women being murdered, after all.

She sometimes thought of the Slasher, when she went out jogging after sundown. Not obsessively, the way her mother would have, but in the knowledge that she shared a common risk with every other woman in the neighborhood. The way a diver thought of sharks while he was suiting up, or hikers thought of rattlesnakes as they were lacing up their boots.

One thing she wouldn't do, and that was let a sick, perverted animal derail her life. There had been several news reports over the past two years of women giving up their jobs and social lives, adjusting how they dressed or styled their hair. Some moved away, pretending danger could not find them in a new location.

Cowards.

She was coming to the park, deep shadows underneath the trees. On impulse, Erin veered off from the sidewalk to the middle of the street. No traffic to concern her, and she did not mind the small precaution. It was cheap insurance, and she never even broke her stride.

Determination.

Erin had considered purchasing a gun, but compromised on pepper spray. She wasn't into *killing* anyone, for God's sake, though the thought had crossed her mind. Imagining what she would do if someone broke into her home, for instance. Could she reach the carving knife in time to make a difference, much less plunge it into living flesh? At what point did survival instinct override the years of terse reminders to be ladylike?

A half block past the park, she cut back toward the sidewalk. Never missed a beat. Not bad.

So much for living in the shadow of a maniac.

Her mind went back to Todd, imagining what it would be like when they finally made love. *If* they made love. She wasn't ready yet, by any means, but if he didn't blow it on the next few dates, he had a shot.

She didn't yearn for Todd the way she had for others, in her college days and afterward, but he was . . . cute. Not drop-dead handsome, mind you, but a girl could only set her sights so high before it got ridiculous.

Make that pathetic.

Erin knew an old maid when she saw one, and she hadn't seen one in her bathroom mirror . . . yet. A few more years, though, and she would be forced to think about it seriously.

Hell, she took it seriously *now*.

How many of her Berkeley classmates had achieved their dreams? She had lost touch with most of them, but there were still a few who wrote or called from time to time. Most were married now, with children underfoot or on the way. Some days, she pitied them for losing track of all their aspirations. Other times, she felt the ugly pangs of envy.

Seven years since graduation, and she hadn't set the world on fire either. The teaching had been a nightmare, seventh grade in Frisco, with a principal who looked on discipline as someone else's problem. Children who could quote the songs of Megadeth and Motley Crue from memory but didn't give a damn about their native language, much less history or math. Three years of talking to the walls had been enough for Erin. She had never missed the classroom once since walking out, not even when her mother mailed those snippets on the rising cost of health insurance for a single woman over twenty-five.

Let someone else prepare the Leaders of Tomorrow for their future pumping gas or flipping burgers at McDonald's. Erin Gerber had moved on to greener fields.

Before she knew it, she was almost at the railroad underpass. Dark ivy clinging to the arch of stone. A black maw waiting to receive her. It was barely fifteen feet from one end of the tunnel to another, but in wintertime it seemed to swallow light, like one of those black holes in outer space. She could imagine jogging in and never coming

121

out the other side, sucked through a time warp from her own dimension to the next.

But it was just a tunnel, after all, and she was nearly home.

Her legs felt limber now. A few more days and she would be in shape again. Start pushing it from there. Consider tacking on another mile if she felt up to it.

Why not?

Emerging from the pitch-black tunnel, Erin saw another jogger coming her way on the same side of the street. A man. It was unusual, but not unheard-of. Last time had been . . . when? In August? No, September. She remembered, now, because—

The man was running with his head down, baseball cap, his face in shadow. Erin tried a smile for size, in case he glanced up as they passed each other. Never snub a fellow jogger.

But he wasn't looking up. Ten yards between them, and he ran as if he had the road all to himself. Another solitary soul, with mundane worries on his mind or snapping at his heels.

Five yards, and Erin drifted to her right to give him room. Too late, it clicked: the empty car ahead of her.

She never really saw him veer toward a collision course, but then a hand closed tight around her arm, the fingers digging in. She gasped, her free hand groping for the pepper spray, as something jabbed her in the back.

A knife? Too dull. Oh, Jesus, please don't let him—

Forty thousand volts surged through her body, radiating outward from the contact points above her spine, and Erin Gerber stiffened, staggered. Saw the asphalt rush to meet her face.

When she could see again, the next thing she beheld would be a nightmare come to life.

Black holes were everywhere.

He had waited, ticking off the seconds in his mind. This was the hard part, estimating Erin's progress. She would not be visible again until she cleared the tunnel, and a premature approach could ruin everything. If Starr was hasty, made his move too soon and met her on the wrong side of the underpass, it meant that he would have to carry Erin twice as far to reach the Chevrolet. More risk of being seen, and with a woman on his shoulder, any sighting would most likely be relayed to the police.

A minute passed, then thirty seconds more, before he started jogging back in the direction of the railroad arch. The plastic stun gun filled his hand. It should be close enough, unless there was a problem. If her shoelace came untied, for instance, or she paused along the way for any other reason, he was screwed. The lift was critical to all that followed, and—

She cleared the tunnel right on time, some thirty feet in front of him. Starr kept his head down, navigating with a hunter's instinct. If he met her eyes right now, she would sense danger. Bolt for safety. He did not intend to lose her in a footrace.

Closing.

Erin drifted to her right, Starr's left, to keep some space between them. Simple courtesy. She would have seen the car by now, but would it register? Set off alarm bells in her mind?

Starr felt her sudden hesitation, knew that he could not afford to waste another second. Lunging with his left hand, he caught Erin's arm and held her, brought his right around behind her back. As she recoiled from Starr, began to struggle in his grip, the stun gun found her spine an inch or two above the waist.

He pressed the trigger with his thumb and saw her stiffen, jerking as the voltage hit her. Two full seconds blitzing her, and she slumped toward the pavement. He caught her. Pulled her upright. Ducked in front of her and lifted Erin to his shoulder in the fireman's carry.

Simple.

Starr's adrenaline was flowing, adding strength to muscles pumped from countless hours on the Nautilus machine. It felt like he was carrying a rag doll, Erin nearly weightless as he turned and ran to his car.

The trunk had room enough, once he positioned her to suit him. Knees drawn up against her breasts, arms pulled behind her back. He snapped the handcuffs on her wrists and tightened them. Secured her mouth and ankles with a roll of silver duct tape. She could lash out with her legs if she came out of it before they reached their final destination, but her posture in the trunk would not allow much leverage. Her back was to the latch, and there was no way she could spring the lid.

Experience told Starr that he had fifteen minutes, minimum, before she came around. The drive took twice that if the lights were with him, but he wasn't worried. If she woke ahead of time and started getting noisy, he could always find a side street, stop and let her have another jolt. Full dark, now, and he had no fear of being recognized if he should have to pause and poke around inside his trunk. No one would give the dark-haired motorist a second glance. And, if they did . . . so what?

He had it covered, nothing left to chance or guesswork. All he needed now was time and privacy.

Starr had the perfect place, a mile outside of town. No neighbors close enough to spoil the fun.

For weeks, he had imagined Erin Gerber on his operating table. Soon, in just a few more moments, his daydreams would become reality. Starr hoped that she was strong and durable, with an abiding will to live. She had no chance, of course, but it would help prolong the game, enrich the pleasure he derived from stealing Erin's final breath.

Starr hoped she was a screamer.

He was looking forward to a little music in the night.

CHAPTER

12

———•———

Through Monday night and Tuesday morning, Adam Reed kept waiting for the telephone to ring with Michael Sturgess on the line. The only call he got, though, was from Roy McKeon at the Santa Rosa task force. It was nearly 6:00 P.M. when Adam heard the sergeant say he would be flying into LAX at noon. Was Reed available to meet with him and a detective from the Pasadena force?

He was.

Reed kept the news from Dana overnight, and she was gone—a shoot with Chick, in Venice—by the time he got around to breakfast. It felt strange, deceiving her with silence, but he knew that she would worry if he briefed her on the Sturgess call, McKeon's plan to tap their line and trace the next call, if and when it came.

Not *if*, Reed told himself, on second thought. The stranger's tone of voice had matched his letters: calm, self-confident, controlled. *I'll be in touch.*

Adam tried to work on Tuesday morning, gave it up at half-past ten without a single new word added to his manuscript on Bender. Pacing didn't help, and he got nowhere paging through his notes. The only voice inside his head belonged to Michael Sturgess, possibly a murderer of thirty women, who might just call him up to chat at any time.

He didn't even know the bastard's real name.

It should have been a comfort, knowing the police were on their way, but what had they accomplished in the past three years? No suspects. No hard evidence. They couldn't even bag their man when he showed up to claim his mail. McKeon telling Reed, *We had a little problem, there.*

Translation: Sturgess had somehow outsmarted them and left them in the dust. They blew it.

Adam meant to ask about that when he saw McKeon. In the meantime, he was edgy. Painfully exposed. He took a moment and replayed the final argument with Dana, New Year's Eve. She thought the Santa Rosa cops were using him as bait. She could be right, but Reed preferred to think he was cooperating, paying dues to clinch the story of a lifetime. If their suspect turned out to be someone's wacky uncle, no connection to the Slasher crimes, Reed's personal investment would be minimal.

But if his instinct was correct . . .

He had mixed feelings about pursuing Sturgess, even from a distance. There was apprehension, certainly, inspired as much by Dana as by any private fear on Adam's part. Beyond that feeling, though, he registered excitement. Standing near the center of a major homicide investigation, working with police to bag their one and only suspect. It was quite a change from prowling on the outside, looking in and begging for a word or two that he could use in print.

Who else had ever found his way inside a case like this? There had been Jimmy Breslin in New York, with Son of Sam, but he wound up at odds with the police, had never actually *spoken* to the killer. It was ancient history, his book—a *novel,* mind you—so long out of print, it may as well have been the Dead Sea scrolls.

No competition.

It was straight-up noon when Adam made himself a roast beef sandwich, thinking that McKeon should be on the ground by now, unless his flight from Santa Rosa was delayed. He shouldn't have much in the way of luggage, flying home that afternoon or evening. Call it half an hour, minimum, to meet his ride and buck the traffic leaving LAX, then fifteen miles between the airport and his destination, as the crow flies. Say another hour, minimum, on L.A. surface streets. They might improve that time a little, on the freeway, but it meant a zigzag course, at least ten extra miles through noontime traffic.

Half-past one before Reed should expect his callers, then. He took his time with lunch and washed it down with a Corona. Not that Adam *needed* alcohol to face the interview. He knew what he was doing, understood the hazards. Now that Pasadena's finest were involved, he had two law enforcement agencies covering his back.

And neither one of them would recognize the suspect if he walked in to surrender.

Maybe one more beer, before his company arrived.

The standard "unmarked" car pulled up outside Reed's house at 2:05 P.M. He watched from the front window as the occupants unloaded. From the driver's side, a sandy-haired athletic type in polyester, six-foot-three or -four, with mirrored aviator shades. Reed placed him somewhere in his early thirties. His companion might have been six-one, but posture and a stocky build made him seem shorter. Olive skin and dark hair thinning at the crown. He wore a navy blazer, slacks that nearly matched, a spotted tie that somehow failed to tie it all together. He was carrying a stainless steel attaché case.

Reed did not move to greet them on the porch. He felt a little silly, watching through the window like a neighborhood voyeur, but something made him wait until the officers were on his doorstep, jabbing at the bell. Reed took his time responding even then, as if afraid to let his callers know he had been following their progress from the street. It bothered Adam that his hand was trembling slightly as he opened the door.

The sandy-haired detective got things rolling. "Mr. Reed?"

"That's right."

"Steve Driscoll, Pasadena P.D., homicide."

The handshake was perfunctory, and Reed turned toward the officer with the attaché case. "Sergeant McKeon?"

"Right." A dry, firm grasp. Brief smile.

"Come in, please. Can I get you anything to drink? Some coffee?"

Both declined, and Adam steered them toward the sofa, settled in his BarcaLounger. Driscoll's eyes were mousy brown behind his mirrored glasses. Roy McKeon placed his briefcase on the floor beside his feet.

"The sergeant's filled me in on what you're doing," Driscoll said. "It doesn't seem to impact my department, but I'll be coordinating just in case."

Reed didn't like the sound of that. "I see."

"It's just procedure."

Roy McKeon sat hunched forward, elbows on his knees. "No word from Sturgess since we talked last night?"

"Not yet."

"Okay. The plan, as I explained, involves a trace next time he calls. We get his number, find out where he's calling from, with any luck at all it leads us to his doorstep."

"That's a tap?" Reed asked.

McKeon shook his head. "Whole different thing. On taps, we need an order from the court to listen in, and neither party knows we're on the line. It gives us dialogue, but doesn't trace incoming calls. With your cooperation, though, we don't need any paper from the judge. I wouldn't mind if you could tape this joker, but the first priority is tracing him."

Reed frowned. "That takes some time, I understand. I'll have to keep him on the line."

"It used to," said McKeon. "We've got marvels of technology these days. You've heard about the Caller ID system?"

"Bits and pieces. Wasn't it designed to stop harassment calls?"

"That's it." McKeon lifted his attaché case and set it on the coffee table. "Right away, your ACLU types start raising hell about the so-called right to privacy. We nail a breather terrorizing women in the middle of the night and we're infringing on his sacred right to use the telephone as he sees fit." The sergeant forced a smile. "Don't get me started, 'kay?"

He opened the attaché case, removed a plastic box approximately half the size of Adam's answering machine, with insulated wires attached. It could have been a digital alarm clock, from the general shape and size.

"Your basic phone trap," said McKeon. "Plug it into any wall jack in the house. Somebody calls, you get a readout on their number, even if you don't pick up. It lets you dodge your in-laws, they don't even know you're home."

"Sounds useful."

"Yeah, it can be. In the old days, tracing calls, we had to use an operator, run the trunk lines. Hell, it took forever. Nowadays, you dial, you're dusted."

"What about long distance?"

"Doesn't matter," said McKeon. "Each display includes the area code. He calls from Santa Rosa, you should see that 707 up front."

"I understood that you were *counting* on long distance," Driscoll said.

"That's right," McKeon told him. "We've got nothing to suggest our man's a traveler. Three years, the FBI's been looking at his work, and they've got nothing similar from any other jurisdiction."

"What we don't need," Driscoll said, as if McKeon had not spoken, "is to drag some headcase in from out of town. You get my drift?"

"I hear you," said McKeon. "All we're looking for is this guy's number. We can drop in, have a little chat. Odds are, he's just some psycho groupie, but I'd like to scratch him off the list."

Reed knew that wasn't strictly true. He could not picture Roy McKeon leaving Santa Rosa, getting on a plane to fly 450 miles one-way and bring the phone trap with him, if he didn't have at least some hope that Sturgess was the Slasher.

"What about the postbox?"

Driscoll frowned. McKeon almost cringed. "We ran into a problem, there," the cop from Santa Rosa said.

"That's it?"

McKeon met his gaze and shrugged. "We spotted someone picking up the mail," he said, with obvious reluctance, "but we lost him on the road. His license plate was stolen,

129

traced back to an old man with an airtight alibi. We're checking on the car through DMV, but it's a needle in a haystack."

"Photographs?" Reed asked.

"No time," McKeon said, "plus, it was raining. We've been sitting on a sketch. I hate to scare him off, when all we've got him on so far is petty theft and reckless driving."

"No, of course not. Could I get a copy, just in case?"

"I didn't bring one with me," said McKeon. "I could send it down."

"That's fine."

Reed's voice was steady, but a chill was tickling his spine. On top of everything—the cryptic letters, phony name and address—Sturgess had eluded the police in Santa Rosa. Stolen license tags, for Christ's sake. Everything he did made Sturgess sound less like a harmless flake. More like the Slasher.

Adam didn't know if he should be excited or appalled. The game was heating up, but there was still an unreal quality about it. Distance helped, of course. The guy had covered every base, so far, without a major slip, and Adam didn't see him driving six or seven hours to expose himself on unfamiliar ground.

"The phone trap," Adam said. "It's not a secret."

"Well . . ."

"I mean, if Sturgess reads the paper, chances are he knows about it. Right?"

McKeon shrugged again. "He's got no reason to believe you'd set him up."

"The box?"

"Coincidence. We didn't brace him in the station, and we didn't have a chance to talk. He's using stolen plates and fake ID. For all we know, the car was stolen, too. A guy like that, the cops go after him, my guess would be he has to stop and wonder what we know."

"He won't go back there," Adam said.

"I wouldn't think so."

"And he had the box how long?"

McKeon thought about it for a moment. "Eighteen months," he said.

Reed felt a little better. Sturgess must have used the box

for *something* in the past year and a half, beside the letters sent to Reed and Bender. Each transaction multiplied his risk—and shaved the odds of Sturgess blaming Reed for his betrayal.

"Which day was it, when you missed him?"

"Saturday," McKeon said.

And Sturgess phoned on Monday, two days later. No apparent anger in his voice, though he had been cautious. Kept it short and sweet, refusing to divulge his number. That much was consistent with the use of pseudonyms and false addresses, stolen license plates. The man was either paranoid or he had something to conceal. He would not risk a call if he suspected Adam of betraying him to the police, would he?

Idle speculation was a waste of time. Reed knew that he was chasing shadows, trying to persuade himself that he would face no risk if he continued with the game. The *smart* thing, if he thought about it, would have been to show McKeon out and end it now, but he had come too far for that. He had already volunteered to bait the suspect. Sturgess knew exactly where to find Reed if he wanted to.

Surprisingly, he felt a sense of freedom, knowing he had passed the point of no return. Whatever happened next, he couldn't turn the clock back and relive the past three weeks. If Sturgess called again, so be it. He would log the number, pass it to McKeon, let the task force follow up.

And if the stranger blew him off, what then?

Reed knew that he would always wonder, turn the problem over in his mind and worry it, frustration setting in.

He smelled a story, damn it, and he wasn't letting nerves derail him.

Adam rose and took the plastic box. "I'll put this in my office."

The detectives followed him, with Driscoll bringing up the rear. They stood and scrutinized the titles in his bookcase as he placed the phone trap on his desk, knelt down and plugged it in.

"Okay, I guess we're set."

"You got to know this Bender pretty well, I take it." Driscoll's narrow lips were turned down at the corners, disapproval in his tone.

"That's right."

Reed would have bet the house on what was coming next.

"So, what's the interest in a guy like that? He slaughters women and they stop his clock. You write about him. People pay to read it, maybe watch it on the tube, you catch a break. Where's the attraction?"

Adam answered with a question of his own. "What kind of books do *you* read?"

"Sci-fi, mostly, when I get the time."

Escaping from reality, Reed thought. And what he said was, "Different strokes. You spend your whole life chasing bad guys, and you need a break. Most people never get a look inside your world."

"They're lucky," Driscoll said.

"Agreed, but there's an interest. Call it morbid curiosity. You see them on the highway, slowing down past accidents."

"Like scavengers," said Driscoll.

"That's a part of it," Reed said. "You'll always have a marginal percentage out for blood. They watch an auto race and hope for accidents, or sit around and tell themselves pro wrestling's not a sideshow, but they're still in the minority."

"So, who's your audience?"

"I leave the demographics to my publisher," said Reed, "but I suspect you'll get all kinds. A fair percentage wish they had your job, the way it looks on television. Reading up on monsters and the men who track them down, they get a chance to share the glory."

"That's a good one." Driscoll and McKeon smiled together. "I could use some glory for a change."

"And some of them are scared," Reed said, continuing. "They know about Jeff Dahmer. He's the guy next door. It helps to know he's in a cage and find out how he got there. If he made mistakes, they want to know about it. Maybe they can spot the next one coming."

"Keep your fingers crossed," McKeon said.

"Some people read about a man like Bender and they feel relief."

"How's that?" asked Driscoll.

"Dancing in between the raindrops," Adam said. "The lightning missed them this time. There, but for the grace of God, goes everybody."

"Did you ever stop and think a book like this might just encourage other fruitcakes?"

Standard question Number Two.

"It crossed my mind," Reed said, "and I discounted it. We had sadistic rapes and murders long before there was a printing press, much less a movie camera or a VCR. I don't believe we can protect ourselves through censorship. For every random killer hooked on horror movies or pornography, I'll show you one who got his inspiration from the Bible or detective magazines."

"Myself," said Driscoll, "I don't care *what* makes them tick, unless it helps me do my job."

"Amen to that," McKeon said.

"Well, if we're finished here—"

The last thing Adam was expecting, at the moment, was the sound of Dana calling to him from the living room.

"Hello?"

He felt a sudden urge to duck out through the back door, leave the two detectives to explain themselves.

Too late.

She met them in the hallway outside Adam's office and the master bedroom, blinking in surprise.

"We finished early," Dana said. Translation: *Who the hell are these guys, anyway?*

"Detectives Driscoll and McKeon, Dana Withers."

Women have it easy, Adam thought. It's not a snub if they don't feel like shaking hands.

"I didn't know you were expecting company," she said.

"They just stopped by."

"On business?"

"We're not busting anybody," Driscoll told her, putting on a smile.

"That's good to know."

"You look familiar," he continued, "but I know we've never met. Are you an actress?"

"Model."

"Would have been my next guess. Fashion layouts?"

"Mostly."

"That's it, then. I must have seen you in a magazine."

"It's possible."

"I'm good with faces."

133

"That must help you in your work."

McKeon glanced at Adam, frowned, and said, "We'd better roll. I need to check in early for my flight."

"You're leaving town on business?" Dana asked him.

"Going home," he said.

"And home is . . . ?"

"Santa Rosa."

Dana blinked again and turned a frosty stare on Reed. "Well," she said, "we won't keep you."

Adam trailed them to the door, McKeon picking up his metal briefcase from the coffee table, Dana close behind. She would smile for the detectives, but if Adam turned to face her now, he knew she would be glaring daggers at him.

Disengaging was the hard part. Driscoll was amused by Reed's predicament, and while McKeon seemed more sympathetic, there was no way he could make believe the visit was a social call.

"Well, thanks again," he said, thick fingers squeezing Adam's hand. "We'll be in touch. If you hear anything—"

"I'll let you know," Reed said.

"Take care." A cautious smile for Dana. "Ma'am."

"Good-bye."

Eyes boring into Adam as he stood and watched them go. Another moment, and the unmarked cruiser pulled away. His last excuse was gone.

"Look, Dana—"

He expected her to interrupt him, but she didn't. Standing there in front of him, arms crossed beneath her breasts, she stared him down and waited for an explanation.

"That's the cop from Santa Rosa I've been talking to," he said. "McKeon."

"So I gathered."

Stalling. "Driscoll's with the Pasadena force. He drove McKeon over from the airport."

Stony silence. Dana listening.

"We talked about this Sturgess character."

"It's cheaper flying down than talking on the telephone?" Reed tried a laugh for size and didn't like the fit.

"Well, hardly."

"So?"

"He brought me something."

134

CAT AND MOUSE

"Shall I guess? You want to play twenty questions?"

"A phone trap," Adam told her. "Anybody calls the house in the next few days, it runs an automatic trace and prints their number out."

"When you say 'anybody,' you mean Sturgess."

"Right."

"Is there some reason to expect he'd call you here?"

The worst part, coming up. "He called me yesterday."

She didn't blink, this time. Instead, her eyes went big and round.

"God*damn* it, Adam!"

"Dana—"

"No! You lied to me!"

"You're wrong. I knew you'd worry, so—"

"You kept it to yourself."

Reed felt like he was treading water with an anvil in his hands.

"I'm sorry, Dana. Christ, it isn't like I asked him to call me."

"Didn't you?"

"What's that supposed to mean?"

"You send him letters. He writes back. You're running interference for the cops, and now you act surprised when this guy calls *our home?* A homicidal maniac, for all you know."

"I doubt that very much."

"That's bullshit, Adam. You don't chase a story if it lacks potential."

"This is not a problem, Dana."

"Wrong again. Whatever drives a wedge between us is a problem."

"Please."

"This scares me, Adam. And the worst part is, you don't see that—or maybe you don't care."

"Of *course* I care. There's nothing to be frightened *of.*"

"I hope you're right," she said. "I really do."

And left him staring, as she turned and walked away.

CHAPTER

13

———•———

Five days and counting. By the time noon rolled around on Sunday, Adam had begun to tell himself that Sturgess would not call again. It was a washout. The police had scared him off, or something else had changed his mind.

Tough luck.

He had mixed feelings, watching as the story of a lifetime slipped away. On one hand, Reed could not deny a certain feeling of relief. No call from Santa Rosa meant that he could not pursue the matter—couldn't even write, since Roy McKeon's team had driven Sturgess from his postbox. That, in turn, reduced his risk of contact with the only suspect in the Slasher homicides to something in the neighborhood of zero.

Dana was relieved, of course. She had relaxed a little more with every passing day, and Sunday found her almost back to normal. Following McKeon's visit, she had barely spoken to Reed for the next two days. When dialogue was unavoidable, she kept it terse, and flinched away from Adam's touch in bed. On Friday, they began to talk again: the weather, Dana's work, the household bills. When they made love on Saturday, it felt like unarmed combat, Dana working out her pent-up anger and frustration in a style that left them both exhausted.

There was something to be said for making up.

The flip side of relief was disappointment. Not the worst he had experienced, perhaps, but getting there. Reed had convinced himself the story would be his, a surefire ticket to the *New York Times* best-seller list, and now he came up empty.

Friday's mail had brought the artist's sketch of "Michael Sturgess," with a brief note from McKeon. Thanks again for helping out, and stay in touch. The full-face drawing showed a man of forty-five or so, with hair that drooped around his ears, a bushy mustache covering his upper lip. A short description typed across the bottom of the page told Reed the suspect's hair was graying. He stood about six-foot-one and weighed about 190 pounds. He drove a Volvo, chocolate brown, last seen with stolen California license PBA1035.

It wasn't much.

The artist's rendering was lifeless, vague enough to match at least a million men between Los Angeles and Santa Rosa. Half an hour with some hair dye and a razor would eliminate whatever passing likeness had been captured by the sketch. Reed knew he might not recognize the man if Sturgess rang his doorbell in the next five minutes.

Never mind.

I lost him, Adam thought, as if the manhunt had been his from the beginning. Once a story captured the imagination, letting go could be a problem. The emotional investment had to be considered. It was not enough to simply shrug and walk away.

But what else could he do?

Since Tuesday afternoon, Reed had curtailed his trips away from home whenever possible. He left the PhoneMate on, in hopes of catching Sturgess on the tape, but there was still McKeon's trap to think about. It would not store successive numbers, meaning that if Adam got three calls while he was out, the first two numbers automatically erased. On Friday night, when Dana had insisted that they catch a movie, Adam fumed and fretted through the whole four hours they were gone. Came back and found that no one had called in his absence.

Dana didn't gloat. Relief was written on her face, another dig at Adam for his part in making her feel ill at ease.

Reed's parents had believed—and taught their son—that most things work out for the best. He knew they would have cast their votes with Dana where the Slasher was concerned. Stand back and play it safe. Leave well enough alone.

They never understood what Adam knew instinctively: that no one ever made it to the top by playing safe. His brush with Thomas Bender had been one step up the ladder, but it lacked the drama necessary to propel an author from the grunt work into literary stardom. Reed had seen a hopeful glimmer in the Santa Rosa case, but it was fading fast.

Another long shot staggers home, dead-last.

He smiled his way through lunch on Sunday, making small talk. Dana had some free time coming up, and she suggested that they claim a weekend for themselves. Get out of town and breathe fresh air. Chick had a little place near Ensenada they could borrow, if she asked him nicely.

"I'm surprised he hasn't asked you down before," Reed said.

"Did I forget to mention that?"

"You know damn well—"

Her laugh disarmed him, Adam feeling stupid for his petty jealousy. He trusted Dana, but her beauty still intimidated him sometimes. He didn't have to see her photo in a magazine. Just watching her around the house would do it, make Reed wonder what she saw in him. He wasn't *ugly,* granted, but the source of her attraction still eluded him. When he and Dana first moved in together, there were times when Adam lay awake all night, afraid that if he went to sleep, she would evaporate by morning.

They had discussed the marriage gig on more than one occasion, stalling, more or less assuming it would happen "someday." Dana wanted kids, but not right now, and Adam couldn't argue with her logic. Neither one of them had maxed out on professional achievement yet, or reached a point where backing off felt like the thing to do.

A few more years. Hell, they were young enough to work it out.

It wasn't like they had a deadline, after all. No hurry.

They were clearing the remains of lunch away when the telephone rang. Dana reached it first and listened briefly, handed it to Adam.

"It's for you."

On Sunday?

"Who?" he asked.

Her shrug was casual, disinterested.

"Hello?"

"You recognize my voice," said Michael Sturgess. It was not a question.

"Yes."

Reed glanced at Dana, rinsing dishes. Edged away from her. A chill raced down his spine.

"I said I'd be in touch."

"That's right, you did."

"So, here I am."

"You caught me by surprise." Reed turned in the direction of the hallway leading to his office, thought about the phone trap. Was it working?

"If you're busy—"

"No!" Too quickly. "Not at all."

"But you have *company*." It sounded wicked, coming from the stranger's mouth.

"No problem, honestly."

"Well, if you're sure . . ."

"I'm positive."

"You mentioned something earlier, about an interview," said Sturgess.

"Right."

"There *are* some things I'd like to talk about when you have time."

"Okay. Just let me shift into my office, get a pen and notepad."

"Not today."

Reed frowned, saw Dana watching him. She turned the water off and leaned against the counter, one hip kissing tile. A queasy feeling in his stomach. As a child, he would have called it guilt.

"All right. Say when."

"I'm thinking," Sturgess said. "My schedule's rather hectic at the moment."

"Business?"

"I suppose I'll have to call you back." Ignoring Adam's question. "Don't think I've forgotten you."

Another chill. "I won't."

"I need to put my thoughts in order first. Before we talk."

"Okay."

There were at least a hundred questions Adam longed to ask, but they eluded him. He did not bother asking for a call-back number, knowing it would be a waste of time. Besides, with any luck at all, he had it now.

The marvels of technology.

"Until the next time," Sturgess said. "Farewell."

The line went dead before Reed had a chance to answer, but he said "good-bye" for Dana's benefit and cradled the receiver.

"So?" she asked.

"Hang on a second."

Down the hall to reach his office. Adam went directly to the desk. The phone trap had a number for him, black on gray. He grabbed a pen to write it down, repeating it aloud from fear that something would go wrong. A power failure. Anything.

He had it: (707) 555-1496.

The Santa Rosa prefix.

"That was him."

He turned, found Dana staring at him from the doorway. Saw no way to get around it.

"Yes."

"I guess you've got yourself a *buddy.*"

"Dana—"

"So, what happens now?"

"I call McKeon."

"On a Sunday?"

Adam frowned. She had a point, but the police department never closed. There would be *someone* he could talk to, fill them in on what was happening.

"I'll leave a message. No big deal."

"You still don't get it, do you?"

Dana turned away and left him. She was cultivating quite a knack for that, these days.

Forget it. She would come around, in time, and at the moment he had work to do. He had McKeon's number coded on his telephone. One button put him through.

"Detective Baker."

"Sergeant Roy McKeon, please."

"The sergeant's off today. Is there a message?"

"It's important that I speak to someone from the task force."

"In regard to what?"

"A major suspect in the Slasher case."

"And you are . . . ?"

"Adam Reed. I'm working with McKeon. If you'd call him—"

"Hold."

A click, and silence. He was thankful the department didn't pipe in elevator music, like so many other systems. Turn the telephone into a radio, the tortured logic ran, and people won't mind hanging on the line for ten or fifteen wasted minutes.

Click. Another voice said, "Lou Kominski. Can I help you, Mr. Reese?"

"It's *Reed.*" Exasperation creeping into Adam's tone. "You're with the task force?"

"That's correct."

"I've got a number for McKeon. Sturgess called me back, just now."

"I see. And Sturgeon is . . . ?"

Reed felt an urge to scream. Instead, he started from the top and ran it down, Kominski jotting notes. He held the number back for last and listened while the officer repeated it.

"Okay," Kominski said when he was done. "I'll pass it on."

"That's it?"

"We'll check it out, sir."

"Right. Okay."

"And thanks for calling."

This time, Adam hung up first, but there was no real satisfaction in it. In his mind, he saw the memo lying on McKeon's desk. One of those pastel slips of paper from a pad that read *While you were out* . . . A garbled message scrawled in longhand, barely legible. Suppose McKeon missed it altogether? What would happen then?

141

He made a mental note to call again on Monday, keep on trying till he reached McKeon and confirmed the message. Giving up was not an option.

Dana passed the open doorway, heading for the bedroom. Adam knew that he should talk to her, but he could think of nothing useful to say, just then. If he stood back and gave her space, the anger would subside, in time.

She rarely held a grudge, but Reed knew he was pushing it.

"It's not my fault," he told the empty room. And once again, for emphasis. "It's *not* my fault."

For just a second, there, it almost sounded like the truth.

The diner occupied a corner lot, with windows facing north and east. At first—or even second—glance, it did not seem to be the kind of place where Howard Michael Starr would stop and take a meal. In fact, he almost never ate away from home, except when he was traveling. He was repulsed by the idea of strangers handling his food.

Today was different, though.

This Sunday afternoon, he was conducting an experiment.

It could be wasted time, Starr realized, but he was bound to try. A relatively simple test, and while it might prove nothing either way, at least he would have made the effort.

Nothing ventured, nothing gained.

Obtaining Adam Reed's home number had been easy. Once the scribbler thoughtfully provided his address, Starr only had to call the operator, pose the question, and receive his answer in the stiff, robotic tones that had supplanted human voices these days. That much he had accomplished from his house, secure in the thought that while his monthly bill would show a small charge for directory assistance, it would be extremely difficult—effectively impossible—for even a computer to recall which number he had asked for on a given day.

The later calls, of course, were made from public phones. Starr kept them short enough to foil most tracing mechanisms, but he was aware of new technology, at least in abstract terms. There were devices on the market now, he understood, that locked a phone line open and refused to let the caller break connections, giving the police an infinite amount of time in which to track him down.

CAT AND MOUSE

Assuming he was fool enough to call from home or hang around the scene.

No fool, was Howard Michael Starr.

The first time he had called Reed from a pay phone in a shopping mall. Trace *that,* for all the good that it would do. Gloves would have been conspicuous indoors, but Starr knew all the tricks. A double coat of airplane glue, applied to human fingertips, dried clear and smooth, invisible unless you made a special study of the subject's hand.

And it eliminated fingerprints.

He did not wait around the mall to watch for a reaction, even in the wake of the surprise encounter at his postbox, since he knew Reed was not counting on a phone call. Danger would accrue if Starr called back a second time, a third. Each call increased the risk of apprehension, though the odds were in his favor, even now.

Geography was on his side, for one thing. Say technology permitted Adam Reed to learn the number he was calling from immediately. There would still be lag time while Reed took the call, hung up, reported back to Santa Rosa homicide. Starr knew the local pigs would not assign a man to stay with Reed, and there had only been one number listed for the writer, indicating that his home was probably restricted to a single phone line. He could not alert the pigs while Starr was talking to him, and a call to Santa Rosa P.D.—even if he dialed direct—would take some time.

Enough for Starr to slip away and find himself a comfy vantage point.

And Sunday helped, of course. The hallowed day of rest, when crime rates dipped across the land and law enforcement agencies cut back on working hours. Adam's call from Pasadena, if he made one, would be passed around from one third-stringer to another, sidelined, maybe lost. The Slasher task force might have someone working on a Sunday afternoon, but it would surely be a gofer, shuffling paperwork, collating field reports. Without a recent case to occupy their time—and Erin Gerber didn't qualify, not yet—the *real* detectives would be sitting on their butts at home, zoned out on beer and football.

Starr's disguise was simple, but he had selected it with care. A sandy crew cut, horn-rimmed glasses, corduroy and

143

denim, high-topped sneakers. It was difficult to guess his age, without a ghost of stubble on his face. He could have been an aging college student or a young professor, maybe a computer nerd.

Perhaps a cop.

He chose the second pay phone after scouting several neighborhoods, well out from Willow Run. He needed a degree of privacy—no slack-jawed cretins in the booth next-door, debating the inanity of Howard Stern or Axl Rose—but visibility was also critical. Starr needed a convenient place in which to wait and watch for a police response.

How else could he be sure if Adam Reed was working with the pigs?

His choice had been the pay phone at an Exxon station six miles from his home. The booth was situated in a corner of the lot, some distance from the gas pumps and directly opposite the diner, where he occupied a window seat.

Five minutes, by the time a fresh-faced waitress in her twenties brought a laminated menu, rattling off the daily specials she had memorized. The name tag on her breast read KAREN. Starr amused himself by studying her painted lips, imagining his cock inside her mouth. It would be pleasant, teasing her with promises he never meant to keep. Her freedom. Life. An end to pain.

He ordered Sprite and asked for more time with the menu. By the time she brought his drink, he had decided on a BLT, assuming there was little damage anyone could do to lettuce and tomato. Fifteen minutes coming up, when it arrived with sliced dill pickle on the side. A handful of potato chips.

Starr took his time, the waitress coming back to catch him with his mouth full, asking him if everything was satisfactory. He smiled and nodded, turned back toward the window.

Waiting.

Twenty minutes.

Twenty-one.

The first patrol car came in from the south, behind him. Two pigs rolling past the Exxon station, catching their mistake in time to make a U-turn at the intersection, doubling back. They pulled into the lot, and both got out, hands resting on the fat grips of their service pistols. One of them—a rookie, judging by his age and general demeanor —stuck his head inside the booth and verified the pay phone's number, nodding to his partner. They were idling in the black-and-white, the older pig engaged in conversation on the two-way radio, when yet another squad car pulled into the lot.

Starr watched his adversaries circle wide around the phone booth, checking out the empty lot. They kept their hands off, waiting for the lab technicians to arrive, for all the good that it would do. Starr's gloves were in the Geo Prizm, parked outside.

With four cops on the scene, the station's manager got curious. He ambled over, trailing smoke behind him from his cigarette, struck up a conversation with the uniforms. They humored him. Asked questions. Didn't act surprised when the grease monkey shook his head. He had a poor view of the phone booth from his office—Starr had checked that in advance—and he would not have seen the Geo parked across the street, while Starr approached on foot, from the mechanic's blind side. Nothing left to chance.

Starr finished off his BLT and nursed his Sprite until the waitress came around to take his plate away. Impulsively, he ordered apple pie and got a bright smile in return, the little wage slave hoping he would leave a larger tip. Starr watched her sashay toward the kitchen, wishing he could pay another call at closing time, but that would be a foolish risk.

Stay cool. Stay focused.

He was on a different scent, now. Planning. Looking forward to the next stage of the game.

Reed had betrayed him to the pigs. There could be no doubt on that score. His motive was irrelevant, though Starr suspected greed, professional ambition, seasoned with a dash of public spirit. He could almost read the bastard's mind, pursuing convoluted trains of thought.

If Reed cooperated with police to bag the Santa Rosa Slasher, he would have a million-dollar story in his pocket. He would *be* the fucking story, flavor of the month on tabloid television, while producers lined up, bidding for the movie rights. Precipitating Howard Michael Starr's destruction meant a one-way ticket to the major leagues for Adam Reed.

Unfortunately for the scribbler, he had blown it. Reed had underestimated his intended prey and it would cost him dearly. Everything he had, in fact.

Starr thought about the woman who had answered Adam's telephone. He didn't know her yet, but there was time. No rush in orchestrating his revenge. Smart hunters took their time and relished the pursuit as much as they enjoyed the kill.

His pie arrived with the forensics van, a man and woman dressed in denim coveralls unloading their equipment. Karen spied them through the window, lingering.

"What's that about, do you suppose?"

Starr swallowed, shrugged. "You never know, these days."

He watched them dust the booth and telephone for fingerprints, imagining the dozens they would check in vain. Another secondary project was collecting litter from the ground around the phone booth, each piece tucked inside a separate plastic bag and labeled. Cigarette butts. Scraps of paper. Wads of chewing gum.

A total waste.

Starr paid his bill and left a tip for Karen from the change. Outside, the air was crisp and cool, his breath a plume that fluttered from his nostrils. He did not ignore the pigs across the street—that would have been suspicious in itself—but neither did he stop and stare. A short walk to the Geo, keep it casual, and he was rolling by the time a blue sedan arrived, disgorging plain-clothes officers. No one he recognized from coverage of the manhunt on TV.

The Sunday team.

Starr put an extra ten miles on the Geo, driving home the long way. Making sure he was not followed from the diner. You could never be too careful.

He was clean, no tail. The drive back to his home in Willow Run gave Starr a chance to think about his enemy in Pasadena. Adam Reed had chosen to betray him, when they could have worked together and produced a grand, historic document.

It was a critical mistake.

Reed would regret it for the rest of his short, miserable life.

CHAPTER

14

———•———

Autopsies were the shits. No matter how long he worked homicide, they always soured Roy McKeon's day. He still attended them religiously, believing that he needed every bit of information he could find to solve an open case, but it was getting old.

The Slasher had a lot to do with that.

In many murders—most, in fact—you had a fair grasp of the motive and the perpetrator, going in. Postmortems wrapped it up with scientific evidence: the time and cause of death, specific weapons used, and so forth. It was frosting on the cake for family killings, crimes of passion, even murders spawned by simple greed.

The Slasher was a whole new ball game. He enjoyed his work, took pleasure in refining his techniques and taunting homicide investigators with the grim barbarities inflicted on his prey. And worse, if that were possible, he left no useful evidence behind.

The latest victim was a twenty-eight-year-old named Erin Kathleen Gerber. She had been reported missing Wednesday evening, January seventh, when she skipped her second day of work and friends could find no trace of her at home. Her car was in the driveway, and her relatives in Bakersfield knew nothing of the woman's whereabouts.

It smelled bad to McKeon, even then. Three months and thirteen days without a Slasher killing and their boy was overdue. The longest gap between reported cases, heretofore, had been nine weeks. McKeon had been waiting for another victim, dreading it. Each passing day had given fleeting cause for hope that it was finished.

Still, you couldn't tell with random killers. Nearly one in five, McKeon knew from reading up, were never caught. Nobody had a clue what happened to them, why they suddenly stopped killing. Jack the Ripper. Zodiac. Green River. Useless theories multiplied like roaches. Suicide or accidental death. Committal to a psycho ward. Imprisonment for unrelated crimes.

Or, maybe they got bored. Moved on to find another happy hunting ground and changed techniques deliberately, to stump the cops.

McKeon didn't have to guess about the Slasher anymore. Not this month. Standing in the county morgue's postmortem operating room with Mentholatum smeared across his upper lip to cut the stench of death, he knew that he was looking at the Slasher's handiwork again.

Officially, the young assistant manager of Floral Fantasies was number twenty-four. Toss in the seven missing women, and she made it thirty-one. No end in sight.

A hiker had discovered the remains on Tuesday afternoon, near Austin Creek, eleven miles northwest of Santa Rosa. It was county jurisdiction, but the sheriff's office was cooperating on the task force, and McKeon caught the squeal. Three weeks had passed since Erin Gerber was reported missing, and the forest scavengers had done their best to wipe out any traces of forensic evidence.

Whenever Roy McKeon started thinking that his job must be the worst on earth, he had to stop and think about the county medical examiner. Things *could* be worse, he told himself.

But not by much.

The ME didn't have to deal with grieving relatives and journalists who took "no comment" as a bald admission of defeat. He worked with rotting flesh and shattered bone, but when he laid his scalpel down and switched the tape recorder off, his job was done. He knew the cause of death—most times, at least—and he could tell you roughly when it happened, what the victim ate for supper, whether he or she was drinking, when the maggots came. If there were stab wounds on the body, he could draw a picture of the blade. When poisons were involved, he told you what to look for, where it could be purchased by a would-be killer.

Answers.

In the Slasher case, it all came down to squat without a suspect. Roy McKeon knew the Slasher liked to use a knife, before and after death. He reveled in the agony of women, knowing from the outset that their screams and pleas for mercy would elicit none. Sometimes he masturbated on or near their bodies. A secretor, type A blood, for all the good *that* did.

McKeon watched as Dr. Amos Willingham went through the motions, weighing the remains of desiccated organs, drawing fluids, talking to the microphone he wore on his lapel. The object on his table had once been human. Predation and decomposition might obscure the facts of Erin Gerber's death, but the ID was verified from dental records. There was no more mystery, in Roy McKeon's mind, about the woman's fate.

Her left hand, for example, had been surgically removed, the carpal joint bisected with some man-made instrument resembling a hatchet or a cleaver. That was new, but no surprise. The Slasher always claimed some trophy from his kills.

It was coming up on three weeks, Sunday, since the last contact with "Michael Sturgess"—just a few days after Erin disappeared. They had traced his call back to a pay phone, but the fingerprints collected there, with sweepings from the service station's parking lot, had been no help at all. Of twenty-three prints that were clear enough to read, McKeon's sources matched exactly two: the thumbprint of a sixteen-year-old boy, from DMV, and the left index finger of a female kindergarten teacher who had worked the last eight years in Petaluma.

Worthless.

Each new killing was a personal affront to Roy McKeon, not that anger put him any closer to his man. He couldn't help it though, in spite of everything he knew about the ill effects of personal involvement in a murder case. His objectivity was out the fucking window.

When they found the Slasher, *if* they found him, it would be a challenge for McKeon not to shove his weapon in the bastard's face and pull the trigger. Thirty-one young women savaged, butchered, thrown away like so much garbage. And, for what?

The personal amusement of a monster.

One clean shot, McKeon told himself. That's all I need. But Erin Gerber would not give it to him. Not this time.

The Slasher had another trophy for his shelf, and the police were groping in the dark. As usual.

Next time, McKeon vowed, and prayed that he could make it stick.

Next time.

"Right there! You got it, sweetheart!"

Dana listened to the *whir-click* of the camera, pivoting to show the lens her profile. Wind-swept hair flowed back across her naked shoulders, aided by a large fan mounted on the guardrail of the pier. It was beyond her, why they couldn't do bikini shots without a mock typhoon, but that was Chick. He knew exactly what he wanted, and his pictures always sold.

This afternoon, they were in Long Beach, doing some generic T and A. The skimpy suits were manufactured by a local impressario with dreams of going national, and Chick thought he could help.

In fact, she knew, it didn't matter if the suits made any money. It was all about *exposure,* glossy photos mailed or faxed around the country, maybe landing on the right desk one time out of twenty.

All it took was one, though, for the lucky break.

And luck was part of it, don't kid yourself. She had the looks, but so did several thousand other, younger women, rolling into L.A. every year from Dipshit, Iowa. False modesty aside, it didn't take a rocket scientist to figure out that twenty-nine was pushing it. She worked to stay in shape, and she had done all right—so far, at least—but youth was everything unless you caught a break and graduated into brand-name status.

Supermodel Dana Withers.

It had crossed her mind, of course. She wasn't in the business for the fun of it, although she got her share of ego strokes along the way. While she wasn't a household name, it was a trip the way men fawned around her at the parties, talking nonsense. Hoping.

The generic thought of men brought Adam instantly to mind, as Dana made another turn, leaned forward, showing some dramatic cleavage to the camera.

"All right!" Chick told her. "That's the way."

Things had been strained at home, but they were getting better. Coming up on three weeks since the nut from Santa Rosa last called, and Dana was about to write him off. She had been worried early on, but that was fading. Every day without another call reminded her that kooks had short attention spans.

Some of them, anyway.

Another turn, the T-back showing off her buttocks, smooth and tan. She felt Chick watching her, his camera click-click-clicking. It was cool out, and her nipples spiked against the thin material of the bikini top. A touch-up with the airbrush would be needed, for the goose bumps on her arms. Preserving the illusion.

Dana was in love with Adam Reed, no doubt about it, but he sometimes tried her patience. The Nevada gig with Thomas Bender had been one thing, going in to watch another human being executed, even if the slimy SOB deserved it. Dana had agreed to tag along, support her man and all that good stuff, but she couldn't follow through. Halfway through getting dressed, she started shaking and it wouldn't stop until Reed put his arms around her, kissed her cheek and told her it was cool, she didn't have to go.

"This way, baby! Give it to me!"

Turning, back arched, never mind the nipples. Sex sold posters, magazines, bikinis, sports cars. Hell, it made the world go 'round.

No problem there, where Adam was concerned. They missed a beat or two while she was fuming over his involvement in the Santa Rosa case, but it was coming back. She had a hard time staying angry, even when he wounded her unconsciously. And reconciliation was a kick.

151

Last night, for instance, when he—

"Dana! Are you with me?"

"Right."

She pushed the sweaty images away and used the energy to find her mark, hair swept across one shoulder by the artificial breeze. Hips cocked, a sultry glance back toward the camera.

"That's it! Sell it, babe!"

They always had an audience on outdoor shoots. This afternoon, she counted twenty-five or thirty hangers-on. Most of them male, the aging beachboy type, though one had shown up in a double-breasted suit and several others could have passed for highway trolls. The three young women present stood together, off to Dana's left, and watched with vague expressions of disdain.

So much for sisterhood.

Her thoughts strayed back to Adam as she struck another pose. A part of what she loved about him was his earnest attitude, the way he threw himself into his work, but she could not help wishing he was interested in something *normal*. Let the psycho-killers slide—or make them fictional, like Hannibal the Cannibal. She didn't want the crazy bastards calling up, exchanging recipes.

"Okay, let's switch," Chick said. "We need the green suit, Dana. Sylvie, shake a leg, my darling."

Sylvie Summers ditched her robe and moved in from the sidelines. She was honey-blond and stunning in a sheer black maillot, turning an electric smile on Dana as they passed each other, touching close.

"I'm *freezing*," Sylvie whispered.

"Just pretend it's Honolulu."

"Right."

The dressing room was Chick's blue Chevy Astro van, with blacked-out windows in the back for privacy, a sliding drape behind the driver's seat. She locked the door behind her, making sure none of the sidewalk gawkers blundered in "by accident," and stripped off the bikini, tossed it in the box with several other suits.

It was a creepy feeling, being naked in the van, but you got used to it. She had a clear view of the shoot in progress, but the windows only worked one way. No one could see her, looking in. Not even with their faces pressed against the glass, which happened now and then.

At fashion shows, she knew from personal experience, the models had to change backstage, with total strangers—male and female—traipsing in and out. You either got used to it or you found another line of work.

The van was better, if a trifle cramped. She pictured Sylvie, grappling with the clingy maillot when she couldn't even stand erect, and Dana was relieved that Chick preferred her in bikinis.

Not that she would ever mention *that* to Adam.

He was jealous, in his way, although he tried to cover up. The snide remarks were part of it, the way he looked at Chick when they were thrown together in a social setting. Dana recognized the symptoms, and she took it as a compliment, still wishing that the two men in her life could get along.

Chick wanted her, of course. He wanted two-thirds of the females in Los Angeles, but Dana could not bring herself to think of him *that way*. He had a head for business, and he was the best photographer she knew, but if she really hit the big time, there would have to be some changes. She would need a manager with national—no, *inter*national—connections. Dana felt a pang of guilt, considering the two years she had worked with Chick, but that was life.

She found the green bikini, slipped it on, adjusting it to fit. A muffled rattling noise behind her startled Dana, made her turn to face the door. She had a glimpse of short, dark hair, broad shoulders in a leather jacket, moving rapidly beyond her line of sight. She almost whipped the curtain back, to track him through the windshield, but she hesitated, frightened.

Let it go.

She slipped a robe on, one of Chick's generic terry models, and went back to join the shoot. A glance around the smallish crowd of spectators revealed no leather jackets, no one who resembled the aggressive stranger.

He was gone. Forget it.

Dana could not shake the sense of being watched, but that

153

was only natural. She had been ogled by two dozen neighborhood voyeurs since they arrived and started setting up the shoot. A few of them were staring at her now, and she would have their full attention in a little while, when Sylvie finished up and traded places.

Get a grip, she told herself. A working model has to worry when the men *stop* looking.

She could mention the peculiar incident to Chick, but he would only shrug it off. L.A. was Psycho Central. Everybody knew it. Check the papers out or watch the nightly news if there was any doubt. Sometimes she wondered if the smog had anything to do with it, corroding brains along with lungs and larynxes. Or maybe it was just the laid-back Southern California lifestyle, drawing mentally disordered drifters from around the country and around the world.

No harm, no foul. Some creep had tried the door and gone away frustrated. Screw him.

"Dana, are you ready, babe?" Chick's smile looked plastic at the moment. Irritating.

"Ready."

"Beautiful. Let's get the two of you together in the water, shall we?"

She kept her robe on, told herself it was the January chill that made her tremble as they walked down toward the beach.

The rental was a Buick Skylark, silver, with maroon interior. It cost $165 a week, plus fifteen cents per mile beyond the first two hundred. Not the best deal in Los Angeles, perhaps, but Starr was satisfied. His Visa gold card in the name of "Robert Capshew" covered it, and he could either pay the bill when it arrived or let it slide, as he saw fit.

Identities were cheap and easy to establish when you knew the system. As for plastic, there had been a glut of credit cards in recent years. Most banks and many corporations issued Visa, MasterCard, and more, with competition slashing yearly dues. Starr kept at least a dozen cards on hand in different names, at any given time. Used some and blew the charges off, while others were allowed to gather dust and wait for personal emergencies.

He peered through the binoculars and found the green

bikini, while his free hand toyed with his erection through the fabric of his slacks.

Not yet.

When it was time, there would be no mistake. No witnesses.

He had been reckless, playing with her at the van, but there was no harm done. Something about the woman had excited him, compelled him to approach the vehicle, but he was in control now. Watching. Gathering intelligence.

When Howard Michael Starr made up his mind to visit Southern California, he had planned the outing like a military operation. Drive south in the Volvo, as a gesture of defiance, confident the pigs would not be looking for him in L.A. One suitcase held his clothes, the other his disguises, weapons, video equipment, documents for alternate identities. He found a small hotel in Glendale, west of Pasadena, where he registered as "Howard Michaels," using cash to pay for two weeks in advance. A fresh ID was needed for the Buick, since the rental agencies demanded credit cards, and fifteen minutes put him on the road with brand-new wheels. His Volvo occupied a small garage in Burbank, rented by the month.

L.A. was great, that way. So many suburbs crammed together, most of them with individual police departments, overrun with transients who ignored their neighbors as a matter of routine. There were so many human oddities at large on any given day, that no one gave a second glance to clean-cut strangers.

Howard Michaels wore his brown hair neatly trimmed, with sideburns. Robert Capshew's hair was likewise brown, although the photo on his California driver's license showed a longer style, with a goatee and wire-rimmed glasses. Contact lenses and a shave explained the change, if he was stopped by a patrolman on the street.

No problem.

It was simple, finding Adam Reed at home. A drive-by, first, confirming the address before he parked and took a stroll around the quiet neighborhood. The house was not constructed with security in mind. Reed's neighbors went about their business with a genial disinterest in their fellow man. With proper planning, Starr could slip in, do his job, slip out again. No clues for the police, and by the time reports got back to Santa Rosa, he would be examining a new set of mementos in his trophy room.

It seemed a shame to rush things, though. The whole point of revenge was to exact a price in pain and mental anguish. He was hoping for a chance to play with Adam first, before the kill. Prolong the game.

And then he saw the woman.

She was beautiful, the kind Starr would have chosen for himself in other circumstances. As it was, she met his needs precisely. It was early Friday morning when he glimpsed her for the first time, walking to her car. On impulse, he had followed her to Hollywood, a photographic studio. A cross-check in the yellow pages told him Charles Portelli was the man in charge. Starr waited half an hour, followed when the woman and a long-haired pretty boy drove to a shopping mall in Inglewood. Observed them as they went to work.

A model, living with a writer. They were self-absorbed, pathetic creatures, parasites who lived on adulation from the herd. Between them, they created nothing that would last, reflecting images of what society—the vague, amorphous cesspool of humanity—desired to see or read at any given time.

When Starr removed them, it would be a pleasure *and* a public service.

Friday afternoon, he trailed the woman back to Pasadena, glimpsing Adam for the first time when his target met her on the doorstep. Reed was average height, dark hair, his features unremarkable. He wore a sweatshirt over blue jeans. Casual. He kissed the woman lightly, and the door swung shut behind them, cutting off Starr's view.

That night, he followed them to dinner at a restaurant in L.A.'s Chinatown. They caught a movie afterward, then drove back home and went to bed. Starr sat outside, imagining their naked bodies tangled in the sheets, sweat-slick and heaving in the throes of passion.

And he wished them dead.

The weekend was a monumental waste of time, his targets holed up in the house except for short trips to the supermarket and a neighborhood convenience store. He could not watch them all the time, of course, but Starr had grown adept at physical surveillance in the past three years. He switched cars as the spirit moved him, changed disguises in the squalid rest room of a nearby service station.

Keeping track.

The woman went to work again on Monday, same photographer. They did not leave the studio this time, and Starr was moved to wonder if they had a guilty little secret, maybe fucking on the side. He finally discounted it, considering the pretty boy a cut below the woman's style . . . but you could never really say for sure.

God knew that bitches of her sort were treacherous enough.

By Wednesday afternoon, Starr felt he knew his targets well enough to start the game in earnest. It would not take long, once he began to move against them. Something simple for a start, to rattle Adam's cage. Enough to put him on his guard, believing that he had a chance to save himself.

The idiot.

A warning would increase Starr's risk, of course, but that was all a part of playing in the major leagues. The pigs would do their best to stop him, but they didn't have a prayer. Despite their numbers, it was still intelligence that counted, and they always came up short in that respect.

So be it.

Howard Michael Starr was smiling as he lowered the binoculars and gave a final stroke to his erection.

Let the games begin.

CHAPTER

15

The last thing Adam could recall, before the telephone began to ring, was David Letterman announcing stupid pet tricks on the tube. He must have dozed off during the commercial break and wound up losing half an hour, caught in muddled dreams. The high-pitched shrilling brought him out of it with no clear memories, a vague sense of frustration and uneasiness that he could not define.

Had there been blood and screaming in his dream? A glimpse of Thomas Bender crouched above a woman's naked body?

Adam struggled off the couch, his left foot tingling from a lack of circulation. He had slept with both legs propped up on the coffee table, ankles crossed, and now it felt like he had donned a slipper lined with needles. Dana must have gone to bed without him, damn it, and there would be hell to pay if Reed allowed the telephone to wake her.

Late-night calls were always trouble. No one called that late to simply say hello. Reed's pulse was hammering for no good reason as he crossed the living room to reach the telephone. Who's sick? Who died? He dreaded answering, was frightened not to.

Adam picked up on the fourth or fifth ring.

"Hello?"

No answer.

There was someone on the line. He felt it, like a brooding presence in the room. The lines got crossed from time to time, but this was different. Adam could not hear the caller breathing, but he would have bet the farm that he was not alone.

"Hello," he said again, allowing room for irritation this time.

Still no answer.

"Going once . . . twice . . . gone."

He dropped the handset in its cradle, muttering a curse. Some jerk who got off playing games, or maybe it was just a fumble-fingered moron who had trouble dialing telephones. Whatever, Adam would have loved to call him back and—

Standing in the middle of the living room, Reed froze.

The phone trap.

It was still connected, had been since the day McKeon dropped it off. Reed seldom thought about it now, except to check a number for the hell of it when phone calls caught him at his desk, but he could use it now.

A wicked grin crept over Adam's face. How often did you get a chance to turn the tables, on the little things? Somebody scrapes your new car in a parking lot and drives away without a second thought. Your neighbor plays the stereo too loud. A friend's ill-mannered brat runs through the house and topples everything in reach. A dog shits on your lawn, and you forget to look before you step down off the porch.

The little things.

He switched the television off, set the remote down on the coffee table. Turned lights off behind him as he navigated toward the bedroom. Stopping at his office on the way. Lights on, he moved directly to his desk and stooped to read the number showing on the phone trap.

It was local, more or less. The prefix—818—served Pasadena and at least two dozen other suburbs of Los Angeles, from Burbank to Glendora. Adam did not recognize the number, and he didn't care.

"My turn," he said to no one special, smiling as he spoke.

The only question in his mind was whether he should call immediately or relax awhile and give the bonehead time to fall asleep. Wake up the whole damned family, if he had one. It was nearly half-past midnight, Adam's eyes were grainy from his short nap on the sofa, and he did not feel like waiting.

Right.

His hand was on the telephone when it began to ring again. The sound wiped out his smile as Adam cut the first ring short.

"Hello?"

"You shouldn't have betrayed me, Adam."

Reed's heart stuttered, missed a beat. It wasn't just a euphemism, after all. He *felt* it, in his chest.

"Excuse me?"

Sturgess heaved a sigh of disappointment. "Don't play dumb," he said. "It doesn't suit you."

"Honestly." The word caught in his throat. "If you'd just tell me what you mean——"

"All right then, have it your way." Sturgess sounded almost bored. "You never should have gone to the police."

"I don't know——"

"Have you read Einstein, Adam?"

"What?"

"For every action, there's an equal, opposite reaction. Nature's law."

"Look, Mr. Sturgess——"

"That is not my name."

"What should I call you, then?"

"You needn't call me anything at all."

"Okay."

"But you must understand that every action has a consequence."

"Is that a threat?"

"Consider it a statement of eternal truth."

"I'm hanging up now."

"As you wish."

But Adam kept the handset pressed against his ear, imagining the stranger, trying hopelessly to match his voice with Roy McKeon's sketch.

"What makes you think I went to the police?" he asked.

"You're playing dumb again."

"So, tell me what you want."

"A reckoning. I always pay my debts."

"What's that supposed to mean?"

"Use your imagination, Adam."

And the line went dead.

Before he cradled the receiver, Adam had begun to curse himself for things he should have done. He had not taped the call, although the PhoneMate was within his reach. The bastard took him by surprise, and Reed could use some work on coping with emergencies. A brain glitch. He had blown it, plain and simple.

When it struck him for the second time in fifteen minutes, Adam blinked. The phone trap, Jesus! Even if the creep had used a pay phone, like the last time, there was something to be learned from his selection. Was he calling from a different part of town, each time, or did he like it close to home? This time, McKeon's people might have better luck with fingerprints. You never knew, unless—

Reed checked the phone trap, blinked again. The stupid thing was jammed, apparently. It still displayed the local number Adam was about to dial before . . . before . . .

Before the tricky bastard called him back.

A local prefix. Christ, the guy could be next door!

No, that was crazy. Get a grip. The 818 meant he was somewhere in the northern part of L.A. County, that was all. The closest public telephone was—what? Four blocks away? Reed saw it in his mind, outside the 7-Eleven where he sometimes purchased milk and magazines. If Sturgess drove directly from the store, observing posted limits, he could reach the house in five, six minutes, tops.

Blind panic.

Adam ran back to the darkened living room, avoiding furniture by feel, and stared out through a window facing on the street. He half expected to behold a prowler on his doorstep, maybe slinking up the walk. Was Sturgess fool enough to drive the Volvo he had used in Santa Rosa, with the stolen license plates?

Not likely.

Adam waited, ticking off the minutes in his mind, retreating from the window only long enough to satisfy himself the door was double-locked. He ought to check the back door and the windows, too, but it was hard to tear himself away. If Sturgess pulled up at the curb while he was scurrying around the back rooms, how would Reed defend himself?

A weapon!

There were no guns in the house, by mutual agreement, but he had a baseball bat, and there were always kitchen knives. The options seemed pathetic when he thought about them, but your average home invader had a disadvantage, coming through a window, if the occupant was ready with a bludgeon or a blade.

Unless the prowler had a gun, of course, in which case—
Call the cops!

Reed switched the nearest lamp on, grabbed the telephone, and scanned the short list of emergency numbers affixed to the handset. Skipping 911, he tapped out seven digits, waiting for the switchboard operator. She was female, sounded middle-aged.

"Police Department, may I help you?"

Adam kept his eyes fixed on the street outside as he replied.

"Detective Driscoll, please. In homicide."

Steve Driscoll liked to say that when the war in Vietnam shut down, it moved to Southern California. Not the tanks and planes and napalm, mind you: just the people. Thousands of them. A majority had gravitated toward Orange County, but there were enough to go around, and Pasadena got its share. The upscale immigrants, you might say— politicians, merchants, military officers—who managed to escape from Saigon with their fortunes more or less intact. And they were decent people, for the most part. Peaceful, law-abiding, quiet almost to a fault.

Driscoll knew, however, that some of them had fattened up their bank accounts back home by smuggling heroin, occasionally with cooperation from the U.S. Army and the CIA. When they were forced by circumstance to relocate, the smugglers brought their attitudes and their connections with them, setting up new pipelines to the States for China white. They did not purchase $750,000 homes with income from the grocery stores and service stations they took over on arrival in L.A., and anyone who thought they *did* was living in a fantasy.

Drug money is blood money—in Colombia, in Vietnam, in Pasadena. When you're moving powder at a price of forty, fifty thousand dollars for a *pound,* you have to deal with thieves and sharp competitors from time to time. In the narcotics trade, you deal with enemies by killing them—or, maybe *they* killed *you.* In either case, the homicide investigators caught some overtime, and that was how Steve Driscoll happened to be sitting at his desk at 12:15 A.M. on Thursday, January twenty-ninth.

The victims were Vietnamese and middle-aged, a man and wife. They had been hogtied in their home and murdered execution-style, one bullet in the head for each. The place was ransacked, with a wall safe jimmied open, and the boys in narco had a snitch who named the male decedent as a dealer moving heavy weight.

That information by itself told Driscoll a solution in the case was damned unlikely, but he had to go through all the motions, following the book. Examine crime scene photographs and autopsy reports, interrogate the neighbors, scan financial records that would almost certainly be doctored for the IRS. If a reporter asked him, Driscoll would inform the world that he was making steady progress.

And if they bought *that,* he could always steer them toward some nifty lakefront property in the Mojave desert.

He was studying a floor plan of the murder house and sipping tepid coffee when the phone rang. His extension. Driscoll let it ring again before he hoisted the receiver.

"Homicide."

"Detective Driscoll?" Male, an undertone of apprehension.

"In the flesh. Who's calling?"

"Adam Reed. We met the Tuesday after New Years. You brought Roy McKeon by my house, from Santa Rosa."

"I remember."

"It's about the Slasher," Reed informed him. "Or, the suspect, I should say."

"Specifically?"

"I got another call just now. He threatened me. I mean, he didn't *really*—"

"Mr. Reed, that's not our case." Cut through the crap before he started babbling. "Now, you can file an incident report on the harassing phone call, but you're better off relaying this to Santa Rosa, where—"

"He's not *in* Santa Rosa."

"Say again?"

"I got his number. You remember, from the phone trap?"

"Right." McKeon's half-baked scheme to find out where his man was calling from.

"And it's a local number: 818."

Steve Driscoll frowned. "You're sure about that?"

"Positive."

"You recognized his voice, from when he called before?"

"I did. He talked about some kind of reckoning, said I've betrayed his trust."

"How's that?"

"To the police."

It didn't take a rocket scientist to figure that one out. He had a memo somewhere on the first call Reed received from Santa Rosa. Someone must have fumbled on the follow-up and tipped their hand. It wasn't hard to do. A wrong word to the papers, anything at all. Now Reed was on the spot, and Driscoll had a brand-new problem on his hands.

"I'm sending a patrolman over. What's the address there, again?"

Reed told him, and he wrote it down.

"Hang on."

Line two, a word to the dispatcher, and the nearest black-and-white was rolling.

"Mr. Reed?"

"I'm here." And worried, by the sound of it.

"We've got a unit on the way right now. Sit tight, okay? I'll be there in a little while, but first I want to try and raise someone in Santa Rosa."

"Yes. All right."

"Why don't you let me have that number, while I've got you on the line."

"Oh, right. It's 818-323-1496."

"Okay, we'll check it out. I'll see you soon."

"Good-bye."

He called the operator first, identified himself, and had her trace the number. Waited, drumming fingers on his desk until she came back on the line. It was a public phone on Euclid Avenue. He recognized the address of an all-night restaurant.

Next up, he rolled a second unit to secure the phone booth, followed up with a forensics team. The odds against retrieving useful fingerprints or other evidence were astronomical, but they would try.

He saved the Santa Rosa call for last, 12:47 when he got through to the P.D. switchboard and explained his urgent need to speak with Sergeant Roy McKeon. They refused to give his number out, of course, but promised to relay the message, even if they had to wake the sergeant.

Driscoll smiled and cradled the receiver, waiting for his callback.

"I don't sleep," he told the pile of papers on his desk. "Nobody sleeps."

"You're sending me *away?* I don't *believe* this." Hurt and anger grappled for supremacy in Dana's voice.

"It's not like that."

"What is it, then? Explain it to me, will you, Adam?"

"Dana, please."

"Please *what?*"

She had him cold. He could not meet her gaze, and when he looked away, he found Steve Driscoll watching from the sidelines, following the terse exchange.

"It's for your own protection," Adam said at last. "A day or two, that's all."

"Who set the deadline?" she demanded. "Did your pen pal promise not to come and kill you after Saturday?"

She still looked sleepy, almost childlike. Touseled hair, the long skirt of a flannel nightgown showing underneath her robe, with fuzzy slippers on her feet. She wore no makeup, but the anger brought a flush of color to her cheeks.

"For safety's sake, okay?" Reed said. "It's probably a hoax, but—"

"Fine. If it's a hoax, I'm staying."

"But you never know," Steve Driscoll interjected.

"Chances are, this creep just wants to scare you, but he did take time to come down here from Santa Rosa, so precautions are in order."

"Oh, terrific." Dana turned her wrath on the detective. "What you're saying is, he may pop in here any second with a goddamn chainsaw."

"I've got uniforms outside."

"Which means we should be safe," said Dana.

"But I hate to scare him off."

She stared at Driscoll, flabbergasted. "Right. Now *that* would be a tragedy."

"We need to pick him up and settle this."

"So pick him up, for God's sake. Do your job."

"We're trying. If you'd—"

"Two police departments," Dana interrupted, turning back to Adam, "and they can't track down *one man*. They follow him around in Santa Rosa, and he gets away. You *trust* these people, Adam?"

"What choice do I have?"

"Come with me. We can take a few days off, go somewhere for the weekend." Glancing back toward Driscoll on the sofa. "Let your buddy house-sit, if he wants to."

Adam hesitated, wanting it, then shook his head. "I can't just leave."

"Why's that? You're throwing me out in the street."

"A day or two with Sylvie," Adam said. "It's not like you'll be sleeping in the park."

"And a man's gotta do what a man's gotta do, is that it?" She made no effort to disguise her scorn.

"Not quite."

"So, tell me, Adam? What's the deal?"

"I started this."

"Damn right. You brought it on yourself. On *both* of us."

"And now I have to see it through."

Her eyes were glistening with angry tears. "I told you once, they're using you for bait. Will you believe me, now?"

"I need this, Dana."

"What?" She blinked the tears away. "You *need* this?"

Adam met her eyes, this time refusing to be cowed.

"That's right."

"Oh, God. The story. Psychos *uber alles*. It's the fucking *story,* right?"

"For Christ's sake, Dana—"

"Never mind," she snapped. "I'm going. Satisfied? You got your wish."

She turned away and swept past Driscoll, moving toward the bedroom. Adam heard the door slam, pictured Dana dressing, tossing clothes into her suitcase. She was bound to cool off, given time to think about it. This would pass.

"McKeon's working on a flight," said Driscoll. "Probably be coming into LAX around eleven, give or take. I woke him up."

The homicide detective seemed inordinately proud of that achievement, smiling like the Cheshire cat.

"What did he say?" Reed asked.

A shrug. "Not much he could say. He's . . . concerned."

So, it's unanimous, thought Reed. His own initial panic had subsided, but he still felt nervous, angry at himself for bringing on the ugly scene with Dana. It was an embarrassment, Steve Driscoll watching while they argued, but he also recognized a blessing in disguise. Without a witness present, Dana would have pulled out all the stops and given free rein to her anger. As it was, she could unwind with Sylvie for a while and bad-mouth Adam to her heart's content.

Like therapy.

He thought of Sturgess. *"That is not my name."* Reed could not match the bland face in the artist's sketch to that malignant voice. Was he the Slasher or a psycho groupie with an attitude?

McKeon was "concerned," which could mean anything or nothing. They were dealing with an unknown quantity, three years of stacking bodies up without a solid suspect. After all that time, McKeon and his colleagues on the task force would be praying for a break, and Mr. X could wrap things up, if they got lucky.

On the other hand, if Sturgess *was* the Slasher, Adam had a fucking tiger by the tail. He had the story of his life.

The outrage he had seen in Dana's eyes came back to him like a slap across the face, but Reed was not about to flush his golden opportunity. She would forgive him when the creep was in a cage, and Adam showed her the advance check on his next hot property.

I Caught the Santa Rosa Slasher.

That was stretching it, but he would think of something while he fleshed out the proposal. Picture Roland poring over clippings from the L.A. *Times* and *USA Today.* Heroic writer aids in capture of elusive homicidal maniac.

The sound of Dana's voice inside his head. *I told you once, they're using you for bait. Will you believe me, now?*

Two could play that game. If Adam served as bait, the cops would definitely owe him one, and there was no way anyone could scoop him on this story. Reed would *be* the goddamned story, or a major part of it at least.

"You have a plan?" he asked the homicide detective.

Driscoll thought about it for a moment, then replied, "Let's find out what McKeon has to say."

"That's it?"

"Assume he's watching you," said Driscoll. "There's nobody on the street right now that we can see, but let's imagine."

"Right."

"He has to figure that you'd call the cops, first thing."

"I did."

"Correct, and here we are. We look around, see nothing. Cops are busy guys, you know? We take some notes and drink your coffee, then we split."

"So, *that's* the plan?"

"The plan is that he *thinks* we're gone, because he sees us leaving. But we're not *all* gone."

"Who stays?" asked Reed.

"For now, one of the uniforms. A two-man car goes home a little light."

"And Sturgess doesn't notice that?" The name persisting, even now. He had to call the bastard *something.*

"If he's here at all, he's playing hide-and-seek. I seriously doubt he's got a head count. Anyway, it's all we've got until McKeon gets here."

"You could let me have a gun."

"We don't loan weapons to the public, Mr. Reed. The chief is very strict on that. Go figure."

Dana came back from the bedroom, wearing jeans and

168

boots, a turtleneck and fleece-lined jacket. She was carrying her purse, a suitcase, and a smaller bag, presumably for makeup. Adam thought she looked like she was going off to summer camp . . . or possibly to war.

"I'm leaving now." The obvious.

"If you want me to," said Driscoll. "I can have one of my people drop you off."

"No, thank you." Then, to Adam: "You have Sylvie's number?"

"Yes. Am I allowed to use it?"

Softening, but barely. "If you must," she said. "I have a passing interest, here."

"That's good to know."

She did not kiss him, would not let him help her with her bags. Reed thought the door clicked shut behind her with a note of terrible finality.

What would he do if she decided this was too much and she couldn't take it anymore? It was a strain for him to picture life without her and he did not care to try.

"That's it, then," Driscoll said. "Let's get a uniform in here to baby-sit, and I'll be back to see you when McKeon lands."

"No gun?"

"The officer will have one."

"Right."

Reed checked his watch and saw that it was nearly 2:00 A.M. Sleep was the last thing on his mind. If any of his neighbors were awake, they must be curious about the squad cars parked out front. The local rumor mill would probably be working overtime by breakfast.

No such thing as bad publicity, his agent liked to say.

Unless you wound up as a homicide statistic on the nightly news.

But it would never go that far. If Sturgess showed his face, the cops would scoop him up and slap him in a holding cell. Regardless of his link to any unsolved murders, he would be exposed.

And Reed would have a ringside seat.

Despite the nagging sense of apprehension, part of him looked forward to the show.

CHAPTER
16

——•——

The domestic terminal at L.A. International was a chaotic mess, as usual. Bewildered-looking travelers, including many new additions to the ethnic melting pot, roamed aimlessly around the concourse, singly and in packs. From time to time, they stopped and stared at empty space, while unattended children shrieked and ricocheted around their legs. Gang bangers had their colors on display. Three skinheads stood outside a coffee shop, all dressed in black, practicing sneering at the crowd. A scattering of Hare Krishnas worked the crowd for pocket change, some of them trailed by spit-and-polish Jesus freaks with pamphlets in their hands and strident imprecations on their lips. A fair percentage of the people Roy McKeon saw had seemingly turned out to browse among the airport shops, with no real thought of getting on a plane.

He was reminded of the alien saloon in *Star Wars,* and it struck him that a well-placed neutron bomb would do the state a world of good.

McKeon had been nursing antisocial thoughts since 1:00 A.M. when the dispatcher's call had routed him from bed. Steve Driscoll on the line, from Pasadena. "Michael Sturgess" in the Southland, phoning threats to Adam Reed.

McKeon couldn't do a thing about it at that moment, but the call had ruined any chance of sleep. He made arrangements for a morning flight, called Driscoll back to let him know. Was he imagining the smirk in Driscoll's voice?

He was used to losing sleep; insomnia was in the job description. Right now, what concerned him was a nameless murder suspect who had flown or driven some 450 miles away from home.

If all the bastard had in mind were threats and breather calls, he could have handled it from Santa Rosa. The expense of traveling eclipsed whatever money he would save on phone calls. And, since cost was not a factor in the move, it told McKeon he was seeking access to the object of his wrath.

The whole betrayal thing disturbed McKeon, telling him his men had blown it, somehow. They had tipped their hand to Sturgess on the Sunday afternoon they traced his phone call and descended on the booth. No doubt about it in the suspect's mind from that point on: Reed had to be working with the cops.

Take it as an article of faith that Sturgess knew Reed burned him. Why had he waited nearly three weeks to begin his quest for sweet revenge?

If Sturgess was the Slasher, he would take it all the way without a second thought. Their psycho had not killed a man before—McKeon didn't *think* so, anyway—but this was special. An affair of honor, like some kind of fucking duel. Conversely, if their subject was a simple crank, albeit one who got pissed off when people schemed against him, then he might stop short of violence. Either way, McKeon wanted him.

He had a need to sit across from Sturgess in a drab interrogation room that smelled of sweat and fear and cigarettes. It didn't even matter if the bastard called a lawyer and refused to talk. McKeon wanted him to know the fucking jig was up. No matter where he went or what he did, until they made the case or verified an airtight alibi for each and every Slasher crime, detectives would be following his every move around the clock.

They would have enough to justify a warrant, but if a

judge thought otherwise, he was prepared to wait. Let Sturgess go about his business with a constant shadow on his ass. If Sturgess moved away, pursue him and enlist new agencies to keep the heat on. If he cracked and killed himself, declare an early Christmas. Either way, at least surveillance would reduce the risk of future homicides.

There had been a case in San Francisco some years back wherein a brutal psychopath was knifing homosexuals. He picked them up in leather bars, drew little sketches of his victims as a come-on, prompting someone in the media to christen him the Doodler. As it happened, several of his targets managed to survive their wounds, but they refused to jeopardize their reputations and careers by coming out with public testimony. Homicide investigators knew their man on that one, but they couldn't make a case without eyewitnesses. The Doodler was alive and well, as far as Roy McKeon knew, a brand-new generation of detectives watching every move he made and praying for a relapse . . . or a heart attack.

If that was what it took to nail the Slasher down, McKeon was prepared to spend his golden years on sentry duty. Train some rookies coming up from the academy to keep the ball in play.

Or, maybe there would be a tragic accident.

He spotted Driscoll up ahead, and it was good to see the pouchy bags beneath his eyes. They didn't bother shaking hands this time.

"That's it for luggage?" Driscoll nodded toward McKeon's smallish carryon.

"I travel light."

"Looks like. Let's hit it, then."

They made fair time, all things considered, jostling through the airport crowd. No conversation till they hit the sidewalk. Driscoll's unmarked car was waiting in the red zone, where a disembodied voice warned motorists that unattended vehicles were subject to immediate removal.

Driscoll concentrated on the traffic, pulling out, and saved his breath until they made the interchange and hit Sepulveda. Before he spoke, McKeon felt the young detective's anger simmering.

172

"I don't mind telling you, I'm taking heat on this," he said at last. "Your guy's supposed to be up north."

"You think I *knew* he'd run a play like this?"

"Anticipation's half the game, the way I figure. You've been studying this prick for what? Three years?"

"First thing," McKeon said, "we don't know that he *is* our guy. A phone call's one thing, killing thirty women is another story."

"Thirty-one," said Driscoll. "We get CNN down here, you know."

"And secondly," McKeon said, ignoring him, "there's no way to anticipate a change of scene when we don't even know the fucker's name, all right?"

"From what I understand, you missed him twice."

"The phone booth doesn't count, for Christ's sake. By the time my people got the word and traced the number through an operator, he had all the lead time anybody needs."

"It doesn't sound like he was running," Driscoll said. "Fact is, he's pissed off at your boy for playing ball. Unless you've got a leak up there, I'd say the guy was watching when you hit the phone booth."

"Maybe so." Reluctantly.

"And now, I've got your mess in my backyard. It may surprise you, but my chief's not thrilled about the prospect of the Slasher moving south. We've got enough freaks as it is, okay? They breed 'em in Los Angeles, for export to the suburbs. Now, if your boy starts to play his game down here, it's my ass on the line for putting out the welcome mat."

"I'll take responsibility," McKeon said.

"In Santa Rosa, maybe, but it won't help me. Shit rolls downhill, my friend, and there's enough to go around, if we don't wrap this mother up."

"Let's bag him, then."

"You have a plan?" asked Driscoll.

Roy McKeon frowned. "I'm working on it as we speak."

The target house was in Los Feliz, on a winding street that bordered Griffith Park. Starr had less trouble with surveillance there, than in the quiet Pasadena neighborhood where Adam Reed had put down roots. Topography prevented

173

houses stacking up on top of one another, and the crazy layout of the streets enabled him to scout the area without becoming too conspicuous.

No pigs, so far. They did not seem to care about the woman, concentrating on the Pasadena house, as Starr had hoped. Reed's bitch, meanwhile, apparently believed that she was safe.

Starr held the sweet advantage of surprise.

It would be pleasant, taking out the woman first. Let Reed experience the pain of loss before he faced his private reckoning. A simple bullet in the head or blade between the ribs would be too merciful for one who had betrayed the hunter.

Never mind that Starr was reckless in the first place, trusting Reed to correspond without involving the police. Great men took chances, and they did not always triumph in the short run. It was how you compensated for the setbacks, turned your bad luck upside down, that mattered in the end.

There was no question of allowing Reed to skate on his betrayal. Starr had no truck with forgiveness. He dismissed the concept as a sop for weaklings who were physically or mentally incapable of meting out revenge.

A real man paid his debts in blood.

Starr thought about his mother while he sat outside a drive-in on Vermont and sipped black coffee from a paper cup. It was a short trip back, the time machine of memory transporting him across the years before he had a chance to sip and swallow.

Bridget had been banished from the house when he was twelve years old. A fluke brought Mother home from a dinner date ahead of schedule to find them in the shower, taking turns with soap and sponge. His mind recalled the screaming row with crystal clarity. A tearful Bridget, driven out with barely time to pack her things, no taxi waiting as she started down the driveway with a suitcase in each hand, her shoulders bowed in shame. Starr's mother coming at him with the belt, bright crimson speckling the sheets before she finished.

She was doomed from that day forward, but it took nine years for Howard Michael Starr to execute his plan. He studied every facet of the problem, knowing he would be

174

packed off to relatives or foster care if Mother died while he was still a minor. Even when the voting age was cut to eighteen years, the state of California, in its wisdom, still decreed that legal adults—capable of buying guns and liquor, signing business contracts—must be twenty-one.

Starr waited.

High school entertained him, in a morbid kind of way. His grades and trust fund paved the way to Stanford University, where business courses taught him all he had to know about long-term investments, managing his father's money when the time was ripe. The draft was not a problem after Nixon, but he missed the prime-time bulletins from Vietnam. It had been pleasant, watching soldiers and civilians blown to pieces in his living room.

He stayed away from women, fearing ridicule and rejection when his wig came off. Starr didn't need them, anyway. He had his own imagination, solitary pleasure with the stray cats from the neighborhood. He started hunting as a pastime, taught himself to be an expert marksman, but a quick, clean kill left much to be desired. Starr liked to take his time.

And there were always Mother's little games.

She staged their scenes less frequently as he grew older, but the play grew more elaborate. Refinements might include Starr hiding in her closet—once beneath the bed itself—and he was always in the nude. She never sought him out until her playmate had departed, but Starr caught her looking at him while they rutted, watching *him* watch *her*. Instinctively, he knew that she could only climax with an audience. Her son, the house voyeur.

When Mother came to punish him for watching, she expected him to grovel and confess his vile, disgusting sins. Had he been *jerking off* while he was spying on her? Don't dare lie to me, you filthy little wretch. I want to *see* what you were doing, while you watched.

And Starr would show her. Gladly.

Mother whipped him while he knelt and masturbated in the bathroom, reeling from the heady rush of pleasure-pain. Sometimes, when he had trouble, she would slap his hand away, replace it with her own. Her free hand slashing with the belt.

Increasingly, she drank. A preference for Stoli on the rocks. The days and nights became an alcoholic blur for Lucy Kendrick, but her son remembered everything. He laid his plans in private, worked the details out on paper. Shredded notes and flushed them down the toilet when he had committed every step to memory.

Starr's mother kept a .38 revolver in the nightstand. She had never fired it, but it gave her peace of mind. The day Starr lifted it and hid it in his bedroom, Lucy didn't notice.

Two nights later, in the first week of September, it was playtime. Starr was one month past his birthday, anxious to be rid of her, but he had waited for the perfect player to complete their threesome. On this Friday night, the chosen beneficiary of Lucy's sexual largesse resembled something from a county road gang: coarse, unkempt, with the vocabulary of a semiliterate Hell's Angel.

Starr was waiting in the walk-in closet when they went to bed, dressed only in a pair of rubber kitchen gloves, armed with his mother's .38. He watched them for a quarter of an hour, waiting for the moment when his mother got on top, her back turned toward the closet.

Perfect.

Creeping up behind her with the .38 extended in his right hand, reaching past her, aiming at the sweaty, stubbled face. Starr's first shot drilled the stranger's upper lip and dyed the pillow crimson underneath. The second round gratuitous, perhaps, but he was making sure.

His mother screamed—no one to hear her, in the rambling house—and vaulted backward off the bed. Her lover's cock slid free and spurted on the sheets, a parting shot.

Coitus interruptus.

Starr was on her in a rush, before she had a chance to bolt. He punched her in the face repeatedly, his knuckles burning through the rubber glove, until she crumpled at his feet, her face a bloody mask. It was a short trip to the bathroom, dragging her behind him, careful not to stain the carpet with a pattern that would show. She didn't weigh much, even then, and it was simple to deposit her on the commode, lid down.

Starr longed to fuck her, but he knew enough about

forensics to resist the urge. Instead, he put the shiny .38 revolver in her hand and placed the muzzle in her mouth before he pulled the trigger. Spattering the tile with nasty dreams.

The cleanup was perfunctory: a check for drag marks on the bedroom carpet, rinsing off the rubber gloves and drying them before he tucked them in their proper place below the kitchen sink. A hasty shower, dressing in the same clothes he had worn all day, before he walked back to his mother's bedroom. Standing in the open doorway, Starr had jammed a finger down his throat, spewed vomit on the floor, his shoes and cuffs. Made sure to run, instead of walking, when he went to call the pigs.

The sudden case of nerves he suffered, when detectives came to call, worked out to Starr's advantage. They mistook anxiety for grief and kept the questions to a minimum. His mother had a reputation in the local bars, and no one seemed especially surprised by her untimely death. Police informed the press that she had been assaulted by a man of short acquaintance, shot him dead—perhaps in self-defense—and took her own life in a fit of panic, fueled by too much alcohol.

Case closed.

It was the first and last time Howard Michael Starr had used a firearm to dispatch a human being. He preferred the hands-on method, a protracted kill, but the elimination of his mother had been partly business, and demanded explanation.

All things come to those who wait.

And he was waiting now, for sundown. Darkness would provide the cover he required, and once Starr satisfied himself that no policemen had been sent to guard the woman, he would make his move.

Step one, of his revenge on Adam Reed.

Betrayal had its price, and Howard Michael Starr was eager to collect.

"There's been no further contact with the subject since you called Detective Driscoll?"

Adam took a sip of Classic Coke and shook his head. They

177

sat around the table in his dining room, McKeon opposite, with Driscoll on his left, both clutching coffee mugs. A young patrolman in plain clothes was staked out on the sofa, watching television.

"Nothing yet."

"You're sure it was the same guy calling?" asked McKeon.

"Absolutely. Even if I hadn't recognized his voice, he knew about my link to Sturgess—and the fact I've been in touch with you."

Steve Driscoll frowned and stared into his cup, as if expecting to discover a solution there. McKeon rocked back in his chair and stared off into space for several moments.

"And he definitely threatened you," the man from Santa Rosa said at last. It did not come out sounding like a question.

"He accused me of betraying him and said I never should have gone to the police. He said he always pays his debts, and now there has to be a reckoning. I took that as a threat."

"Okay. You're covered here, I guess."

McKeon spoke to Reed, but turned his face toward Driscoll, waiting for the Pasadena officer's response.

"We're cool," said Driscoll, "for another day or so, at least. I can't leave men on duty here indefinitely."

"If he's coming," said McKeon, "I don't see him waiting long. The prick's away from home, remember. That's disruption of routine, no matter how you slice it. Has to cost him something, staying in L.A. Too many witnesses and questions if he stayed with friends or relatives."

"That's pretty much what I thought," Driscoll said.

"So, this is Thursday," said McKeon. "If he hasn't moved by Sunday night, I figure we can breathe a little easier."

"Hang on," Reed interjected. "I'm supposed to put my life on hold till *Sunday?*"

"Had you planned on going somewhere?" Driscoll asked.

"Well, no . . ."

"That's perfect, then," McKeon said.

"I mean to say, I wasn't leaving town," Reed told them. "No one said I had to spend four days shut up inside the house."

McKeon shrugged. "I don't have any problem with you

going out," he said. "From what I've seen, you don't have any decent sniper nests around the neighborhood."

"We had a look around," said Driscoll. "Nothing vacant in a three-block radius. He'd have to stand in someone's yard or pull a drive-by."

"Adam, I can't tell you how to live," McKeon said. "You were concerned enough to send your lady off with friends, and I think you should watch out for yourself. We'd like to bag this guy, all right?"

"And I'm the bait."

He pictured Dana sticking out her tongue. *I told you so.*

"In essence, that's correct. I wish it wasn't," said McKeon, "but we work with what we've got."

"If I go out?"

"We'll have a man go with you," Driscoll said. "Of course, that tells our subject that you're covered. If he's half as smart as everybody seems to think, he splits and tries another day."

"That's if he's watching me," said Reed.

"And if he's not," McKeon said, "then chances are the threat was just hot air. We're wasting everybody's time."

"But you don't think so," Adam said.

"I don't know what to think right now. At least we've got a shot at taking him this way. Don't ask me what the odds are on a deal like this. I couldn't tell you. But I have to think we've got a better chance to wrap him up if he comes hunting you, than if *we* have to look for *him.*"

They had already proven that twice, Reed thought, but kept it to himself. "Okay," he said, reluctantly, "but Sunday has to be the end of it. I won't live under siege."

"Suits me," said Driscoll. "If he hasn't showed by then, I'll have to pull my people, anyway."

"You're going back this afternoon?" Reed asked McKeon.

The detective shook his head. "I took a couple sick days I had coming," he told Adam. "Thought I'd make a weekend of it, just in case. If one of you can point me to a cheap motel—"

"Stay here," Reed said, on impulse. "I mean, that eliminates the hassle with patrolmen, right?"

Steve Driscoll thought about it, frowning. He was clearly

glad to be relieved of watchdog duty, but it ran against the grain for him to leave a stranger on the job within his jurisdiction.

"I can sell it," Driscoll said at last, "if you agree to stay in touch and keep me posted."

"Fair enough," McKeon said.

"Okay, I'm taking this one with me." Driscoll cocked a thumb in the direction of the living room. "We'll keep a squad car in the neighborhood, but nothing obvious. You need somebody in a hurry, give a shout."

"Will do," said Roy McKeon, pushing back his chair.

They headed for the door together. On the tube, Geraldo had a group of pissed-off feminists explaining why they hated men. Reed thought of Dana, dreading her reaction when he told her she could not come home till Monday. Jesus, would she even *want* to come, by then?

The young patrolman brought McKeon's bag in from the car, and Driscoll shook hands all around, as if he were departing on a trip around the world and didn't know when they would meet again.

"Stay frosty," he advised McKeon, leaving Adam with a silent nod.

"Alone at last," McKeon said, when Reed had shut the door. "You have a guest room here, or what?"

"The couch folds out," Reed told him.

"Great."

McKeon set his bag down on the coffee table, opened it, and took an automatic pistol from underneath a folded shirt. Reed watched him pull the magazine, confirming it was fully loaded.

"Well," McKeon said, "I guess that's everything. You need to work, go right ahead. Don't let me cramp your style."

Reed left him on the sofa poring over *TV Guide*.

He had a call to make, and he was dreading it with all his heart.

CHAPTER
17

---•---

It was approaching midnight when the hunter made his move. The second pass within a quarter hour, coming from the opposite direction this time. Nothing to concern the neighbors if they cared enough to glance outside as he cruised past.

The lights went out at Bimbo Central.

It was time to strike.

There was a house for sale a hundred yards beyond his target, another darkened home between the two. Starr parked his Buick in the driveway, pulled the realtor's sign out of the ground, and tossed it underneath a hedge of prickly juniper. The neighbors wouldn't notice until morning, if at all, and the precaution minimized his risk of a patrolman getting curious about the Buick parked outside a vacant dwelling.

Starr was dressed in black from head to foot: black turtleneck, black jeans, black running shoes, black socks. The long knife hidden underneath the Skylark driver's seat was also black, likewise the sheath Starr fastened to his belt.

He had debated various disguises, finally deciding to forgo the wig and facial hair. Instead, he wore a lightweight ski mask, rolled up like a watch cap on his head. A pair of sâp gloves rested on the seat beside him, jet-black leather, pockets on the palms and knuckles filled with powdered lead.

He left the car unlocked, the key in the ignition. There was nothing in Starr's pockets to identify him, nothing that would make a sound as he crept through the darkness. Only critical equipment. Rolling down the ski mask, tugging on the gloves, he felt himself transformed.

He had become a creature of the night.

His first real obstacle would be the house next door, all dark and silent now. Was anyone at home? Starr didn't know or care. He had to find a way around or through the property without arousing any occupants. His choice was simple: either walk along the street and risk encounters with a passing motorist, perhaps a squad car, or negotiate the intervening yard.

The yard seemed safer, but he had to check it out. Starr walked around behind the vacant house, no padlock on the gate to stop him, and proceeded to the eastern border of the property. A sturdy redwood fence divided one lot from the next. There was no response as Starr climbed halfway up, surveyed the silent yard beyond, and whistled softly toward the sleeping house.

Again.

Five minutes satisfied him that there was no dog in residence. He scaled the fence and landed in a crouch on grass that could have used a mowing. *Better Homes and Gardens* would be passing this one by.

And so would Howard Michael Starr.

Perhaps the tenants shifted in their sleep, aware of Death's proximity. Starr watched the house, alert for any sign of movement at the windows, gliding like a sentient shadow through a corner of their lives. He would have paused to kill them if he had the time, but there was more important work afoot. Starr hoped tomorrow's headlines would destroy their false sense of security.

Another redwood fence, apparently the standard of the neighborhood. He paused and tried another whistle, smiling through his ski mask when the night ignored him. No dogs here.

Just pussy.

Death be nimble, scrambling atop the fence and dropping

182

to the other side. The bitches kept their lawn cut short, unlike the neighbors. Starr imagined how the blonde must flaunt her body for the wetback gardeners. Her roommate, too. Or were they lesbians?

It made no difference. Any cunt could fool the average man with a facade of passion, lead him by his swollen prick into the most ridiculous of situations. Howard Michael Starr would gut a dyke as swiftly as a breeder, but his interest in the occupants of record was peripheral. They were potential witnesses and obstacles, a challenge, but his target was their houseguest: Adam's bitch.

Starr counted off two minutes—*one-one thousand, two-one thousand*—making certain his arrival had gone unobserved. When he was satisfied, he drew his hunting knife and scuttled toward the house.

Sleep wouldn't come, no matter how she tried to clear her thoughts and concentrate on absolutely nothing. Just when she was close, her eyelids drooping, Adam's face would pop up on the blank screen of her mind.

And close behind him stood The Stranger.

Missing home was part of it, she knew. Except for the occasional reluctant visit to her parents in Wisconsin, Dana had not slept apart from Adam for the past three years. They had not done the altar trip because it seemed superfluous. They were agreed that if and when they wanted rug rats, there was ample time to tie the knot.

Now, this.

It was not being sent away that galled her most. She recognized the move for what it was: a caring gesture, Adam trying to protect her. At the same time, Dana knew she wouldn't *need* protection if he had not gone ahead with this insanity in Santa Rosa.

Trying to provoke a psychopath, for Christ's sake, while the cops stood back and waited on the sidelines, offering suggestions, safe behind their guns and badges. Killing time until the freak showed up in Pasadena, phoning Adam, threatening his life.

"You ought to sue the bastards," Sylvie had suggested over Chinese takeout.

"Right."

183

"You think I'm kidding? It's against the law for cops to use civilians on a criminal investigation. You could nail them big-time, Dana."

"Adam volunteered, remember? Anyway, they didn't make a deal with me."

"Same thing. You're on the street because of what they did. It's negligence or something."

"When did you check into law school, Sylvie?"

"Cute. You know I used to date that sergeant from the Wilshire station."

"I remember him," said Monica. An impish smile played at the corners of her mouth. "Armando, with the womb broom."

Sylvie rolled her eyes. "It was Emelio, if you don't mind. There's something to be said for a mustache."

"I'll bet it tickles."

"Tickling's good. Don't knock it till you've tried it."

They dissolved in laughter then, with even Dana joining in. It was a welcome change from brooding, even if she was faking it.

Monica and Sylvie were her two best friends on earth, aside from Adam, and a man was always . . . different. She could tell her girlfriends things that Adam would not understand, complain about the little things he did that drove her crazy, now and then.

Like sisters.

Dana frequently worked with Sylvie Summers on fashion shoots. Her roomie, Monica Glover, was a sometime actress with a few commercials to her credit, waiting for The Break. Red hair and freckles, with a traffic-stopping figure. All they needed was a black woman, Adam liked to say, and they would have a rainbow. Something for everyone.

Dana rolled over, punching her pillow and striving for comfort, coming up short. She had been cool when Adam called at half-past nine, regretting it the moment he hung up. They took a vote on whether she should call him back. It was two-to-one against, with Monica in favor.

"Let him sweat," said Sylvie. "It'll do him good."

But in the meantime, Dana pictured Adam sitting in their house—were there policemen with him?—waiting for a man he didn't even know to carry out his threat.

It pissed her off again, remembering how they had argued over Adam's work with the police in Santa Rosa. Dana understood the urge. He had been seeing dollar signs, but there was more to it than that. A writer's work was for the most part solitary, even when he had a good relationship to back it up. The isolation crept inside, where it could fester if you let it. It was easy to get caught up in a story, shift from observation to participation, never mind the risk. It felt like *living,* for a change.

But it could get you killed.

The other books had all been safe. Two novels and the real-life story of a killer who was safely dead and buried. Dana didn't care for all the morbid details, but she let it go, content with Adam's satisfaction in his work. This time, however, he had crossed a line, inviting danger to his very doorstep.

This time, he could be in trouble. *Both* of them could be in trouble.

Dana gave it up and snapped the bedside lamp on. If she couldn't sleep, she might as well sit up and read. The choices ran to fashion magazines and romance novels. Dana passed on Jackie Collins, reaching for a month-old *Cosmopolitan* with Cindy Crawford on the cover.

Watch out, babe, she thought. I'm gaining on you.

And suddenly—or not so suddenly—she had the urge to speak with Adam. Wake him up, if necessary. Christ, she hated fighting with him. Maybe, if they each made some conciliatory noises, she could get some rest.

The guest room had a telephone, and Dana picked it up. Tapped Adam's number out and waited.

Nothing.

Try again.

This time, she listened for the dial tone, first, and felt the bare hint of an icy ripple down her spine.

The telephone was dead.

Starr's weapon was an engineering masterpiece. The eight-inch fluted blade was forged steel with a black oxide finish and serrated teeth along the spine. The hollow handle was aluminum, matte black and grooved for a secure grip if he struck bone on a thrust. The dark blade's razor edge was suitable for shaving or for surgery, depending on the user's frame of mind.

He stood in shadow, studying the house, and tracked the phone line to its point of contact on the northern wall. No trick for him to slip his blade between the insulated wire and stucco, ripping outward with the saw teeth.

Snip.

He slid the knife back in its sheath and edged around the corner, stopping when he stood outside the kitchen door. It had a dead bolt, but the top half of the door was glass, a quirk that sacrificed security to fashion.

Starr had come prepared. Gloved hands removed a rubber suction cup and its attachment from a pocket of his jeans. Saliva was a last resort, and four steps brought him to a garden hose, coiled loosely near the steps, one end still threaded to a spigot on the wall. Starr held the free end like a flaccid penis, shook it lightly. Two fat drops of water fell into the upturned suction cup.

Enough.

He smeared the moisture with a leather fingertip, affixed the sucker to the backdoor windowpane. A three-inch piece of twine was fastened to the backside of the suction cup, a small glass cutter knotted on the other end. Starr chose his spot precisely, paused a moment, listening, and went to work.

The cutter made a high-pitched rasping sound, but Starr did not allow himself to hesitate. He stood a better chance of waking those inside the house with several halting strokes than one decisive twist. It took a fair amount of strength to cut the glass on one swift pass, but Starr was equal to the challenge.

Done, he tapped around the cut to free it and removed a disk six inches in diameter. He held it in his left hand, crouched, and snaked his right arm through the opening. Released the dead bolt. Turned the knob and let himself into the silent house.

Starr did not close the door behind him. Always leave a ready exit hatch on home invasions, just in case the master plan went awry. No fumbling with a doorknob if he had to flee in haste.

He disengaged the rubber suction cup, returned the

makeshift apparatus to his pocket. Left the glass disk on a counter by the stove. A little keepsake for the pigs to play with. Send it to the lab, for all the good that it would do.

Starr spent a moment savoring aromas in the kitchen. Chinese food, but no utensils in the sink or on the stove. He tried a cabinet below the sink and spotted paper cartons in the trash. The lazy bitches ordered out. He doubted that there was a decent cook among them, always using men to pay their way at high-toned restaurants.

He opened the refrigerator on an impulse, bathed in light while he stood counting bottles, cartons, jars. A head of lettuce and some carrots in the crisper. Juice and dairy products racked on shelves inside the door.

The cupboards, next. He studied flatware, cups and glasses, canned goods, cereal in boxes, party crackers sealed in Tupperware. All useless to the bitches now.

Starr paused, adjusting garments to accommodate the swell of his erection. Standing in a stranger's house like this excited him, a bit of foreplay to the main event. Instead of opening his fly to masturbate, he drew his knife—the next best thing—and left the kitchen. Hesitated, with the living room immediately on his right. Turned left and started toward the bedrooms.

He could smell them now, all warm and cozy in their beds. Death coming for them and the stupid bitches didn't even know it.

It would be a pleasure waking them, Starr thought, and introducing them to nightmares in the flesh.

The clock beside his bed showed 12:16 A.M. when Adam gave up staring at the ceiling fixture, wishing he could fall asleep. The queen-size bed felt cold and empty, even when he shifted to the middle—neutral ground—and tried to make believe that everything was normal.

Less than three hours since he had spoken to Dana, and the tone of their conversation haunted him. She had been distant, while Reed felt awkward, groping for his words and making small talk like an adolescent schoolboy. They had skirted any meaningful discussion of the problem, stuck to generalities. The sign-off had been worst of all.

"I'll see you later, then."

"Okay. Good night."

Reed told himself that he should call her back, despite the hour, and apologize for everything. The whole damned mess was his fault, anyway. He couldn't change the situation now, but past experience had taught him that a little groveling could save a world of heartache later on.

And she was definitely worth it.

He was sitting up in bed, with both feet on the carpet, when he thought about the time again. If they had gone to bed, a call meant waking everyone. Chances were he would have to go through Monica or Sylvie, piss them off before he even got to speak with Dana. Get off on the wrong foot when he started fumbling for words.

On second thought, perhaps he ought to wait for morning. Breakfast time. Catch Dana with her mouth full, maybe dressing for the day. Distracted. He could take her by surprise and spill his guts, claim full responsibility and beg forgiveness. Reed was fairly certain she would buy it.

But he could not bring her home. Not yet.

McKeon had affirmed his first reaction to the threat from Mr. X. It might be nothing, but the risks were multiplied with Dana in the house. Her presence gave their man another target and divided Reed's attention. It was safer, all around, if she remained with Monica and Sylvie through the weekend.

Christ, but Adam missed her.

It was sobering, this sense of virtual dependence on another person for your happiness. In some respects, it troubled him, subverting his self-image as a "real man" who could look out for himself, confront the daily obstacles and challenges alone. Still, there was something to be said for sharing. When he looked at Dana, when he touched her—

What he *didn't* need right now was an erotic fantasy to make things worse. The fact of Dana's absence—and her anger—was enough to spoil his sleep, without imagining the way her round breasts filled his hands, the way she tasted when he—

Call her.

He reached out for the lamp, then pulled his hand back. Darkness fit his mood, and turning on the lights would be the ultimate concession to insomnia. It wasn't like he had to punch a time clock in the morning, after all. The best part of a writer's life, Reed sometimes thought, was making up the hours as you went along.

He thought of Roy McKeon, camped out on his couch, 450 miles from home. Their conversation over dinner told Reed that McKeon was divorced, no children, coming up on sixteen years in law enforcement. If he read between the lines, Reed saw McKeon as a man who let his job fill in the blank spots in his private life . . . or tried to, anyway. He did not speak with bitterness about the wife who left him for a high school physics teacher or the fact that he had lived alone for almost seven years. McKeon seemed to focus all his anger on the men he hunted.

One man, in particular.

Reed didn't need a Ph.D. in pop psychology to understand the role the Slasher had assumed in Roy McKeon's life. They might be polar opposites, in terms of good and evil—though it rarely worked that way, in life—but the detective was dependent on his adversary, in large part, for definition of himself. Unless he caught a more sensational investigation somewhere down the line, McKeon would inevitably be remembered as the man who caught—or failed to catch—the Santa Rosa Slasher.

Adam found it fitting, in a way, but there was a depressing side to the reality. It must be galling, when he thought about it, for McKeon to be inextricably connected to a monster. Holmes and Moriarty. Beowulf and Grendel.

Years from now, would Reed look back on these days as the apex and the nadir of his own life? Would the Thomas Bender–"Michael Sturgess" case define his impact on the literary world?

And would he be alone?

He switched the lamp on, grabbed the telephone, tapped Sylvie's number out from memory. It wouldn't wait for morning. Adam had to speak with Dana now.

The clock read 12:19.

A high-pitched squealing made him wince and pull the handset from his ear. Behind the noise, a woman's bland recorded voice.

"The number you have dialed is not in service at this time."

He tried again, took extra care to get the digits right. Recoiled from the ungodly squeal and hung up on the voice.

Now, what the hell?

He tried the operator, waited through five rings before a nasal voice came on the line. Explained his problem. Heard the same shrill whine and tinny explanation of the failure to connect.

"You'll want to check that number, sir," the operator said. "We've got a disconnect."

"But that's impossible," said Adam. "It was working perfectly at half-past nine."

"In that case, sir, there may be a malfunction on the line." She did not sound convinced. "I can report that for you, and the service team will check it out tomorrow. If there's nothing else . . . ?"

Reed slammed the telephone receiver down and bolted for the living room, propelled by sudden dread. He found McKeon watching television with the lights off and the sound tuned almost to a whisper. The detective turned and blinked at Adam when he hit the lights.

"I think he's after Dana," Adam said.

Starr's first hint of a problem was the sound of water flushing in a toilet bowl. It caught him halfway down the hall and emanated from the next room on his right. Directly opposite, a bedroom door stood open, darkness beckoning.

He took a chance, swept forward, veering to his left. Inside the bedroom, he could mount an ambush. Take her coming through the doorway, clap a hand across her mouth, and slit her throat before she had a chance to warn the others. It would barely slow him down.

The door behind him opened.

"Sylvie?"

Filthy little bitch! She didn't even take the time to wash her hands.

Starr whirled and rushed her, knowing he was blown. The only hope now was a quick, clean kill.

The woman screamed.

His left fist slammed into her face, the leaded knuckles cracking bone and cartilage. She staggered, hit the door-jamb, reeling to her left, Starr's right.

The knife was there to meet her, piercing silk, flesh, muscle. Starr was swift and thorough, twisting, ripping outward. Felt the saw teeth snag a rib, shear through the fragile bone.

Without the penetrating blade to hold her upright, she slumped backward, sprawled across the threshold to the bathroom with her sleek legs tangled in the hall. Starr's powerful erection strained against the fabric of his jeans, but there was no time now.

He lunged back toward the open bedroom doorway, groped inside and found the light switch. Flicked it on. The rumpled bed was empty, waiting for its occupant's return.

One down.

Starr moved along the hallway, took the next door on his right. Barged in and hit the light switch with his left hand, smearing crimson on the wall.

The blonde was sitting up in bed, bewildered, squinting at the light. She wore a baggy purple T-shirt with an iron-on portrait. James Dean's sultry face distorted by the ripe swell of her breasts.

"Hey, what—"

Starr threw himself on top of her, the sap glove slamming twice into her nose and forehead. She was down before the knife fell, pierced the velvet curve between her jaw and clavicle. Again. The grating sound of steel against her vertebrae. Blood spouted from her open throat and sprayed the hunter's face.

Starr licked his lips and tasted salt.

A sudden frenzy overtook him, straddling the woman's body, slashing at her while she lurched and heaved beneath him, in a parody of intercourse. He hacked at James Dean's face, revealed her naked breasts. Kept slashing, while his free hand pinned her head against the bloodstained pillow. Starr could feel his climax coming, when she suddenly went limp and cheated him.

Disgusting bitch!

He came back to himself a moment later, kneeling in her

blood, remembering the essence of his mission. Rolling off the bed, he almost lost his balance, saved it with momentum as he hit the threshold running.

One left. Adam's whore.

In front of him, the last door was ajar, her pale face gaping, wide-eyed.

"Shit!"

The door slammed in his face. Starr threw himself against it, bruised his shoulder. Fumbled at the knob with blood-slick fingers. Found it locked. He stepped back, raised a leg, and put his weight behind a jarring kick. Once more. A third time, and the door flew open, pieces of the shattered locking mechanism scattered on the carpet.

Starr rushed through and stumbled on a suitcase standing in his path. He caught himself with outflung hands, re- trieved the hunting knife at once, and braced himself for an assault.

The cunt was gone.

Four choices.

Crossing to the bedroom window, Starr drew back the curtains and confirmed that it was latched. Backpedaled for a hasty look beneath the bed. Dust bunnies breeding under there.

That left a closet on his right, and what appeared to be another bathroom, on his left. Both doors were closed.

The closet, first.

He did not hesitate, excited at the prospect of resistance. If the bitch was armed, she would have met him coming through the doorway, shot or stabbed or bludgeoned him while he was still off-balance.

She had missed her chance.

He slid the closet door back, crouching, with the long knife poised in front of him. Three pairs of slacks and half a dozen shirts on hangers. Nothing that would hide a human being.

Starr turned toward the bathroom, almost leisurely in his approach. He knew that he was running overtime, but he was past the point of no return. His prey was waiting for him, just beyond one final, flimsy door.

"I'm coming, bitch," he told her, almost whispering. "Get ready."

Try the knob. She had locked it, of course. Starr smiled behind his mask of blood and wool. He felt the power coursing through his veins, the red heat radiating from his groin.

"Don't start without me."

He was grinning as he plunged his knife into the center panel of the bathroom door.

CHAPTER
18
———•———

Steve Driscoll hit the ground running, wrestling with a jacket as he covered thirty feet between his front door and his car. One of the sleeves was inside-out, and Driscoll finally gave up, cursing. Dropped the rumpled jacket on the seat beside him as he slid behind the steering wheel.

Five minutes since the call had jarred him out of fitful sleep, and Driscoll knew that wasn't bad. He would not take a prize for neatness, but he had himself together, more or less.

The hell of it was knowing that he might already be too late.

Police work was reactive, for the most part, meaning that the good guys always started out at least one step behind. When different jurisdictions were involved, communication was an added problem, making even simple tasks a major drag.

McKeon's call had been logged by the Pasadena P.D. switchboard at 12:22 A.M. Because the source of the complaint was in Los Feliz, Pasadena had to call L.A.P.D. and bring the night dispatcher up to speed on what was happening. The nearest squad car was a mile away and cruising in the opposite direction when the "unknown trouble" call came through at half-past twelve. By that time, Driscoll had been called at home and was already struggling into his clothes.

He told himself it might be nothing. Phones went out of order all the time, and Reed was obviously nervous, jumping at the worst-case scenario up front. There was no hard evidence that Mr. X was even serious about his threat, much less that he was capable of tracking Dana Withers to her home away from home. In any case, the threat had been to Reed, not to his squeeze.

Yet Steve Driscoll was a firm believer in the sixth sense cops developed over time, from working on the streets and rubbing shoulders with the denizens of darkness. Cops—the best of them, at least—could spot a bad guy by his walk, the way he cocked his head or acted just a bit too casual around a uniform. They knew the smell of death and picked up vibes that a civilian couldn't hope to understand. Sometimes, with luck, that instinct could prevent a tragedy.

This time, his gut was telling Driscoll they had trouble on their hands, but it had gone down in Los Angeles, reducing him to mere observer status. If it went to hell, L.A.P.D. would flip a coin, deciding arbitrarily if information should be shared or classified as need-to-know.

The bullshit politics you had to mess around with on the job; Steve Driscoll sometimes wondered why he even tried. And then, he thought about the victims, watched his doubts go up in smoke.

He had a route in mind before he backed out of the driveway. Colorado Boulevard through Glendale, to the edge of Griffith Park. Pick up the Golden State, a mile or so due south, and get off on Los Feliz. After that, it would be down to watching street signs, maybe checking out the map he carried in his glove compartment. One way or another, he would get there.

One way or another, Driscoll had a feeling he would be too late.

Forget it. Bagging Mr. X was all that mattered, now. Let L.A.P.D. have the collar *and* the paperwork that went along with shipping him to Santa Rosa. When he thought about it, Driscoll almost felt like he had caught a lucky break.

Almost.

It would have been a feather in his cap to bust the Slasher, even so. Three years, they had been looking for him up in Santa Rosa. Driscoll would have been amused to steal their thunder, maybe get his picture in the papers, rate a chapter in the paperback, but that was all beyond him now. He would be lucky if he got to see the prick before they sent him north.

He had no light or siren on his private car, but Driscoll made good time, jumped red lights when he had to, ready with his shield if he was spotted by a cruising black-and-white. It would be over by the time he got there, but a sense of urgency demanded speed.

No time to lose.

If anything had happened to the woman, Driscoll could expect some pointed questions from his chief. But questions were the easy part.

The answers were another story.

Better if they wrapped it up right here, tonight.

He kept the pedal down and crossed his fingers as he drove.

Just let us take this sucker down, and make it stick.

Another light turned red in front of him, and Driscoll barreled through it, following his instinct to the killing ground.

"Slow down a little, will you?" Roy McKeon had his seat belt fastened, one hand braced against the dash. "I'd like to get there in one piece."

"No time!"

The light went yellow half a block in front of Adam, and he stood on the accelerator, gunned his Sunbird through the intersection with a microsecond left before the signal switched to red. He checked the rearview, watching out for cops.

So far, so good.

Eight miles from home to Sylvie's house, and it felt more like eighty, with pedestrians and traffic. What the hell were all these people doing on the street at half-past midnight? They should be at home, for Christ's sake, making sure their families were safe and—

"Watch it!"

Adam swerved to miss a motorcycle coming out of nowhere. Stupid bastard didn't even check the street before he pulled out into traffic, trusting someone more responsible to watch his ass. Reed slammed a fist down on the Sunbird's horn and saw the biker flip him off as they roared past.

"You run somebody over, I can't help you," said McKeon.

"We're all right."

But Dana wasn't. He could feel it.

Reed had listened, trembling, while McKeon placed the call to Pasadena P.D. from his living room. Los Feliz lay outside their jurisdiction, but the call would be relayed. Detective Driscoll would be notified.

McKeon tried L.A.P.D. while Adam finished dressing. He was put on hold, then somehow disconnected. Cursing, he was just about to try again when Adam grabbed his car keys off the breakfast counter, headed for the door.

"You coming?"

They were making decent time, all things considered, but it seemed to take forever. Adam wished that he were living in the *Star Trek* universe, where he could beam across the miles and reach his destination instantly. Grab "Michael Sturgess" by the throat and squeeze until his eyes bugged out.

What if it was all a hideous mistake?

Phones *did* go out of service now and then, with nothing sinister behind it. There *was* such a thing as pure coincidence.

But not tonight, Reed thought. Not this soon after *he* called, with his threat of retribution. Coincidence was when a song kept running through your head, and then you heard it moments later on the radio. Or when you had a nice, romantic weekend getaway all planned, and uninvited relatives blew in from out of town to make your day.

Not this.

If he was wrong, he would apologize to all concerned and pay his fine for turning in a false alarm, whatever, with the greatest of relief. If he was *right,* though, then he knew that they were almost certainly too late.

The cops would be there, Adam told himself. They had a

fair response time in L.A.—white neighborhoods, at least—and when the call came from another law enforcement agency, it had to take priority.

Suppose the cop was chowing down on doughnuts, flirting with the waitress, out of earshot from his radio? Suppose the lazy prick was cooping in his car and missed the call?

Slow down.

He was anticipating nonexistent problems, running on a mix of fear and guilt. If Dana came to any harm, it would be his fault, plain and simple. She had tried to warn Adam off the Slasher story from the start, but he had listened to his ego, gambled everything he had on one hot story.

"Shit!"

The light ahead went crimson, but he kept the pedal down. To brake now meant a broadside skid into the intersection, maybe stalling out in front of north-south traffic. With a bit of luck and extra speed—

"God*damn* it!"

Roy McKeon closed his eyes and clutched the seat, white-knuckled, as they cleared a city bus with something like a foot to spare. Horns blared behind them, quickly Dopplered out of hearing.

"Jesus, Adam!"

"Freeway coming up," he warned McKeon, veering toward the on-ramp. "Get a grip."

The first rule of survival as a motorist in L.A. County: Distance is a fluid concept, mileage versus time elapsed. The straight-line rule applied in theory, but negotiating surface streets could turn the shortest jaunt into a marathon. Conversely, if you used the freeways, chose your time judiciously, you had a decent shot at driving twice as far in half the time.

The question now: How fast was fast enough?

And how would Adam face himself tomorrow if his fears were realized?

Starr hesitated when he heard the first, faint siren drawing closer. He had carved a fist-size porthole in the bathroom door, but it was too small, yet, for him to reach inside and trip the lock.

Too late.

The siren's wail was closing rapidly. Starr checked his swing and stood with one hand braced against the door. It might be nothing, some emergency entirely unrelated to his mission. Possibly an ambulance.

He couldn't take the chance. To let himself be trapped inside the house was suicide.

Starr pressed his face against the bathroom door, peered through the ragged opening his knife had made. A mirror on the wall, directly opposite. A woman's pallid face reflected in the lower right-hand corner, staring at the door and waiting for her executioner to set her free.

"This isn't over, bitch!" he shouted. "I'll be back! You hear me? Coming back for you!"

He turned and sprinted down the hallway. Cleared the redhead's outstretched legs in one long stride. Turned right, into the kitchen, sliding on the polished vinyl floor. The siren moaned and died out front, as Starr burst through the kitchen doorway to the yard. Leaped off the concrete step and tore across the lawn.

They would be coming up the walk by now, with pistols drawn and ready.

Starr attacked the redwood fence as if it were a living adversary, scrambled over. Lost his balance, sprawling in the neighbor's yard. A bedroom light came on, the sleepers roused by danger noises on the street. Starr scrambled to his feet and sprinted past before they had a chance to reach for robes and look outside.

The second fence. He slammed one knee, a bolt of white-hot pain that turned his leg to rubber, folding under him as he collapsed into the yard behind the vacant house.

Get up!

As soon as the patrolmen saw his work, they would request assistance. He was running out of time.

Starr hobbled toward the gate, his left leg dragging. Christ, it hurt! No broken bones, but nerves controlled the muscles, movement, everything. He needed time to sit, massage the knee, but they would have him if he did not clear the neighborhood at once.

He made it to the Skylark, slid behind the steering wheel.

His right hand groped beneath the driver's seat, retrieved the Smith & Wesson automatic he had stashed there. Safety off, the pistol in his lap for easy access.

Backing out, he left the headlights off deliberately. The road curved just behind him, and he could not see the squad car, but he took no chances. Roll dark for a block or two, and then proceed as normal. Take your time.

Starr's eyes were on the rearview mirror as he shifted into Drive. His foot was barely touching the accelerator when he saw the second black-and-white approaching from the south. The pigs had doused their headlights, creeping down the street, but Starr could see the light bar bolted on the cruiser's roof.

So much for stealth.

He switched his headlights on, your basic absentminded motorist. In front of him, the squad car did the same. No sudden burst of speed or screeching tires. They were apparently content to let him pass, unless—

From twenty feet, he saw the two pigs staring at him. They were cautious men. The worst thing he could do was hesitate, act guilty or suspicious.

Move along, before—

A spotlight blazed in Starr's face, blinding him.

The mask! Goddamn it!

In the time it took to grasp his peril, Starr scooped up the Smith & Wesson, closed his eyes, and fired. His first shot took the driver's window out and gave him room to aim. The next four came out as a single burst, in rapid fire. One bullet found the spotlight, but its image lingered on his retinas as Starr swept past the black-and-white, still firing at the startled faces of his enemies.

He glimpsed a splash of crimson, couldn't tell if it was real or an illusion triggered by the spotlight. Standing on the pedal, blinking rapidly to clear his vision, Starr had covered half a block when he looked back and saw the squad car veer off course and come to rest, nosed in against the curb.

Starr hoped the pigs were dead, but there was no way he could count on it. By now, they could have broadcast a description of his car to every cruiser in Los Angeles. With radio and fax machines, the fucking APB could go statewide in half an hour. Granted, cops were rarely that efficient, but his luck had turned, and Starr was bracing for the worst.

There was a steady flow of traffic on Los Feliz Boulevard. Starr took his turn, no screeching-tire theatrics, and remembered to discard the bloody ski mask while he waited for the light to change. A hasty check for squad cars, east and west, revealed no pigs in the immediate vicinity.

What next?

He had to ditch the Skylark soon, but he was not prepared to walk from Griffith Park to Burbank, where he had the Volvo stashed. It meant abandoning his gear, the clothes and personal belongings back at his motel room, navigating unfamiliar streets by night, unarmed and undisguised. He might get lucky with a cab, but he would have to kill the driver, a potential witness for the prosecution.

Shitshitshitshitshit!

He still had no idea of what had given him away to the police, back there, before he had a chance to finish Adam's whore. It was entirely possible that he would never know. The best laid plans, and all that rot.

For now, Starr had to concentrate on his escape. It took raw courage to refrain from racing down Los Feliz, jumping red lights as they came, to put some space between himself and the police. No one would notice him if he was cool. There was a chance that he could make it all the way to Burbank, swap the Skylark for his Volvo, double back to the motel and get his things. Three weeks to go, before his rent ran out on the garage and anyone came snooping. By the time pigs found the car, it would have been reported stolen by the rental agency, a warrant issued for the nonexistent Robert Capshew, late of Petaluma.

Perfect. All he had to do was—

Jesus! Coming up behind him, flashers in the rearview mirror. Red and blue. It seemed impossible that anyone could spot his car from two blocks back, but Starr was not about to take the chance.

He stamped on the accelerator, cut his wheel hard left and veered across the double yellow line. Oncoming traffic swerved to miss him, grinding fenders, flashing headlights, blaring horns. Starr shouted curses at them till his throat was raw, cut back into his own lane after passing several slower cars.

Like playing leapfrog, where the stakes are life and death.

He checked the rearview, watched the flashers dwindle. Saw an intersection coming up and braced himself for impact. Slowing down was not an option. Capture was unthinkable. The pigs would never take him in alive.

He grazed a minivan and left his bumper in the middle of the intersection, fought the Skylark back on course with muscles screaming in his arms and shoulders. Starr's adrenaline was pumping. He could barely hear the siren, with his own pulse throbbing in his ears.

A sign alerted Starr that he was coming to a freeway. One-half mile to reach the Golden State. I-5. He stood a better chance of ditching the police on surface roads, but there was something to be said for speed. Less opportunity for them to box him in.

So be it.

From the freeway, he could take off into Glendale, Burbank, keep on going if he had to. Drop the Buick in Sun Valley or Pacoima. Anywhere he found himself another set of wheels.

But first, he had to get there.

Half a mile and closing, with the needle kissing seventy.

Riverside Drive was the last major cross-street, no question of stopping. To hell with the traffic. Starr leaned on his horn, kept his foot on the floor. Kamikaze time. Going for broke.

Too late, he glimpsed the giant tanker truck approaching from his left. It had the green light, clocking sixty, minimum. The driver didn't see him coming.

Christ!

Instinctively, against his will, Starr mashed the brake and felt the Skylark start to skid. He fought the wheel and rode it through a full one-eighty, coming broadside with the tanker on his right.

He fumbled at the door latch, cursing, and the world exploded into thunder, smoke, and flame.

CHAPTER

19

———•———

...CHAPTER 19...

Waiting at the hospital was hell.

No fault of the designers. Queen of Angels was a stylish, up-to-date facility, complete with color schemes intended to relieve anxiety and give a boost to flagging spirits. Skilled psychologists had pondered long and hard, selecting just the right shades of pastel, debating contrast, color's subtle impact on the mind.

The only problem was, it didn't work.

To Adam Reed, at least, the waiting room seemed garish, done in circus colors, more inclined to breed a headache than engender peace of mind. He felt like screaming, picking up his molded plastic chair and smashing it to pieces on the floor. Instead, he sat and waited, did his best to eavesdrop on the four detectives huddled on the far side of the waiting room.

They were Driscoll and McKeon, plus two suits from L.A.P.D. homicide. The older of the L.A. cops was Sergeant Amos Guthrie, big and black, with salt-and-pepper hair. His partner, Frank DiGiorgio, was a slender thirty-something, compensating for his early baldness with a thick mustache. Professionals, all four of them. They frowned and nodded, spoke in muted tones, discussing grisly death the way most men would talk about last weekend's football scores.

The worst was over by the time Reed and McKeon reached Los Feliz. Squad cars blocked the street, lights flashing, forcing Reed to park a block away. McKeon's badge got both of them past the patrolmen guarding the perimeter, but they were not allowed inside the house. Reed stood and stared, his mind in turmoil, while McKeon made the rounds and tried to pick up information from the officers on hand.

One ambulance was at the scene when they arrived, another rolling in five minutes later, Driscoll close behind it. He was standing with McKeon, out of earshot, when the coroner arrived and Adam felt his spirits plunge.

He couldn't say how long it was before the women started coming out. A stretcher first, with red hair and a bloody face just visible. Could that be Monica, for Christ's sake? If they left her face uncovered, did it mean that she was still alive? Her stretcher disappeared inside the nearest ambulance, doors slammed, and she was gone. The siren wailed.

Then Dana, walking on her own, supported by a para-medic. Adam ran to meet her, dodged a uniform that tried to hold him back. She wore a baggy sweatshirt over jeans, no sign of blood or other injury. At first, she did not seem to recognize him, looked right through him, as if Reed were made of glass. It took a moment, with the paramedic nudging him aside, and then her eyes came into focus. Dana met his gaze, recoiling.

"You."

It sounded like a curse.

When she was gone, he drifted back to the perimeter and watched patrolmen stringing yellow tape around the proper-ty. Reed knew there had to be one woman still inside the house, but no one hurried to remove her. Suits arrived and homed in on the coroner, reluctantly including Driscoll and McKeon in their circle. After some preliminary conversa-tion, they went in the house, left Adam standing in the yard. The odd man out, surrounded by patrolmen who regarded him with thinly veiled suspicion.

Twenty minutes later, Driscoll and McKeon came back out, spoke briefly on the step, and went their separate ways. McKeon crossed the yard to where Reed stood and took him by the arm.

"You know where Queen of Angels is? The hospital?"

"I think so. Yes."

"Let's go."

In transit, Adam learned a few stark details of the crime.

"Two dead, so far," McKeon said. "The roommate, Summers?"

Sylvie, Jesus.

"And a cop," McKeon added. "Way it looks, the second car arriving on the scene surprised our boy two houses down. They caught him driving with his lights off, and he opened fire. The driver took a head shot, stalled the cruiser's engine. Never had a chance. His partner got off easy, cuts from flying glass, and managed to describe the shooter's car. A gray or silver Buick Skylark."

"Did he get a look at Sturgess?"

"Said he had some kind of mask on, but they're looking for the car." McKeon paused a moment, and his tone was bitter when he spoke again. "Now that the motherfucker shot a cop, they want his ass as bad as I do."

The hour helped him park at Queen of Angels. There were no cars left, to speak of, in the lot reserved for visitors. They jogged a hundred yards to the emergency receiving entrance, breezed in through the automatic sliding doors, and found a dozen would-be patients waiting dolefully for a physician to relieve their suffering.

On Adam's left as he came in, a young L.A. patrolman whispered something to a weeping teenage girl. Her face was bruised, and she had lost one shoe. Reed noted that her bulky sweater did not match the skirt she wore, as if she might have borrowed it in haste.

A rape or mugging? Adam wondered. What about the others, young and old, who watched him apathetically or managed to ignore him altogether? One, a man of middle age, had wrapped his left hand in a grungy-looking bath towel, dribbling blood around his feet. A woman in her thirties sat beside a six- or seven-year-old boy, both looking dazed, but neither showing any outward signs of injury. An older woman, morbidly obese, had pulled two chairs together, scowling over something that displeased her in the latest *People* magazine.

The weary-looking nurse on duty checked her clipboard

and informed them Monica had gone directly into surgery with Dr. Redenbaugh—"He's *very* good."—while Dana was awaiting her examination by a Dr. Cowden. No, she couldn't speak with visitors until the doctor finished up. With any luck, it shouldn't be too long.

There was a separate, smaller waiting room for friends and family of patients undergoing surgery. Reed and McKeon had it to themselves until Steve Driscoll wandered in some fifteen minutes later. He was followed, after roughly half an hour, by the L.A.P.D. team. Still no sign of Dana.

Reed was getting nervous, wondering if he had overlooked some hidden wound when he had briefly glimpsed her at Sylvie's house. With Sylvie dead and Monica requiring surgery, it seemed impossible that Dana could have walked away unscathed.

Of course she hadn't, Adam told himself. Whatever had gone down inside the house, she was a witness to the carnage. How would it affect her mind? Her attitude toward him? Toward everything?

At first, he had been so relieved to see her walking upright, seemingly unharmed, that he was flooded with relief. The guilt set in a moment later, with the understanding that whatever had gone down inside that house of death was *his* fault. Sylvie's murder, the policeman, Monica still fighting for her life. None of it would have happened but for Reed, his eagerness to cash in on the Santa Rosa Slasher case while it was hot.

He picked up bits and pieces from the four detectives, losing most of it in his distraction. There had been some kind of highway accident, more people dead. A Buick Skylark in the middle of it. They were checking license plates and hoping that the dead man in the driver's seat turned out to be their fugitive.

Coincidence, or karmic justice?

Either way, Reed thought, the case was closed. Whatever doubts he may have had about a link between the Santa Rosa crimes and "Michael Sturgess," they had been erased tonight. Who but the Slasher would attack three women in the middle of the night, slay one and nearly kill another, gun down a policeman fleeing from the crime scene? A harmless crank might threaten on the telephone, but he would never follow through. Not this way.

Sylvie's killer clearly had experience. He was—had been —propelled by a consuming hate for women, for society at large. His death would spare the public a protracted, costly trial. The trail of carnage ended here.

And that, at least to some extent, was Adam's doing, too. If he had not cooperated with McKeon, lured Mr. X away from Santa Rosa on a mission of revenge, how many women would have fallen to his knife within the next twelve months? The next *three years?*

McKeon had been clueless, groping in the dark, when Adam dropped the Sturgess letters in his lap. Whatever flowed from that, for good or ill, was Adam's work, as much as that of any homicide detective on the force.

Reed caught himself before he turned the whole mess upside down and made himself a hero. He could think about a damned book later, see if there was anything to think about at all. Right now, he wanted Dana safe and sound.

He got his wish ten minutes later. She was pale, exhausted, looking almost waiflike in the floppy sweatshirt. Sneakers on her feet, no stockings. Adam rose to greet her, and she let him put an arm around her shoulders, pull her close.

"How are you?"

"Sylvie's dead," she told him.

"Yes, I know, hon. How are *you?*"

"They don't know yet if Monica will make it. She's in surgery."

He wasn't getting through. "Are *you* all right?"

She turned to stare at Adam, studying his face as if he were a total stranger, possibly an alien from deepest space. He half expected her to burst out crying, maybe slug him. In the circumstances, neither would have been an inappropriate response, but Dana simply stared.

They were surrounded by detectives in another moment, Guthrie and DiGiorgio asking questions, Driscoll and McKeon listening. Had Dana seen the prowler? Yes. Could she identify him? It was dark, and he had worn a mask. What tipped her off that he was in the house? A scream. She couldn't say if it was Monica or Sylvie. Did the man say anything?

"He said, 'This isn't over, bitch. I'm coming back for you.'"

DiGiorgio frowned and turned away. His partner asked, "Have you got someplace you can stay tonight?"

"She lives with me," said Adam.

Dana disengaged his arm and took a short step to the side.

"I'm staying here," she said. "Somebody has to wait for Monica."

Three hours later, Amos Guthrie stood before a smallish audience at Parker Center, sipping tepid coffee from a plastic cup. His captain and DiGiorgio were among the group, along with half a dozen other L.A.P.D. bulls, the Driscoll kid from Pasadena, and McKeon from up north.

"It's been a busy night," he said. "Here's what we've got so far."

He spent a moment glancing over hasty notes, collecting scattered thoughts, before he spoke again.

"The hit went down at 2107 Chislehurst. We can't be sure what time the perp arrived, but we have solid confirmation that the phone was dead by twelve-nineteen A.M. He cut the line and came in through the kitchen door. Glass cutter, probably a suction cup. He left the cut-out glass inside the house, no tape."

"You'll want to check that for saliva traces," Captain Brundage said. He swung his bulk around to face McKeon, on his left. "You have a blood group on your man up there?"

"Type A," McKeon said.

"It's on the list," said Guthrie, slightly irritated that the captain felt a need to push the obvious in front of strangers. "Lots of fingerprints inside the house, but it will take some time to screen the women. Our coherent witness thinks the guy had gloves on."

"Thinks?" The captain, sounding dubious.

"She's pretty sure."

"Keep checking, anyway."

"Yes, *sir*. Inside the house, we've got one DOA, identified as Sylvia Ann Summers, twenty-five. Preliminary cause of death described as multiple stab wounds to the neck, chest, abdomen. What it is, he nearly took her head off."

"Sexual assault?" asked Captain Brundage.

"None apparent. Probably, there wasn't time. Guy had his hands full, three babes in the house."

"Hey, I should have such problems." That was Mulligan from Wilshire, trying for a laugh. He blew it.

"Victim number one, the way it looks, is a survivor. Monica Glover, twenty-six. She's split the rent with Summers there, the last three years or so. She's got a fractured nose and cheekbone, mild concussion, and a stab wound on her left side, through the ribs. It got her lung, but Queen of Angels says she ought to be okay."

"You said she's number one?" The captain, frowning.

"Right. From what we've pieced together, Glover came out of the bathroom and surprised the perp. He punched her out and stuck her, left her where she fell. Summers had the next room down the hall. He runs in there and waxes her. One of them screams—we don't know which—and Dana Withers sticks her head out just in time to see the perp approaching bedroom number three. She slams the door and locks it, hides out in the bathroom. Meanwhile, we're already getting calls from Pasadena P.D. on the trouble with their phone, foul play suspected. The dispatcher rolls a couple black-and-whites to check it out. The sirens must've scared him off."

"That's lucky for the woman," Captain Brundage said, "but I'm not clear on why we got the call to start with. Anybody want to fill me in on that?"

McKeon cleared his throat and gave a brief recital of the Santa Rosa murders, Adam Reed's connection to the case, the circumstances that convinced him suspect "Michael Sturgess" had a bone to pick with Reed in Pasadena.

"So, this guy's a *writer?*" Brundage made it sound like Reed was somewhere down the evolutionary scale from lepers and the IRS.

"That's right," McKeon said. "He helped me set the suspect up."

"Great work. And Pasadena P.D. went along with this?"

Steve Driscoll's face was deadpan as he answered. "Reed

and Santa Rosa worked this deal out on their own," he said. "I got involved when Sturgess started phoning Reed in Pasadena, strictly as liaison. Last I heard, it wasn't in my job description to discourage private citizens from helping the police catch criminals."

"Nice speech," said Brundage. "Trouble is, you let your dog-and-pony show get out of hand. Your subject didn't do his thing in Pasadena, did he? I've got five dead people in *Los Angeles,* including a policeman. Now it's *my* mess, thank you very much, and you'll excuse me all to hell if I'm not tickled pink." He swiveled back toward Guthrie, scowling. "Please continue, Sergeant."

"Right. Our perp skins out the back, across the yards. Got his car parked in the driveway of a vacant home for sale two houses down. First unit on the scene arrived at half-past midnight, checked the house, and radioed for homicide. Their backup came in from the south and met the perp just pulling out, no lights. He cut loose when they put the spotlight on him. That's Patrolman Gary Redman, DOA. His partner made the shooter's car and put it on the air. A Buick Skylark. We found three nine-millimeter casings in the street."

"Which brings us to the wreck," said Brundage, shifting in a hopeless search for comfort on his metal folding chair.

"Twelve thirty-five A.M.," said Guthrie, reading from his notes, "we started getting calls about a pileup on Los Feliz, where it crosses Riverside. In case you're unfamiliar, that's a mile or so from where the hit went down."

"Mile and a half," DiGiorgio said.

"Close enough. The way it reconstructs, we've got a Buick Skylark blowing through the light, hit broadside by a tanker. Gasoline. Four other vehicles involved, the tanker blows. It looked like fucking Sarajevo when the fire department got there. Three dead in the wreckage, two of them incinerated. One appears to be the trucker, tentative ID as Archibald Wayne Kirlin, thirty-seven, with a Bakersfield address. Another roast inside the Skylark. It's a rental. Avis records make the driver Robert Arnold Capshew out of Petaluma."

"With a false address," McKeon interjected. "No such number on the street he listed, nothing else from DMV or county records. My guess is, we'll come up empty all around. Another fake ID for Mr. X."

"No way we're getting any prints out of the Buick," Guthrie said, "but we've already found a semiauto pistol . . . and a knife. Big mother."

"Christ, that's lucky." For the first time since he showed up for the briefing, Captain Brundage sounded pleased.

"You mentioned three fatalities." Steve Driscoll, looking curious.

"Oh, right. Some old guy in a Plymouth had a heart attack. They lost him in the ambulance. Tough break."

"At least we got the prick who killed Patrolman Reddick—"

"Redman, sir."

"—and cut those women," Brundage finished, glowering at Guthrie. "Maybe we can turn this mess around and see some positive reporting for a change."

"Does anybody know what made him jump the light?" McKeon asked.

"There was an ambulance a couple blocks behind him," Guthrie said, "responding to an overdose. Smart money says the jerk mistook it for a black-and-white."

"Dumb shit." DiGiorgio was amused.

"What can we hope for in the way of an ID?" McKeon asked.

"Not much. We're talking crispy critter time, okay? No prints, for damn sure. Maybe height, but weight will be a guess. No eyes or hair. You'll have to ask the ME what he gets as far as blood type. If you had some dental records—"

"Then I'd know the bastard's name," McKeon said.

"Be happy that he's dead," snapped Brundage. "We can draft a press release and try to make this look like something other than a total cluster fuck. Less heat on your department, running games outside your jurisdiction, if we've got the bastard nailed."

McKeon looked as if he were about to answer Brundage, but he changed his mind and kept it to himself. Beside him, Driscoll wore a thoughtful frown, digesting Guthrie's information, looking for a loophole.

"Are you *sure* it's him?" he asked.

"We're hoping for ballistics," Guthrie told him, "but the pistol we recovered may not fire. I'd say the odds are pretty steep against *two* crazies driving Buick Skylarks in the neighborhood, with knives and automatics."

"Steep?" The captain sneered. "The odds are fucking astronomical, is what they are. You're not in Dallas with the fucking grassy knoll, for Christ's sake."

"Maybe you can help us on the knife," McKeon said to Guthrie, carefully ignoring Brundage. "I've got twenty-seven bodies, most of them with cuts and stab wounds. Any kind of match at all would sew this up."

"I'm sure—"

"You'll get the knife," said Brundage, interrupting, "when we're finished with it. First, we have to check against forensics on the Sumpter woman."

"Summers," Guthrie said, correcting him.

"Whatever. Shouldn't take more than a week, ten days. Put the request through channels, will you? Stick with the procedure for a change."

"I'll do my best." McKeon's voice told Guthrie he was running out of steam.

"So, are we finished here?" The captain was already on his feet. "Good deal. I'll get the PR boys to work on this, feed something to the papers for their afternoon editions. Fair enough?"

When no one contradicted him, the captain nodded to himself and left the conference room, beelining for the nearest telephone.

"You wanna bet who shows up on the tube tonight?" DiGiorgio asked the room at large.

"No bet," said Guthrie, pocketing his notes. The whole department was aware of Captain Brundage's ambition. Chief of the department in a few more years, elective office after that. *Mayor* Brundage, maybe. Why stop there?

The captain was adept at kissing ass when it served his purposes, but he also stepped on people. At the moment, Amos Guthrie thought McKeon and the Santa Rosa task force looked like perfect stepping stones.

"I'll see what I can do about that knife," he told McKeon, as the L.A. bulls began to drift away. "Meantime, you wanna watch your back with Brundage."

"Thanks." McKeon seemed distracted. "I was getting that."

"You still don't think we got your man?"

McKeon shrugged. "It's just a letdown, I suppose. Three years, and we don't even get a chance to question him." He forced a crooked smile. "But what the hell, it's like your boss said. Who else could it be?"

CHAPTER
20

———•———

All right, we're coming back in forty seconds, and I want to talk about the Santa Rosa Slasher. Get some local color in the picture, 'kay?"

Reed forced a smile and nodded. "Fine."

The jock had tuned him out already, concentrating on the taped commercial for an acne cream that promised purchasers a whole new social life. He called the shots, assuming Reed would play along with any whim that struck his fancy.

And why not?

The trip to San Francisco was the first leg of a nine-day tour promoting *Deathwork* in the western states. Talk shows —the low-rent locals, nothing national so far—and something like a dozen signing parties. Bookstores, shopping malls. The stuff that sales are made of.

Paying dues.

Deathwork had startled everyone, his editors included, when it cracked the *New York Times* best-seller list at number twelve its third week in the stores. That kind of a surprise, while pleasant, also had its downside. Overnight, a new campaign was mounted to promote the title, boost those sales, and Reed became a one-man road show, slated for appearances from San Diego to Seattle, Denver, Salt Lake City, and Las Vegas.

San Francisco was the launching pad on Friday, August ninth. The jock was Ricky Wade, a poor man's Howard Stern, best known for drive-time interviews with UFO abductees, teenage prostitutes, and self-styled victims of police brutality. A throwback to the sixties in his dress and grooming, Wade was wise enough to know exactly what his audience enjoyed. They wanted sex and violence, with a local slant if possible.

The Rickster aimed to please.

"We're back with Adam Reed," he told the pintle-mounted microphone that hovered inches from his face, "the best-selling author of *Deathwork*. Changing gears for just a second, here, I understand you played a major role in smoking out the Santa Rosa Slasher."

"Well . . ."

"Why don't you fill us in on that?"

Reed hit the basics, knowing it was his imagination that the soundproof booth had suddenly grown smaller, verging on the claustrophobic. There were windows all around, a steady flow of air-conditioning, and Adam still felt trapped, constricted, short of breath.

The story did that to him, even after nineteen months.

He got it out though, skating over details of the murders in Los Feliz, wrapping with the pileup that incinerated Mr. X. His underarms felt clammy when he finished, his mouth was dry.

"So, after all that carnage, even with a body in the morgue, we still don't know exactly who this wacko was?"

"That's true, Rick."

Keep it on a first-name basis, Adam had been told. We're *family*.

"Can you believe it, people?" Ricky playing to his audience. "The cops are on this guy for what, three years or something, and they can't come up with squat. Now, even with a *body* in the *morgue,* they still don't have a notion. That's efficiency, my friends. Your tax dollars at work."

Wade eyed the wall clock, half turned toward the bank of phone lines. One light blinking on the board. A smallish monitor displayed the caller's name, but Adam couldn't see the screen from where he sat.

215

"We've just got time for one more call," said Wade. "It's Michael, from Vallejo. What's your question, Mikey?"

"Adam?" Something in the voice. Was it somehow familiar?

"You're on the air," Wade interjected. "Time's a'wasting."

"Adam, I'm just curious. What did it feel like, setting up a total stranger for the pigs?"

Wade leaned into the microphone before Reed could respond.

"Wake up and smell the coffee, friend! We're talking psycho-killer on a major homicidal rampage in your own backyard, okay? You wanna start a fan club for this creep, I know some fruitcakes in Atascadero who'll be glad to join."

A *click*, and he was gone.

"That's all the time we have unfortunately," Wade was saying, "but I want to thank my guest for stopping by. In case you're interested in finding out what makes these weirdos tick, the book is *Deathwork*, now available wherever blood and guts are sold. Tune in tomorrow for a little something different. Lesbians in politics, I kid you not. We're naming names!"

Theme music coming up, a heavy metal remake of the classic "Purple Haze." Reed smiled to keep from laughing, took his earphones off, and rose to shake Wade's hand.

"Good show," the jock was saying. "Glad we had a chance to rap." His thoughts were clearly elsewhere as he herded Adam from the booth and left him with a blonde who might have been nineteen. She led him through a maze of office cubicles to reach the elevators. Six floors down, and out.

It wasn't hot outside, exactly—San Francisco rarely simmered—but he felt it after all that air-conditioning. The morning traffic hummed along Divisadero, people running late for work or early for their shopping errands. Sidewalks swarming with pedestrians.

Twelve blocks to his hotel on Lombard Street. Reed started walking north.

The interview had run for sixty minutes, minus the commercials. Seven callers, most of them with questions that a first-year journalism student might have asked, but

Reed could only think about the last one. Michael. His familiarity, and—yes, admit it!—the familiar sounding voice.

"What did it feel like, setting up a total stranger for the pigs?"

Reed had expected something of the sort, before his tour was finished. Every lunatic appeared to have a following, these days, and San Francisco was the city where Richard Ramirez, the infamous "Night Stalker," had been deluged with nubile groupies in the county lockup, while his fifteenth murder trial was pending. It would have been remarkable, Reed knew, if there had *not* been idiots on tap to speak up for the Slasher . . .

He heard the caller's voice addressing him by name, as if they were the best of friends—or old, familiar enemies. Wade introducing him: *"It's Michael, from Vallejo."*

That was north of San Francisco, Adam knew, twenty miles or so. Still close enough to catch the broadcast and respond. Wade's program had a toll-free number to encourage callers. Freaks spiced up a broadcast, boosted ratings. It was business, plain and simple.

Michael from Vallejo. As in Michael *Sturgess*?

Adam felt a sudden rush of dizziness and caught himself before it overwhelmed him. That was crazy thinking. "Sturgess"—Mr. X—was dead, cremated in a five-car pileup, buried in an L.A. pauper's grave when no one claimed the body after ninety days. Case closed.

There had to be at least ten million Michaels in the state of California, if that even was the caller's name. A psycho groupie would have read the clippings, maybe picked up on the Slasher's alias for "fun."

Reed picked up his pace, approaching Lombard, wishing he had spent the money on a cab. It was a bright, clear morning, but a shadow seemed to haunt him now. Like one of those cartoons in which a tiny cloud pursues one individual and rains incessantly on his parade.

For nineteen months, he had done everything within his power to forget about the Santa Rosa Slasher, wipe the whole case from his mind. It was impossible, of course, but he had learned to do a fair impression of forgetfulness.

At least when Dana was around.

It had been rocky for the first two months or so, no guarantees that they would make it. Sylvie's funeral was grim, her parents down from Oregon, a brother from New Mexico. They stared at Adam off and on throughout the ceremony, more with curiosity than overt bitterness, as if they could not figure out exactly who—or what—he was. The family shared its grief with Dana, whispering and weeping at the graveside, Adam hanging back, unwilling to intrude. He told himself it was a gesture of respect, but wondered, afterward, if he were really looking out for number one. Avoiding any confrontation that would put his guilt up front, for all the world to see.

Reed saw it for himself in those days every time he looked in Dana's eyes. He half-expected her to leave him, pack her bags and flee, but they continued sharing quarters. Even so, she wasn't *really* there. Her work and visits to the hospital consumed her daylight hours, and the nights were mostly silent. Dinner, or a movie now and then. A cocktail party thrown by one of Dana's cronies in the business. Going through the motions.

Wondering if Dana had it in her to forgive him.

Monica spent three weeks in the hospital, went back twice more for reconstructive operations on her nose and cheek. Externally, she was as good as new, but she was also still in counseling a full year after the attack. Her first shot at a feature film, ironically, had been a slasher movie with a graphic shower scene. She turned it down, and fired her agent when he tried to change her mind.

After the assault, the first time Adam reached for Dana she froze him with an arctic glare. He moved into the guest room, gave her "space," afraid that she would always blame him, never take him back. Reed was confused, not understanding why she stayed, afraid to ask in case the very question drove her out. One April evening, when she came to Adam in the middle of the night, they coupled in a frenzy, lay together afterward and wept.

After that, he never mentioned Michael Sturgess or the Slasher case in Dana's presence. In truth, there wasn't much to say.

Detectives in L.A. and Santa Rosa had continued working

on the case, though all—or most—of them believed their man was dead. McKeon seemed to have his doubts at first, but nothing ever surfaced to suggest that Mr. X had pulled a fast one, somehow managed to survive the fiery crash and slip away.

The blaze had damaged "Robert Capshew's" semiautomatic pistol, but a local gunsmith carefully rebuilt it, using the original barrel and firing pin. Ballistics tests confirmed it was the weapon used to kill Patrolman Gary Redman, moments after Dana and the others were attacked. The Smith & Wesson's serial number was traced to a gun shop in Oakland, where it had been purchased by a black bus driver in December 1987. Almost two years later, it had been reported stolen in a residential burglary. There were no fingerprints, no way at all of tracking it beyond November 1989, until it turned up in the ruins of a burned out Buick Skylark at the intersection of Los Feliz Boulevard and Riverside.

The car itself had yielded one more lead, although it ultimately came to nothing. Routine circulation of the Buick's license number led police to a motel in Glendale two weeks after "Capshew's" fiery death. They learned that he—or someone else—had paid for two weeks in the name of "Howard Michaels," with a false address in Fresno, printing out the Buick's license number on the registration card. Two out of three handwriting analysts agreed that "Michaels" *probably* filled out the rental card for P.O. Box 1165 in Santa Rosa eighteen months before the action in L.A.

And there, for all intents and purposes, the trail went cold. It was a fact, forensic experts said, that "Capshew's" knife, recovered from the Skylark, had inflicted several of the deeper wounds observed on Sylvie Summers. The results from Santa Rosa were equivocal, decomposition getting in the way, but Roy McKeon had his eye on two specific skeletons with marks that seemed to match the blade's serrated teeth.

They knew the Skylark's driver was Caucasian, male, age indeterminate, approximately six feet tall. His weight— around 180 pounds before the fire—had been an educated guess. It fit McKeon's glimpse of "Sturgess," back in Santa Rosa, and it seemed to be the best that anyone could do without a fingerprint or dental charts.

The capper took four days, considering the charred condition of the corpse. The medical examiner used marrow from a femur to complete his test, informing the police on February first that "Robert Capshew's" blood type had been A. The Slasher's type.

"That covers forty-two percent of everyone in the United States," McKeon said, the last time that he spoke to Reed, "but what the hell, I'll take what I can get."

It struck Reed that he had not spoken to McKeon since the weekend after Sylvie's funeral. Nineteen months and counting, Jesus. It did not seem possible, but there it was.

What of it? Reed had not expected an enduring relationship with the detective following their brief collaboration. They had vastly different backgrounds, lived in different worlds. Reed would have been surprised to learn that Roy McKeon ever thought of him at all these days.

What bothered Adam, really, was the way time slipped away. For several weeks, McKeon and his nameless murder suspect had been central figures in Reed's life, dictating actions, straining his relationship with Dana close to the breaking point. Times change though, in the twinkling of an eye. Old loves and fears evaporate, new feelings take their place.

And life goes on. For some.

Reed's work had helped him through the past year and a half. It may have saved his sanity when things were bad with Dana, giving him an outlet for the guilt and rage he kept pent up inside. Reed poured his feelings into Thomas Bender's story, struck a silent bargain with a dead man to present his wasted life with every bit of empathy at Reed's command.

Not *sympathy*, which would have been a task beyond his capability. Reed could not sympathize with Bender in adulthood, even knowing where he came from, but he could and did begin to *empathize*. It was peculiar, even frightening, to crawl inside another mind and probe the shadows lurking there, turn over slimy rocks and see what wriggled underneath. Peculiar, frightening . . . but possible.

Reed came to understand the hatred that had powered Thomas Bender through his days and nights, compelling him to hunt for human prey. A measure of that hatred lived in Reed, directed toward the dead man who had nearly torn his life, his world, apart. Reed had only lived in dread of Michael Sturgess for a few short days, before the bloody script played out. What must it be like, living with that fear and hate for years on end?

He was done with Bender now, except for chatting up the talk show jocks and putting on a happy face at signing parties. Bender was, would remain, a piece of history. A few more weeks or months, and *Deathwork* would begin to gather dust on bookstore shelves.

But what about the Slasher? Roland had been nagging Reed to tell the story, go back to the first day of the case with victim number one, and carry through his own involvement in the killer's fiery end. There had been several offers, and with *Deathwork*'s unexpected showing on the *Times* best-seller list, Nash promised he could push the bidding into numbers Reed had only dreamed about.

He had been stalling Roland, so far out of fear. Reed was afraid to bring the subject up with Dana, worried how she might react. They had been making progress, slowly getting back to where they started, and he did not wish to jeopardize their personal relationship a second time. Beyond that, there was Monica to think of, Sylvie's relatives . . . and Reed himself.

Before he put that story down on paper, he would have to think about it long and hard. He also had to speak with Dana, find out how she felt about the project, whether writing it would ultimately cost him more than any New York publisher could pay. He wasn't sure exactly how to bring the subject up with Dana, but he felt no sense of urgency. Perhaps, if he let interest wane, the problem would resolve itself.

The ostrich option, right.

Reed almost passed the hotel entrance, walking with his head down, lost in thought. It would not be mistaken for the Ritz by any means, but it was clean and economical, in fair proximity to KROC radio and the Embarcadero shopping mall where he was scheduled for a signing party later on that afternoon.

The morning desk clerk was a redhead in her twenties. No resemblance at all to Monica, but Adam saw it anyway. The last time they had spoken, back in April, Monica had squeezed his hand and smiled at Adam, almost shyly. Told him not to worry, everything was fine.

He wondered whether that was true, if *any*thing was fine, or ever would be.

Passing by the desk, he glanced beyond the redhead, noticed something barely visible, protruding from the little box that bore the number of his room. A slip of paper? He had been advised to stay alert for messages, adjustments to his schedule on the road. The publisher's PR department had been working overtime the past few days to schedule extra signings or appearances on Adam's list of stops.

The price of fifteen minutes in the spotlight.

Veering toward the desk, he tried to match the redhead's smile and came up several kilowatts behind.

"Yes, sir?"

"I seem to have a message." Pointing. "Adam Reed, in six-thirteen."

"I'll check, sir."

She retrieved an envelope about the size one would expect to hold a greeting card attached to flowers. Adam's name was printed on the front in blue ink, square block letters. Someone else, perhaps the clerk herself, had written "#613" below his name, in black.

The little envelope was sealed. He tore it open, turning from the desk in the direction of the elevators. Drew a folded piece of paper out and opened it, eyes losing focus for a heartbeat as he read the simple message.

TRAITORS DIE

He turned back toward the redhead, hoping that his face did not betray emotion.

"Sir?"

"Is there some way of telling when this was delivered?"

Handing her the envelope, without the note. She turned it over in her hands and frowned.

"It doesn't say." She placed the envelope between them, on the desk. "I haven't taken any messages since I came on at nine o'clock."

"Could anyone describe the man who dropped it off?"

Still frowning. "That was Julie, I suppose. She's gone. Was there a problem with the message, sir?"

"It isn't signed," he told her, covering. "I'll have some trouble calling back."

"Oh, that's a shame." She seemed sincere. "I hope it wasn't anything important."

"No." He palmed the envelope and stuck it in his pocket, with the card. "Not really."

Moving toward the elevator, Adam wondered how he should proceed. The call had been unnerving, but he wrote it off to general weirdness. That was public radio, a sounding board for cranks.

The note was something else.

It meant that someone had found out where he was staying, and they cared enough to pay a visit, leave a message for him at the registration desk. There was no ambiguity involved. Within the context of his recent past, the threat was crystal-clear.

He had a "fan," perhaps a stalker. Someone meant to see him squirm, if only for a moment.

Adam glanced around the lobby, hoping to catch someone watching him or acting just a bit too casual. Unless the nameless correspondent planned to call him back, the next best thing would be to watch him read the note, enjoy the shocked expression on his face. See Adam scurry in an effort to identify the sender.

Screw it. He was leaving San Francisco first thing in the morning, bright and early. Let the creep congratulate himself on getting under Adam's skin if that was how he got his kicks. This time tomorrow, he would have to call long-distance, leave a message in Seattle, if he wanted to prolong the game.

Reed thought of Dana, staying on her own in Pasadena while he made the circuit. They had switched to an unlisted number following the incident with Sturgess, thereby minimizing nuisance calls. No way a creep from Frisco could disturb her.

Not unless he had the Pasadena address from an old directory or clipping in the *Times*.

It was ridiculous, Reed knew, but who could say how far a psycho groupie would extend himself in tribute to a fallen idol? He recalled a girlfriend of the Hillside Strangler who had tried to stage a carbon-copy homicide, complete with semen traces, in a bid to get her lover out of jail.

It was beyond the realm of possibility for anyone to resurrect the Slasher, but revenge was something else. A screwball with a cause and spare time on his hands might do some homework, jot down the address, and maybe pay a visit to the "traitor" who had sold his hero down the river.

Adam waited for the elevator, wishing it would hurry, careful not to turn around and check the lobby one more time. Upstairs, he hesitated in the hall outside his room, with key in hand.

Suppose the creepy bastard came *upstairs*?

The room was empty, undisturbed. He had returned before the maid arrived. Damp towels festooned along the shower's curtain rod. The bed unmade. Torn candy wrappers in the trash can.

Nothing in the way of booby traps, as far as he could see.

Reed checked the closet, just in case.

Call Dana. She might still be home, and he could pass it off as simple loneliness. A call to say he loved her, ask how things were going. Any calls? A simple question, business-oriented. If he kept his wits about him, watched his tone of voice, she didn't have to know that anything was wrong.

Because there isn't, Adam told himself. I'm getting worked up over nothing.

He dialed the Pasadena number. Two rings before the PhoneMate answered, Adam's own voice droning in his ear. He tried to think of something cute to say, but gave it up and cradled the receiver. The machine would automatically reset, and Dana never had to know that he had called.

There was no way for police to analyze the note, assuming they were interested in trying. Any fingerprints were long since smudged by Reed or one of several clerks, no reason to believe they would have been on file, in any case. Despite the massive files maintained in Washington, along with count-less local agencies, most residents of the United States had not been photographed or fingerprinted for official records. In the modern age, despite his fearsome rep, Big Brother looked like something of a clutz.

Again, he told himself: *Forget it.*

Reed had books to sign, a city to enjoy while there was time to see the sights. With all that he had been through, he was not about to let some spineless jerk-off with a taste for melodrama spoil his day.

He crumpled up the note and was about to drop it in the trash can when he changed his mind. Retreated to the bathroom, dropped it in the toilet bowl, and pressed the handle.

"Fuck you," Adam told the swirling bit of flotsam, as it disappeared.

And once again, for emphasis: "Fuck you."

CHAPTER

21

The secret of survival, Howard Michael Starr decided, was a mixture of tenacity, preparedness, and pure dumb luck. He had considered it from every side the past year and a half, and he could not rule out the element of random chance.

Or was it Fate?

He had been reckless in L.A. The papers told him so, if he could trust the words of fawning lackeys to the pig establishment. The flashing lights behind him on Los Feliz had been mounted on an *ambulance,* for Christ's sake, but he couldn't know that, couldn't take the chance. It had been only logical for him to run. Bad timing, certainly, but how could he predict a trucker speeding on his way to reach a service station in the neighborhood of Silver Lake?

The trucker's name was Archie Kirlin. He was thirty-seven when he fried, and it was nice to think of him engulfed in flame, trapped in the wreckage, screaming out the final moments of his worthless life.

Starr hoped it hurt like hell.

A second dead man in the pileup had been Robert Ogilvie, age sixty-eight. His heart gave out when he collided with the car in front of him. He was a cipher, less than nothing in the cosmic scheme of things.

Still, if he had the option, Starr would happily take credit for his death.

The one that saved his ass, almost restored his childish faith in miracles, was number three.

The crash itself was still a blur, all grinding noise and jerky motion, with the wind knocked out of Starr on impact. Looking back, he reckoned that was part of what had spared him, kept him from inhaling smoke and flame that would have seared his lungs.

The fire was everywhere in seconds flat, a rush of heat and light that nearly blinded him. It would have singed his hair and eyebrows off, if he were not already bald. At that, his turtleneck and jeans were smoking, bright flames licking at his left arm, down his side, along one hip, when he was thrown clear of the Skylark, bouncing like a rag doll on the pavement.

Normally, Starr wore his seat belt when he drove, but there had been no time to think about it fleeing from the crime scene. When the tanker struck his rental car at something close to sixty miles an hour, Starr exploded from the driver's side like a projectile, trailing smoke and flame. He cracked two ribs, flayed palms and knees against the pavement, but his bouncing, rolling exit from the Skylark also doused the flames that nibbled at his flesh.

He barely saw the rest of it, three more vehicles sliding into the inferno, passengers and drivers—all but Mr. Ogilvie, of course—unloading in a panic. Howard Michael Starr was on his feet, prepared to run, when his salvation tottered past him, moving toward the flames. A highway troll, for Christ's sake, hair like greasy spikes, a tattered raincoat flapping over filthy blue jeans. The guy was either drunk or crazy, lurching toward the bonfire with a Windex bottle and a squeegy in his hands.

Starr recognized his opportunity and seized it, coming up behind the animated scarecrow, one arm thrown around that scrawny neck and twisting, snapping vertebrae. The corpse weighed next to nothing, with the new rush of adrenaline. Starr hoisted it by crotch and collar, ran back toward the funeral pyre, and pitched his stand-in through the open driver's window of the burning Skylark.

Off and running then, with screams behind him. He

moved up toward the point where Griffith Park pressed up against the highway, leafy darkness covering his tracks. He paused there, turned and watched the conflagration from his hiding place. Cars stopping, four lanes blocked by twisted metal and a lake of burning gasoline. Dark silhouettes against the background of the fire.

And in another moment, sirens coming.

It was time for him to go. The park concealed him, vast and silent in the hour after midnight. Starr was not alone, of course. He crept past rutting lovers, kept an eye out for patrolmen, wondered if he would be challenged by a mugger stepping from the shadows.

God help anyone who tried to stop him if they were not armed.

The pain kept Starr alert. His burns, raw palms and knees, the spastic throbbing of his ribs. Without the pain, exhaustion might have claimed him on the spot, compelled him to lie down and sleep until the pigs came by to roust him with a flashlight glaring in his eyes.

Unarmed and ragged, bruised and burned and bleeding, Howard Michael Starr traversed the width of Griffith Park on foot. Two miles and then some, in the dark. He had no map to guide him, but he kept the I-5 freeway on his right, forever northbound. Watching out for squad cars, anything or anyone who might betray him to the pigs.

He reached the L.A. Zoo at half-past one A.M. and heard the big cats snarling in their pens. Starr would have liked to scale the wall and join them, move among his fellow predators, but he had neither energy nor time. The clock was his relentless adversary, robbing him of precious time, each moment he delayed another point in favor of his enemies.

He skirted wide around the zoo, avoiding lights and watchmen, coming back on course when it was well behind him. The Ventura Freeway stood in front of him, last stop before the park gave way to Burbank, sacrificing shadows to the city lights and traffic. Underneath the freeway, sleeping rough, a small but aromatic village of the homeless. Starr passed through their ranks like an avenging angel. Anyone who noticed him was wise enough to turn away.

The park had been his refuge, but he could not spend the

night. Whatever Starr accomplished toward his own salvation, he would have to work in darkness, while the pigs were busy counting bodies in Los Feliz, sorting out the wreckage back on Riverside.

The worst mistake that he could make was standing still.

It was a brand-new problem, even so, emerging from the darkness onto Western Avenue. More lights, for one thing, even though the vast majority of businesses were closed. Cars everywhere. Each street he crossed had the potential for a chance encounter with police, but if he stood and watched too long, disheveled as he was, some passing motorist might turn him in. With cordless telephones, they didn't even have to stop and find a booth to make the call.

His second saving grace, Starr calculated, was the weird, erratic quality of life in Southern California. After twenty years of bleak recession, homeless bums and "street people" were everywhere. Police in the exclusive enclaves tried to run them out, but it was tantamount to spitting on a brushfire. Beggars thronged the Sunset Strip, slept on the pier in Santa Monica, smeared windshields for a living on Rodeo Drive.

One more in Burbank, give or take, would pass unnoticed if he did not draw attention to himself.

To that end, Howard Michael Starr became a flitting shadow, crossing streets when traffic waned, against the light if necessary. Alleys lined with Dumpsters took him where he had to go, a glimpse of street signs at the crossing all he needed to maintain his course. The one time he encountered cruising pigs, Starr made a show of sifting through some trash behind a supermarket, swallowing the pain from broken ribs and lacerated hands until the black-and-white was gone.

Another forty minutes and he reached the small garage that he had rented west of Victory, below Magnolia. Fishing in his pocket for the keys, he cracked fresh scabs and stained his ruined jeans with crimson from his palms.

No matter.

In the Volvo, there were driving gloves. Starr slipped them on, to keep from smearing blood around the steering wheel, cleaned up behind himself with tissues from the glove compartment. Resting for a moment in the driver's seat, he almost lost it, giving in to the pervasive weariness. It would have been so easy to relax and sleep around the clock. The pigs would never find him here, and—

No. Not yet.

He still had work to do.

Step one was cleaning up enough to pass unnoticed on the street. He bent the rearview mirror at an angle, used more tissues and his own saliva to remove dry blood and smudges from his face and scalp. He had a jacket in the Volvo, slipped it on, ignoring angry protests from his ribs, the raw flesh on his arm and flank. He couldn't help the knees until he had a change of pants.

Tough shit.

The Volvo started up immediately. With the engine running, Starr got out and opened the garage door, checked both ways along the alley, satisfied himself that it was safe before returning to the driver's seat. Backed out. Took time to close and lock the door behind him. Nice and tidy for the landlord. Let him wonder what had happened to his tenant when the month was out.

Starr found an all-night service station on Verdugo, pulled around in back. His tank was nearly full, but he was looking for a rest room, running water, paper towels. A string of lawsuits filed by homeless vagabonds with nothing else to occupy their time insured Starr's right to piss or wash his hands without a purchase at the gas pumps.

Liberal democracy was wonderful.

He guessed that it had been a day or two since anybody checked the rest room. Cigarette butts had accumulated in the urinal, the toilet needed flushing, and the floor was tacky. Starr felt soiled, just standing there, but it would have to do.

He locked the door behind him and removed his gloves. Turned on the faucet and adjusted it until the water ran lukewarm. It stung like hell when he began to wash his hands, and worse when he applied the liquid soap, but Starr was not deterred by pain. When he had done the best he could, he dried his lacerated palms by blotting them with paper towels. He left moist, red handprints that he wadded up and threw away.

He couldn't help the burns yet, but he dabbed his bloody

knees with moistened paper towels and finished cleaning up his face. It helped to have some light, a mirror large enough to see himself without examining one fractured segment at a time.

Still not presentable, but he was getting there.

Outside, he passed the Volvo by and walked directly to the station's public phone booth, pleased to find the Burbank yellow pages more or less intact. He scanned the page of pharmacies, found one that never closed, ripped out the page in lieu of memorizing the address.

The pharmacy was on Magnolia, in the opposite direction from his chosen route of travel, but he had little choice. The graveyard shift consisted of an old man with a sagging basset face, who stood behind a chest-high counter with a sheet of glass ascending to the ceiling. He surveyed the new arrival, followed him with mirrors mounted at strategic points around the shop while Starr made his selections from the shelves.

He mixed it up to blur the old man's memory, in case police came calling in the next few days. Burn ointment. Condoms. Antiseptic cream. Roll-on deodorant. Adhesive tape and gauze. Nail clippers. Aspirin. *Guns & Ammo* magazine. Starr paid in cash and left without a backward glance.

The dashboard clock read 4:03 when Starr pulled up outside his room in Glendale. Daybreak was still at least three hours off, full light another thirty, forty minutes after that.

He still had time.

Inside the room, he stripped and left his ruined clothing in the middle of the floor. Proceeded to the bathroom with his recent purchases and checked himself from head to toe. The burns were raw, second-degree. He treated them with ointment, swallowing the pain, then covered them with gauze and tape as best he could, one-handed, to protect them from the chafing of his clothes. The knees took antiseptic salve, more gauze and tape. Starr left the hands alone until he finished putting on a fresh disguise.

Brown hair and matching brows, a thin mustache. Long practice helped him get it right, despite his clumsy, aching hands. When he was finished there, Starr squirted antiseptic cream into his driving gloves and slipped them on, then chose a fresh shirt, jockey shorts, and jeans to wear. His tattered, bloody clothes went back into the suitcase, earmarked for disposal when he had the time and opportunity. A final check around the room, including one last wipe for fingerprints, and he was ready for the road.

As far as he could tell, no one observed him taking bags out to the car. He left his room key on the bed, drove past the dark and silent office. East on Colorado to the Glendale Freeway. North from there to catch the Foothill Freeway, circumventing Burbank. Half an hour on the road to join I-5 again, a few miles west of Sylmar.

It was easy after that. He simply had to watch his speed and check the mirror frequently for cop cars. Bits and pieces on the radio about the killings and the pileup, nothing helpful to the porkers. In Valencia, he drove through a McDonald's, bought a hasty breakfast, ate it on the highway. Bakersfield was well behind him when he stopped to fill the Volvo's tank, self-serve, and paid the bill in cash.

He knew the pigs might follow him as far as the motel if they were lucky, but there was no paper trail beyond that point. The room and rental car were two dead ends, a sacrifice of one ID, but that could not be helped.

There were a thousand more dead babies' identities waiting for him. All Starr had to do was pick and choose.

Fatigue was catching up with Starr as he continued north on Highway 99. He stopped for coffee in Delano, and again in Selma, driving with the windows down and turning up the radio to sweep the cobwebs from his brain. In Sacramento, he bought gas again, took Highway 80 to Vallejo, followed State Road 37's loop around the north end of the bay, and picked up Highway 101 to Santa Rosa. With his several stops, it put him back in Willow Run by 5:15 P.M. Not bad.

He spent the weekend resting, eating, watching television news. By Friday night, authorities "suspected" links between the Santa Rosa Slasher and the latest violent outbreak in L.A. No comment on specific details. The investigation was continuing.

At 12:03 P.M. on Saturday, a special bulletin delighted Howard Michael Starr. The pigs had found a man's charred body in the Buick Skylark. Pending further confirmation, homicide detectives were described as "hopeful" that the Slasher was no more.

It was bizarre to hear his own death announced on television, sandwiched in between a Bogart classic and a douche commercial. Starr considered it a privilege, denied to common men.

On Monday night, police reported that forensic evidence confirmed the Slasher's death. Next morning, "sources close to the investigation" told the L.A. *Times* that "Robert Capshew's" blood type and the Slasher's were identical. A DNA comparison would not be possible because of damage from the fire, but homicide detectives working on the case were satisfied.

Starr watched and listened, grateful for his brand-new lease on life.

He was supposed to be a dead man. Fine. The easy part of death was *staying* dead once the official word came down. It would require self-discipline, of course, but that was not a problem.

Patience was the hunter's stock in trade.

If Starr the Slasher were deceased, he must refrain from hunting in the neighborhood of Santa Rosa, shy away from old behavior patterns that would set alarm bells ringing with the local pigs or with the FBI at Quantico. Revise old tactics, choose new weapons and techniques. Take special pains to clean up any evidence that might provide forensic links between a dead man and ensuing crimes.

At first, Starr had been disappointed that he could not hunt in Santa Rosa anymore, but then he recognized the challenge. It was more expensive hunting on a wider range, but he was set for life, a man of means. He would expand his list of pen pals. Use a Berkeley mail drop for security and check it once or twice a week. When visiting, take care to make each kill seem individual, distinct.

No problem.

While he waited, healing, Starr had his trophies to distract him—and his visions of revenge.

Aside from damage to his ribs, which Starr wrapped tightly with elastic bandages, his injuries were superficial. There was pain involved, of course, but given Starr's

233

peculiar background, even that had certain pleasant aspects. Any scars would be concealed when he was dressed, no problem as he went about his daily business under different names. No living soul had seen him naked since the last time with his mother. Starr was bashful that way.

Waiting.

Healing.

Looking forward to revenge.

Starr thought of Adam Reed each morning when he woke. The traitor and his bitch. *Her* name was Dana Withers, the reporters told him. Starr amused himself with fantasies of torture, rape and sodomy, dismemberment. A punishment to fit the crime.

Reed had betrayed him to the pigs, but Dana's crime was worse. She had embarrassed him, unwittingly, and thus became a heroine to all the whining bitches of the world. One so-called journalist gave Dana credit, indirectly, for the Slasher's death.

That much, at least, was true.

In foiling Starr, Reed's bitch had paved the way for his "destruction" and rebirth. However inadvertently, she had compelled him to revise his lifestyle, find a new technique of hunting that would dazzle his committed adversaries, give him years and years in which to savor and refine the game.

Starr ought to thank the bitch . . . but he preferred to kill her.

Nineteen months of waiting and recuperating, marking time. He kept track of his quarry from a distance, undismayed when Adam changed to an unlisted number. Six months after the Los Feliz incident, Starr paid another visit to the Pasadena neighborhood, found Reed and Dana still residing at the same address. He wore his postman's costume, checking their mail to make sure.

From there, he kept in touch with them obliquely. Purchased stationery in the name of Blue Star Marketing Associates and paid his eighty bucks for one of Pasadena's "special" street directories that listed addresses numerically and named the occupants. A new directory was issued quarterly, but he could spare the cash. He didn't need to call them. It was ample for his needs, just knowing where they were at any given time.

The next time Starr addressed himself to Dana, it would be in person, face-to-face.

In nineteen months, he had allowed himself one victim. Sarah in Chicago, chosen from among his growing stock of pen pals. She was bashful, trying hard to change, afraid of opening herself, her heart, to lovers in the flesh. It seemed to be much easier with Adam Reed, from Berkeley. He was gentle, patient, every inch a gentleman. As they became more intimate, he brought her out and taught her things about herself that she had never dared imagine.

Sarah would have given anything to meet her new Prince Charming . . . and, in fact, she did. The night Starr showed up on her doorstep—one block east of Clark Street, two flights up—he took her absolutely by surprise. He wore the uniform of a deliveryman, a box of flowers for the lady. Used the stun gun when she had her hands full with the box, his clipboard, a defective ballpoint pen. Some twenty minutes later, when she woke to find herself spread-eagled on her bed and gagged, a naked stranger straddling her torso with a razor in his hand, his turgid penis snuggled in the valley of her breasts, Starr introduced himself.

As Adam Reed.

He did not bother searching the apartment afterward. It pleased him to imagine the police discovering his letters, tracing them to an abandoned mail drop. It would take a wild deductive leap for them to sniff Reed out in Pasadena, but the point had never been for him to be arrested. Rather, Starr enjoyed the sense of commandeering Adam's life at will, without his knowledge.

That was power, in a nutshell.

He kept track of the investigation through the *Tribune,* purchased at his favorite newsstand. Sarah's death got three days' coverage before it vanished into limbo. Starr clipped out the articles and dated them, preserved them in his scrapbook.

He preserved her ears in formalin and kept them in his trophy room.

At last, when he was close to giving up, came news of Adam's book on Thomas Bender. Starr procured a copy on the first day it appeared and read it through that night. The prose was adequate, Reed's insight into Bender's childhood

235

something less than revolutionary. In the end, he seemed to miss the point.

A hunter *chose* his avocation. He was not compelled by circumstance or by heredity. It was a *pleasure,* stalking bitches. If you understood the nature of the world, it could become an *honor* and a *duty.*

Starr decided he would have to raise that point with Adam when they met, attempt to educate the scribbler in the final moments of his life.

He was surprised to see the book achieve best-seller status, but it played into his hands. The tour was advertised on radio, a poster hanging in the shop where Reed would sit and scrawl his autograph for strangers on the afternoon of Friday, August fifth.

The rest was simple. Starr had called around on Wednesday night, checked seventeen hotels before a clerk on Lombard Street advised him that he had his dates wrong; Mr. Reed was coming in *tomorrow* evening and departing early Saturday.

No problem.

Starr allowed himself two hours for the drive to San Francisco, forty miles one-way. It gave him time to park and wait for Adam to emerge from his hotel, ahead of schedule for his tête-á-tête with Ricky Wade. Starr crossed the street, went in, and left his note with the insipid desk clerk. Listened to the KROC broadcast on his Walkman. Used a phone booth in the corner drugstore to complete his call as "Michael from Vallejo."

He resisted the compelling urge to loiter in the hotel lobby, afterward, and witness Reed's reaction to the note. Starr could imagine the expression on his quarry's face, the nervous agitation as Reed did his useless best to find out who had left the note, and when.

Step one, but he was far from finished.

Howard Michael Starr was only getting started.

CHAPTER

22

———•———

Howard's Book Store, in the Bayfront Shopping Centre, was a block south of the foreign trade zone, at the point where Front Street merged with the Embarcadero. Something like two miles from Reed's hotel, and he had walked it on a whim, to test himself against the famous San Francisco hills. His legs were killing him when he arrived, reminding him that he was badly out of shape.

The PR team at Simon and Schuster had blown up a vacation photograph of Adam smiling enigmatically, with redwoods in the background. It was two years old, and Adam, winded from his grueling hike, decided he looked younger than he felt. It was a kick, though, standing in a mall with people moving past him, staring at his frozen likeness in a bookstore window. Never mind the crude, hand-lettered poster that accompanied the photograph. It was his face, his name, his work.

He had "arrived," whatever *that* meant in the modern world.

The manager of Howard's was a tall man in his forties, with a ponytail and a receding hairline. Adam thought it looked as if someone had grabbed his hair and yanked it backward, somehow, to expose more of his scalp. A pair of granny glasses, with a thin mustache and beard, completed the impression of a hippie past his prime.

Reed introduced himself, shook hands, and was escorted to a point just off the entrance, to his left. A small card table and a folding chair were waiting for him, near the window where a couple dozen of his books were on display.

"Two hours, right?" the manager inquired.

"So I was told."

"Okay. Need anything to drink?"

"Whatever's handy."

"Coke all right?"

"It's fine."

The hippie sent a teenage sales clerk out to fetch Reed's fountain drink, while Adam settled in to wait for the arrival of his fans. He had done local signings on his other books, recalled the tedium and sluggish sales, but *Deathwork* was a different story, with the *Times* behind him and a firm push from his publisher.

He hoped so, anyway.

In fact, he sold three copies in the first full hour, spending half that time with an obese crime buff who tried to interest Adam in the story of a neighbor who had knifed his boyfriend in a lover's quarrel, dismembering the corpse to hide it in his deep freeze. Several months had passed before the killer's parents came to visit. Mama wanted to surprise her baby with a rump roast from the freezer. She was startled to the point of cardiac arrest when she unwrapped the chosen cut of meat.

Reed smiled and took the bozo's number, knowing he would never call. There were a million stories in the naked city, but the vast majority were either too mundane or too grotesque to qualify as book material. You had to strike a balance, somewhere in between the boy-kills-girl scenario and headlines for *The National Enquirer*. Thomas Bender's life was such a story.

And, Reed thought, there was the Santa Rosa Slasher.

It had all the classic elements: a body count and kinky sex, detectives stymied by a clever maniac, a nice Rod Serling twist that left the killer dead but unidentified. Advance publicity, on top of everything, to drive the advertising budget down. Reed's personal involvement in the case would be a special hook for sales.

The problem was, he didn't know if he could write it.

Living through events was one thing, but reporting them objectively required a special discipline and personal detachment Adam was not sure that he possessed. To stand outside the story and describe the monster who had nearly stolen Dana's life, on top of more than thirty documented murders, all without a shred of biographical material . . .

Too much.

But, on the other hand, could he afford to pass it up? Trust someone else to get the story right, interpret how it felt to be the stalker's chosen prey?

The second hour managed to distract him from his morbid thoughts. New shoppers fresh off work were starting out their weekend at the mall. Reed wound up staying late by popular demand. He signed and sold a dozen copies in his last half hour at the shop before the brief rush tapered off. His final customer was thirtyish, dark hair that fell across his collar, sideburns that were in or out of style, depending on the past week's television trends. He brought a copy of the book from home for Reed to sign.

"That's quite a story."

Adam smiled. "I'm glad you liked it, Mr. . . . ?"

"Howard. Mitchell Howard. Mitch."

"Okay, Mitch." Signing on the title page.

"It must have been a challenge, winning Bender's confidence that way."

"It just worked out," said Reed. "He had a story he was interested in telling. I was handy."

"Now you're being modest."

"Well . . ."

"A man like that, he wouldn't share his secrets with just anyone. There must have been a special bond between you."

Was there? Adam asked himself. While he was working on the story, it had almost seemed mechanical: recording Bender's statements, looking for corroboration in official records. Bender had an itch to tell his story while he still had time, and Reed was looking for a ticket to the Big Time. They had served each other's needs in that respect. It had never really crossed Reed's mind that there was something more between them till the night of Bender's execution. Looking back on that event, the feelings it produced, Reed still had trouble labeling their personal relationship.

"I wouldn't go that far."

"What *would* you say?"

Reed shrugged. "Right place, right time. A few days, either way, I might have caught him when he felt like clamming up."

"That's it?"

"'Fraid so."

Nonwriters—even would-be writers—had a tendency to view the process as a kind of magic. They bent over backward seeking art and inspiration, but ignored the grunt work that was ninety-five percent of writing. Query letters. Research. Reading microfilm until the fine print blurred and ran together. Scouring the manuscript for typos. Sweating deadlines. Sweating blood.

"I understand you're working on another story."

"Nothing definite," Reed said.

"The Santa Rosa case? I saw it in the papers."

"That was blown out of proportion."

"But—"

"I'm glad you liked the book," Reed said again, "but I'm afraid I have to go now. Running late, you understand."

The manager appeared beside him as he pushed his chair back.

"Finished?"

"Just about."

Reed glanced back toward the fan and found him gone.

"You made a decent showing. Normally, unless the author's gay, we don't sell half this many copies on a personal appearance."

That was something, anyway. Reed fumbled for an exit line, came up with: "Thanks for having me." He left the shop and made his way out of the mall. Still daylight, but the temperature had dropped off five or six degrees while he was busy pushing *Deathwork*. He would need his jacket when the sun went down, and Reed was glad that he had worn it, even with the hike ahead of him.

But first, he wanted food.

CAT AND MOUSE

It was a fair walk north on the Embarcadero to
Fisherman's Wharf, but he could always ride the trolley
back from there to Lombard if fatigue caught up with him.
Meanwhile, two hours on a metal chair encouraged Reed to
stretch his legs. The walk would whet his appetite.

He felt like lobster, maybe shrimp or clams. Perhaps all
three.

He crossed on Union Street and walked north with the
flow of traffic at his back, the azure sweep of San Francisco
Bay immediately on his right. At one point, halfway there,
he paused to watch a sailboat gliding past, eastbound toward
Treasure Island. Someone on the deck—a woman, sleek and
tan in her bikini—blew a kiss in his direction, swiftly fading
out of sight.

Praise God for leisure time and summer days.

There was a new vitality in Adam's step as he continued
on his way. It was absurd, he realized, but there was
something in a stranger's smile that blew the cobwebs out.
Reed could not put his finger on it, but the evidence was
undeniable.

He thought of Dana, wishing she had joined him on the
trip. They could have made some memories tonight, but she
was shooting in L.A.

So be it. They had time. They had forever.

Dana made him think of Santa Rosa, and the Slasher
made him think of Mitchell Howard. Mitch. At *Howard's*
Book Store. It was a coincidence, of course. What else?

"I understand you're working on another story."

After nineteen months, the damned thing wouldn't die.
There must be something, after all, to Roland's "feel" about
another breakthrough book.

Reed thought about presenting it as fiction, wondering if
he could pull the monster's teeth that way, but Roland had
his heart set on a true-crime opus that would knock their
socks off in New York.

So, think about it. Take some time and mull the details
over. There would never be another story quite like this one.
Not for Adam. It was foolish—even cowardly—to bar the
door when opportunity came knocking with a guaranteed
best-seller.

Dana was a big girl. She would understand.

241

Maybe not.

He had a few days left to think about it yet, before he brought the subject up. See how she takes it. Go from there.

Reed thought about the note he had received at his hotel, imagining a stranger sick enough to wish him dead. For what? Because another maniac had failed to kill him nineteen months ago?

It was a crazy world all right, where Thomas Bender preyed on helpless women, and the law-abiding citizens paid hard-earned cash to learn the graphic details of his crimes.

God bless the crazies, Adam thought. Without them, I'd be teaching English for a living, working on an ulcer. There it was, the silver lining.

Reed was smiling as the wharf came into view, his stomach growling anxiously. It never crossed his mind to turn around and see if he was being followed. "Michael from Vallejo" might as well have been a man from Mars.

He had a few short hours left in San Francisco, and he did not mean to spend them underneath a cloud.

The freaks could take a flying leap.

As long as they came back to buy his book.

It was a nuisance, being forced to leave the Porsche behind, but Starr could not have followed Reed at walking speed without attracting notice to himself. Horns bleating. Angry drivers giving him the finger. Better just to stretch his legs and blend in with the crowd. If Reed suspected he was being followed, he concealed it well.

There was a certain sense of satisfaction, standing close enough to touch your quarry in a public place, allowing him to live. The stupid bastard didn't even realize how close he was to death. All smiles and small talk as he signed Starr's book.

To Mitch. Best wishes, Adam Reed.

Another trophy for his private stash. It would be even better when he added something special from the scribbler and his whore. A set of bookends, maybe. Pickled hearts in matching jars.

The first thing Starr had done, on leaving Adam in the bookstore, was to find a public rest room in the mall and strip off his disguise. He had to rush, afraid of losing Adam, worried that a stranger might walk in and catch him working at the mirror, but he got it done. Dark hair and sideburns swapped for blond, a shorter cut, no facial hair. He left the eyebrows, donned a pair of wire-rimmed spectacles with plain glass lenses, and the transformation was complete.

Voila!

His jacket was reversible, from black to gray. The wig and sideburns went into a J.C. Penney shopping bag with *Deathwork*, out of sight. It would require a solid double take, up close and personal, for Adam to identify "Mitch Howard," and the hunter did not plan to let him have that chance.

He met Reed coming from the bookshop, exit bound, and made a show of window-shopping, letting his quarry pass before he turned to follow. On the sidewalk, Adam paused to look around the parking lot, took time to zip his jacket halfway up. Starr wondered if his note was preying on Reed's mind, the possibility that someone he had never seen might sidle up to him unnoticed on the street and slip a blade between his ribs.

It pleased Starr to imagine Adam running scared, but there was no clear evidence of agitation as his prey struck off across the parking lot toward the Embarcadero. Crossed the busy street and started walking north, along the bay side.

Starr pursued him, keeping his distance. Nothing obvious. He didn't have a clue where Reed was going, and it hardly mattered. No one would disturb his Porsche back at the mall, and he could always take a cab or streetcar back if he felt tired on his return.

They walked a mile and then some, north and west, with stops along the route of march while Adam studied fishermen at work or ogled sailboats on the bay. The breaks were perilous for Howard Michael Starr. He bent to tie a shoelace once, pretending fascination with the loading of a cargo ship the second time. When Reed stopped yet again, around Pier 35, Starr had no choice. He walked on past, continued for a hundred yards or so, then paused to thumb the pages of a San Francisco guidebook carried as a prop. It took some time, but Reed caught up with him, passed by, and Starr fell in behind him once again.

They wound up on Fisherman's Wharf, Reed browsing past open-air markets where fish were displayed on beds of crushed ice, crabs and lobsters alive in their buckets and tanks. Starr hung back, watched his quarry slip into a restaurant. Saw the door close.

It was risky to follow. Starr went with discretion, retreated to Cappy's, a haven for diners who liked their fish fried and served up on paper. From his stool at the counter, Starr had a clear view of the restaurant's entrance, some fifty feet distant. He ordered the crab cakes and chased them with Mexican beer. Went for seconds when Reed made it clear he was taking his time.

Starr was waiting when the scribbler showed himself again. Reed glanced directly at him, turned away, oblivious. Starr smiled. He may as well have been invisible.

It was a half mile from the wharf to Lombard Street, another mile and change from there to Reed's hotel. Starr knew that he could manage it, but Reed gave up and waited for the cable car at Jefferson. Starr had a choice to make: give up, or stand in line with Reed and half a dozen other drones to catch the trolley.

Backing off was prudent, but it smacked of fear.

He got in line.

The cable car arrived on time, unloaded ten or fifteen passengers, and waited for the rest to board. Starr sat beside a fat Hispanic woman, three warm bodies separating him from Reed. The car pulled out, bell clanging. They were on their way.

Starr let his mind take over, picturing the havoc that would reign if he stood up, produced a pistol, leaned across the peasants seated on his left, and shot Reed in the head. Jump off the trolley, running for his life, and vanish while the witnesses were busy cringing, dabbing fresh blood off their clothes and faces.

Slick.

One problem with the fantasy was that he didn't have a pistol. Even if he had been packing, though, a head shot would have been too quick and clean for Reed. The traitor had a lesson coming, all about the high price of betrayal. He would learn it one step at a time.

The slaughter in Los Feliz would have been Step One, if it

had not gone sour. As it was, Starr now considered the attack a diversion, lulling Adam and his whore into a state of apathy. They felt invulnerable at the moment, confident their mortal enemy was dead and buried. It would be Starr's pleasure to dismantle that assumption. In fact, he had already started with the call to Ricky Wade and the note at Reed's hotel.

The first moves in a brand-new game.

Reed left the cable car at Lombard, hiking west. Starr let him go, concerned that it would be too obvious to follow him from that point on, since no one else unloaded at the Lombard stop. No matter. Reed was clearly headed back to his hotel. He would check out in the morning, bound for Denver. He had mentioned that much on the radio while Wade was yammering about his busy schedule.

Starr considered staying over in the city, driving out to San Francisco International and having Adam paged before his flight to Colorado. Hang up when he lifted the receiver, leave the bastard guessing.

A part of playing with the enemy was subtlety. He would let Adam go about his business for the next few days, forget about the unsigned note some crank had left for him in Frisco. He would find a different kind of message waiting for him back in Pasadena when his tour was done.

Step two.

He had not planned the move in detail, yet, but Starr was working on it. Dana figured prominently in the next phase of his plan. The bitch would not be spared when he began dispensing justice in his own inimitable style.

The stop for Union Street approached, a straight shot eastward to the mall and his waiting car. He stepped from the trolley, waited while a balding black man took his place, and watched the quaint vehicle pull away. Starr pictured it accelerating, hurtling off the tracks and crushing stray pedestrians before it jumped the curb and smashed into a shopfront, grinding bodies into bloody pulp.

The vision made him smile before he turned away and flagged a taxi.

Starr was tired of waiting, but he could not rush the game. Revenge, according to an English proverb, was a dish best eaten cold, but Howard Michael Starr preferred his meat served up at normal body temperature. It spoiled the game if he could not look in his quarry's eyes and register the sense of hopeless panic there, feed on the precious nectar of his victim's suffering.

A gourmet meal of agony took preparation, planning. Patience.

Starr was not about to ruin everything by rushing it. If he could not contain himself before the time was right . . . well, there were always drones available for sacrifice. He wouldn't even have to leave his signature. A day trip out from Santa Rosa, maybe into Oakland. Bag himself a Zulu on the hoof.

But for the moment, he was satisfied to watch and wait, construct his plan with infinite attention to detail. Early Sunday morning he would make the long drive south to Pasadena one more time.

Starr had a message for the traitor's bitch and he intended to deliver it in person.

Service with a smile.

CHAPTER

23

The supermarket on Los Robles was crowded with shoppers when Dana walked in at 5:40 P.M. She was running late from a studio session with Chick, but she had time to spare. Four hours, yet, before the San Diego flight touched down at LAX—assuming it came in on time—and probably an hour after that before the cab brought Adam home.

She would have met him at the airport, but he didn't want her driving through the city after dark if she could help it. Frankly, Dana didn't care for the idea herself, and was glad when Adam volunteered to take a cab.

The fear of going out alone at night was something new, since the attack. Before that night at Sylvie's, Dana had been game for anything, regardless of the hour. She had recognized the dangers that were part of living in L.A., of course, and took the usual precautions—locked her doors and mostly kept the windows up when she was driving, watched for shifty types in parking lots, around her favorite ATM—but she had managed to survive unscathed.

She had been dancing in between the raindrops, Dana realized these days. Her charmed life had a price tag, and the awful bill had come due in a single night of madness. Sylvie . . . Monica . . .

For God's sake, stop it!

Dana tried three shopping carts before she found one that would roll without obnoxious squeaking, rattling sounds, and aimed it toward the gourmet section. Trying not to think as she maneuvered through the teeming aisles.

They had been shooting lingerie that afternoon, and several of the pieces would have been ideal for Sylvie, with her golden hair and lustrous tan. It seemed ridiculous to think about her after all this time, but Dana couldn't seem to shake the habit. She could sometimes pass a day or two without remembering—her record was a week, so far—but then, the image of her dead friend crept up on her in some unexpected way and pulled her back into the middle of the nightmare.

Part of it was guilt, she knew, for bringing lethal violence down on Sylvie's head. The Slasher—Christ, they didn't even know his *name*—was after Dana when he broke into the house. For Monica and Sylvie, it was just bad fortune, tantamount to living in the path of a tornado.

No, she told herself, that wasn't right. Tornados, earthquakes, and the like were classified as acts of God. Unless the guy upstairs was crazy, like so many of His children, natural disasters did not stem from malice, and they weren't directed at specific individuals. The slaughter in Los Feliz had been totally *un*natural in that respect, albeit fairly normal for L.A.

And it was *her* fault Sylvie died.

Well, *Adam's,* really, when she thought about it, but the danger had been clear to Dana when she called on Monica and Sylvie for a place to stay while Adam played Dick Tracy with the cops. She could have spared the money for a hotel room, but she preferred to stay with friends. Now, one of them was dead, and she could never look at Monica without remembering her pain, the reconstructive surgery that left her swathed in bandages.

The worst part, Dana sometimes thought, was coming out of the attack unharmed. If she had just been cut—or bruised, at least—she would have felt more like a victim, rather than the instigator of a tragedy. There was some ghoulish irony at work there, but she didn't like to think about it.

Browsing on the gourmet aisle, she found pâté, beluga

caviar, smoked oysters, truffles. Adam would have eaten sometime prior to leaving San Diego, but she felt like celebrating. He had worked so hard, and now that he was really making it, she had to be there for him. Even if it hurt.

Champagne would do the trick, she thought. Two bottles, just in case. They would relax, enjoy some high-priced snacks, and bolt some bubbly.

It had been difficult for Dana, getting close to Adam after the attack. There was an element of conscious blame to deal with—it had been *his* work with the police that led to Sylvie's death and Monica's horrific injury—and in the early weeks, she cringed whenever Adam tried to touch her. Later, though, when she had managed to "forgive" him, there was still a barrier between them. Vague, invisible, but very real.

She dreamed of the attack each night for three weeks after Sylvie's funeral, rejecting Adam's urgings that she "see somebody" to discuss the problem. Dana couldn't share the worst of it, the nights—and there were several—when she dreamed of ripping off the madman's ski mask just before he stabbed her, and revealing Adam's face.

One night, the face behind that mask had been her own.

She understood the symbolism of her dreams and didn't need a shrink to charge a hundred bucks an hour while she spilled her guts out, nodding from behind his desk and asking how she felt about the fact that she was still alive. Some days she felt like shit, but mostly she was grateful . . . and the gratitude itself inspired more guilt.

Dana knew enough about psychology to understand that it would pass with time. If not entirely, then at least enough to let her lead a normal life, whatever that meant. She still loved Adam, obviously. It would be a grave mistake to hold the actions of a psychopath against him and destroy the one relationship in her experience that had left her feeling truly satisfied.

Whatever difficulties lay ahead, the two of them could work it out.

And so they had.

The nightmares hardly troubled her at all now. Maybe once a month, if that, and Dana never saw the killer's face these days. The worst part, lately, was his voice.

This isn't over, bitch! A promise. *I'll be back! You hear me? Coming back for you!*

An empty threat, considering his fiery end short moments after the attack, but Dana's nightmares brought the bastard back to life. She woke up in a sweat, her muscles rigid, teeth clenched to the point that dull pain radiated through her jaw.

But only once a month, she told herself. If that.

The longer he was dead—the nameless, faceless piece of shit—the less intrusive power he exerted over Dana's life. At this rate, in another year—six months, if she was lucky—she could relegate him to the mental storeroom where she kept unpleasant memories from childhood, adolescence, growing up.

According to the experts, everything that happened in a person's life, however trivial, was filed away, recallable at need, but few possessed the mental gear to make full use of memory. In fact, the vast majority of information "learned" from birth was worse than useless. If the conscious mind was flooded with a billion random images at any given time, the whole damned human race would swiftly go insane.

And maybe that was part of it, thought Dana, as she navigated toward the liquor section. Maybe the demented individuals who ran amok were simply overcome by nightmare images they couldn't block or tolerate. Perhaps the rise in random, violent crime was part of human evolution. Men and women tapping in and turning on to memories that sent them screaming through the streets with any weapons that were handy.

Maybe, in a few more generations, *everyone* would be insane. *Homo berserkus,* preying on his next of kin. There goes the neighborhood.

She saw it in the papers every day, on television. Brutal acts that seemed to make no sense at all. When Dana was a child, the crimes she heard about were fueled by greed, revenge, racism, jealousy—emotions anyone could understand, if not condone. Today, though, every other story on the news involved a maniac like Jeffrey Dahmer or the Slasher, maiming total strangers in a homicidal frenzy. When the shrinks began to probe for answers, they got gibberish or dull, blank stares.

And no one ever saw it coming. Last week's lunatic was always such a nice boy, so polite and shy, respectful of his elders. Who would ever guess that he was cooking children in the basement? What about that *smell?* Hey, we just thought somebody left his dinner on the stove too long. No biggee. Happens all the time.

The market's stock of alcoholic beverages was long on beer and dinner wines, but rather limited in terms of hard stuff and the more expensive brand names. Dana was unhappy with the prospect of a second stop. She chose two bottles of the best champagne available and hoped that it would be all right.

Of course it would. Why not? It wasn't Château Rothschild, but it still cost forty bucks a bottle.

Never mind the cost, she told herself. They didn't have a smash best-seller in the family every day.

It startled her a bit to think of Adam in that way, as "family." With all their time together, he was obviously more than just a boyfriend, still less than a husband or fiancé. Recently, since Sylvie, they had tiptoed wide around the wounded heart of their relationship and occupied themselves with trivia, the sluggish healing process. Their respective jobs provided an escape to some extent, but there was time for sharing, too.

The first few months, it had been difficult for Adam, knowing what to say and what to leave alone. He learned by trial and error, picking up the pieces, slowly gaining ground. She couldn't help him much, not knowing what would set her off from one day to the next, until a certain word or gesture brought back images of Monica and Sylvie, their assailant rushing down the hallway with a huge knife in his hand.

I made it, Dana told herself. Survival in a crisis wasn't something that required apologies. She was a victim who got lucky, not the instigator of the crime. As far as Adam was concerned, she recognized the pain and guilt he carried with him every day, did what she could to help him cope.

She hadn't come around to reading *Deathwork* yet, might never bring herself to open it. The book's success was gratifying, certainly, and she was proud of Adam, happy for him, grateful for the money.

It was impossible, however, for her to think of Thomas Bender without bringing up the Slasher. They had merged in Dana's mind, identified as symptoms of the same incurable disease. She wished that Adam would explore another field of interest, leave the maniacs to someone else, but it was not that simple. Writers could be typecast, just like actors, just like models. Sell a hundred thousand copies of a murder story, and the publishers demanded more next time around. More blood. More bodies. More insanity.

She knew the arguments by heart. If people didn't want to read about the slashers and the stranglers, didn't want to watch them on TV and in the movies, there would be no market for the stories. Art reflected life, and factual reports of crime did not *produce* the crimes. There had been thousands, millions of sadistic homicides before the VCR, the movie camera, or the printing press were patented.

The fact remained that she would still have felt more comfortable with Adam writing romance novels, Westerns, cloak-and-dagger stories—almost anything at all, besides the sort of thing where he had gone with Thomas Bender.

And the Santa Rosa Slasher.

Dana knew he was considering a book about the case. In fact, she was a bit surprised he hadn't signed the deal already, what with Roland nagging him about it every week or so. She didn't mean to eavesdrop, truthfully, but Adam rarely closed his office door completely, and she couldn't help but overhear one-sided snatches of his conversations, now and then. She knew when it was Roland on the line, from Adam's tone, the things he said, and she could tell when they began to talk about the Slasher, Adam lowering his voice in hopes it wouldn't carry. Adam never brought the subject up, and always tried to steer the conversation into other avenues when someone started asking questions, so she knew Roland must be pushing.

Adam would discuss the subject with her when he got around to it. She knew that he was stalling on the book for her sake, and she loved him for it, his consideration, but it also made her feel uneasy. Did she really seem that fragile to him, that he couldn't even talk about an incident she had survived without a scratch?

She slipped into the checkout line behind a woman slightly younger than herself, observed the infant squirming in the other woman's shopping basket. Where were those on sale? she asked herself, and smiled. The world would be a great deal easier for all concerned if there were baby markets, something in the vein of pet stores, where selections could be made without the side effects of morning sickness, labor, all the rest of it.

Charles Darwin would have said her sudden yearning for a baby was instinctive, possibly genetic. Females wanted children; males got horny at the drop of a brassiere. Their urges worked together for survival of the species, but the *modern* woman did not have to put her life and dreams on hold for someone else. You've come a long way, baby.

The young mother was writing a check for her purchases, standing in profile to Dana. She had another baby on the way—six months along, from all appearances—and Dana's yearning gave way to relief. She thought of stretch marks, lower back pain, rushing to the toilet every twenty minutes.

Better her than me.

When it was her turn, Dana used her Visa card. Buy now, pay later. The cashier was all of twenty, but she still had braces on her teeth. She smiled at Dana's choice of items as she placed them in a plastic bag.

"Some kind of party."

Although it wasn't really a question, Dana answered out of habit. "More or less."

It didn't feel like August in the parking lot. Perhaps October, with a cool breeze that was out of season, but the city had been sweltering for weeks, and it was a relief. She didn't really need the shopping basket for a single bag, but used it anyway. It kept her hands free for emergencies, the right one bristling with keys.

She knew the rules of street survival in Los Angeles, had practiced them religiously before The Incident, but self-defense seemed more important now. There was a can of pepper spray in Dana's purse, acquired through friends. It was illegal in the state of California, where a drug-crazed mugger had more rights than his intended prey, but Dana didn't care. Her brush with sudden death had solved *that* question. If confronted with the choice of being brutalized or coughing up the money for a misdemeanor fine, she was prepared to pay the money with a smile.

She was driving Adam's Sunbird, his request, to keep the battery from running down while he was on the road. She put her gourmet goodies in the trunk, wedged in between the spare and several items she had purchased at the mall on Washington, before her final stop. Emerging from the market's parking lot, she drove south on Los Robles, east on Mountain, heading homeward. She had covered half a mile or so before the left front tire began to rumble.

Christ, a flat!

She limped into the parking lot of a convenience store, imagining the wait before a driver from the Auto Club arrived to help her out. Another car pulled in behind her, drove directly to an open slot outside the entrance to the store. She registered an older man emerging from the vehicle, his glance in her direction, but her mind was focused on her wallet, searching for the plastic Triple-A card. She was startled by the sound of knuckles rapping on the window, close beside her. Turned to find the stranger smiling at her, saying something Dana couldn't hear.

She cranked the window down an inch or so. "Excuse me?"

"Need some help?" he asked again.

She sized him up as early fifties, brown hair shot with gray around the temples, thinning out on top. Still fairly decent, if you went for older guys, and he appeared to keep himself in shape. He wore a short-sleeved shirt and khaki trousers with a fabric belt.

You never know about a stranger in Los Angeles, but this guy looked okay. Broad daylight on a busy street, no more than thirty paces from the clerk in the convenience store, his telephone, surveillance cameras. It was as safe as you could get.

"I have a flat," she told him, feeling stupid even as she spoke.

"I see that." Smiling. "May I help you change it?"

May I? It was perfect. She was being rescued by an English teacher.

"Well, I hate to put you out . . ." The window coming down a few more inches, almost of its own volition.

"That's okay. You have a spare?"

She took the plunge, got out and took her keys.

"Sure thing."

She guessed that he was six-foot-one or -two, athletic looking. If it wasn't for the hair and crinkly lines around his eyes, she could have shaved a decade off his age.

"You've saved my life," she said.

"Not yet. Let's see that spare."

She walked around behind the Sunbird, opened up the trunk. The good Samaritan leaned in and pushed against the spare tire with his right hand, leaning on it.

"Feels all right," he said. "I can't be sure until I get it out, of course."

She stood aside and watched him shift her packages aside, remove the spare, lug wrench, and jack. He bounced the spare and listened to it, frowning.

"Seems okay," he said at last. "You ought to have the pressure checked before you drive too far."

"I will."

It took him twenty minutes, setting up the jack, inserting it beneath the Sunbird on the driver's side, and pumping till he had a few clear inches underneath the flat. Pried off the hubcap, spun the lug nuts free, removed the tire and placed it in the trunk before he slipped the new one on. Replaced the lug nuts, tapped the hubcap into place, removed the jack and stowed it in the trunk beside the flat.

"All done."

"You *really* saved my life," she said again. It was a toss-up whether she should pay him, kiss his cheek, or simply say good-bye.

"My pleasure."

"Listen, if you're getting something at the store—"

"Forget it." Stepping back a pace, retreating from her. "I'll consider it my good deed for the day."

"The week, at least," she said. "Well, thanks again."

"You're welcome."

Dana saw him in the rearview mirror, disappearing into the convenience store, as she prepared to pull away.

Take *that,* L.A.! They weren't *all* creeps and thieves and lechers. The majority, perhaps, but there were still a few good apples in the barrel, even now.

Another fifteen minutes saw her home. She parked the Sunbird in the driveway, took her packages inside, and went directly to the kitchen. There was nothing to prepare, in terms of cooking, but she wanted everything to look *just so* when Adam saw it. That meant opening the tins and jars, creating a display of sorts. Some toast for the pâté and caviar, but that could wait, so it would still be warm. Or fresh, at least. For now, it was enough to empty out the shopping bag, select the serving dishes she would use.

She lined her goodies up beside the double sink, prepared to wad the plastic bag up for recycling. Two scraps of paper fluttered out and landed on the counter. One of them was obviously her receipt. The other seemed to be a note of some kind. Square block letters printed with a marker that had soaked the paper through in places.

What the hell?

She picked it up and turned it over in her hand, felt suddenly light-headed as she read the seven printed words.

IT ISN'T OVER BITCH. I'M COMING BACK.

CHAPTER

24

The flight down from Sonoma County Airport to Los Angeles was long enough for Roy McKeon to relax, doze off, and dream. "Relax" may not have been the right word, though, because his dreams were dark and troubled. He was chasing someone through a graveyard, fresh soil underfoot, and every time he took a step his feet sank down into the earth. It was a struggle pulling free, each new disturbance of the sod releasing clouds of noxious gas. The stench of rotting flesh.

McKeon tried to keep his balance, but it felt like walking on a giant sponge. In front of him, the figure he was chasing seemed to have no difficulty vaulting over headstones, sometimes kicking them aside as if they had no substance. He was close enough to try a shot, but when McKeon aimed his pistol, squeezed the trigger, there was no response. The sharp *click* of the hammer falling on an empty chamber.

Shit!

His quarry heard the sound, stopped dead, turned back to face McKeon. Mist and shadows still concealed his features, all except the glowing crimson eyes. Like portholes in a furnace or a glimpse of hell.

He moved toward McKeon, long strides eating up the rugged ground. McKeon felt a sudden rush of panic, turned to run away, lost his footing, and went down on his face. The empty pistol spun away from him and disappeared. No time to get it back before a strong hand clasped his shoulder, flipped McKeon over on his back.

Up close, the Slasher's face was still a blur, as if the wily bastard had been sitting for a photograph and jerked his head just as the camera's shutter clicked. The nose and mouth all ran together, dominated by those incandescent eyes. He had a long knife in his right hand, poised to strike. McKeon watched the blade descend and simultaneously felt the earth give way beneath him. He was falling, falling, fall—

His eyes snapped open, blinking in the sudden glare of sunlight from the window on his left. The plastic cup of ice cubes on his snack tray finished dancing as the Boeing 737 pulled its nose up, leveled off. The pilot's voice came out of nowhere.

"Just a bit of turbulence, but it's behind us. We'll be over LAX in just about twelve minutes."

Roy McKeon checked the landscape from his window, but he didn't recognize a thing. All wooded mountains down below, perhaps the Calientes or Sierra Madre range. He didn't know their cruising speed and didn't really care. They were on time, and that was all that mattered.

Six months earlier—hell, *yesterday*—he would have laughed at anyone who told him he would have to make this trip again. The sense of déjà vu upset his stomach, made him wish he had some Coke left in the plastic glass, instead of melting ice.

Forget about it. It was probably a false alarm.

He had been watching Arnold Schwarzenegger kick some righteous butt on cable when the squeal came through from a detective on the night watch. Adam Reed had called from Pasadena asking for McKeon, stressed as hell. Some crap about a theory that the Santa Rosa Slasher was alive.

McKeon almost put him off till morning, let it slide, but something nagged him into calling Adam back. He sat there in his living room with Arnold on the tube, the sound turned off, and listened while the writer ran it down. A phone call and a note in San Francisco, back on Friday morning. Next, the stranger helping Dana with her car that very afternoon.

The note slipped in her shopping bag. Who else could have done it?

The Frisco note was gone, of course, flushed down the crapper. Adam had the second note from Dana's grocery bag, but they would never match it to the "Sturgess" letters, all of which were typed. No realistic hope of fingerprints. There was an outside chance KROC might have a tape of Friday's broadcast, with the voice of "Michael from Vallejo," but they had no tape of "Sturgess" for comparison.

It was a nice, fat goose egg, all the way around.

As far as recognizing Mr. X, they had an excellent description of the man who rescued Dana from a long walk home. She made him fifty-something, glasses, gray hair thinning out on top, six-one or -two. The height aside, that did not match the stranger Roy McKeon and his men had glimpsed in Santa Rosa, and the standard profile placed their subject fifteen, even twenty years below the estimated age of Dana's not-so-good Samaritan.

So what the hell was going on?

McKeon had been up all night, considering the possibilities. One option was a psycho groupie looking to avenge the Slasher, but would anybody with a grudge like that wait nineteen months to make his move? A variation on the groupie theme involved a possible accomplice in the Santa Rosa murders, like the Hillside Stranglers, but the same objection came to mind. Why wait a full year and a half if he was pissed enough to seek revenge?

There were several possibilities. The hypothetical accomplice-groupie could have been locked up on some unrelated charge and only recently discharged from custody. Same thing if he was booked into a sanitarium. Or his hero-partner's flameout could have frightened him so badly that it took him all that time to find his nerve.

Roy McKeon had a problem with the "Second Slasher" notion, starting with the fact that there had never been a shred of evidence suggesting two men were involved in any of the Santa Rosa homicides. What little evidence they had from Mr. X, stray semen and saliva traces, all suggested one man, operating on his own.

Which left McKeon with a copycat, some joker with a fucked-up sense of humor, or . . . he didn't want to think about the third alternative. It played like science fiction, something from the Twilight Zone. Roy McKeon liked to keep his big feet planted firmly on the ground. He had been taking bad guys off the street for sixteen years and change, without resorting to a séance, Ouija board, or crystal ball. If they were talking ghosts now, it was time for him to pull the pin and find another line of work.

Yet the Slasher's fiery death was one thing—some might even call it justice—but it had left McKeon feeling empty and unsatisfied. He didn't mind the bastard frying, but a part of him still yearned to know exactly who the Slasher *was,* fill in the blank spots with a history that helped McKeon understand the crimes.

He started with the "Robert Capshew" alias and traced it back. Their man was eight weeks in the ground before McKeon verified the issuance of a duplicate birth certificate on Capshew, mailed from Vital Stats in Sacramento to a Santa Rosa postbox. It was Box 1165, in fact, eleven months before McKeon ever heard of Adam Reed or "Michael Sturgess."

With a copy of the birth certificate in hand, McKeon knew that Robert Capshew had been born December 14, 1956, in Healdsburg, north of Santa Rosa. Figure Mr. X was concentrating on the local papers for the sake of personal convenience, watching out for births a year or so on either side of his. That placed him somewhere in the range from thirty-five to thirty-seven when he made his run at Dana, well within the FBI's established profile.

It was easy for McKeon, tracking Robert Capshew down. He had the date and place of birth, parental names, the hospital and doctor. Rather than pursue the family, though, he paid a visit to the library and scanned some microfilm, discovering that Capshew had survived for all of three days in his first life. Never left the incubator. Never suckled at his mother's breast. He had been four weeks premature, with a defective heart. Case closed.

Except that you could never keep a good man down.

Reborn in January 1993, the *second* Robert Capshew had gone on to get himself a California driver's license and Social Security number, Amex and Visa cards, using them twice each before the Los Feliz excursion and paying his bills off on time. Money orders, no checking account. Despite the driver's license, he had never registered a vehicle in California, and he never got around to paying taxes. How he made his living would be anybody's guess.

A guy like that, you had to wonder.

Curious, McKeon had gone back to run another check on "Michael Sturgess." Zip. No birth certificate from Sacramento, none of the supporting documents that constitute identity. Which told McKeon . . . what?

For starters, Mr. X was smart enough to differentiate between a solid cover and the names he used as throwaways, secure that no one cared enough to check them out. ID was not required to rent a postbox, but you needed some to buy a car or open up a bank account. How many alternate identities was "Robert Capshew" holding, when it all went up in smoke?

McKeon knew it would be hopeless, making any kind of random check for birth certificates. The paperwork in Sacramento was horrendous, and his man had fifty states to choose from. Check the papers from Chicago, New York City, Birmingham, New Orleans. Find a tiny corpse that meets your needs and drop a letter in the mail. No big surprise that he had changed locations sometime in the past three decades, when you had a whole damned country on the move.

The average fee for birth certificates, these days, fell somewhere in the four- to seven-dollar range. With stamps included, you could pick up twenty new identities and still get change back from a C-note.

Smart was one thing, but it didn't make the bastard fireproof. There was *someone's* body in that Skylark, sure as hell, and Roy McKeon could not find his way around that obstacle, no matter how he tried. Of course, when he was still a bluesuit on patrol, he had seen crashes where the drivers were ejected from their vehicles, sometimes with nothing but a few small cuts and bruises. Anything was possible.

But who the hell was *in the car?*

A chime alerted him that it was time to buckle up for safety. When they started filing out eleven minutes later, he retrieved his carry-on and got in line behind an old man with the kind of dandruff normally reserved for a shampoo commercial. Children whining close behind him, fidgeting against his legs. McKeon took a short step backward, heard a startled yelp, and smiled.

A body in the fucking car. How could that be, if the Slasher was alive?

He found Steve Driscoll waiting for him at the gate, no smile. Those nineteen months had put some new lines on the youngster's face, but most of Driscoll's sour mood, McKeon guessed, came courtesy of Adam Reed and Mr. X. His handshake was perfunctory.

"I thought we finished this," said Driscoll.

"So did I." McKeon matched his frown. "I guess you never know."

"The thing is," Driscoll said, "we don't have anything to work with."

"What about the note?" asked Dana, leaning forward with her elbows on the dining table.

"That's harassment, granted," Driscoll told her. "It's a local misdemeanor . . . *if* we knew the guy responsible."

"A *misdemeanor?* Threatening my *life?*"

"You want to read the note again, you'll see he didn't really threaten anything. He says, 'It isn't over,' and 'I'm coming back.'"

"We both know what it means." An angry flush suffused her cheeks.

"A *judge* won't know," said Driscoll. "Even when we bring him up to speed, you have to understand, with all the major crimes that happen every day, a thing like this . . ."

He didn't finish, didn't have to. Reed could see it in his eyes. With L.A. County on the verge of anarchy at any given moment, nasty notes ranked somewhere close to littering in their importance to the cops and courts. It would be different if the note had been addressed to someone rich and famous, like the mayor or Sly Stallone, but little people lived with vandalism and harassment every day. For all the good it did Joe Average in Los Angeles, The System might as well pack up and move.

"There could be fingerprints," Reed said.

"I'll check it, if you want," said Driscoll, "but it's pretty small. Cheap paper, fairly porous, and we know the two of you both handled it."

"I wish you'd try it, anyway," said Reed.

"Will do. Don't get your hopes up, though."

"About the note you got in San Francisco," Roy McKeon said. "Did it resemble this one?"

Adam frowned to cover his embarrassment at having flushed the evidence. "Block letters, printed. It was in an envelope, of course, but yes, I'd say they're similar."

"And it said, 'Traitors die'?"

"That's right."

"Which you interpreted to mean . . ."

"The deal with Sturgess, obviously."

"No one else around who might imagine you've betrayed them, somehow?" Driscoll asked.

"You're missing it," said Dana, cutting in. She reached across the table, nudged the scrap of paper with a perfect fingernail. "It's in the wording, dammit! This is what he said to me that night with Sylvie."

Adam saw the link and made his grab. "That's it, then. It was never published, right? There's no way anybody on the street could know what Sturgess said to Dana if he wasn't there."

"Slow down," said Driscoll. "It was never published, but there may have been a leak, you know? I've got the incident reports on file, along with L.A.P.D., Santa Rosa—hell, for all I know, the FBI may have a copy back in Quantico. That tells me several dozen people have free access to the statements."

"So you think a *cop* may be harassing us?" The scorn Reed felt was echoed in his voice.

"I didn't say that. People talk. They want to turn a girlfriend on or get the conversation rolling at a cocktail party, some of them tell stories from the office."

"And the audience just happens to include a psycho who writes notes in San Francisco, then comes down to Pasadena three days later and—"

"We can't prove any link between the notes," McKeon told him.

"It's *coincidence?* Is that the party line?"

"I didn't say that."

"Great. What *are* you saying?"

"Off the record?"

Adam caught a frown from Driscoll, eyes downcast. Beside him, Dana sat, hunched forward, elbows on the table. She was almost trembling, like a pointer straining at the leash.

"Get on with it!" she snapped, before Reed could reply.

McKeon took another moment, even so, as if he had to organize his thoughts. "I'm wondering," he said at last, "if Sturgess might have had a partner. Something like the Hillside Strangler, or those cousins down in Florida a few years back."

"There's nothing to support that," Driscoll said.

"And nothing to disprove it, either," said McKeon. "It would help explain some things."

"Such as?" Steve Driscoll's tone was frankly skeptical. Reed had the feeling they had covered this ground previously.

"Such as the divergence in descriptions," said McKeon. "You're forgetting I saw Sturgess once, myself, in Santa Rosa. Can you tell me how he put on ten or fifteen years in nineteen months?"

"He didn't," Driscoll said. "You're talking like the guy's *alive,* for Christ's sake. What am I, the only one who still remembers he was burned to death last year?"

"I never said he was alive. I said he may have had a partner on the killings."

"But you never found a single piece of evidence—"

"Suppose he was?" said Reed.

"Was what?" McKeon asked.

"Alive."

Steve Driscoll rolled his eyes. "Oh, brother. Here we go."

"They found a body in the car," McKeon said. Was Reed imagining the audible reluctance in his tone?

"Somebody else."

"Like who?" asked Driscoll. "You suppose he stopped, while fleeing from a double murder scene, and gave some guy a ride? Get real."

"The partner," Adam said.

"Again, the phantom partner. There was *one* man in the car when L.A.P.D. spotted him."

"One man they *saw,*" McKeon said.

"That's right. He had a ski mask on, black shirt and gloves. That sound like anyone we know?"

"Somebody *else,*" Reed said again. At once, he wished that he had kept his mouth shut.

"Tell me more," said Driscoll. "I'm all ears."

"In the collision," Adam told him, thinking fast. "You had the gas explosion, bodies flying . . ."

"Everybody was accounted for," said Driscoll. "L.A. checked it out, first thing."

"They could have missed someone." A light winked on in Adam's head. "The truck!"

"No way. The driver bought it in his cab. We got a firm ID from dental records."

"What about a passenger?"

"It's funny you should ask," said Driscoll, "since I checked that angle out myself. It crossed my mind, you know, what with the elevation of the cab and all, there might be one chance in a million someone was ejected and he fell into the Skylark, through the busted windshield."

"So?" McKeon prodded.

"So, I called the company in Bakersfield and ran it down. They've got an iron-clad rule on hitchers, something in their liability insurance. Drivers know they've got a pink slip coming if they're caught with passengers."

"And no one ever breaks the rule," Reed scoffed. "Is that the story?"

Driscoll shrugged. "You're asking me if people cheat and lie? Hell, yes, they do. But there's no *evidence* that anybody broke the rule *that night.* You're bending over backward to accommodate a theory, but you've got no *proof.*"

"We have a stranger threatening our lives, Detective." Adam's voice was taut with anger. "If you think back to the last time, maybe you'll agree there's cause for some concern."

"I had some thoughts on that," McKeon said. Three pairs of eyes regarded him with curiosity and skepticism. He returned the gaze of each in turn before he spoke again, directing his remarks to Reed and Dana. "Is there anything to stop you taking a vacation for the next few days?"

Reed thought about it, shook his head and glanced at

Dana. "I can probably free up my schedule," she replied. "What's on your mind?"

"I'd like to get you out of here," McKeon said, "in case this joker makes a move."

"You think he will?"

McKeon's turn to shrug. "I don't know who he is, what's on his mind. Right now, I wouldn't like to bet against it."

"For the next few days, you said."

"A week should do it, anyway."

"Do what?" asked Driscoll.

"What I've heard," McKeon said, "your pen pal's heating up. Two notes within four days, almost five hundred miles apart. He was in town this afternoon. I'd guess he's still around."

"Oh, God." The color leeched from Dana's face as the detective spoke. She reached for Adam's hand and clutched it tight enough to make his fingers ache.

"We can protect you here," said Driscoll.

"Or," McKeon plowed ahead, "I have a cabin up at Calistoga. That's in Napa County, east of Santa Rosa. Mountains. Trees. You'd like it there, I think."

Reed frowned. "I'd rather take my chances in the city, thanks. At least it won't take half an hour for the cops to find us if we need them."

"That's affirmative," said Driscoll. "We can beef up the patrols and—"

"What I had in mind," McKeon said, "you wouldn't be alone."

"How's that?" Reed asked.

"Last time, with Sturgess, it came out that he was watching you. We think so, anyhow, the way he followed Dana to Los Feliz."

"So?"

"I'm thinking, if he had a partner, maybe sick minds work alike, you know?"

"You think he's watching us *right now?*" As Dana spoke, her fingernails gouged Adam's palm.

"I really couldn't say, but it's a possibility."

"In that case," Adam told him, "leaving town would be a waste of time."

"You got that right," said Driscoll.

"Not exactly."

"Oh?"

"Thing is, I'm *hoping* he might follow you."

"We're bait," said Dana. "Just like last time, damn you!"

"Wrong," McKeon said. "Last time, we waited for him *here* and didn't cover *you* at all. I'd say he got it on a silver platter. Now, with both of you together, under guard . . ."

"He'll see the guards," said Reed.

McKeon smiled. "Not if I play my cards right."

"This is crazy," Driscoll said. "We've got him here in town, and now you want to lead him back up north. Why complicate the play?"

"Home court advantage," said McKeon. "That's for me. Unless I miss my guess, he's bound to feel the same, start laughing up his sleeve. That's when they make mistakes."

"You hope."

"Of course, I could be wrong." McKeon cocked a thumb in the direction of the living room. "He could come waltzing through that door tonight, tomorrow, any time at all. Your baby, Steve."

Reed turned to Dana, found her watching him. She answered all his silent questions with a nod.

"We're going north," he said.

Steve Driscoll frowned. "We need to leave somebody in the house," he said.

"You want to move in while we're gone," said Reed, "I won't object."

"You've got my vote," said Dana.

"Jesus Christ," the young detective said, "I ought to have my head examined."

"Hey," McKeon told him, smiling now, "you'll have to get in line."

"Terrific."

"While you're at it, maybe you could fix me up with wheels?"

"You need a car," said Driscoll.

"I forgot my jogging shoes."

"This blows up in my face, I'm holding *you* responsible."

"It wouldn't be the first time," Roy McKeon said. He turned to Reed and Dana, wiping off the smile. "How soon can you be on the road?"

CHAPTER

25

"You're sure he's back there?"

Adam checked the rearview mirror, frowning at a sliver of his own reflection. "I'm not sure of anything," he said.

"Oh, thanks. That's very reassuring."

Dana checked her own side mirror, watching for a tail. McKeon was supposed to be behind them, somewhere, keeping watch.

"You know, we really shouldn't see him, if he does it right," said Adam.

"Even so, he could have missed us. What if he's still sitting back there, waiting?"

"*He* picked out the checkpoint," Adam said. "You know that. We were right on time."

"I wish we knew for sure, that's all."

"He's back there."

"If he's *not*, though—"

"Dana."

"Sorry."

It was coming up on 3:00 P.M. when Adam left the Foothill Freeway, merging with the northbound traffic on I-5. They had discussed the route with McKeon beforehand, spent the best part of an hour packing, sat and waited while he went with Driscoll to retrieve a loaner from the Pasadena P.D.

268

motor pool. Their bags were in the Sunbird when he called at 2:15, and Adam gave him ten more minutes to assume his station at the point where Allen Avenue crossed Colorado Boulevard. Reed didn't know what he was driving, and it hardly mattered. For his own sake, and for Dana's, he would cling to the belief that Roy McKeon was behind them, covering their backs.

They had a long drive north to Calistoga, in the wilds of Napa County. Four hundred miles, or thereabouts, not counting detours to connect with major highways. If he drove the posted limit, factored in at least one stop for fuel and food, it would be pushing midnight by the time they reached their destination. Reed felt stiff and tired just thinking of it.

At least they had a plan this time, and Dana was beside him. Hating every minute of it, possibly, but she was *there*. Whatever happened next, they would be facing it together.

Adam tried the radio, scanned through the rap and heavy metal to an "oldies" station. Music from the seventies, for God's sake. In another year or two, the music from his adolescence would be playing on the prehistoric channel.

"Hey, do I look old to you?"

"A little," she replied.

"Gee, thanks."

"You asked."

He looked at Dana, found her smiling. It was good to know she still remembered how.

"I love you," Adam said, impulsively.

"Me, too."

I-5 rolled north through Saugus and the Angeles National Forest, past Gorman, Lebec, Wheeler Ridge. Reed bypassed Highway 99 and Bakersfield, taking the long, straight run through Buttonwillow, Lost Hills, and Kettleman City. It was high August in the San Joaquin Valley, sprinklers hissing in green, humid fields on both sides of the freeway, reminding Adam that this portion of the state produced eighty percent of the nation's fresh vegetables and melons, half the fruit and almonds. He forgot about the other California, sometimes, living underneath a cloud in L.A.'s manicured backyard.

There was a whole, wide world outside of Pasadena,

where the farmers, truck stop waitresses, and gas pump jockeys didn't know or care a thing about his problems, whether Adam lived or died. If they recalled the Santa Rosa Slasher, he was last year's news. In the meantime, there had been other monsters to contend with. Mother Nature kicking butt and taking names with earthquakes, mud slides, brush and forest fires.

It was refreshing, in a way, to realize that life went on, regardless. At the same time, it was also humbling. Adam felt like a tiny fleck of lint on God's lapel, completely on his own.

No, that was wrong. He still had Dana, and the two of them had Roy McKeon, bringing up the rear and watching out for anyone who might have followed them from Pasadena. It could take a while to spot and verify a tail, but what the hell. They had all afternoon, all night. A stop or two en route, and anyone who stuck to them from Pasadena all the way to Calistoga was the enemy. Coincidence be damned.

According to his map, there was a long empty stretch after Kettleman City, some eighty miles without another town, before they got to Santa Nella. Going on six hours since they picked at lunch without enthusiasm. Reed could hear his stomach growling, audible above the Beatles singing "Yesterday."

"You want some dinner?"

Dana thought about it for a moment. "I could eat."

"Okay, pick something."

"Should we stop?"

"The plan allows for stops."

"He might drive by us."

"Streetside parking," Adam said. "He's a detective, right?"

"This doesn't look too bad." She pointed to a diner on the right. The sign out front said ROSA'S FINE ITALIAN RISTORANTE.

"Well . . ."

"What happened to your spirit of adventure?" Teasing him.

"You're on."

He nosed in to the curb, got out and stretched. Four cars were backed up waiting for a red light at the nearest intersection, but he couldn't spot McKeon with the sun reflecting off their windshields. Christ, suppose they *had* eluded him, somehow?

It made no difference in the long run, Adam realized, because McKeon knew where they were going. Even if he lost them on the highway, they should all wind up together in the end. But it would blow his grand surveillance plan, and no mistake.

Relax. Consider it a paid vacation.

"Coming?"

"Right behind you," Adam said, and followed her inside the diner.

Driscoll's loaner was an Oldsmobile Ciera from the impound lot. Less paperwork that way, and Roy McKeon didn't mind. There was a musty smell about the car, but after half an hour driving with the windows down, it blew away.

He had been waiting in the lot outside a strip mall west of Allen when the Sunbird passed him by with Adam at the wheel. McKeon gave it forty seconds on the clock, assuming a pursuer would take pains to keep his prey in sight, at least until they hit the open road. There were a dozen cars between McKeon and the Sunbird when they reached the Foothill Freeway, seven of them peeling off before he hit I-5. He lost two more in Burbank, one at Mission Hills, another passing San Fernando.

That left one, McKeon feeling somewhat optimistic till he got up close and saw it was a woman driving. Still, it could have been a wig, but she got off in Saugus, damn it, leaving him alone with Reed and Dana.

No, scratch that. They weren't *alone* on California's longest superhighway, but the motorists surrounding them were clean, as far as he could tell. It would have been impossible for anyone to guess where Reed was going, get ahead of him and choose the proper freeway.

McKeon checked his rearview mirror, wondering if maybe he had jumped the gun. Suppose the stalker was *behind* him, running one or two cars back. McKeon would have missed him, and it didn't help to check his mirror now, with several dozen cars back there, all headed north.

Okay, no problem. They were right on track, and everything was still the same, in principle. If anyone was trailing Adam's Sunbird, they would have to follow every move he made. Pull over when he stopped, pursue him when he left one highway for another. If McKeon kept his wits about him, hung back just a little, trusting Adam not to deviate from their selected course, he still might spot the tail.

Assuming there was anything to see.

And what if he was wrong? Suppose the freak who slipped the note to Dana let it go at that or waited several weeks to make his next appearance on the scene. What then?

McKeon thought about it, cast his mind back to the first attack on Dana Withers. That assault had come within a day of "Michael Sturgess" phoning in a threat to Reed. The bastard didn't waste much time, and something told McKeon that his partner—if it *was* a partner—might be every bit as rash, once he committed to a course of action.

That was stretching it, of course. He was imputing motives and behavior patterns to a total stranger, flying blind. A part of it was instinct, something in the back of Roy McKeon's mind or in his gut that told him he was close. Not close enough to grab his quarry, yet, but getting there.

And this time, if his plans jelled, they would play the game out in McKeon's own backyard. He had no legal jurisdiction, once he crossed the Napa County line, but that was not about to slow him down. It was a damn sight better than attempting to coordinate with Driscoll and his playmates down in La-La Land. If nothing else, McKeon was entitled to protect his property and guests. Beyond that, he had friends in Napa, people in the sheriff's office who had seen the Slasher's work and wouldn't mind allowing him a little slack.

The Slasher.

He was coming back to that again, in spite of Driscoll's argument—backed up with bones, for Christ's sake—that the guy was dead and gone. McKeon knew it was ridiculous, like housewives spotting Elvis at the supermarket.

Except, the Slasher had a way of using death to his advantage. Borrowing his various identities from lifeless children. Taking home grim souvenirs of butchered women. When McKeon thought about it, he would not have been surprised to learn that Death had done another little favor for the man who stirred up so much business in the undertaker's trade.

But how? It still came back to that, and he was stymied, damn it. Let it go.

They might be dealing with a silent partner in the Santa Rosa killings, but McKeon wouldn't mind if it turned out to be a copycat or freaked-out psycho groupie. Anyway you sliced it, he was looking for a bust, to take this bastard off the street and out of decent peoples' lives.

He owed that much to Reed and Dana, after all.

The guilt Reed felt for what had happened in Los Feliz nineteen months ago was multiplied and amplified in Roy McKeon's mind. It didn't help to say that he had done his job within the limits of the law. He had encouraged Reed to bait the Slasher, draw him out, because McKeon had been hungry for a break. Whatever flowed from that initial conversation, his encouragement of a civilian meddling in police work, was more his fault than it was Adam Reed's.

He couldn't make it right, too late for that when people died, but maybe he could get a leg up on redemption if he solved *this* problem with a minimum of sweat and strain. It wouldn't balance out, but what the hell. At least it was a start.

He was a block behind the Sunbird, dawdling along to catch the light, when Adam parked outside a small Italian restaurant. It must be dinnertime. McKeon drove on past and watched his rearview, making sure he had an unobstructed view of Rosa's from the A & W drive-in's parking lot, a short block north.

It was amazing what you had to go through, looking for a decent chili dog these days.

Steve Driscoll cracked his second beer and started channel surfing on the Zenith console, searching for a program that was worth his time. It stood to reason there should be a *TV Guide* somewhere around the house, but he had long since given up the search. Whatever caught his eye from that point on would have to do.

Madonna had a concert underway on HBO, but Driscoll flicked on past it. You could keep the bullet bras, shaved eyebrows, and the zombie makeup, women dressed like something from the night of the Teutonic living dead. Bruce Willis in the middle of a shoot-'em-up on Cinemax, which ranked as an improvement, but the violent choreography struck Driscoll as a turnoff. Finally, a local channel gave him giant ants pursuing soldiers through the L.A. sewer system.

Better.

He felt stupid, drinking beer and watching television in a stranger's living room, but it was part of his agreement with McKeon. Driscoll's boss had gone along with the decision, figuring they didn't need another bungled "incident" to make the force look bad.

In fact, the Slasher business had not damaged Pasadena P.D.'s image overall, as far as Driscoll could determine. L.A.'s finest came out looking sloppy, and McKeon took his share of lumps in Santa Rosa, but there were no casualties in Pasadena proper. Driscoll's captain had been pissed off at McKeon—meaning he was pissed of at *himself* for letting Driscoll get involved—but it could easily have been a great deal worse. Nobody filed a lawsuit, all the blood was spilled in someone else's jurisdiction, and if L.A.P.D. didn't like it, that was too damned bad.

It was the kind of thing you didn't like to see on instant replay, even so. Unfortunately, freaks and lowlifes called the tune in Driscoll's business, leaving him to chase around behind them, picking up the pieces. This time, if they got the chance to head a bad guy off and save some lives, it had to look good on the nightly news.

And, if McKeon's guess was right . . . well, then the heat would all come down in Napa County, way to hell and gone up north. Odds were, it wouldn't even make the L.A. papers.

Either way, the plan had Driscoll standing in for Adam Reed and hoping Dana's playmate from the supermarket was a bigger fool than anybody gave him credit for. No matter who he was—a Slasher groupie, silent partner in the Santa Rosa killings, or a drool case coming out of nowhere—he would have to be an idiot to crash the house. That didn't rule it out, of course. On any given day, Steve Driscoll would have bet his paycheck that the idiots outnumbered normal, thinking people in L.A.

So, he was sitting on the sofa with a cold Bud in his hand,

watching giant ants devour James Whitmore in a storm drain. You could tell it was the 1950s even if you overlooked the cars and hokey uniforms. These days, if monster bugs were snacking in the sewers, they would get so fat on trolls they couldn't move, much less chase Jeeps around at fifty miles an hour. It was one solution to the growing homeless problem, sure, but who had any giant ants to spare?

So much for pest control.

As far as Driscoll was concerned, the one-man stakeout was a waste of time. It had been so long since the murders in Los Feliz, nothing to suggest the Slasher had a sidekick, much less that the crazy bastard was *alive*. McKeon was a decent cop, but Driscoll had a hunch that he had lived with one case preying on his mind until he couldn't let it go. Some years ago, in San Francisco, one of the detectives hunting the elusive Zodiac had been so disappointed when the killer pulled a fade that he had started writing crazy letters to the media himself, above the killer's signature. Shrinks called it job related stress, and they would get no argument from Driscoll. God knew there was stress enough to go around.

He switched the television off and checked his watch: 11:55 P.M. McKeon's threesome should be pulling into Calistoga any time, and Driscoll had to wonder if they were alone up there. *Had* someone followed them from Pasadena? *Would* there be another incident before the week was out?

He almost hoped so.

Let McKeon bag his man—hell, *any* man—and put the goddamned case behind him. Driscoll had his own apartment waiting for him, and he didn't need the overtime for watching Adam's house.

What Driscoll really needed, at the moment, was a shower.

Rising from the couch, he took his beer along and headed for the bathroom. If a prowler dropped in on him later, one of them, at least, was going to be squeaky clean.

The other would be in for a surprise.

Starr made his second pass at 12:05 A.M. Lights out in Adam's living room, this time, but they were clearly not asleep. For safety's sake, he knew that he should wait another hour, maybe two, before he made his move, but Starr was itching—*aching*—for a shot at Adam and his bitch. Her Fiat in the driveway, but he couldn't see the Sunbird, reckoning that it was parked in the garage.

He had deliberately avoided staking out the house that afternoon. Too risky after his encounter with the whore on Monday. Dana would have read his note and called for help at once, but Starr was not tremendously concerned about the pigs. He had been "dead" for nineteen months, his charred remains interred without a name, and no detective worth his salt would waste five minutes on some cunt's hysterical report of threatening communications from beyond the grave. The pigs would write it off as a pathetic crank in action, maybe tell Reed's bitch to take some Mydol and relax.

And he was right, of course. No matter how he searched the neighborhood, Starr found no evidence of spotters, uniformed or otherwise. He recognized a number of the locals from his other visit, knew damned well they weren't police. The strangers all had dogs or children trailing after them, no jackets hiding sidearms in the August heat.

So far, so good.

It had occurred to him that Adam and the bitch might flee at once, when Reed came home and saw the note, compared it to the one in San Francisco, but he took the chance. Hung back and waited, out of sight. It was a gamble, but he had to try.

And it was paying off.

Lights told him there was *someone* in the house, and Dana's Fiat parked out front would indicate that she had not run off alone this time. Her last experience with Howard Michael Starr, the price her two bitch friends had paid, should keep her close to Adam's side this time.

He drove around the block once more and parked his rental car outside a darkened house that shared a common fence with Reed's, their backyards juxtaposed. Again, he checked the street for watchers, came up empty. Rummaged underneath the driver's seat for his equipment: ski mask, sap gloves, picks, a custom hunting knife. The Ruger Mark II automatic with its homemade silencer attached.

Starr had resolved to take no chances this time. It was
probable that Adam would have armed himself, the typical
reaction of a novice following a brush with violent crime. It
scarcely mattered that the incident was long behind him, his
assailant dead and buried. Victims—the survivors, anyway
—were big on locking barn doors once the horse had gone.
It would have been unusual if Reed had not rushed out to
buy a firearm in the wake of their encounter. Starr, for his
part, would prefer to take his time, but he did not intend to
be the one who showed up empty-handed for a gunfight.

Through the side gate, hinges squeaking slightly, and he
waited with the Ruger cocked and ready in his hand. No
yapping dog to deal with, no reaction from the house. He
left the gate ajar and crossed the yard, sidestepping scattered
toys. Around the swing set, and a glance back at the house
before he scaled the fence.

Standing on the grass in Reed's backyard, Starr paused,
breathed rose and oleander, studying the house. There was a
pale light showing from the side, a frosted bathroom window by the look of it, but nothing else. The back door was
directly opposite, some thirty feet from where he stood.

Starr closed the gap with long, swift strides and knelt
before the door. He set the Ruger down where he could
reach it instantly and drew the set of lock picks from his
pocket. Made his choice and went to work.

Lockpicking was a skill like any other, learned by application and consistent practice. Ninety seconds put him in the
scribbler's kitchen, standing with the Ruger in his fist. He
stood beside the microwave, bent down and sniffed. Lasa-
gna, probably a frozen dinner.

Starr could hear the shower running, moved along a
corridor to reach the bathroom. Pale light bled into the
carpet from beneath the door. He felt an urge to double back
and check the bedrooms, but it was imperative to neutralize
the shower's occupant before he dealt with any sleepers. If
his luck held, Starr might even catch the two of them
together, soap-slick, fucking.

There was no resistance when his fingers closed around
the knob. He stepped into the bathroom, blinking at the
steam. A mirror fogged with condensation on his right,
above the sink. The shower had a simple plastic curtain,

rippling with the change of pressure as the door was opened. He stood rooted on the threshold as a hand snaked out and whipped the curtain back.

A naked stranger stood before him, gaping at the black-clad apparition that had interrupted his relaxing shower.

"Who the fuck—"

Starr shot him in the chest from twelve feet out, the .22 a whisper through his silencer. Blood spouting from the tiny entrance wound. His target staggered, blinking, but he wasn't done. Not yet. Starr gave him three more rounds in rapid-fire, the spent brass flying, one shell rattling in the sink. The stranger went down on his backside, coughing blood, warm water drumming on his head and shoulders. Crimson swirled around him, flushing down the drain.

Starr crossed the room, leaned in to place the final shot between his target's eyes. The stranger's head snapped back and made a hollow _clonk_ on impact with the tile. It didn't matter that his eyes were open, staring. He was past seeing anyone or anything.

Five shots remaining in his pistol, if he needed them. Starr rushed back down the hall, checked out the bedrooms, one of them converted to an office for the scribbler.

Nothing.

He was all alone.

Starr walked back to the bathroom, spent a moment picking up his brass and stuffed the shells into a pocket. Stared down at the dead man, hoping for a spark of recognition, but it wouldn't come. He knew that Adam and his bitch still occupied the house. Her car was sitting in the driveway right outside.

But who was _this?_

He backtracked, sought out the connecting door to the attached garage. Instead of Adam's Sunbird, he was looking at a Chevy Cavalier. The glove compartment yielded registration and insurance papers in the name of Steven Driscoll, with another Pasadena address.

What the hell?

Back through the house, a quick scan of the bathroom, seeking anything he might have missed. From there, he made another visit to the master bedroom, found the dead man's slacks laid out across the bed. The wallet had a badge and his police ID inside.

Go*ddamn* it!

He was stronger than the rush of panic that enveloped him. He stood and waited for the feeling to subside. If there were more pigs on the property, he would have seen them coming in. This oinker was alone, and he was dead.

Which meant that Adam and his bitch had run away. But where?

Starr couldn't wait around for them to wander home. It might be days or even weeks before they came, and someone would undoubtedly be checking on the dead man—Driscoll —long before that happened. Christ, for all Starr knew, there might be scheduled check-ins through the night, to let his supervisors know he wasn't sleeping on the job.

Starr made a final circuit of the house, unplugging telephones. It was a misdemeanor in Los Angeles for anyone to leave a handset off the hook, and while Starr didn't give a shit about the law, he knew the operators had a way of tracking phones disabled in that way. When you unplugged a telephone, however, it *appeared* to ring, and any callers would assume that Piggy Steve was on the toilet, maybe checking out the yard.

If nothing else, the ruse should buy a little time.

His last stop was the kitchen, where he had to pry the damned phone off the wall to disconnect it. Starr was ready to evacuate the death house when he spied a piece of paper on the counter, underneath the telephone. Bent closer, reading it.

McKeon, Calistoga. Followed by a number.

Starr was smiling as he palmed the slip of paper, stuffed it in his pocket with the brass. McKeon. That could only be the task force sergeant who had tried in vain to snare him for the three years he was active as the Santa Rosa Slasher. Roy McKeon, quoted in the L.A. *Times* and other papers nineteen months ago, when he pronounced the Slasher dead.

The Calistoga reference was a puzzler for about five seconds, then it clicked with Starr and stretched his smile from ear to ear. A safe house, obviously. Something personal, outside McKeon's Santa Rosa jurisdiction, close enough that he would feel at home. Familiar ground.

For both of them, in fact.

It irritated Starr that Adam and the whore had given him the slip, but they had not escaped in any lasting sense. Not yet. He had a long, dark drive ahead of him, but that was fine. He had no fear of dozing at the wheel, and darkness was a trusted friend.

Starr switched the shower off and killed the bathroom light, locked up behind him when he left. The pig was history. With any luck at all, it might be late tomorrow when they found the body. Even if it was discovered earlier, the hunter's intuition told him Pasadena would have trouble reaching out for Roy McKeon at his safe house.

It was all that he could do to keep from whistling as he left the house, retreated through adjoining yards to reach his waiting vehicle. Too late to drop it at the rental agency. He meant to leave it on the street, near the garage where he had parked the Porsche. Head north from there, to finish off the game that had been interrupted nineteen months ago.

I'm coming. Beaming it across the miles to Reed and Dana. *Just you wait.*

CHAPTER

26

———•———

Someone was calling Jacob in the dark, outside his bedroom window.

JA-cob. JA-cob.

No, that wasn't right.

On second thought, it sounded more like *WAKE-up, WAKE-up.* When they started firing random bursts from a machine gun, Adam's eyes came open and he jolted upright in the narrow bed. Beside him, Dana muttered something and rolled over in her sleep.

Machine guns? That was stupid. Maybe a pneumatic drill, if they were working on the street.

It took another moment for his mind to clear, and he remembered where he was. Slipped out of bed and padded to the window. Drew the curtain back just far enough to glimpse the first gray light of dawn.

Outside, no more than twenty feet away, a small redheaded woodpecker was staring at him with a black eye ringed in white. It seemed to find him curious, perhaps mistaking him for someone else.

JA-cob! WAKE-up!

The strident, almost human cry was followed by a rapid drumming sound, the small bird hammering its beak with lightning speed against the tree trunk where it clung.

281

"You'll get a headache doing that."

"Say what?"

He turned back toward the sound of Dana's voice and found her watching him. "I'm talking to our neighbor."

"Who?"

"You won't believe it. Woody Woodpecker. We're hiding out in Toon Town."

"Wonderful."

"Go back to sleep."

"Too late. What time is it?"

He checked his watch. "Six-thirty."

"Jesus."

They had reached the cabin shortly after midnight, following McKeon's hand-drawn map, and spent the best part of an hour settling in. Fatigue had carried Dana off as soon as she crawled into bed, but Reed was barely dozing at 1:30, when he heard another car, glimpsed headlights bobbing on the unpaved access road. McKeon's second, smaller cabin lay in that direction, separated from the quarters Adam shared with Dana by a hundred yards of rugged ground and trees.

He wondered what had kept McKeon, then he wondered if it *was* McKeon. That thought kept him up till 2:15, when he surrendered to exhaustion and the draw of muddled, half-remembered dreams.

He sat down on the bed and felt the mattress sag as he leaned over, kissed her forehead lightly. "You should get some rest. We're on vacation."

Dana stroked his cheek. "You need a shave."

"My thoughts, exactly."

"Not so fast," she told him. "I suggest you crawl back under here and show me how it feels."

An hour later, shaved and showered, Adam stood outside the cabin, breathing in the Christmas smell of evergreens. He wasn't much on botany, but he could recognize the lodgepole pines and taller ponderosas, alders, quaking aspen, bigleaf maple. Squirrels were busy in the trees, collecting nuts and leaping branch to branch like monkeys, chattering in righteous indignation at the stranger on their turf.

For something like a minute, Adam told himself no one could touch him here.

It was a fallacy, of course. The whole point of retreating to the mountains was to draw their enemy away from Pasadena, into territory where he could more easily be spotted, run to ground, and caged.

Or killed.

It startled Reed a bit, to wish a stranger dead that way and really mean it, but he instantly recalled the feeling of relief he had experienced on learning that the Santa Rosa Slasher had been killed. The way courts operated nowadays, with so much emphasis on the protection of sadistic criminals and virtual indifference to their victims, an arrest and trial was no real guarantee of punishment, much less security. Once they were dead, though . . .

Adam shrugged the morbid thoughts away and concentrated on the woods surrounding him. Birds called and rustled in the trees. A chipmunk darted out into the yard and froze, examined Adam for a moment, then retreated in a blur. He caught a glimpse of something smaller, possibly a lizard, slipping out of sight behind a fallen log.

They were a world away from L.A. now, but not so far from Santa Rosa. If McKeon's supposition was correct, and two men had participated in the Slasher crimes, their flight from Pasadena placed them less than twenty miles from where the second stalker must reside. It was an eerie feeling, standing in the woods alone, anticipating the approach of a demented killer. Adam wondered if the local deer felt this way at the start of hunting season.

Roy McKeon owned a wedge-shaped plot of thirty acres, with the narrow western boundary fronting on a smallish lake. A man could pass his whole life here, Reed thought, and never think about the chaos in the cities. Disconnect the phone, shun television and the daily papers. Back to nature with a vengeance, living off the land and shopping once a week or so at Calistoga's general store. Who needed malls and movies, freeways, beaches jammed with oily tourists frying in the sun? They had electric power in the boonies. He could plug in his computer, concentrate on fiction for the next few decades. Stories with the kind of upbeat happy endings that were favored in the Good Old Days.

And he would lose his mind. No doubt about it.

Adam was a city boy, and while he loved to get away from time to time, it was a different story when he thought of permanently giving up libraries, concerts, take-out restaurants, his small but cherished group of friends. It would mean giving up on Dana, too, for she would never be a pioneer.

Forget it.

Adam's stomach rumbled, brought his mind back to the fact that he had eaten nothing but a truck stop doughnut in the past twelve hours. It was breakfast time. He turned back toward the cabin door—and froze.

A twig snapped, and another seconds later. Closer.

Something—some*one*—was approaching through the trees.

The night had seemed interminable for McKeon. He had wasted thirty minutes after Reed and Dana passed through Calistoga, sitting in his car outside the local Texaco and waiting for another car to come along. When none appeared, he gave it up and trailed them off the main road to his private hideaway, unloaded his provisions from the car and made a walking circuit of the property. He gave a wide berth to the larger cabin, navigating with a flashlight and a bright three-quarter moon. The pistol on his hip was a reminder of his mission.

This was no vacation from the office. He was hunting.

It was close to 3:00 A.M. before he got back to his cabin, but McKeon couldn't sleep. Instead, he made a pot of coffee, drank it black and strong, relaxing on the covered porch. Raccoons came out to stare at him and sniff the air before they turned away to seek a free meal elsewhere. Bats wheeled overhead, collecting insects from the night.

McKeon waited for a different kind of predator and watched the sun come up. Despite the season, it was cool here, in the mountains, and he wore a sheepskin jacket as he rose to make another round by daylight. For the hell of it, he took the short High Standard riot shotgun with him, six rounds in the magazine.

He never really thought about the Napa County property

284

as a retirement home. Still short of what society called middle age, McKeon had at least a decade on the job ahead of him, if he was lucky. Anything could happen working homicide, but he refused to dwell on the acquaintances who had been killed or physically disabled in the line of duty. It would be the same in any job. These days, according to the press, a postal worker stood about the same chance as a cop of being shot and killed in uniform.

He ignored the trail, struck off directly through the trees in the direction of the lake. Reverse directions on the circuit he had walked in darkness, more or less, and stay alert for any signs of human movement in the woods. If Reed and Dana were awake when he passed by their cabin, he would stop and say hello. If not . . . well, it could wait.

The hunt was nothing new to Roy McKeon, though today's approach was rather different from the usual. He was accustomed to pursuing leads on paper, reaching out by telephone, collecting evidence to justify a warrant. Find your man or woman, mount surveillance if they stonewalled on the interviews, and make your bust when all the pieces fell in place. Sometimes it never came together, and the file stayed open, waiting for that extra clue, a tip to put you on the scent.

Win some, lose some.

But they were losing more these days, McKeon realized. Solution rates for homicide were down across the country, California leading with the ones who got away. It wasn't quite as bad in Santa Rosa as the larger cities—anyway, before the Slasher came along—but Roy McKeon had his share of mysteries that nagged at him relentlessly, reminding him that he was less than perfect.

So, what else was new?

McKeon did not hunt for sport, though he enjoyed a fishing trip when he could find the time. The Calistoga acreage had been a steal at $1,300 per, five years ago. It was his father's parting gift, the old man's life insurance covering the purchase and a number of improvements on the cabins, with enough left over for the first year's tax. McKeon never failed to sense his father's presence when he walked around the property. Not spooky, like a script from Holly-

wood, but *comforting*. Louis McKeon's grave was down in
Tucson, but his son could always find him when he wanted
to, within an hour's drive of home.

Off-trail, McKeon walked through thistles, horehound,
columbines, and brome. He loved the forest smell, so
different from the city where he lived and worked. You had
to stop and listen for a vehicle out here, and it was mostly
wasted effort. None of the adjacent property was occupied
year-round. McKeon's closest "neighbors" hailed from San
Francisco, Sacramento, Stockton, San Jose. They came on
weekends, holidays—the Fourth and Labor Day were
favorites—to get in touch with nature for a few short hours,
make believe they were not shackled to a desk and tract
house in the 'burbs.

But none of them, McKeon reckoned, ever came up on an
errand quite as strange as his.

What would he do if his intended quarry took the bait?
Would it be worth the trouble, jailing him in Napa County
on a misdemeanor trespass charge and working overtime to
build a case in Santa Rosa or Los Angeles? Why not just
settle it right here, and leave the bastard in a shallow grave?

McKeon knew about the "thin blue line" that stood
between a civilized society and anarchy or vigilante justice.
He had manned that line himself, since he was twenty-three
years old, but there were times when law and justice parted
company. How many times had he seen vicious criminals
walk free to rob and rape and kill again? What misery could
be averted, now and then, by an efficient firing squad?

He recognized the warning signs of cynicism, shared by
most of those in his profession. There were some cops who
could put in twenty, thirty years of wading through the slime
and come out with their faith intact, but they were few and
far between. You started with an honest urge to help
mankind by taking bad guys off the street, but grim experience destroyed childhood illusions. Crime *did* pay. The bad
guys often won. Most cops, at least in his experience,
became as cynical and calloused as the scumbags they were
paid to put away.

A few were even worse.

McKeon spotted Reed from fifty yards away, a flash of
color through the trees. His flannel shirt, fire engine red. He

made a perfect target, even though he stood a bit beyond the riot gun's effective range.

Reed heard him coming well before he saw McKeon, standing still but casting all around him, for a handy weapon. Recognition changed the look on Adam's face from apprehension to relief.

"You made it."

"Absolutely. Sleep well?"

Adam shrugged. "I thought I heard your car around one-thirty."

"That was me. I sat awhile in town to see if anyone was tailing you."

"Spot anything?"

McKeon shook his head, felt Adam staring at the shotgun tucked beneath his arm, the pistol on his hip. "If you had company, the SOB's invisible."

"I never saw you on the road," said Reed.

"You weren't supposed to."

"Right." He found a rock and skimmed it off across the lake. "You think we're wasting time, then?"

"No," McKeon said, with more conviction than he felt. "It's early yet."

"But, if he didn't follow us—"

"Then Driscoll has a decent chance to bag him at the house. You needed relocation for a few days anyway, and what the hell, the price is right."

"Okay."

"If I were you, I'd just relax." He caught Reed staring at the guns again. "You have a weapon?"

"Do I need one?"

"No," McKeon said, "I wouldn't think so."

"Just as well, then. Have you eaten breakfast?"

"Coming up. I want to stretch my legs a bit."

"I'm heading back," Reed said. "Why don't you come around for lunch or dinner?"

"Dinner's good," McKeon told him, counting on a nap that would consume the afternoon. "What time?"

"How's seven?"

"Suits me fine. Who's cooking?"

Adam grinned. "We haven't talked about it, yet. May have to flip a coin."

"I'll take my chances," said McKeon. "See you later."

"Right."

He stood and watched as Adam moved along the trail and disappeared from sight. Alone once more, he waited for the birds and squirrels to pick up their activity where human voices had disrupted it.

A stranger in the woods sent shock waves out in all directions, left his mark for those with eyes to see. McKeon was a far cry from a woodsman, but he knew this property by heart, and he could track intruders by their spoor. On two occasions—once in 1989, and then again in '91—he had evicted squatters from the land without much difficulty.

This time, though, he was prepared for something else.

In the middle of a big-game hunt, sometimes the tables turned, positions were reversed. The hunter could become the hunted, lose it all if he was careless, even for a moment.

The odds told Roy McKeon he had missed his prey. If he got lucky, somehow, and the stalker showed in spite of everything, they would be playing on McKeon's court. No rules, no substitutions.

And the game was sudden death.

Starr drove straight through the night, three stops for fuel and junk food, talking to himself. It was an eccentricity that he indulged in in times of stress, convinced that verbalizing plans, debating them with an imaginary audience, would help him work the bugs out in advance, thereby avoid mistakes. He did not rave or ramble in the ordinary sense. His terse, one-sided conversations always had a point, pursued with all the concentration of a bulldog worrying a rat. Most often, when he finished talking to himself, Starr felt relieved, his concentration focused like a searing laser beam.

And so it was on Wednesday morning, August tenth, when he pulled into Calistoga. It was 8:13 A.M., according to the dashboard clock, and Main Street bustled with a steady flow of pickup trucks, four-wheelers, station wagons. Locals on their way to work or dropping kiddies off at school. His highway atlas pegged the small town's population right around four thousand souls, and from the evidence before him, close to twenty-five percent of them were on the road right now.

The Porsche was a mistake, Starr realized. It stood out from the Blazers, Jeeps, and pickups like a fashion model at a fat farm. He had pondered the advisability of driving back to Santa Rosa, swapping for the Volvo or another of his cars, but the idea of wasting so much extra time repulsed him.

Let the dumb hicks feast their eyes if they were so inclined. The Porsche was wearing stolen plates, his registration sticker up to date. He was a tourist passing through. If anyone remembered him tomorrow, there would be no reason to connect him with a murder in the neighborhood.

And they would have to deal with his disguise.

He was a blond this morning, hair just long enough to brush his ears and collar, with a full mustache and brows that had been sculpted into subtle peaks, like accent marks above each eye. The general effect was one of openness and curiosity, encouraged by the charming smile that Starr could turn on like a spotlight when the need arose.

He felt it coming, even now.

The note he had retrieved from Piggy Driscoll back in Pasadena gave him Roy McKeon's number and the town where he was hiding, but the address still remained a mystery. Starr's first stop, coming into Calistoga, was the Texaco, where he paid cash for premium unleaded and perused the scrawny telephone directory.

No Roy McKeon listed, damn it.

The omission came as no surprise. Pigs like their privacy, avoiding private contact with the people they harassed from day to day, the pissed-off relatives of men and women sent away to prison. Piggies on vacation would be even more protective of their solitude. Starr had the number, he could dial it if he chose, but what would that accomplish? He could hardly call up and demand an address or directions to the house. Indeed, a simple hangup might be all it took to start McKeon's paranoia working overtime and make him bolt, with Reed and Dana, well before Starr had their hideout spotted.

For the moment, he assumed they still felt safe. It must be obvious they couldn't hide forever, but McKeon's plan would count on Piggy Driscoll to complete the circuit down in Pasadena, drop a net on anyone who showed unusual interest in the scribbler's whereabouts. It was a fairly decent scheme, all things considered, but McKeon had not reckoned on the hunter's skill. His genius.

Problem: He could not use Roy McKeon's telephone to trace his quarry, and a thorough search of Calistoga was impractical. In fact, it struck him that the sergeant had most likely spent his piggy paycheck on a place outside of town, the kind of dump where "real men" go to get away from normal hygiene for a while. Starr reckoned he could cruise the streets of Calistoga till his clothes went out of style and never even glimpse his prey.

Which left the obvious solution: He would have to ask around.

But where to start?

With basics. Sergeant Pork would need supplies for any visit to his home away from home. Assuming that he didn't haul his Dinty Moore and Charmin all the way from Santa Rosa, he would shop in town, rub elbows with the local yokels. Hicks were known for being nosy, and a stranger sleeping over could expect a gentle third degree. Before he got the groceries home, Starr calculated half the town would know his name and how he earned his living.

It was perfect.

All Starr had to do was choose his mark and pitch a decent cover story. Nothing too elaborate, considering the audience. He didn't want a lot of gossip circulating in the first few hours. Afterward, when he was finished . . . well, the local wags could go and fuck themselves for all he cared. They would be chasing shadows in the dark.

He struck out at the Texaco. Dumb bastard on the pumps considering his question, frowning, going through the motions of attempting to retrieve a conscious memory. McKeon? Nope, it didn't ring a bell.

His next stop was the general store, which featured everything from canned goods to a sparse line of cosmetics, automotive tools, and camping gear. The ancient crone behind the counter had blue hair, thick glasses, and a shriveled dewlap.

"Can I help you?"

Starr turned on his most ingratiating smile. "I wouldn't be surprised."

He kept the story simple. Roy McKeon was a friend from school. They planned to spend a few days fishing, reminisce about the glory days, whatever. Good old Roy had given him directions on the telephone, but darned if he could follow them, and he had lost McKeon's number somehow. It was stupid, really, but you know how these things happen.

She was smiling as he finished, evidently pleased to help a city boy who didn't mind admitting he was ignorant. Starr listened and repeated the directions, got it right the first time.

"There you go," the old hag said. "It's twenty minutes, give or take, depending on your vehicle."

"Well, I appreciate your help."

"No trouble."

"If you see Roy, I'd prefer he didn't know that I got lost. He might think there was something wrong with his directions."

"Mum's the word."

"Hey, thanks again."

And he was almost out the door when she called out, "I didn't catch your name, young fella."

Howard Michael Starr could not suppress a grin as he replied, "It's Reed, ma'am. Adam Reed."

CHAPTER

27

———•———

McKeon woke up from his nap at 4:15 P.M. without relying on the small alarm clock he habitually carried on the road. Six hours sleep had cleared his head, and he was ready for another night of sitting up and waiting for the enemy to show himself.

He made a sandwich, ate it standing at the sink, and washed it down with Michelob. The woods outside were fresh and dripping with a rain that must have fallen while he slept. Almost three hours until his dinner date with Reed and Dana. From the way he felt, McKeon knew that he would have no problem eating when the time arrived.

The country always did that to him, let his nerves unwind, increased his appetite. He didn't starve himself in Santa Rosa, but he had a tendency to wolf down what he could as time allowed. Days off, he leaned toward frozen dinners, maybe takeout, nothing that would pass for *haute cuisine*. His definition of a homecooked meal was something from the microwave, with salad on the side.

McKeon found himself anticipating dinner with his "guests," and frowned at the suggestion that he might be getting soft. It wouldn't do for him to lose his focus, start believing they were on some kind of camping trip and everything was cool. It had begun to look like Dana's bad

Samaritan had blown it, let them slip away unnoticed, but McKeon would not let his guard down.

Not just yet.

At five o'clock he started double-checking hardware. Pulled the magazine from his Beretta Model 92 and pumped the live round from the chamber. Stripped it down for cleaning, even though he had not fired the gun in three weeks, give or take. When he had finished oiling it and wiped the excess oil away, McKeon reassembled it, reloaded, eased the hammer down against the firing pin, and started on the shotgun.

Better safe than sorry, right.

It was approaching 6:00 before he satisfied himself that everything was perfect, or as nearly so as he could make it. You could never absolutely rule out misfires, but he wasted no time sweating out the one chance in a million that a given round of ammunition in his weapon was defective. Christ, as quiet as it was so far, he may as well have left the guns at home.

But he was glad to have them, all the same.

At 6:15, McKeon rose to make his final check around the property before he met with Reed and Dana. He considered carrying the riot gun, but finally left it in his cabin to avoid disturbing Dana any more than necessary. If he had to shoot at someone in the woods, before he stopped for supper, sixteen rounds in the Beretta plus his two spare magazines would have to do the job.

No sweat.

He locked the cabin door behind him, feeling slightly paranoid, and took a different trail this time. Rule number one while on patrol: Avoid distinctive patterns that allow the bad guys to predict your movements. Not that there were any bad guys in the neighborhood this evening, but McKeon kept his skills in shape by practice.

He circled north and eastward from the cabin, following a narrow deer trail toward the access road. It had been sprinkling while he slept, no cloudburst, but enough to make the ground a trifle softer. Had he been a tracker, Roy McKeon could have spotted squirrel and rabbit spoor along the trail, perhaps some larger animal like fox or feral cats. There was a problem with abandoned dogs in the vicinity, discarded on a whim by tourists, sometimes forming packs to hunt for prey outside of Calistoga proper. Two or three large dogs could kill a deer—or maul a child, if parents let the little ones play unattended, out of sight and earshot. Twice, in summers past, McKeon had experienced disturbing close encounters of the canine kind, and he was grateful for the automatic on his hip.

He reached the narrow, unpaved road a few yards from the eastern boundary of his property. Stepped out and checked both ways, like any citified pedestrian. No traffic sounds. McKeon knew that he could stand there all night long, perhaps for days on end, and never see a car.

It made him smile.

He was about to leave, retrace his steps, when something made him glance down at his feet. The smile evaporated in a heartbeat.

There were tire tracks on the muddy road.

Beyond his property, three-quarters of a mile, Joel Curry out of San Jose had bought himself a cabin two years back. McKeon knew him well enough to nod and say hello if they should meet in town, but that was all. Of course, Joel always drove a Jimmy four-by-four, with wider tires than these, but there was no law saying an insurance salesman couldn't change his taste in cars.

No law at all.

McKeon guessed the vehicle was headed east, toward Curry's place, because its tracks held slightly to the right of center on the narrow road. One lane or not, most drivers fell back on their early training, keeping to the right whenever possible. It was a guess, of course, but still . . .

One thing was obvious: The car had passed by *after* it had rained. What time was that? Somewhere between the time McKeon fell asleep, say half-past ten, and when he woke at four-fifteen. The ground had dried enough to hold a set of decent tracks without dissolving into muck. One set of tracks, approaching. None returned.

McKeon frowned, decided he should check it out. He still had ample time before his dinner date. If it was Curry with a new car, he could put his mind at ease.

McKeon started walking eastward, keeping to the shoulder of the road. He made a hundred yards or so before he found the Porsche parked in a turnout, pointing back the other way. No passengers, no luggage visible. He called out several times, in case the driver had stepped out to take a bladder break, but there was no response.

McKeon tried the doors. Both locked. His frown became a scowl.

He memorized the license number, knowing he would have to call it in.

But first, he meant to have a better look around.

The trick was waiting, when your chosen prey was close enough to smell his sweat and taste his fear. A fool would rush the job, take chances, make mistakes. The veteran hunter knew which risks were viable and therefore worth the effort.

After checking out the general store, Starr went to breakfast at a diner three doors down the street. He ordered scrambled eggs and bacon, buttered toast, black coffee. There was time to kill, and he would need the extra energy when he prepared to make his move.

He had the layout plotted in his mind, but it would not be totally revealed until he drove along the narrow back roads, found his target, started gliding through the trees on foot.

A proper hunt.

It started raining as he paid the breakfast tab, and Starr decided he would wait it out. A drizzle, more than anything. He dawdled past the stores on Main Street, window-shopping, let himself be seen. It didn't matter now. Let them recall the smiling stranger, if they could. When he was safe at home, Starr would retire the wig and its accessories. A place of honor in his trophy room.

The rain blew out of town two hours later. Starr considered picking up another snack, but settled for a paper cup of coffee from a drive-in at the far end of the street. He drank it walking back to where the Porsche was parked, outside a smallish grocery market.

Following the hag's directions, Starr drove out of town, a two-lane road that took him north toward Angwin. Less than halfway there, he saw the unpaved access road and slowed to make an easy right-hand turn. McKeon's property was one mile back, a numbered mailbox standing on the road directly opposite his driveway, but the hunter kept on going, looking for a place to hide the car.

And found it on his left, three-quarters of a mile beyond his target. Nothing special, just a turnout someone had prepared for those occasions when two vehicles confronted one another on the narrow track. Starr motored past and found another driveway, used its mouth to turn the Porsche around.

He had already changed, while Goober filled his tank up at the Texaco. Black jeans and turtleneck, black gloves, the ski mask rolled up like a watch cap on his scalp until he needed cover. If it all played out according to his plan, he had a special treat in mind for Dana Withers.

He would let her see his face, before he went to work.

Around his waist, Starr wore a pistol belt. The Ruger automatic on his right hip, in a canvas holster he had altered to accommodate the homemade plastic silencer. Two extra magazines in Velcro pouches, at his back. A long knife on his left, honed razor-sharp. He knew McKeon would be armed —perhaps all three of them, by now—but Starr was confident that he could do the job with what he had.

Starr spent the next three hours reconnoitering the property by sections, moving carefully among the trees. The woods were not his normal element, but he made do. There were no fallen leaves to speak of, but he watched his step regardless, taking all the time he needed. Straight down to the lake along a game trail, half expecting fishermen but meeting no one on the way. He circled west again and found a smallish cabin with an Oldsmobile Ciera parked in front.

Not Adam's car, unless the scribbler had exchanged his Sunbird for the Olds. A possibility.

The risky part was sneaking close enough to peer in through the window, picking out a solitary figure on the bed. No woman in the place, that much was obvious. The man lay on his right side, with his back turned toward the window.

Adam?

The size was wrong, his choice of clothes incongruous. There was an automatic pistol on the nightstand, and a shotgun stood beside the bed.

McKeon.

Starr was tempted to complete the first part of his business then and there. Creep in and shoot the pig while he was sleeping. Maybe slit his throat instead, so he could wake up choking on his piggy blood and glimpse his nemesis before he died.

Slow down.

If Adam and his bitch weren't here, where were they? He could always double back and take McKeon, now that he had found the piggy's hideaway and caught him napping. It was all in vain, unless he found the couple he had come so far to punish.

Starr retreated cautiously, avoided walking past the windows, even though McKeon was asleep. No point in taking foolish chances. Pausing to consider which direction he should choose, he spied another trail and followed it. Ten minutes later, he was crouched beside a looming ponderosa pine and checking out a second, somewhat larger cabin.

Parked in front was the Sunbird.

Starr did not approach the cabin, fearing Reed or Dana might emerge without sufficient warning, maybe glance outside and spot him. Telephone and power lines were visible, but he would have to wait for sundown to approach the dwelling. If they saw him coming, if they had a gun, if they were able to alert McKeon . . .

He made a circuit of the cabin, staying well back in the trees, to satisfy himself that there was only one way in or out. The windows didn't count. He traced the driveway back until it branched, one section veering off to serve the cabin where McKeon slept.

He had the layout now, with time to watch and wait. A brisk walk brought him to McKeon's rustic hovel, and he sat among some ferns, his back against a sturdy oak. Starr watched McKeon rise and feed his piggy face, inspect and clean his weapons. He was waiting when the sergeant stepped outside, surveyed the woods without detecting him, and set off toward the road.

Starr gave his prey a hundred-yard head start before he followed, careful not to make a sound along the way. He saw McKeon step into the road and look both ways, glance down and spot the tire tracks at his feet. Starr was behind him, almost close enough to use the Ruger, as McKeon wandered eastward, found the Porsche and tried the doors. He was McKeon's shadow when the pig retreated to his cabin, moving briskly through the forest. Left the door wide open when he went inside.

To get the shotgun?

Now or never.

Starr went in behind him, blocking out the twilight as he filled the doorway. Roy McKeon pivoting to face him, wary, one hand edging toward his sidearm.

"Can I help you?"

Howard Michael Starr was smiling over gunsights as he said, "I wouldn't be surprised."

"He's late."

"I know." But hearing Dana say it made him nervous.

"Well?"

"Well, what?" Reed knew what she was getting at, but he played dumb.

She turned the flame down on the propane stove. The smell of chicken frying filled the cabin, making Adam salivate. Peas boiling. Summer squash. The bounty of McKeon's freezer.

"Maybe he forgot."

Reed shook his head. "I doubt that very much. He's not exactly overrun with prospects for a dinner date up here."

She hesitated. "Adam—"

"Nothing's wrong," he interrupted. "Give him ten, and if he isn't here, I'll get him."

"Ten? The chicken's almost done."

"Ten minutes, Dana. No big deal."

At 7:20, Reed went out to do the manly thing. Find Roy McKeon somewhere in the woods and bring him back to supper, PDQ.

Reed was betting that their tardy host had overslept, recuperating from his night on watch and morning hike around the property. He would not be surprised to find McKeon snoring in his bunk, dead to the world.

Okay, poor choice of words.

It got dark early in the forest. That was an illusion, Adam realized, trees blocking out the sun before it fully set, but the result was brooding twilight well before it would be dark in town. The shadows made him jumpy, walking by himself on unfamiliar ground, and Adam stopped, not once but several times, to check out rustling noises in the undergrowth beside the trail.

I'm getting paranoid, he thought. But, then again, why not? He was four hundred miles from home, staked out as bait to catch a lunatic who might—or might not—be involved in thirty brutal murders. Last time out, his playing footsy with McKeon had come close to getting Dana killed.

The odds were excellent that they had given Mr. X the slip in Pasadena. It was Driscoll's baby, now. Reed made a mental note to ask McKeon if they ought to call and find out what was happening at home. For all he knew, the case had broken overnight, and they were roughing it for nothing.

He thought about that morning, in the narrow bed with Dana, and decided he could rough it for another day or two, all things considered. Live on love, if they ran short of food, or maybe go to town for groceries. Take it nice and easy while he had the chance.

No lights on in the cabin as he came out of the trees. Reed wondered if McKeon had gone off to check the property again before he kept their date. He could be sitting down with Dana this very minute, making small talk and awaiting Reed's return.

So, check it out. If there was no one home, he would go back, tell Dana. Eat without McKeon, if he didn't have the simple courtesy to check his wristwatch. He would be there when he got there. In the meantime, Adam could not be expected to conduct a search alone, with full night coming on.

McKeon was a big boy with at least two guns and he could take care of himself.

The door was standing open. Dark inside. Reed lingered in the yard, beside the Oldsmobile, and called out to the cabin.

"Roy? Hello? It's getting late. Don't want to let the food get cold."

No answer.

Adam swallowed, glanced around him at the creeping shadows. Climbed the wooden steps without enthusiasm.

"Roy?"

The silent doorway mocked him. Adam's skin was crawling as he stepped across the threshold, groping for a light switch on his left. He found it, switched it on, and drove the darkness out. Blinked twice at Roy McKeon, staring at him from behind the redwood dining table.

No, that wasn't right. McKeon lay *beside* the table, stretched out on his back, feet toward the door. But how . . . ?

Reed's stomach knotted, bringing up the remnants of his lunch. He doubled over, retching. Managed to control it when the sudden shock of fear kicked in and overrode disgust.

McKeon's *head* was sitting on the table, staring at the door. The eyes weren't merely open, Adam saw, but *lidless*, the result of cunning surgery. A small hole in the center of McKeon's forehead could have been mistaken for a third eye, weeping crimson.

As for the discarded body, it had been laid out for burial, with heels together, arms crossed on the chest. A pool of tacky blood had formed in place of Roy McKeon's head, as if his mangled neck was blowing bubbles.

Jesus fucking Christ!

The full reality of that tableau came through to Adam in a chilling rush. He couldn't tell how long McKeon had been dead, but there was no dispute about the cause. Whoever killed him would be close at hand, perhaps already shadowing the other cabin.

Dana!

Adam bolted, caught himself before he cleared the steps outside, and doubled back. He stepped across McKeon's legs and bent to check the holster on his belt.

Still there.

Reed took the pistol, clutched it awkwardly as he retreated from the cabin. He was running by the time he hit the ground, a mad dash for the game trail that would take him back to Dana.

Jesus God, don't let me be too late!

She heard the footsteps coming back a moment after Adam left to find McKeon. Clumping on the porch, knob turning, and the door swung open.

"What did you forget?" she asked him.

Turning from the stove to face a stranger dressed in black from head to foot. He wore a too-familiar ski mask that revealed his hateful eyes and wicked smile. The awkward, bloated-looking pistol in his hand was pointed at her face.

"We had a date," he said. "Remember?"

God, that voice!

"You're dead," she told him, wishing that pronouncement of the words would make it so.

His smile seemed artificial in the ski mask, grafted on a blank face like that toy she used to play with as a child. Mr. Potato Head.

"Reports of my demise," he answered, reaching back to close the door behind him, "were exaggerated."

Where was McKeon? Adam?

"You can't do this," said Dana.

The intruder blinked, as if someone had thrown a cup of icy water in his face. She saw the corners of his mouth turn down. "I'm *doing* it, you stupid bitch!" The heavy muzzle of his weapon dipped below her waist. "The only question is, do you prefer to make it easy on yourself or would you rather lose your kneecaps?"

Dana swallowed hard to clear her throat. She had no doubt that he would carry out his threat. Nor was there any question that he meant to kill her, probably in some horrific way, before he left. Somehow, against all odds, this *was* the man who murdered Sylvie, who had nearly finished Monica. The only plan that she could think of in her panic was a stall for time.

"What do you want?"

"Let's start by getting naked," he replied. "You first."

Of course, what else?

These psycho shits were all alike. They couldn't find a willing partner, couldn't even get it up unless they had a woman bound and terrorized. She knew from reading some of Adam's notes and clippings that a fair percentage liked their "lovers" dead. It was less threatening that way, and there was no critique of their performance afterward.

Removing clothes was no big deal; she did it all the time. Pretend you're at a showing, changing clothes backstage, with cameramen and God knows who else wandering around. Forget about false modesty and get it done. Do *anything* to buy some time and stay alive.

She fumbled with the buttons of her blouse and shrugged it off. Stepped out of sandals. Skinned her Levis off and stood before the madman in her bra and panties.

"Everything."

Stay calm.

She reached around in back, unhooked her bra, and dropped it. Rolled her panties down, stepped out of them and tossed them somewhere to her left.

"Not bad."

Two steps, and he was in her face, the muzzle of his weapon pressed against her navel. Dana had expected icy metal, but it felt like plastic. Curious. Up close, his breath reminded her of cinnamon. She wondered what it felt like, being shot at point-blank range.

His left hand, in a black glove, stroked her naked breast. She felt the nipple pucker in response to friction and her fear. The gunman smiled behind his mask, mistaking the reaction for excitement. Slowly, almost lovingly, he rolled her tender flesh between his thumb and index finger.

"See? We're friends already."

Even as he spoke, his fingers tightened, twisted. Dana gasped, felt tears of pain slide down her cheeks.

"You need to loosen up a little, Dana."

She stood, trembling, as he walked around behind her. Losing contact with the pistol. What she felt next was the flat steel of a knife blade, razor-edged, beneath her breast. His free hand slid around her hip to rummage in between her legs. The gloves were off. She tried to squirm away from the invasive fingers, but his body blocked her from retreating, and the cool blade nicked her breast.

"Relax," he hissed. "We need to get acquainted."

Dana closed her eyes and concentrated on the simple act of drawing breath. What was the trick for going out-of-body? Yoga masters did it all the time, and people who survived near-death experiences. She was having one of those right now, for Christ's sake, but she couldn't stop her flesh from feeling everything he did.

"You're getting wet," he whispered. "See?"

He brought the hand up from between her legs and shoved two fingers in her mouth. She gagged, half choking, and he slapped her with an open palm. The impact made her ears ring.

"Nasty little bitch!"

He marched her toward the redwood dining table. When her thighs met wood, he put a hand between her shoulder blades and shoved her forward, flattening her breasts against the tabletop. Cool wood against her cheek. He wedged a knee between her legs, kicked Dana's feet apart until her full weight rested on the table. When his hand came back, she tried to clench her buttocks, but he stopped her with the knife blade pressed against her face.

"You want to play? Pretend you don't enjoy it? That's okay. We both know how you like it."

Dana clenched her teeth against the pain, denying him the satisfaction of a scream. She wasn't really injured yet. She still had time, if only—

"Dana!"

Adam's voice, outside the cabin.

"Dana?"

Her assailant hesitated, drew his hand away. "Oh, dear," he said, "it seems we have a visitor."

He grabbed her by the hair and drew her upright, turned and guided her in the direction of the door. The knife was sharp against her throat.

"This won't take long," he promised her. "We've got all night."

Reed froze with one foot on the bottom stair, as Dana stepped across the threshold. Naked, leaking crimson underneath one breast. Behind her, all in black, the Slasher gripped her hair and held a long knife to her throat. The pressure forced her head back at an awkward angle. Adam raised his pistol, tried to aim. His hands were trembling violently.

"Are you all right?" A stupid question, but the choice was speak or scream.

"She's doing fine," the Slasher said. *That voice.* "We were about to have some fun. You're interrupting."

"Let her go. It's me you want."

"I'm not a *faggot*, Adam. Look at her, for Christ's sake. Where's the contest?"

Thinking fast, Reed blurted, "*I* betrayed you. It's revenge you're after."

"Ah." The Slasher took his blade away from Dana's throat and ran its edge along the soft curve of her breast. "Revenge takes many forms."

It happened in a heartbeat. Dana had been standing with her arms down at her sides. The left hand slid around behind her as her captor spoke, the fingers curling into talons, clutching at his genitals. She twisted, squeezing, as her right arm jarred the knife away and whipped around to strike the Slasher's temple with her elbow.

Bellowing and clutching at his wounded crotch, the man in black lashed out at Dana, missed her with his long knife as she tumbled down the steps. Reed couldn't fire with Dana in the way and had no faith in his ability to hit a moving target. Lunging for the porch, he swung McKeon's pistol at the Slasher's head. Connected with a solid jolt.

The bastard grunted, staggered, but he kept his balance, lashing out at Adam with the knife. Reed dodged in time to save his face, but cried out as the sharp blade gouged his thumb above the knuckle, peeling flesh. He whipped his hand back, spraying blood, and heard the pistol clatter at his feet.

The Slasher rushed him, sweeping with the blade. Reed lurched back from the flashing steel and felt his balance going as his foot met empty air. He tumbled off the porch, one hand thrown out to catch himself. The impact sprained his wrist, shot bolts of pain from Adam's elbow to his shoulder. Scrabbling backward like a crippled spider, he had time to raise one knee before the Slasher launched himself into a shallow dive.

More pain, the hip and knee this time, but he had spoiled the Slasher's aim. The knife slid past his face with something like an inch to spare and scraped the dirt. His knee was in the prowler's stomach, winding him, and spittle flew in Adam's face. The bastard wheezing, retching, while the knife came up again, descended in a slashing arc.

Reed blocked it with his left arm, struck out with his

bloody right. And *more* pain, Jesus, as his fist connected with the Slasher's skull. It rocked his adversary sideways, Adam twisting underneath him, shoving with his knee to help the prick along. Another moment saw him out from under, rolling free, but he could hear the Slasher scrambling to his feet and coming back for more.

Reed turned to face him empty-handed. Knowing he was dead.

The first shot missed, but it was loud enough to startle both men. Dana kneeling on the porch, McKeon's pistol braced in both hands as she sighted down the slide, her elbows locked. The Slasher saw it coming, tried to dodge, but he was nowhere fast enough.

She fired six times, and Adam heard at least two bullets find their mark. A slapping sound, distinct and separate from the bark of gunfire, like a mallet pounding steak. The Slasher jerked and did an awkward pirouette before he went down on his face.

Reed found the knife, retrieved it, stuck it in his belt. He moved toward Dana, took her in his arms, and felt her shuddering against him like the victim of an arctic chill. He took the pistol from her trembling hands and dropped it, led her back inside the cabin.

Smoke came out to meet them.

"God! The chicken's burning."

Seemingly unconscious of her nudity, she went to turn the stove off. Adam found her jeans and picked them up. A few feet to his right, her shirt lay crumpled on the floor. He stooped down to retrieve it.

"Nasty fucking bitch!" It didn't feel like being shot, the way he had imagined it. More like the stinging lash of a wet towel against his buttock, like they used to do in gym class. *Deep* pain, though, a white-hot burning in the muscle, and a snorting sound behind it, coming from the open doorway.

Adam turned to find the Slasher lurching toward him with a funny-looking pistol in his hand, blood soaking through the side and shoulder of his turtleneck. He moved with jerky steps, like Frankenstein's creation, but his aim was steady. Adam hit the floor and felt the next round whisper past his scalp.

"You *bastard!*"

Dana gripped the skillet like a giant tennis racquet, seared her palms and never even seemed to feel it as she brought the pan around, its greasy contents spattering the Slasher's face. He screamed and dropped the pistol, bringing both hands up to shield his eyes. Too late.

Reed drew the long knife from his belt and vaulted from a crouch to hit his adversary like a blocker on the line of scrimmage. Driving underneath his rib cage with the blade and feeling hot blood mingle with his own. The Slasher grabbed his ears and shouted something incoherent, stumbling backward with the force of Adam's charge.

They struck the doorjamb, held there, Adam leaning on the knife and twisting, putting all his weight behind it. Someone screaming.

"Die, you motherfucker! *Die!*"

It took another moment, but the Slasher seemed to melt, and Reed could feel the life run out of him like sand escaping from a broken hourglass. Knees buckled, and the two of them went down together, Adam clinging to the knife, refusing to break contact.

Dana brought him out of it, a soft hand on his shoulder, drawing him away. He left the knife, no point in taking chances. Put his arms around her. Pulled her close.

"McKeon's dead," he told her.

Dana leaned back far enough to look him in the eye. "But we're alive," she said. "We made it."

"Right," he answered, and it almost sounded like a prayer of thanks. "That's right."